BLOOMIN'

BLOOMIN'

A Novel in Three Acts

by

Maria Ciaccia

Excalibur Publishing
New York

Copyright © 1990 by Maria Ciaccia
All rights reserved. This book, or parts thereof, may
not be reproduced in any form without permission.
Published by Excalibur Publishing,
434 Avenue of the Americas, Suite 790,
New York, New York 10011.

Lyrics to "When You Fall Asleep in My Arms"
© 1986 Rhett Judice
All rights reserved. Used by permission.

Lyric to "Only a Dream in Rio"
© 1985 Country Road Music Inc. (BMI)
All rights reserved. Used by permission.

Library of Congress Card Catalogue Number: 90-84036

ISBN 0-9627226-0-X

Printed in the United States of America

1 2 3 4 5 6 7 8 9 10

Acknowledgements

The accuracy of the old adage "truth is stranger than fiction" certainly was emphasized to me as I wrote *Bloomin'*. Although the characters in this book are entirely fictional, some of the situations were inspired by original material.

For their contributions, I would like to thank Kathleen Fogarty, Stan Bartosiak, Matt Bartosiak, Betsy Mulderig and Martha Rand Mahard. Sharon Good, Stan Bartosiak, Diane Tarleton and QED Transcription provided me with much-needed technical assistance.

I wish to thank the following people for their input, support and unfailing good humor: John Ahearn, Eloise Klombies-Paris Akerberg, Monica Ambrose, Pat Ambrose, Isabelle Bartosiak, Dr. Marlene Caroselli, Celeste Ciaccia, Mary Jo Ciaccia, Vic Ciaccia, Tony Ciaccia, Howard "JIB" Cutler, Barry Donaldson, Joan Dornemann, Marilyn Dornemann, Marie Fogarty, Dr. Joanne Foster, Sheila Field, Sharon Good, Dr. Rose Hayden, Maureen Kerrigan, Pat Jackson, Jack Jenkins, Catherine Lamy, Maralyn Lowenheim, Sharon McGuire, Ned Putnam, Peter Puzzo, Raymond Sepe, Jim Shewalter, Barnet Shindlman, Robert Trentham, Bill Tripician and Michael Yoder. And, of course, Cecilia and "Big Al" Ciaccia.

No acknowledgments section of mine would be complete without a heartfelt thanks to my editor, Alexis Greene.

Finally, I am eternally grateful to the brilliant author Barry Paris for his generosity, advice, friendship and inspiration.

Dedicated to Dameon Fayad
1946-1985

"Love's final gift, remembrance"

BLOOMIN'

Overture

1967 – 1971

Youth is blessed with clear-mindedness and simplicity of goals, born of a belief that all things are possible. I was no different from any other stagestruck seventeen-year-old; I wanted to: a) get away from home as fast as I could and leave my parents and Rochester, New York, in the dust; b) become a superstar of the first magnitude in New York; and c) have a million passionate love affairs.

These were lofty ambitions and, if one looked closely at my life, there was no indication that any of my dreams had a basis in reality. Convincing my parents that I should leave Rochester to study singing and theater in Boston was going to be no easy task, since Rochester had one of the best music schools in the country, The Eastman School of Music ("The Eastman"). As to being a superstar, I was talented enough, but at 5'7", even though I was slim and pretty, with long, honey-brown hair, I still couldn't get the lead in my high school production of *Brigadoon* because the male lead was 5'5". Pursuant to the million passionate love affairs, I'd been in Catholic girls school for twelve years. Enough said.

Eastman, I explained to my parents as if they were idiots, didn't have a musical theater department. My parents didn't want me to attend school in Boston, but to me, Boston seemed less dangerous than New York and almost as exciting. Besides, since Boston was a college town, there were sure to be Men. (I did not mention this reason to my parents.)

I skated through my audition for the Boston College of Music and Drama, but immediately encountered an obstacle to the rest of my game plan: female students were expected to live in the dorms their freshman and sophomore years. The "dorms" were rat-and-roach infested buildings on The Fenway. In my few weeks there, I never saw a rat or roach; what put me off were the dorm mother, the curfew and the rule about no men in the rooms.

This would never do.

The problem was, how to wriggle out of it. My parents had already paid the semester's room and board. I talked it over with my new best friend in the world, Sulynn O'Reilly, whom I'd met in the registration line the day after I arrived in Boston. Sulynn's real name was Susan Ellen O'Reilly, but she intended to be known professionally as "Sulynn Reilly."

"Don't you think it makes me sound more exotic?" she had asked me.

"I think it makes you sound Japanese-Irish," I answered.

"Right," she agreed. "Exotic."

Sulynn had no particular commitment to a theatrical career. She originally wanted to be a grammar school teacher, until she found out that in order to practice teach, she had to get up at 6 a.m. Good-bye, teaching ambitions — hello, show biz.

Sulynn lived at home. She, too, attended Catholic girls school and not only that, had spent most of her life fat. Now that she was slender, she wanted out of her parents' house.

There was another reason we wanted an apartment: The Gaines Brothers.

Sulynn saw them the first day we walked into drama class. She grabbed me and we rushed to the seats next to them, nearly knocking over another girl headed in the same direction.

"Excuse me," Sulynn said in what sounded suspiciously like a southern drawl. "Is this Mister Hardenburgh's class?"

"Yeah," grunted the sandy-haired one on the far end, without turning around or looking up.

He didn't know with whom he was dealing. "I'm Sulynn O'Reilly," she said, "and this is Margo Girard."

The two objects of our virginal affection now faced us. "I'm Arthur Gaines," said the dark-haired one next to me, shaking my hand, then Sulynn's.

"Bobby Gaines," the grunter said.

"Are you brothers?" Sulynn asked.

"We're twins," Bobby Gaines said, pivoting his very tall body sideways and casting his gray eyes over every inch of Sulynn.

"You don't look anything alike," Sulynn said.

"That's because we're fraternal twins."

"Still spewing that twin crap?" I looked to my right, and there stood a very odd-looking person in tie-dyed clothing, a purple bandana and with brick-red hair. At first I thought it was a girl.

"Oh, shut up, Fred," Bobby said.

"Fred" plunked down next to Sulynn. "I grew up with these slobs, and they're a year apart," he advised us.

"What kind of name is Girard?" Art asked me.

"Italian. Ghiardelli. Changed at Ellis Island. I'm Irish on my mother's side."

Art nodded. "We're Polish on our mother's side. Lots of our relatives had their names shortened."

"Where are you all from?" I asked him.

"Yarmouth, Mass."

"So we're not twins," Bobby interjected. "We're half brothers. We had different fathers."

Art chuckled. "Don't listen to him. We're full brothers. I spent a year in Europe after high school, that's all."

"Wow," I said. A man of the world. As class began, Sulynn and I exchanged desperate glances.

We had to get our own apartment.

"This will be easy," Sulynn promised as we conferenced later in my dorm room. "If you live with a relative, you don't have to stay in the dorms. Tell the bursar you have to take care of your grandmother, who lives in Boston."

"But what if he wants to meet her?"

"She's a helpless invalid. I do a great old lady voice. Don't worry about a thing."

The bursar heard me out, then told me he needed a letter from my parents. I typed one up and sent it to my married brother in Rochester to mail for me.

Everything set to go, I called my mother and laid on the hysterics. "I found a dead rat in my room!" I sobbed.

"Oh, my GOD!" she screamed. "What kind of a hellhole is that place? You've got to get out of there!"

"Well," I said between gasps, "I think it's going to be okay. They're giving me a refund to hush it up, and I have a friend here, and we're going to get an apartment together." That didn't sit too well. I explained about Sulynn, how her family lived nearby, and that her sixty-five-year-old Uncle Roger had an apartment in the same building (a lie).

My mother wanted me to come back to Rochester immediately rather than get an apartment (these were the days when Albert

DeSalvo, the supposed Boston Strangler, was fresh in the minds of mothers everywhere). "Don't forget," she reminded me. "All he did was meow like a kitten to get girls out of their apartment. You know how you love cats." Fortunately, Sulynn's mother was a bit more progressive than mine, having had several birds fly the nest; her mother wrote to mine and assured her we'd be carefully policed. I wonder if my mother noticed that Mrs. O'Reilly didn't mention Uncle Roger.

We found a tiny one-bedroom apartment on Park Drive and immediately started cultivating Bobby and Art Gaines. "I hope you like Art," Sulynn said one day before school, brushing her thick brown hair, "because I'm taking Bobby."

"That's fine," I told her. I really didn't know how I felt yet. Art seemed nice, and polite. It never occurred to either Sulynn or me that they might not want us.

We got to know each other through our various performance classes. Art was a character actor with a singing voice that lent itself to patter songs. To judge by his appearance, he was compulsively neat.

Bobby, on the other hand, was a dancer-singer whose acting exhibited a strong James Dean influence. Quiet and introspective, he always promised more than he gave (on-stage as well as off), a talent that gave him an air of mystery.

Art and Bobby were opposites: Art was tall and dark, Bobby taller and blond; Art fastidiously groomed, and Bobby his wrinkled shirtsleeves hanging; Art always ten minutes early, Bobby at least an hour late, if he even bothered to show up.

Sulynn and I settled on a non-threatening strategy and included Fred Corso, their bizarre friend in the Carmen Miranda headgear, in our casual "let's go to lunch" suggestions and invitations to our apartment. Soon, we were all hanging out together, but only as friends. "We're where we should be," Sulynn assured me. "It'll be easy from here on out."

We learned that Art and Bobby were part of a show-biz family. Their mother, Lettie, was the daughter of Polish immigrants who settled in Cambridge, Massachusetts, where Lettie grew up. Lettie was gorgeous and became a Broadway showgirl at the age of 16. She quit the business to marry Mr. Gaines and moved to Yarmouth, Mass., where she instilled her love of an audience into Bobby and Art. About Mr. Gaines we could learn nothing, and I for one assumed he was dead (I found out eventually from Fred that he had deserted the family and later died). Art and Bobby never talked about him.

Fred Corso was the funniest man I ever knew. His favorite line was, "Mass Mental — make it quick!" According to Art, when Fred was in seventh grade, he dyed his hair butterscotch. Now, each week his hair was a different color and a different cut, depending on his present mood. One day I walked into speech class and there was Fred with a Beatle-type haircut, complete with bangs.

"Don't say it," he warned me, holding up a hand. "I look like Jane Wyman in *Johnny Belinda*."

Art and Bobby lived together on Beacon Street in a huge apartment that had been in their family for years. Their maternal grandmother owned the building, but didn't actually live there. Their apartment became Party Central, and there was a party for any excuse: cast parties, Halloween parties, special-movies-on-TV parties (Psycho with the lights out being a big one), snowstorm parties, parties-when-there-was-no-school-the-next-day. Parties were always BYOB (bring your own booze), and the "booze" consisted of either Ripple or GIQs, which were Canadian quarts of beer. Everyone always ended up sleeping on the floor to the tune of "Does Anybody Know What Time It Is?" and the next day, one had to walk over bodies to get anywhere. Some of those bodies belonged to total strangers.

But the good times ended abruptly when Art and Bobby's grandmother moved into the apartment below theirs. Fortunately, she was only there from April until November, since she spent the rest of the time in Florida, but our social activities were strictly curtailed whenever she resided in Boston. Their grandmother did not approve of overnight guests.

One such guest was Art and Bobby's high-school friend Toni, who showed up at their door one day after quitting her stewardess job because of sexual harassment. "Panic City" was her favorite term, and Panic City was what she called her present situation, having only her cosmetics case with her and a terrible toothache.

I was at the apartment when she walked in. We both had on the same makeup: frosted lipstick, white base, black eye-liner. Her mini-skirted stewardess outfit was in some kind of psychedelic pattern, set off by white vinyl boots and a Carnaby Street oversized cap. Around her neck was a gold chain. A true '60s Fuck-Me outfit, courtesy of the airlines.

She was in agony from her tooth. "I'll go down and see if my grandmother has anything," Bobby offered.

Art stayed with her, and Bobby and I went down together. "I don't want my grandmother to know she's here," he said, "so I'll tell her Art has the toothache."

His grandmother let us in and Bobby spun his tale. "Art's got a horrible toothache, Grandma Jania. Do you have anything for it?"

"I vill mek something," she announced, and went to work over the stove with dozens of bottles. The smell was horrendous beyond belief; at one point, I put my hand over my mouth to keep from gagging. Bobby got two kitchen towels, gave me one, and we sat with them over our mouths.

After what seemed like an eternity, she was finished. "Thank you, Grandma Jania," Bobby said, and put out his hand to take it.

"Oh, no," she told him. "Dis fery peculiar medicine. I must apply it to Art myselv."

"I'm sure we can figure it out, Grandma Jania," I assured her.

She wouldn't hear of it. Up the stairs we went, conversing at the top of our lungs so Art would hear us and hide Toni. When we reached the apartment, Toni was nowhere to be found. "Grandma brought you something for your toothache, Art," Bobby said.

Art's eyes at this point were crossed from the smell, which instantly permeated the apartment. Bobby and I replaced the towels over our mouths. "Sit down," Grandma Jania ordered. "You must hold this on your tooth for vone halv hour. Vich vone is it?" Art pointed aimlessly at his left side. "It's hard for me to tell," he said. "The whole side of my mouth hurts."

After soaking this gunk in a cloth, she placed it inside his mouth. Art made an inhuman sound. I went looking for Toni. She was under the bed in Art's room, waving to me frantically. "I have to go to the bathroom," she whispered. "And my mouth is killing me."

"You'll have to wait," I hissed back. "Their grandmother is still here."

When the ordeal was finally over, Art went into the bathroom and threw up. Grandma Jania left some of the concoction, after carefully instructing Art in its use. Toni groaned and cried a lot as he applied it, but strange as it may sound, her toothache disappeared. I never did know what was in that mess.

The small, one-bedroom apartment Sulynn and I rented on Park Drive was reserved for gabfests on school nights for Bobby, Art, Fred, Sulynn and myself.

As I look back, it's apparent we were a bunch of naïve high school students thrown into college too young. We were in Boston, which was rampant with '60s promiscuity, and yet stupid Sulynn and I were entertaining gentlemen callers under the most platonic of circumstances.

Sulynn and I discussed at great length what was going on between

Bobby, Art and ourselves. Over the months, a loose pairing had evolved that consisted of Bobby-Sulynn/Art-me. After an evening of overindulgence on grass and booze, there would be some kissing, some fondling. But otherwise, we were like brothers and sisters. Truth to tell, we didn't know what was supposed to be happening, but it did seem to us that every other female student was getting laid on a regular basis.

"I know nothing," Sulynn admitted. "I once asked my mother what a blow job was."

Between everyone else's sexual promiscuity and everyone else's student unrest, Sulynn and I felt a bit out of the college mainstream. We were *in* the '60s but not *of* the '60s. We attended a myriad of protests on the Common, more to see what they were like than to actually participate. Music school students tended to be insulated from politics, although, once the war in Vietnam heated up, there was a big assembly in the auditorium; the more radical among the students — drama majors, mostly — declared a moratorium from classes for those who wanted to protest. But try as they might, it was difficult to whip the small school into much of a frenzy. An attempt to take over President Lambini's office fizzled. Considering all that was going on around us, this was the stuff of wimps.

Sulynn and I, selfishly, were interested in love, not war. For a time, we let the foolishness with Art and Bobby go on and then, as we began to date others, analyzed the situation every night from our beds on opposite sides of the room. There was obviously mutual attraction, but the signals emanating from the four of us said the same things: I like you more than I should, I came to Boston to have fun, I'm not ready for anything serious, let's just be friends for now.

Accepting the friendship message for what it was, Sulynn and I started looking elsewhere. We didn't even bother with guys at the college. We went to mixers at Harvard on weekends, two virgins dying to get the deed over and done. Finally, I met a cute guy named Rich, a law student, and decided he would be the one to break the seal. I was, by this point, totally desperate — Sulynn had lost her virginity on the previous weekend.

I brought Rich back to the apartment, where he started kissing me passionately. The two of us rolled off the couch and onto the floor. As he kissed and bit my neck, I looked sideways. I couldn't believe how much debris — crumbs, lint, bits of paper, were in the rug, and I'd vacuumed before I left. Boy, I said to myself as Rich unzipped my skirt, I need a new belt for that vacuum cleaner. Then I felt something that sort of hurt, and my mind went off the rug and onto my pain.

"RELAX!" Rich screamed at me. "You're not a virgin, are you?"

"No," I groaned. Boy, did it smart. I found when I released my pelvis, the pain almost went away, and when I moved my pelvis around, it actually felt not half-bad. Rich must have known I was a virgin; I didn't know what the hell I was doing. The whole thing ended soon, with a sweaty Rich collapsing on top of me, nearly crushing me.

I felt like bursting into song: Peggy Lee's "Is That All There Is?". Anyway, it was over, and with practice, I might even get to like it.

Besides this new and exciting aspect of my social life, there was the weekly activity with "the gang" of going to old movies at the Revival Cinema in Cambridge. It became a ritual. Every Friday night, no matter how poor we were, we always found the money to have dinner at Ken's of Copley Square. All of us, that is, except Sulynn. She routinely ordered a Pepsi and stole food off of everyone else's plates. Fred always referred to Sulynn as "Veda," after Joan Crawford's brat daughter in *Mildred Pierce*.

The only drag about our trips to Cambridge was that we always traveled by subway, although occasionally, Bobby brought his old Volkswagen into Boston, which he normally garaged at his mother's house in Yarmouth. But the parking situation made it impossible for him to bring it in too often.

Parking was so bad that people did just about anything for a spot. Once, Bobby had his Volkswagen in town and found a place along the park across from the school. Just as he was getting ready to back in, another car drove straight across the park, on the grass, and got into the space first.

Another time, when I was in the car with him, he looked for a parking space for about an hour. At last he found one, started to back in, and a car drove into the spot from behind him. Just to make things worse, the girls who got out of the car thought it was funny.

Bobby didn't say a word. We toured around for ten minutes and found another spot. Then we walked back to the previous spot. "That's not a rental car, is it?" he asked me.

"It doesn't look like one from the license," I said.

His voice was as noncommittal as ever. "Good," he said, jumped on the hood and, with his dancer's feet, smashed in the windshield. Sitting on a stoop a few houses away were some kids who'd evidently seen the whole incident. "Right on, man! Far out!" they applauded. Bobby held up his fingers in the peace sign, and they doubled over in laughter.

Eventually, I wanted more money than my parents were sending me, so I took a job as a replacement receptionist for a busy office; one hour a day, during lunch. The head of the company felt he couldn't spare his other employees to answer the telephone while the regular receptionist was at lunch. But one day, I reported to work and was told that during my hour the day before, I had received nine more personal calls than the president of the company. So that job went. But not before I met Prince Kandra of Sri Lanka.

One day, I arrived at work early, and since it was a nice day, I sat on the bricks near the subway and enjoyed the sun. A short Indian guy wearing shiny, patent-leather elevated shoes came up to me and said, "You wouldn't be the model, Jean Shrimpton?" He spoke with a marked accent and a small, squeaky voice.

This was a total absurdity, but I just said, "No, but thank you. I'm not a model."

"I could have sworn you were a model," he said. "What do you do?"

"I'm a singer and an actress."

"I have a theater company, actually," he said. "My name is Prince Kandra. Pleased to meet you."

I said, "Did your parents name you Prince?"

He tittered. "No, no, that's a title. I'm the Prince of Sri Lanka."

I gave him the office number. A week went by, and I didn't hear from Prince Kandra, nor were there any messages from him.

One day I got a phone call. "Hello, this is Prince Kandra."

"Oh, my God, hi — Prince." The conversation went on for a bit, until I realized it was Bobby, not my Prince. I slammed the phone down, and a half hour later, I got another call.

"Hello, this is Prince Kandra."

"Drop dead, Bobby, I already know it's you. It's not funny the second time. It wasn't funny the first time."

"This is Prince Kandra. Is Margo Girard there, please?"

"One moment, please," I said, and putting down the phone, I took five deep breaths, then answered in a lower voice. "Hello?"

"Margo, I'm sorry it took me so long to call you. I've been very busy, and so on and so forth." He said "and so on and so forth" every other sentence. "I'm going to send my chauffeur over to pick you up after work and take you to my place for an evening drink or tea or whatever. Is that all right?"

I had a date, so I said no, I couldn't.

"Then the next day, you will come. Come after work, at 1 p.m.?"

I said fine, that he didn't need to send a chauffeur, I would walk. I went over the next day carrying tapes of my voice. I knew he was a phony, but I figured it was worth finding out just how phony. Sulynn was especially anxious for me to see if he had any money and/or any wealthy or titled friends.

"Prince" lived in an apartment building on Front Street, near the water. On the walls of his pint-sized apartment were huge photos of Prince standing next to Picasso, President Johnson, Raquel Welch and other celebrities.

I sat down, and he began listening to my tapes. He said, "Well, very good. We will be doing a musical together. You're very talented, and so on and so forth."

I went back four different times. The fourth time, when I went there with a recent tape of a voice lesson, he put his hand on my knee and said, "I want to get to know you."

I said fine. He was so short, I thought he would be easy to overpower.

Then he said, "Come here in front of the mirror for a minute." We stood in front of the mirror. The Prince came up to about my belly button.

"You have very beautiful cheekbones," he told me. "And a very beautiful bone structure, and so on and so forth. I want you to be in some of my movies. I also produce movies."

"Oh," I said. "That sounds great."

He cautioned, "But I want you to be able to act. Are you a passionate girl? Can you produce passion?"

I said, "Well, that depends."

"In order to be in movies, you've got to be relaxed and loose. For instance, if I kissed you..." He proceeded to stand on his toes in an attempt to cram his tongue down my throat. I pushed him away. "No, Prince, it's not going to work. I'm not interested in that at all." So we sat down.

He said, "Well, you know, if you're going to be working with me, and if you're going to be doing movies and musicals — although you have to relax more, obviously — we'll work on that — but if I'm going to produce a musical for you, my contract would be exclusive. I don't want anyone else in on this."

"My father's a lawyer," I answered, "and he'll definitely be in on it. I'm not signing anything."

"No, no, no," he screamed, standing up. "I detest lawyers. I will not have nothing to do with lawyers."

I also stood and gazed down at him from my lofty 5'7" height. "You know, Prince, in that case, let's call it quits now. There's no way I'm going to make a move without my father."

"You cannot be this immature," he yelled. "You cannot be hanging on daddy's coattails, and so on and so forth. You sit back down here, and we'll get to work. You will not have a lawyer. Also, you will RELAX, so that you can be PASSIONATE and be in my movies."

"Prince, really —" I headed toward the door. "It's been nice meeting you. Thank you very much."

He slammed his fists on the table and said, "You — you little nothing — are saying NO to me, PRINCE KANDRA OF SRI LANKA? I am royalty, and you, you little nothing, are saying no?"

"That's correct, Prince. You speak English very nicely."

"GET OUT! HOW DARE YOU!"

I left. By this time, he had my home phone number, at the insistence of Bobby, Art, Fred and Sulynn, and that night, he called and apologized, "Come back tomorrow, and we'll get to work both relaxing you for the movies and working on the musical."

"Fine," I said. Then, to rile him, I added, "In fact, I might even bring my father."

I got the desired reaction. "NO! ABSOLUTELY NOT. IN THAT CASE, THE RELATIONSHIP IS TERMINATED." He slammed down the phone.

Occasionally, as the years went on, I would see the Prince hanging out in Government Center in his patent leather elevated shoes.

Another time, Sulynn met a Frenchman at Harvard, and we both went to a party for Harvard French students. They had all just smoked their first pot (they split half a joint among seven of them) and were completely wrecked; they threw cous-cous across the room. Sulynn and I spent most of the evening ducking.

At one point, I looked out the window at the beautiful view of the campus, wishing that I were outside, and one of the French guys came over and said, "Excuse me, you know I would like to suck your blubber." I said, "What?"

He said, "I would like to suck your blubber."

I said, "That's okay, I'd like to kick you in your balls."

He called his friend over and indicated I was to repeat what I just said. I repeated, carefully, I-want-to-kick-you-in-your-balls. His friend translated what I said into French and the other man said, "Then get out of my house."

These were the horror stories. But there were some nice guys along the way, guys I slept with, all the time feeling more and more attracted to Art and getting nowhere with him.

Sex was accompanied by Roman Catholic Guilt. I was always sure I was pregnant, and every month I waited in terror for my period.

Finally, I went to the gynecologist everyone was going to, to be fitted for a diaphragm. The sight of the diaphragm traumatized me; I was sure I'd never be able to insert it. The gynecologist suggested I try it while in her examining room. I picked up the diaphragm. It was so greasy, it flew out of my hand and bounced against the wall. The doctor was exceedingly patient. Finally, I succeeded, but I wasn't sure it was going to be worth the trouble.

Thus armed for action, a confident me returned to school on Monday, and instead of running into an attractive, available man, I ran instead into the awful Amalia Hayes, my arch-enemy. It was apparent from the first that Amalia and I were destined to be in competition. She also possessed a strong singing voice and, with her dark hair and strong features, was similar physically to me. What's more, she made no bones about the fact that she was after Art and Bobby. And on that score, I silently wished her good luck.

One day, problems with Amalia extended off stage. We banked at the same bank, Shawmut Savings, and on this particular day, on my way over there to deposit a check from my mother, I met her at a "Don't Walk" sign on Boylston Street. She, too, was on her way to Shawmut Savings. She allowed me to get ahead of her in line and stood directly behind me. When it was her turn, Amalia stole the teller's name plaque, proudly showing it to me when we got outside.

A few days later, I went back to the bank and was accosted by a security guard. They had studied the security camera film and fingered me as an accomplice, since I had stood and waited to walk out with Amalia. I played dumb about the sign and approached one of the tellers.

"You were with a girl who stole a name plaque," she said. Now I knew what Peter felt like the night he denied Christ. The situation was obvious: either get the plaque back or change banks. I went to Amalia, who shrugged and laughed. "They'll never see me again. I closed my account that day. I took the plaque as a souvenir. I doubt they'll send the police for me." No, just harass me to death, I thought.

"You'd better get it back," Art teased me, "or you'll become the sex slave of some dyke warden in prison."

I got it back by going to Amalia's dorm when I knew she was in class and telling her dorm mother that Amalia sent me to retrieve a book. Great security — the dorm mother directed me to Amalia's room, and after I conducted a search that made police drug searches look amateur, I found it under her mattress. I then returned it to the bank. For some reason, Amalia never mentioned the incident.

I didn't seriously worry about Amalia competition-wise, because my singing voice could blow her out of the water. My voice teacher was Madame Lutrice Duboniet. She was an excellent teacher, and my voice developed from a big, raw soprano to a beautiful sound, and I managed a grade of A– every semester. I sang operatic arias at my vocal juries. Madame Duboniet and some of the other teachers encouraged me to switch to the Opera Department.

One teacher who urged me toward an opera career did so for his own reasons. Mr. Hal Winslow, one of the Performance Class teachers, hated my guts, thanks to Amalia's intervention. He was a has-been actor-singer at the age of 30 and had no business teaching, but given the salaries the school paid, he was all they could get.

Winslow and Amalia were having an affair, although it was unknown to us at the time. But his crush on her was obvious, as was the preferential treatment she received. He gave me a terrible time in class, perceiving me as a threat to her. He told me to go into opera because "you're not a very good actress and your voice doesn't sound good in musicals."

At one point, Winslow decided I was having "problems" and invited Madame Duboniet to class to see if she could figure out what was wrong with me. I was working on a scene from *The Most Happy Fella*, which ended with the beautiful song, "Somebody, Somewhere." In front of the class and Miss Duboniet — and, of course, Winslow told everybody why she was there — I did the scene and finished with the song. There was a long, tense silence afterwards.

Winslow stood up. "Well, aren't you something," he sneered. "AREN'T YOU SOMETHING. Aren't you just like my air conditioner I've got at home?

"Now, everyone has had this happen to them. It's ninety-five degrees out with one hundred percent humidity. You're sweatin' to death. Everything you can think of, you try to get this air conditioner to work. You call a repairman — two weeks wait. For two weeks, you sweat. No air conditioner.

"Doorbell rings." (He made a buzzer-type sound.) "It's the repairman. And just at that moment, the air conditioner starts working. Isn't that always the way? As soon as the repairman shows up, it's working perfectly.

"Same thing with MISS Girard. I bring the repairman here in the person of Madame Duboniet, all of a sudden, MISS Girard is fine."

From that point on, I was known as "the air conditioner."

Winslow, of course, had dug his own grave. I didn't care that he hassled me in class, because I knew the reason was mad passion for

Amalia. I planned to draw the line and go to the administration if he gave me a bad grade. However, after inviting Madame Duboniet to class and having her witness that there was nothing wrong with me, he couldn't give me a low mark.

Despite being encouraged to go into opera, I was more interested in musicals and was busy working on my acting. For my freshman second-semester jury, I did a scene from *The Miracle Worker*, as Annie Sullivan. Sulynn played Helen Keller, which she practiced for weeks by blindfolding herself, putting cotton in her ears and falling over chairs. The jury didn't hold her performance against me and gave me an A–. No one ever got an A in performance subjects.

Music Theater Department students had two major goals: to get a great role in the annual musical once one was an upperclassman; and, following senior year, to be part of the paying summer stock company that the school ran in Cofis, New York. This was the beginning of a résumé, which would lead to fame and fortune in New York. It was with these goals in mind that we all worked to impress the faculty.

I went back to Rochester the summer after freshman year, but after that, I stayed in Massachusetts. In February of sophomore year, I became aware that Chick Dawson, a piano major, was interested in me. I looked him over and found that the interest was mutual. Chick introduced himself to me by knocking on the door of my practice room and complimenting my singing. After that, whenever I used a practice room, Chick, by some coincidence, was using the room right next to mine, and often ended up accompanying me and coaching me. There got to be less and less of the musical accompaniment, and more and more of a piece of cardboard taped over the little window, and the sound of smooching, rather than song, emanating from the room.

Chick wanted to put together a group of singers to work on Cape Cod during the summer. The group would then work in Boston performing at functions during the school year. That's how Sulynn, Bobby, Art and I ended up as singing waitpersons at a restaurant in Dennis, Massachusetts.

Being a singing waiter or waitress is great so long as you're under twenty and have the superhuman strength to do five shows a night plus serve dinner and drinks, six nights a week from 6:30 p.m. to 2 a.m. The restaurant was owned by two men, unaffectionately known as The Simons Legree. Bobby did the choreography, Chick did the music direction and was the accompanist, and we called ourselves, in an imaginative twist, The Cape Codders. Sulynn and I lived together in a rented house two miles from the restaurant; Chick lived close by in a house he shared with our drummer (we were hardly serious enough to live together). There was another reason for me to stay free: the availability of men on the Cape. And Chick was aware of the availability of women, so there was little discussion of living together. Sulynn and I shared our place with three college students who came down on weekends, and the town we worked in was near enough to Yarmouth so that Bobby and Art could commute from their mother's.

Sulynn's mother made our Cape Codder outfits: short blue skirts, white blouses and red vests and the male equivalent of blue pants, white shirts and red vests. There was always a contest among the four of us to see whose uniform smelled the worst. Each morning, upon arriving home, Sulynn and I threw our uniforms in the kitchen sink in a Lestoil presoak. We were due at the restaurant at 6:30 p.m., and at 5:30, hair in hot rollers, we took turns at the iron, attempting to make our uniforms presentable.

I was assigned several character songs: "Adelaide's Lament" from *Guys and Dolls*, "Gooch's Song" from *Mame*, plus every song Ethel Merman ever sang. The pretty soprano part of my voice wasn't needed, since Sulynn was singing all the ingénue and leading lady numbers. Art and I did "Anything You Can Do I Can Do Better." The last night of the show was considered kind of a cut-up night, and the restaurant was mainly peopled by regulars. Art and I did the number, and when we got to the part about baking a pie, I let him have one in the face, courtesy of the guys in the kitchen. He retaliated by picking up the pie pan and slathering me with what was left.

It was during this job and living on the Cape that my oats were sown in a way I never dreamed possible. I found lust on the Cape. But I also found romance. There's something about a resort area, with the beach nearby and the balmy nights, that lends itself to such things as outdoor lovemaking. After seeing *From Here to Eternity*, love in the sand with the water nearly drowning me became a fantasy which turned into a reality that summer. However, I couldn't help but notice that in the movie, Deborah Kerr was not shown itching herself to death the next day.

My days off were never boring, especially when I was in Yarmouth with one or both of the Gaines brothers. On one such memorable occasion, Art went into Boston, Sulynn to her family's in Framingham, and I went to Yarmouth with Bobby. We decided to get some beer and "hang out" at a nearby pond and listen to music. Bobby asked Fred to drive. He very often passed driving chores to someone else, and I never cared. It was usually safer.

But if Bobby was an atrocious driver, Fred had him beat. It must have been the driver's ed in Yarmouth. We drove down a path that Fred and Bobby knew from childhood, and Fred turned the car over sideways in a ditch. Bobby climbed out of the car first, hoisted me up, and then Fred.

Devastated, Fred apologized continually. Once back on the main road, we hitched a ride in an open-backed truck with three other college-age kids. Fred was beyond consolation, but Bobby and I started to laugh as we hunched down in the back and felt every bump.

I tilted my head against Bobby's and, à la Roy and Dale, we sang the theme song from their TV show. Fred stared into space. "God, I'm so sorry," he said over and over. "I'm so sorry."

"You have great voices," the girl across from Fred said. "Sing 'Fire and Rain.'"

We bellowed, and she joined us. Fred was catatonic.

We asked the truck driver to drop us off at the Yarmouth Sands Motel so we could call for a tow.

No luck. There had been a huge accident somewhere and all the tow trucks were busy. We had to wait at the motel. Fred was too depressed to get into the spirit of adventure, so he sat on the steps before the entrance, resting his chin in his hand. Bobby and I looked around. We ended up crashing a wedding reception that was in session in one of the front rooms and met some very nice people. However, it was winding down by the time we arrived, and before we knew it, we were back with Fred on the steps.

Bobby performed "All I Need Is the Girl" from *Gypsy* for us, a number he was getting ready to do at the restaurant, and then he and I danced up and down the steps like Ginger Rogers and Fred Astaire. Fred, usually the life of the party, wasn't amused. "I'm exhausted," he said finally. "I've got to find a place to lie down," and headed for the parking lot.

"Is he crazy?" I said to Bobby. "He's not going to break into a car, is he?" We followed him, and sure enough, Fred was trying door after door, with no success at first. Then he hit one. He opened the door.

"GET THE FUCK OUT OF HERE," we heard a man yell from the depths of the car. I saw the tops of two heads surface in the back seat. The three of us ran like hell.

The tow truck arrived at around midnight. We all piled in. The tow truck pulled Bobby's car out of the ditch as if it were a toy. We pooled our money to pay the driver, then took Fred home.

By the time we got back to Lettie's, it was daylight. I conked out on the couch, and when I woke up, Lettie was cooking breakfast. "What did you do last night?" she asked me.

"Nothing," I said.

When we got back to school in the fall, Chick asked us to come over to his apartment to audition for a booking agent. We did "It's Today" as a group. Then Bobby and I performed "The Beguine" from *Dames at Sea*, and Sulynn sang "And This is My Beloved."

"You're great," the agent told us. "I can get you all kinds of work. You'll need photos and evening clothes."

Evening clothes were no problem; performers always have plenty of them. But we didn't have any group photos.

"Wear gowns and tuxes in the pictures," the agent said as he left. "I want to book you as a sophisticated act."

"I've got it!" Chick said. "Come to the Montmartre Club during the day while it's closed, and I can take the photos there. They'll be gorgeous." Chick managed the club, which was very glamorous and catered only to an exclusive membership of Boston Brahmins and their guests. It had been a men's club for years, but had recently admitted women.

We dragged all our belongings over there on the appointed afternoon — Sulynn and I with our hair in rollers, and our heads wrapped in scarves. Chick greeted us with all his camera equipment. The club was sunny and elegant — chandeliers, crystal and huge draperies which closed off sections of the dining room to give members privacy.

Sulynn and I went into the small ladies' room to fix our hair and to change, and we were just about finished when Art walked in. "Stay here," he whispered. "One of the members just brought a charity board of directors here for a meeting."

"Suppose one of them wants to get in here?" Sulynn asked him.

"Just stay here for now." He poked his head out, and as he did so, Bobby forced his way in.

"Maybe we can take the photos in here," I suggested, only half-kidding.

Minutes later, Chick came in. The place was beginning to look like Groucho Marx's stateroom in *A Night at the Opera*.

Chick's face was white with fear. "I can't believe this. Of all days. Okay, one at a time, I want you to sneak out and go right behind the curtain. I've closed off the nearest section. Bring all your stuff with you."

One by one, crouched as if to avoid enemy fire, we made it behind the curtain. The section was in front of a massive picture window which looked out onto Prudential Center. I could hear the usurpers on the other side of the club, near the bar.

After hiding our street clothes under the table and pulling the tablecloth down over them, we posed for photos. It was about as relaxed as being in front of a firing squad. Rather than talk and reveal our hiding place, Chick made signs with elaborate hand motions when he wanted us to change our positions, and he indicated what our expressions should be with his rubber face.

Finally, it was over, and we were forced to change our clothes in the small space, in front of all of Boston. Then we crawled out and ran for the elevators.

After all that, there was only one picture that was any good, but at least it was something the agent could use for publicity.

The agent was good as his word and got us jobs all around the Boston area. Our first big engagement was New Year's Eve 1970 in Framingham. It didn't start too auspiciously, however. As our names were called, a spotlight was supposed to shine on our faces. But the light man was confused. "Art Gaines," the announcer called, and the spotlight shown in my face. Undaunted, he yelled, "Sulynn Reilly" as Bobby's face was illuminated. The audience thought they were going to see a drag show or, at the very least, a comedy. The show was not a brilliant effort, but fortunately, the audience was too drunk to care.

Our agent was a low-life named Joe Waters, who kept the bookings coming, and we were happy for the money and experience, not to mention all the new music we were learning. One never knew when, during our professional careers, goyem like ourselves were going to be called upon to sing from *Fiddler on the Roof*.

However, somewhere along the line, Joe, a skinny, totally disorganized individual, unofficially put Bobby in charge (he had Bobby somehow confused with the much more reliable Art). Joe constantly gave Bobby the booking information and the directions to our engagements. A big mistake.

Sulynn's parents let her have their old, two-passenger second car when they were ready to junk it. She left it parked at her parents and, whenever we had a "gig," she went to Framingham and picked it up. Her parents let Bobby park out there, too. When we had a performance that took us out of Boston, the guys rode in one car and Sulynn drove the other, with me as passenger.

Bobby never had the right directions. Most of the time, he didn't even have the right town. I explained to him more than once that if he at least got the name of the town right, we had a fighting chance of reaching our destination.

One Saturday, we drove in circles. It was obvious we were going to be late for our job at a shopping mall in Billerica — at least, Bobby had told us it was in Billerica. Lost, Bobby stopped at a "yield" sign without warning, and I, driving Sulynn's car while she was putting in contact lenses, drove into him. Art and Bobby used to put their cardboard coffee containers on the dashboard; that incident marked the last time they did it. When they got out of the car, they both had coffee all over their faces and down the front of their clothes, as did Chick, who was drinking coffee in the back seat and spilled it all over his music as well. A shouting match ensued, which attracted a policeman, who finally escorted us to the mall, one town over.

Joe caught me at school one day and told me he had arranged a job for us in Portland, Maine, on a Sunday afternoon, all expenses paid. The others could drive up on Saturday, but I couldn't because I was singing "Ave Maria" in the church across the street on Sunday morning, a job Chick got for me. "No prob," Joe said. "This place is loaded. They'll pay to fly you in." We set a rehearsal for one o'clock in the afternoon. The show was at four, but my plane was late, and I showed up forty-five minutes late for rehearsal, only to find that rehearsal hadn't even started yet. There was no piano and the sound man, who had a broken leg, didn't have four microphones that worked.

The manager of the hotel had his finger glued to the panic button at all times — no acetone to get it loose. He was always out of control and hysterical, as was his staff, and he and Art fought non-stop.

Art was ready to quit when he saw there was no piano. "Haven't you guys ever hired singers before?" I asked.

"Well, yeah," the manager said, getting all huffy. "We had Peters here. We hired Peters."

"Roberta Peters, the opera star?" I asked.

"Yes." He puffed out his chest. "Roberta Peters."

"Roberta Peters? From the Metropolitan Opera?"

"Yeah, that's right. We hired her to come up here."

"And she brought a piano with her?"

"No, we got her a grand piano."

I nodded. "I see. You got her a piano. Okay, fine, just checking."

Joe took me aside. "You're going to have to talk to Art," he said. "He's got to understand."

"Well, you've got to understand," I said, loud enough for the manager to hear. "We come from a very different situation. We're used to working for professionals."

"As far as I'm concerned, you can leave now," I heard the manager say to Art.

But they were stuck with us, and they needed a show for a group of

VIPs, so a piano surfaced, as did some working microphones.

We finished rehearsing at three. At that point, I found out we were a ten-minute drive from the hotel where we were staying — the hotel where we were to sing had no available rooms. Chick needed to be back at the hotel at 3:30, and after changing into his performance clothes, he was obviously going to be late. We singers had to be back at 3:45, and it was 3:10 when Sulynn and I walked into the hotel room. At 3:30, the phone rang. Sulynn and I had electric rollers in our hair and no clothes and no makeup on. But Art was on the phone screaming: "We have to go now. They're ready for us."

There were only forty-three people in attendance, and the manager wanted everyone to be "surprised" we were there. We were told to walk in and mingle with this *huge* audience, grab mikes and start singing "Wilkommen." The audience looked at us with the unspoken question, "What the hell is this?" on their faces. Then we sang "Cabaret" with huge high notes at the end, jumping around with personality plus. No applause. They all resumed their conversations. Then, when we finished the show, all forty-three people followed us out, trying to hire us.

The four of us agreed it was the worst show we'd ever done. It was as if Dracula himself had drained the blood from Art's body. There was just barely a pulse when he was doing the show. His "Impossible Dream" was the most desultory thing ever performed. And Chick was not exactly on uppers — more like Sominex. He played everything at half speed. When I sang "Musetta's Waltz," I kept breathing in the middle of words, because the tempo was so slow. Yet we ended up with ten more bookings.

Hotel jobs paid the most money, so Joe got us a lot of those. One memorable gig was for a brand new hotel in Boston. Twenty limited partners heard how the hotel was so successful, because these fabulous entertainers were here — big New York singers, the manager told them. Sulynn and I had never been to New York, and Art and Bobby had gone with Lettie only once, to see Pearl Bailey in *Hello, Dolly*.

Joe and this particular hotel manager put a lot of pressure on us to do a great show. On show night, we were nervous and exhausted. Our show set-up changed from time to time, but normally, we stood behind the stage while Chick played numbers like "The Bells of St. Mary's" on the marimba. This was intended to warm up the audience.

Chick always drove Art insane. "Okay," he'd hiss, "Chick's finished. Here's the microphone. Get ready." Then, inevitably, Chick would go into another number, the Italian version of "Rhapsody in

Blue," for instance, on yet another instrument. No matter how many times we thought it was our cue to start singing, Chick had another number literally up his sleeve.

This particular night, we knew definitely that since the owners of this hotel were there, and it was supposed to be a "big" show, that Chick would play seventeen numbers. So, at the end of "The Bells of St. Mary's," Sulynn meandered over to the opposite side of the microphones, picked up a lipstick and applied it, figuring we had a long wait.

Chick faked us out. He decided to only play one number. After "The Bells of St. Mary's," we heard our one-note introduction for "Hello, World," an opening song Chick wrote especially for the Cape Codders. Sulynn was supposed to begin by singing, "Hello, sun..." She could never get the first note. I always sang it in her ear. Each time, she used the musical introduction to walk over to the microphone, lipstick in hand. I then sang her note to her, and in her flattest, dullest tone she would sing the line, "Hello, sun..." Then she would leave the microphone and amble back to her hairbrush on the other side.

Art was so nervous this time that he couldn't take it. "GET OVER HERE," he signaled to her, mouthing and waving his hands. Sulynn and I started laughing. "Don't yell at me," she squeaked in between laughs.

Chick was still playing his one-note introduction, and we couldn't get Sulynn to start singing. She was completely spastic with laughter. I couldn't step in for her, because I was laughing, too, and hoping to get composed by the time my phrase occurred. Sulynn's music was totally out of Art and Bobby's vocal range.

Suddenly Sulynn started jumping up and down and squealing, "I wet my pants. Can you see it? Can you see it?"

Chick continued his one-note introduction. In vain, I hummed the note. "Get over here," Art growled, teeth clenched. "Get over here. I swear I'm going to kill you. I'll beat the shit out of you. Get over here." Sulynn continued to jump around. "I wet my pants, I wet my pants."

The one note was still playing. I hummed the note again. Finally, Sulynn went to the microphone. "Hello, SU..." — she ended in a gail of laughter and doubled over. "Hello, MOO..." — Art covered his hand with his mouth and laughed, unable to finish the line.

I actually got through my phrase, "Hello, earth." Then it was Bobby's turn: "Hello, world." He choked on "world." The band started playing, and we all ran out to our microphones on stage. We were then to sing together the phrase, "Hello, world." We managed to sing "Hell," then started laughing again. We never sang the opening number. None of us could stop laughing. The band played on. We did our choreography, laughing all the time, and managed some sort of ending on "Hello, World." Complete silence — no surprise. Then a spattering of applause. There were thirteen people there, all on one side of a long table. It looked like the Last Supper. They just stared at us, waiting for us to be fabulous. It never happened.

Partially because we worked so closely together, my romance with Chick proved to be an enduring thing, and soon he was my steady boyfriend. I was aware that Art resented it and was often hostile to Chick. But Art didn't seem pressed to do anything about it, either, as I pointed out to Sulynn.

Sulynn and Bobby had some sort of subliminal understanding between them. Although they both dated others, they never became serious with anyone. One night, she asked me if I had slept with Art, knowing full well that if I had, she would have been the first to hear about it.

"No," I said. "Have you slept with Bobby?"

"No, but close."

I shrugged. "Past a certain point, close doesn't count. I've come close with Art, too. The Gaines brothers don't seem big on commitment, do they?"

She didn't reply. "Are you in love with Chick?"

"I doubt it. I like Chick. Chick is a nut. Chick is a great musician. Chick is fun to be with. Am I in love with Chick? No."

"Probably because you're in love with Art. The same way I'm in love with Bobby."

But Sulynn's love for Bobby was obviously a lot more painful for her than mine was for Art. "Maybe you should talk to him."

"Wouldn't do any good."

She was probably right, at that.

Things with Chick were never boring. He was highly accident prone, for one thing. Once, after hurting his hand with a knife, he disappeared into the bathroom for forty-five minutes, rinsing, using hydrogen peroxide and witch hazel. When he came downstairs, the wrong hand was bandaged.

For a musician who had to be cool under pressure (especially playing for a group like the Cape Codders), Chick wasn't cool under any circumstances. He demonstrated this when my cousin Carol came to live in Boston and stayed with me for a time.

Carol had had her personality surgically removed. She was, at one time, a fabulous person, very funny and gregarious. She was also at one time about two hundred pounds overweight. Then, deciding she had an addictive personality, she flushed out her personality along with her fat cells and became the most morose person I ever met in my life.

Carol showed up in Boston and, while she was looking for an apartment, stayed on Park Drive and got a job in a hair replacement salon. Sulynn at this point was never home nights, having picked up with an oboist from school. (She was making a big point of the romance for Bobby's benefit.) I was spending a lot of nights at Chick's.

Carol came home one night when no one was home, and she somehow lost the set of keys I gave her. She went across to the Napoli Bakery and asked Anthony, who was later convicted of armed robbery but at that time lived behind the store, if she could use the phone. She called Chick and said she was locked out of the house, and was I there. I wasn't, as a matter of fact. We were all rehearsing for the school production of *Guys and Dolls*. Amalia and I were double-cast as Adelaide, Sulynn was Sister Sara (double-cast, of course), Bobby was Sky Masterson, and Art was Nathan Detroit.

Chick was a great panicker and fed into Carol's already growing hysteria. "I can't get in, and it's midnight," she wailed. "Someone's going to get me; I don't know what to do."

"All right, all right," Chick said. "This is what I'm going to do. Are you near a phone?"

"I am talking to you on a phone."

I walked by the bakery at that point and noticed the lights were on at midnight. I saw Carol inside and waved. She hung up on Chick, never finding out what he intended to do. When she finally got an apartment in Little Italy, I was happy to help her move.

Guys and Dolls was directed by Miss Sandra Fossey, one of the acting teachers on staff at the school. My nemesis, Mr. Winslow, appeared at every rehearsal and took notes on my performance and coached Amalia in private. Miss Fossey was a very talented woman, and no one was quite sure why she had given up a promising career as a New York actress to teach in Boston. At one Park Drive gathering, we'd all seen her on an episode of "Hawaii Five-O." When I mentioned it to her at the school elevator the next day, she blushed. "I hope no one else saw it," she said.

"All my friends did," I informed her. "You were very good."

"Oh, dear," she said, and blushed even more.

Guys and Dolls was to be our crowning glory, the culmination of four years hard labor at the school. For my money, they could have chosen something that showed off my abilities a bit more, but I put my heart and soul into it and tried to forget I was double-cast with Amalia. It wasn't easy, with Winslow making such a big deal of every little thing she did.

Bobby was having terrible stomach problems and was out of active rehearsal for a time, sitting on the side and taking notes. Winslow said to him, "Look at Amalia. She has a slipped disk and is in excruciating pain all the time, and yet she's able to do rehearsals."

Bobby wondered about this, since Amalia was going to bed with Winslow and about five other guys, and in rehearsals, the day before Winslow told Bobby what a martyr she was, Amalia had been fooling around by doing back-flips across the floor.

I put in my almost-last coffin nail when Amalia showed up for a rehearsal — for which she was not called — instead of going to her grandfather's funeral. That night, Miss Fossey threw a little party at her apartment, and Winslow attended. Amalia was there, too.

"Can you believe it?" Winslow said to me. "Can you believe the dedication she has? She showed up at rehearsal instead of going to her beloved grandfather's funeral."

"You give someone credit for that?" I said. "You think that it's *good* that she didn't go to her own grandfather's funeral? Her grandfather, who paid her tuition? Rather than be with her family, she showed up at a rehearsal where she wasn't needed? Hal, I think you have priorities all screwed up."

I thought that was the last coffin nail, but there was one more to come. The school had scheduled three performances of *Guys and Dolls*: Friday night, Saturday night and Sunday afternoon. The cast that got the opening and closing performances was considered the better cast. Since the men were single-cast, the competition existed only among the women, but during rehearsals, there was never a hint from Miss Fossey as to who would be giving which performances, or even what combination would make up one cast or another. The tension was unbearable. Dress rehearsal for Cast I was scheduled for Tuesday night; Cast II, Wednesday night; tech run-through, Thursday night; opening Friday.

On Monday, the cast lists were posted. Sulynn and I had the Friday and Sunday performances. Art stood behind us as we looked at the list.

"Listen," he said. "Can you hear that noise?"

I couldn't hear a thing.

"Listen carefully. It's Amalia grinding her teeth."

The show was a great success, and Miss Fossey again held a party, a cast party, at her large apartment on Boylston Street. During the evening, she made it a point to sit next to me. "I'm going to be directing at Cofis summer theater this year, Margo. Are you planning to audition?"

"Sure," I answered. We all were. "Do you know what shows they're doing yet?"

"That hasn't been set. Well, that's not true — one show has." She stood up. "I'm glad you'll be auditioning." Art, sitting on the arm of the couch next to me, said, "Sounds like she's got you earmarked for something."

Whatever I was earmarked for — whatever Bobby, Art, Sulynn and Fred and I did that summer — it was only to be a stepping-stone to New York. How many nights we passed discussing our grand plans to blow Boston and move to New York!

"I heard," Bobby said, "that thousands of people show up at these New York auditions, and everybody runs onto the stage at once."

"I heard," Sulynn said, "that no one, including your friends, will even tell you where an audition *is*. They'll tell you the wrong place and time."

"I heard," I said, "about a girl who sat next to another girl at an audition, and the girl she was sitting next to opened a bottle of gas or something so the other girl couldn't sing her audition."

"People get into summer stock if they have tap shoes," said Art. "If it's between you and another person, if you have tap shoes, you'll get in."

"I heard," Fred said, "that the way to get a job is to skip the audition, then call the music director or whoever's hiring and say you missed it and could you audition at their apartment. I heard you *always get hired* if you do that, because they get to really audition you, and they're not rushed."

The move to New York, of course, was not to be immediate; there were minor difficulties, like money and finding apartments. We planned to work in Boston doing our shows, drive down to New York for auditions en masse, and only move when we got work. And, like all other performers, we'd have a *New York answering service*, the lifeline to employment.

"All we need is a home base," Art said. "Just one of us has to land something, then each of us will have a place to stay until we get settled. But we've got to save our money from the Cape Codders."

It was fine to lecture Sulynn, who was tighter than Scrooge anyway, and me, who was always pretty good at saving money;

Bobby would never save a dime. But he had other talents. Like freeloading. Bobby made it his business to know who was flush and who wasn't, and he knew Sulynn was flush after stealing a look at her bankbook. Later, when she was complaining about money, as she always did, he said, "I don't know what you're griping about. You have $500 in the bank." Her normal high color paled. "How do you know that?" she demanded. "Have you been looking through my things?"

"Your bankbook was on the table here. If it's such a secret, why'd you leave it out?" Sulynn fumed about that for days. When it came to money, she played things close to her chest and didn't part with a penny easily. Her Christmas gifts were straight from Woolworth's.

One January, we did a show, and Sulynn and I went to her house to pick up the cars. Her sister, Peggy, was in the house and showed me the pocketbook Sulynn had given her for Christmas. "It's already torn," she said.

"Can't you take it somewhere and have it sewn?"

"Sew plastic?" She threw it down on the table.

I knew when we got to New York, Sulynn would have no problem with such details as security deposits, phone deposits and utility deposits.

Each week, Bobby bought *Back Stage*, the New York trade paper that listed all the auditions, and we studied it.

"I could do this..."

"Oh, I wish I was there *now*."

"This would be perfect for me."

"Listen to this. Doesn't this sound like me?"

But before the glorious New York auditions, there was to be compensation for four years of Boston College for the Performing Arts: lead roles in their summer stock company in Cofis, New York.

Cofis Summer Theater was open, by audition, to seniors. Sophomores and juniors, those who wanted to, worked as chorus people and apprentices. (Because of the Cape Codders, none of my crowd had ever done this.) Salaries for the leads consisted of room and train fare, plus twenty-five dollars a week.

Cofis was a wonderful way to get experience, and as far as the school was concerned, you couldn't beat the cost of labor, with the Cofis locals working for the joy of it, the apprentices basically slaves and everyone else getting as little as possible. Productions were directed by school staff, such as Miss Fossey and Mr. Winslow. Leads and supporting roles were played by seniors, the occasional teacher and non-Equity alumni.

Joining Actors Equity, the theatrical union, was, after moving to New York, the most important thing a young performer could achieve. Actors Equity was an entrée into Broadway shows and high-paying, prestige productions all over the country.

Miss Fossey explained it wasn't advisable to try to get into the union right away. "You'll have many more opportunities to work out of the union," she explained. "And when you're young and starting out, you need the experience that only a lot of performances can give you — summer stock where you play five different roles in a summer, dinner theater where you go off and do the same part for eight weeks, off-off Broadway experimental plays. Don't be in a rush to join the union. Once you're in it, it's much harder to get work."

This didn't keep Sulynn and me from plotting different ways of getting our Equity cards. We'd heard all of them: crashing Equity auditions and, once hired, taking the Equity contract to the union and "buying in"; joining a sister union, which then entitled you to join Equity or the other unions; Broadway "open calls," which could lead to an Equity contract. As far as we were concerned, once we were in New York, and the producers and casting people realized the talent before them, the card was in the wallet. Bobby and Art felt the same way. Ah, the cockiness of youth.

The Cofis season list was posted in March, and Sulynn and I broke our necks getting to the Department bulletin board. The shows to be done the summer of 1971 were: *Showboat, Oklahoma, The New Moon, The Odd Couple*, and "a new musical by Sandra Fossey," *Bloomin'*. Shows ran for one week, with two weeks of rehearsal allotted for the first production, *Showboat;* the entire season was six weeks.

I stared and stared at the list, trying to figure out what there was for me in that season. There was no cast breakdown of *Bloomin'*, but it seemed obvious that Miss Fossey had something in mind for me in that show, since she had approached me about working at the theater.

That night, Sulynn and I dissected the season. "Magnolia for me, Julie for you in *Showboat*," she began.

I shook my head. "No one will cast me as Julie. I have the legit voice, but you know how they are here. They're just interested in my belt voice, and they never cast me in any kind of legit leading lady role."

She paid no attention. "Laurie for me and Ado Annie for you in *Oklahoma*."

"Maybe."

"*The New Moon*," she continued. "What the hell is it?"

"It's an operetta like Romberg. I guess you would do Marianne. There are a couple of parts I can do in that." But I wasn't excited. I'd been hoping for *Gypsy*, *Annie Get Your Gun*, *Carnival*, something along those lines. I could sing "legit" very well but didn't fit ingénue roles, and character parts like Ado Annie were really too flimsy for me.

"*The Odd Couple* — well, guess who they have in mind for *that*. Are there female parts in it?"

"The Pigeon sisters. Art and Bobby are going to have a field day."

Sulynn concentrated on the scrap of paper in front of her. "This *Bloomin'* is a wild card." She nudged me. "Cheer up! What are you going to audition with?"

"Oh, what the hay — "Bill" and "I Can't Say No.""

"I've got to go to the library and get a record of *Showboat*," Sulynn said, throwing on her maxi coat. "I wonder who my Gaylord will be. Bobby?"

For someone who aspired to a career in musicals, Sulynn's knowledge could fill half a thimble. "There's a big dance role for Bobby, Sulynn. Didn't you see Gower Champion in the movie?"

"You mean Bob Fosse, don't you?" she called out, and left the apartment.

Three days later, I stood in the school theater, accompanied on the piano by Chick, and sang "Bill" from *Showboat* and then did a completely staged rendition of "I Can't Say No." The auditioners were President Lambini, Miss Fossey and Mr. Winslow.

After singing, I read a scene from *Oklahoma* with Bobby, who read Will Parker (the role was already his, I was certain), and then I did a scene from *The New Moon*, as Clotilde, with Art.

The cast lists were posted a week later. The only shock was just how poor my roles were: Gigglin' Gertie Cummings in *Oklahoma* (Amalia was doing Ado Annie); CHORUS in *Showboat*, understudying Julie — and who the hell was playing Julie, I asked myself, since across from the name, it just said ALUMNI; zip in *The Odd Couple* (Amalia would be sporting a British accent as a Pigeon sister in that vehicle); and Clotilde in *The New Moon* (Amalia had the role of Julie in that — a better role than Clotilde, as far as I was concerned). As for *Bloomin'*, a typewritten note said, "This production will be cast during the summer." Sulynn tied up all the ingénues — her arch-rival off to do summer stock elsewhere; Bobby had the dance roles; Art the good character roles; and Fred was cast in some supporting and character parts. With the exception of my own shafting, the cast lists were predictable.

After I cried for four days, I declared to anyone who would listen that I was not going. Chick and I would instead do a lounge act on the Cape. Chick was supposed to be the musical director for Cofis Summer Theater, but when he saw how upset I was, he agreed to go along with me.

Word reached the mucky-mucks, evidently, that Chick was thinking of defecting along with me, and I was directed into the teacher's lounge by Miss Fossey after a performance class.

"You're disappointed with the roles you got for the summer," she stated.

I started to cry. No amount of consolation the past few days was able to keep me from sobbing at any provocation.

Miss Fossey gave me a fresh hanky from her purse. "What hurts most of all," I choked, "is doing *chorus* in *Showboat*."

"We had some hard decisions to make," she said. "But you're very much needed there this summer. We need your beautiful, versatile voice, your energy, your talent..."

"You need Chick," I said, blowing my nose.

"I'm talking about you now. You remember that I asked you if you were planning to audition for the season." I nodded. "So I'm sure you were confused when you saw some of the casting. I asked if you'd be there because of my show, *Bloomin'*. There's an excellent role in it for you, a role that will require a lot of preparation that you won't have time for if you're doing too much else."

I wasn't mollified. "That's fine, except I notice I don't *have* the role."

"No, you don't, and there's a reason for that. I have some partners in this project, and they couldn't be here for the auditions. They're coming to the theater this summer, and they'll see everybody then. I can assure you that they will defer to me in casting, but of course, I couldn't make any decisions without them here. Please, Margo, don't cut off your nose to spite your face. All your friends are going to be there, it's going to be a good experience and a fun one. And you have an opportunity to do a brand new show, which, if I say so myself, is pretty darn good." She stood up. "So think about it." She left me sitting there.

That night I announced to Sulynn, Art, Bobby and Chick, "I'm doing summer stock." Everyone jumped up and cheered. "It's going to be a great summer!" Art declared, lifting his beer bottle.

My parents came for graduation and sat in the audience with Mrs. Gaines during the concert that was held the night before graduation. The concert involved all of the departments, and the

Dance Department regaled the audience with a modern dance involving folding chairs.

"If I had a child in the Dance Department, and I'd just spent four years tuition on her, I'd kill myself," my mother told me after the performance.

"That good?" I said. The Musical Theater Department did a number from *Carnival*, and the school chorus sang, accompanied by the student orchestra. All in all, neither my parents nor Lettie Gaines was impressed. A lot of hoopla, I thought, for a graduating class of forty. Eight people were graduating from the Musical Theater Department.

I brought Chick with us when we went out to dinner with the Gaines family, and my mother was not enamored of Chick. However, she couldn't stop talking about Bobby and Art — especially Art.

"We're just friends," I said, giving the standard fan magazine answer.

"That can change," she pointed out.

"It hasn't in four years," I replied. And not, I said to myself, for lack of trying.

My mother wasn't finished. "He doesn't seem too friendly with Chick."

"He's not. They both have Hitler complexes."

"I thought perhaps it was because Art liked you and was jealous of Chick."

I once thought that, too, but instead of saying that, I took a deep breath. "I don't think so, Mother." I changed the subject. If Art "liked" me, he had a strange way of showing it. Had he said the word at any time, I would have dropped Chick, and I was sure Art knew that.

Art and Bobby were very careful not to introduce Sulynn and me to their dates or include them in our social gatherings, and vice versa. I knew some of the girls they dated and when they dated them. They'd stop coming around so much. But the relationships never lasted and really couldn't be called anything more than casual dates. That Art and Bobby never talked about their sex lives with us, more than anything spoke to the fact that there were sexual tensions and unresolved conflicts.

Sulynn and I had stopped trying to figure the situation out long ago. After psychoanalyzing them to death, we decided they feared commitment because of their father's abandonment and wrote them off as potential lovers. I wasn't sure if my sexual attraction to Art was real or had to do with the fact that our relationship was never consummated. Sulynn admitted she wondered the same about herself and Bobby. But at this point, after four years of attending school and doing shows together, they were more like family than anything else. And the "family" was about to embark on another adventure: summer stock. "The big time," as Bobby put it.

Unless, of course, Uncle Sam intervened.

Student deferments were dust, and the lottery system was in force. Art had gone through the army physical after high school and had plenty to say about it, to any cannon fodder who wanted to listen.

"I've never been through anything so traumatic," he would begin to a poor soul whose unfortunate birth date came up number four in the lottery. "We were called by city and had to be at the Yarmouth post office at 5:30 a.m. An army bus arrived at 6 a.m. to drive us to the army base in Boston, at South Station.

"The place looked like factory after factory, with those glass-paned windows — huge warehouses. We were divided alphabetically and put into these rooms that were separated by partitions. You could hear everything that went on in the other rooms." Eyes generally widened and faces paled at this point in the narration.

"They hand you a questionnaire. There must have been a thousand questions. It took about an hour to complete it. And they warn you that you have to answer truthfully. They ask the same questions over and over in different ways, to try to trap you. 'Have you ever wanted to dress up like a woman?' 'Have you ever had sexual thoughts about men?' 'Have you ever had a sexual experience with a man?' — stuff like that. A psychological profile. Trying to trick you.

"You hand that in — there was a carbon underneath which got torn off — and you get sent to a place where you are told to strip to your underwear. But you still have your papers with you. Then you stand in lines and go through a physical. They make you urinate in front of everyone, and some guys were too nervous. But you stand there till you pee.

"Then you go into a cubicle for an ear test. Finally, you get to where you left your clothes, and they give you back the rest of your papers. Some people were sent to psychiatric. I got sent to a doctor — it turns out I have an ear problem I didn't even know about. I ended up with a 1Y, which means I only go if they call all the 4Fs."

The panic for many was on. Bobby was number 360, so there was no chance he would be called. Fred, on the other hand, was number five, and while he would be called, there was no chance he would be chosen. Some of the students declared themselves conscientious objectors, stating that the war in Vietnam was illegal and that they refused to serve in any capacity.

There really wasn't much for the army to get at our school, but those the army could grab made their escape plans craftily: they joined the National Guard; bought diseased urine; rehearsed insanity scenes in order to get a 4F; and faked suicides. Getting out of the army was more organized and rehearsed than any school production.

In the end, our merry band got to stay together and go to Cofis.

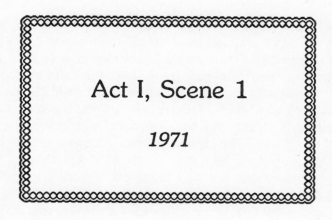

Act I, Scene 1

1971

Cofis Summer Theater was nothing more than a small stage in the center of a barely-converted barn, the doors of the barn covered with drapes. Somehow, though, with an audience, lights, costumes and music, there would be magic — I supposed. It was hard for me to get any real enthusiasm going.

The first day, we went right from the train station to the theater for our cast meeting. The entire school contingent was on the train, and the meeting was set to begin at 6 p.m., to accommodate the train schedule.

The man who ran the theater was an ex-actor named Grant Masters, who once taught at the music college and now lived in Cofis year-round. Art gave us the low-down on him. "My mother knew him when she was in New York. He was in a lot of musicals and quit the business because he went on for someone he understudied and was so good, the star had him fired. Sometimes he sings in the shows here." That turned out to be an understatement, as it was announced at the cast meeting by Miss Fossey that Grant Masters was to play Curley in *Oklahoma*, Gaylord Ravenal in *Showboat*, Robert in *The New Moon* — all leads — and one of the poker players in *The Odd Couple*.

"He'll be the oldest Curley and Gaylord Ravenal in history," Sulynn said under her breath.

"You'll have to gray your hair," I giggled.

"Well, we do have to age in *Showboat*. Maybe it'll work."

I whispered, "I doubt it."

Then we were introduced to Cindy Hopkins, who was to play Julie Laverne in *Showboat*. Julie had been the one role I really wanted.

More from Sulynn. "Her name isn't Cindy Hopkins. I heard at school she's in the Union and changed her name to do this so she wouldn't get caught. There's a big fine or something."

When I saw the "cast house," a rundown place in a shabby part of town, I almost went back to Boston on the next train. I shared a room with Sulynn and another girl, Betsy, a junior who was at the theater as an apprentice. There was one bathroom, with a hose-type thing instead of a shower. The kitchen looked as though eighty high school boys had taken up residence there.

The day after our arrival, I found out something else that was horrifying: we were expected to do children's theater. They didn't tell us at the first meeting, because they knew there was another train out the same night. Children's theater was a big source of revenue for the theater and one of the ways the school kept the place going. It was also used to train aspiring directors.

My first role was that of the Blue Fairy in *Pinocchio*. Sulynn was cast as Pinocchio, and Bobby Gaines played Geppetto. Rehearsals were held after normal rehearsals, and most of the time, I was so tired that my voice was raspy. The word soon got out that I was doing "Bette Davis as the Blue Fairy." It was unintentional, but exhaustion was breaking my voice up into a Bette Davis-à-la-*All About Eve* type of rhythm.

Shortly before opening *Pinocchio*, the director brought me two little blonde girls who were to be the gnomes of the Blue Fairy. It was a nice day, and rehearsal hadn't started yet, so I walked out into a field of weeds across from the theater. When I turned around, the two little girls were behind me. I didn't think anything of it and eventually returned to the theater, and again, the "gnomes" were with me. When I went to the ladies' room, they were still there behind me. Finally, I heard one say to the other, "He said to follow her wherever she goes."

"I think," I said, "that he meant in the play."

I always wore my hair very long, and Sulynn helped me iron out the waves. For the Blue Fairy, I decided I wanted something pert, so I went to the costume barn and found a short, curly brown wig, about two shades darker than my natural color. I thought it looked good and put it on for the rehearsal. When I got up on stage to do my first scene, the director stopped me.

"Take it off," he commanded. "You look like Herman Munster."

This particular version of *Pinocchio* began with a scene in which the Blue Fairy swoops in (with her gnomes behind her, of course), does an incantation, and sweeps off the stage amidst drum and piano rolls. The lights then go up, and there is Geppetto asleep next to the puppet, Pinocchio.

It happened a bit differently at the Cofis Summer Theater. The Blue Fairy swept in all right, but when she left the stage and went back to the dressing room, Pinocchio was there, rather than on stage, her fake nose sitting on the dressing room table and her suspenders half on.

"I don't know who called places," Sulynn said, "but I'm not ready." Ten minutes later, Scene Two took place to the absolute fury of the red-faced student director.

We were all underrehearsed and overtired, so perhaps it wasn't surprising that when the second scene started, Bobby as Geppetto really was asleep on the stage and had to be awakened by loud piano music. Upon regaining consciousness, he was disoriented and forgot the words to his first song, singing, "I'm proud, I'm proud, I'm proud, I'm proud, I'm proud, I'm proud, I'm proud, I'm proud," all the way through, instead of "My son, you make me proud to be your dad, I love you so."

By now, the student director, who was hopeful of directing one of the major productions, was wild. Unfortunately, hard as he tried, there was always a major problem in one or two performances of the children's shows. By major problem, I mean lost costumes, lost actors, forgotten lyrics. You name it.

But strange as it may seem, the audience never seemed to notice. The kids loved the shows and the place was always packed, even when the temperature soared.

The heat in Cofis never let up. One excruciating night during *Showboat*, I looked over (from my position in the chorus) at Sulynn as Magnolia, and sweat was pouring down her chest and face. At that same performance, Bobby did a series of turns on the stage, whipping sweat out into the audience and spraying them as he spun around.

The next show was *Oklahoma*, and in my first actual role of the summer, I decided to steal the show as Gigglin' Gertie Cummins. Stealing shows from Amalia was easy even if one had no lines. Gertie isn't a big part, but it's fun and in the hands of the right actress, very showy. A "guest" director arrived to do the show, and he was the busiest director I'd ever seen. "Okay, Gertie, you'll come out, carrying your picnic basket in one hand, and the other arm will be linked with Curly. You'll look to the right and smile..." Every move, every gesture — choreographed. "I Can't Say No" was an endurance test for Ado Annie. He had her doing everything from sitting in a chair and kicking her legs in the air to running to every corner of the stage. Amalia wasn't up to it and panted through her song each night.

Amalia wasn't the only one with a breathing problem — our lead, Grant Masters, was indeed a rather elderly Curly. But there was the matter of the aging portrait in his closet. We all knew he had one, and referred to him as "Dorian Gray" behind his back. According to the folklore, the portrait didn't kick in until Grant did a performance. Offstage he was aging, gray-haired, flabby and unenergetic, huffing and puffing his way through rehearsals and humming his music rather than singing it. Come opening night, he would practically need help to hobble to his first entrance. Before mounting the steps to the stage for the first time, Grant always took a deep breath. Then, leaping onto the stage, he inevitably dropped thirty years and thirty pounds.

All the men shared a dressing room, and Bobby studied Grant up and down. "There's nothing about make-up or girdles he doesn't know," Bobby told us.

"I'd love a peek in his closet," I said. "That portrait must be a *mess*."

I wanted a peek in his closet for another reason — I suspected Grant himself was in it. He was married with four children, but I was sure he was having an affair with Fred, *Showboat*'s Captain Andy. Art, Bobby, Fred and Chick were living in a house near the theater. While staying with Chick one night, I definitely heard Grant talking in the next room, which was Fred's. Grant's baritone voice was unmistakable. He was not there in the morning, and Fred never said a word. Such were the intrigues of summer theater. I asked Bobby and Art about it, and they claimed to know nothing, although I doubted it. When I told Sulynn, she made it her business to take special note of Grant and Fred whenever she could.

The production of *Oklahoma* was disrupted when Art had to leave Cofis on "family business," and a local took his part of Ali Hakim. That "family business" was so unusual and amazing, it made *The Cofis Press*.

The incident involved Lettie Gaines' older sister, Joûzia, and later, the entire Gaines clan. Joûzia agreed to take in a sick man from Poland who needed a heart operation but, according to the parish priest, couldn't come over to the States unless he had a sponsor. The Communists had agreed to let him out so long as his young wife and baby stayed in Poland. He arrived to stay with Joûzia at long last. But it was too late. The doctor who had begged to do the free heart operation was on vacation in Canada and couldn't be reached when the Pole finally reached the States. The man was lying ill in Joûzia's house and losing ground fast.

When the doctor finally returned and did the operation, the Pole died on the table. It was then, it seemed, up to Joûzia to get him back to Poland. But first, a funeral needed to be held, since it had to be documented by not only the United States but also Poland that he was indeed dead. Joûzia ran all over East Cambridge, digging up little old ladies, professional funeral attendees and members of her own family to attend his funeral, for which she paid. She also provided flowers. Art went back home for it, as the "man of the family."

There was an open casket at the wake, and someone photographed the event for documentation purposes. Joûzia then arranged to ship the body back to Poland to the man's mother. Representatives of the Polish Consulate and American Consulate were there for the sealing of the casket, and he was shipped back, with photos of the funeral and autopsy.

Three years later, in 1974, Art, Lettie, Joûzia and Mania, Lettie and Joûzia's younger sister, visited Poland. Joûzia hired a convoy of taxis to drive them and some of their Polish cousins to meet this man's mother. Down the dirt road the taxis went, in a line, into a sixteenth century village surrounded by fields and shacks.

When the dead man's mother saw Joûzia, she crawled on her hands and knees to her and would not look up, crying and kissing Joûzia's feet. Art got out of the car. The mother crawled on all fours to him and kissed his feet. She knew him, as did the entire village, from the pictures of the funeral.

Everyone went into the shack. There were gifts, there was Polish crystal, there was a ham, vodka — the family had spent their life savings on this meal. The family did not eat, but watched Joûzia and the group eat. The guests got smashed as the family continued to fill their glasses with vodka.

There was a trip past the church where the man had been baptized, then on to a huge granite mausoleum. Encased in the mausoleum were pictures of the funeral, with Art's face up there for all eternity.

Later, the Gaines family heard the whole story of this woman's poor dead son and how the Communists persuaded a young girl to seduce him while he was in his last year in the seminary. As her payoff, after his death, she married a Communist bigwig and moved to Warsaw with the child.

In 1981, Lettie's mother, Grandma Jania of Beacon Street, went to Poland, and the scenario was played out again. Jania appeared in the little village wearing her K-Mart dresses and Eva Gabor wigs and was revered, particularly because she was bilingual.

Art returned just in time for my personal favorite that summer, *The New Moon* — not a show to be done in a barn. Also, we found out the hard way, it was not a show to be done seriously, being much more playable as a camp classic.

Sulynn, not at her acting peak, played the desirable heroine, Marianne. She had a big line before the rousing number, "Stout Hearted Men:" "Rally — rally." She said it in the same vapid monotone she used to say "Judd — Judd" during Judd's attempted seduction of her in *Oklahoma*. "Rally-rally Judd-Judd" became a saying within the company.

Then came the big battle scene. Bear in mind that *The New Moon*, most of it, takes place on a ship. Needless to say, at the Cofis Summer Theater, the big battle had to take place off-stage. As a matter of fact, it took place outside so the audience couldn't see it. One night, the wind swept the main entrance curtain up and the audience saw ten guys, jumping up and down, yelling and pretending to swing swords.

During the run of *The New Moon*, there was a special cast meeting called so Miss Fossey could talk to us about her creation, *Bloomin'*. She passed out a cast list with a physical, vocal and personality description of each character and told us the story.

Bloomin' concerned a bunch of kids from the same neighborhood and what happened to them in the '60s. When the play begins, the characters are thirteen years old. As they develop, one ends up in an underground movement that blows up buildings, one becomes a priest, one a drug addict, one a rock singer, one a politician. I really didn't listen to her with much concentration. The only thing important to me was that I get the decent role promised me to make up for the inferior ones I'd had the rest of the summer. So, while Miss Fossey was rattling on, I was staring at the cast breakdown:

MANDY MORGAN: Feisty, lead/character type. Strong belt with legit, combo of Joan Baez/Judy Collins. Becomes a radical member of the underground movement.

ROBIN GUTHRIE: Ingénue, folk voice, flower child, Marianne Faithful type.

ZIDA HOGAN: Character role with comedy, militant, tough, strong belt voice. Lainie Kazan type. Mandy's friend in the underground.

RON CLARK: Leading man, tenor or high baritone. Must be strong, presidential. Becomes an idealistic politician, à-la-John Kennedy.

KEITH MAYERS: Young character actor, true hippie, baritone/rock, Frank Zappa type. A sweet quality.

LARRY ZYDEK: Young character actor, no singing, good
acting ability required. Shy in the beginning, he becomes bolder
and more assertive as the play progresses. Woody Allen type.

Miss Fossey obviously copied her cast descriptions from any issue
of *Back Stage* that we passed around at school. The cast lists in *Back
Stage* were always a scream, leaning heavily on TV and movie actors
to make their point. "A singing Susan St. James type," "A redheaded
Bette Davis," "A brunette, but with a Marilyn Monroe vulnerability."

Auditions were a week away, and I was in a good position, having
the accompanist in my hip pocket, as it were, and a strong sympathy
vote. I took scenes and music for the role of Mandy, and Chick and I
went off with my tape recorder to study.

Chick made tapes for everyone of their audition songs, but worked
with me, Bobby and Art back at their place, where there was an
out-of-tune upright piano. Chick had the entire score and played some
of the ensemble numbers for us.

"The music's kind of pretty," Bobby said. It had a folk-jazz quality
to it that was different. I loved Mandy's big number, "Sweet Times,"
and decided to use that as my audition number.

According to Miss Fossey's innuendo, I had no competition, but I
wasn't fooled. There would be others judging the audition besides
her.

Sulynn was sure to audition for Robin. My competition was
Amalia — nothing new there. I didn't know Mr. Winslow's
involvement, but he certainly had used his influence to get her good
roles so far. "You have no problem," Sulynn assured me. "Foss
practically *told* you that you have it." No good getting too cocky,
though. I decided to be totally prepared.

Chick and I had a date the night the songs and scenes were passed
out. We went to see *The Out of Towners* at the drive-in, which was
enough to make me decide not to move to New York. It was about a
couple, Jack Lemmon and Sandy Dennis, and the horrors that befall
them when they come to Gotham.

It was rather difficult for Chick and me to be alone — he had his
own room, but I was uncomfortable with both Bobby and Art living
there. Fortunately, his car seat flattened all the way down.

Over dinner at the local burger joint, Chick gave me his view of
the casting situation. "You were obviously brought up here to do the
lead in this," he announced. "As a matter of fact, I'll go a step further,
Margo — I think Foss wrote the role for you."

I nearly choked on a piece of lettuce. "Why do you say that?" I grabbed for my water.

"I've studied the entire score and read the script. It's you. What the hell are you doing here, then? They didn't do one show you were right for, but she wanted you here. You've got the best voice, and yet you weren't really used to your ability. It seems obvious. It's been obvious all along, so you've got no problem."

"I could have done Julie in *Showboat*."

"Forget Julie. This part was *written for you*. Look, Margo, a part like Julie is not really right for you. You're not a true leading lady. And see, neither is Mandy Morgan. She's a leading lady with a twist — that's you. I see the way the music is written and the humor in the script — Fossey intended it for you."

"We'll see."

"See, I think this audition is for verification purposes only. The thing is cast. It has to be. She couldn't do it unless she was sure she had the people for it here."

Instinct told me Chick was right. Still, I wasn't taking any chances. I practiced reading my scenes, using Bobby to rehearse with, and I memorized not only my scenes, but my song.

I was scheduled to audition at 2:00 p.m. I spent a lot of time on my hair and makeup. First, the face: a ton of eye make-up. I carefully penciled in eyelashes on my lower lid. I then put on pale lipstick and tied a scarf around the top of my newly-curled head, gypsy style. Wearing full black pants and a shiny white blouse, I threw a lightweight black shawl over my shoulders. After I held one earring after another up to the mirror, I decided on gold hoops.

I vocalized very carefully, something I hadn't done all summer. I could hear Amalia downstairs, doing the same thing. Then I heard her go into "Sweet Times." Amalia was going for Mandy, too. Her audition was first, and I watched her leave from the bedroom window. She was wearing a peasant skirt and off-the-shoulder blouse. I looked over at my closet. Maybe I should change to a skirt. No, I decided.

I put on my platform shoes and took my time getting to the theater. It was boiling hot. The scarf drove the sweat glands in my scalp insane. I sat outside the theater on one of the benches with Bobby, while Amalia was inside singing.

Bobby patted my hand. "She's not nearly as good as you."

"Thanks, pal. You've got nothing to worry about."

"I've got Golden Boy Grant Masters to worry about, and he auditioned at eleven o'clock this morning."

"Grant Masters is going for a part in this? He's not a tenor."

"Have you looked at the music? It's not that high."

"Still, they must want a tenor quality, which he doesn't have. Also, he can't play young. He's too burly."

"Yes," Bobby reasoned, "but he might be able to blackmail them. He thought he was getting Oscar Madison. He wanted that part worse than anything. When he found out I had it, he hit the ceiling."

"This isn't The Grant Masters Theater. He can't have everything."

"They need him here to run the place. If he makes enough of a scene, he'll get this show."

Art arrived a few minutes later, in the middle of Amalia's audition. "She sounds like shit," Art said, sitting next to me on the bench.

"She's a no-talent," Bobby agreed, on the other side of me.

A minute later, Sulynn happened along. "What time are you people auditioning?" I asked. "I'm at two o'clock. Sulynn, weren't you this morning?" She very thoughtfully hadn't come back to the room afterwards, to give me time to prepare.

"I came to hear you," she said, plopping down next to Bobby.

"I auditioned at 11:30," Art said.

"I'm after Margo," Bobby said.

By the time I went in, Fred was there, too.

I reflected as I walked in that, although I hadn't even begun my professional career, I was already sick of auditioning. Miss Fossey introduced Zack Vincent and Tom Scardini as her "partners." Tom, it was revealed, wrote the script.

I was terrified that all the words and music would fly out of my head, but they didn't, and the song, "Sweet Times," went really well, Chick supporting me on the piano as he had hundreds of times. When I finished, they put their heads together. Chick and I exchanged glances. Chick gave me the thumbs up sign on his knee under the piano.

Tom Scardini read with me, and the threesome was definitely impressed that I had memorized the scene, and bowled over when we did the second scene and that was memorized, too.

"I'd like to hear you sing something else, Margo." It was Zack Vincent. "I'm sorry we didn't make more of the music available. Miss Fossey knows your voice, but I don't. I'd like to hear a belt number."

Chick fumbled through scores on the piano and pulled out *Gypsy*. "How about 'Some People?'" he asked.

"Great," Zack said, and Foss and Scardini muttered in agreement.

I walked over to the piano. "I'm not sure of the words," I said. "Would you mind if I sort of watched the music?"

"Not at all," Zack said.

I gave it everything I had, and then some. Chick took off on the piano as if possessed. It was one of those rare moments when it all comes together and you know you've done it, almost as if you are watching yourself from outside. When I sang the last line, going up the third on the end instead of the traditional ending, there was complete silence.

"Fabulous." Zack.

"Thank you, Margo." Did Foss sound relieved? "We'll be having some more readings in a couple of days so we can match people up." It was over.

Bobby could barely contain himself when I got outside — and he was next. He squeezed my hand so hard, it nearly broke.

"You were Victoria Page," he said, referring to *The Red Shoes*. "Dancing at that little theater while Lermontov watched her."

The final cast list for *Bloomin'* was to be posted on closing night of *The Odd Couple*. I knew I had it — but, ever insecure, I was nervous anyway.

I was also nervous for Bobby. He really wanted the role of Ron. The readings may have been a formality, but not in Bobby's case. Grant Masters was under heavy consideration, although I couldn't figure out why. I read scenes with Grant and Bobby two days later. I hoped the chemistry between Bobby and me shifted the auditioners in Bobby's direction.

On the night of the final performance of *The Odd Couple*, Sulynn and I sat in the men's dressing room, waiting for the list to be posted. We could hear the audience roaring with laughter from where we sat. Art and Bobby were knocking them dead.

The men's dressing room was adjacent to the business office. There was a window between the two rooms, covered by a curtain. Hearing voices, I glanced up from my Nero Wolfe mystery to see Sulynn signaling me to come over to the window. She was kneeling on a chair, peeking through the curtain.

I tiptoed over, and she parted one curtain a little more. There were Foss and Grant Masters, in his *Odd Couple* outfit and makeup, arguing, but trying to keep their voices low. Between them was a piece of paper with typewritten words on it.

Sulynn grabbed me by the neck and lowered me below the window. "I think it's the cast list," she whispered. "Can you read it?" (She needed glasses but refused to wear them.)

I inched my way back up to the curtains and parted them with my nose. Grant was holding the list out to Foss. His hand was shaking a little, and he was pointing at it. I saw what I wanted to see. Sulynn and I crawled over to Bobby's dressing table on the other side of the room.

"We all got parts," I said. "Bobby got it — he got it!" We hugged each other, knees on the hard floor, Sulynn half-squealing. We crawled to the door and went outside, running away from the building into the field across from the theater.

"Grant was furious," I said. "Could he have cared that much about a part?"

She looked at me in amazement. "Margo Girard, you are as dense as they come. Where have you been all summer? He wanted *Fred* to play the part of Keith, and he wanted to do Ron. He wanted to do *The Odd Couple* with Fred, too. What did Fred get?"

I closed my eyes and tried to see the list, then shook my head. "I can't remember all the characters, but his name was on the list. The important thing is Art and Bobby have the male leads, and we have the female leads and Amalia has *crap*." We started jumping up and down in the field, applauding and laughing.

The next day, we picked up our scripts and music. Sulynn noted with glee that Amalia only had one song in the entire show. The script showed something else I hadn't quite realized: Mandy Morgan was the lead role and far superior to the ingénue or the male leads.

One small problem — the show began with Mandy singing the song, "Sweet Times," accompanying herself on the guitar.

When we gathered for rehearsal, I told Miss Fossey I couldn't play the guitar.

"Chick will play it from the side, you'll just finger," she said.

Maybe by opening night I could play for myself, I thought. And that detail out of the way, I threw myself into the rehearsal process. It was a remarkable experience. No preconceived notions, no stars who had played the roles before as role models, no stage business passed from production to production, no original cast recording to hear. There were just our own creative processes, our own chemistries, our blocking dictated not by stage manager notes in a Samuel French script, but evolving from our own physical impulses.

The score written by Foss was captivating. So now we knew why she'd given up her acting career: it was to pursue her career as a composer and lyricist. "I've been writing music for years. I was trained as a pianist," she told us. "A lot of these songs were not written with any show in mind, and then I got together with Tom, and he wrote a script. It was backwards, perhaps, but we think it came out rather well."

As we rehearsed, lines were changed, songs were shortened or verses added, scenes eliminated, rewritten, added. The changes required us to be on our toes and concentrating every second.

"Not like singing "Wilkommen" for Teamsters, is it?" Art reflected one day on a break.

"Yeah, you can't do your grocery list while this is going on," I said.

I was so intensely involved in the rehearsal process, I can't remember when I began to notice Holly Morrison hanging around the theater. The Morrison family was not the richest family in Cofis, it was the only rich family in Cofis. Her father owned the single Cofis industry, a glove factory. The family gave money to the theater, hosted fund-raisers for it at their home, and housed the alumni who came to perform.

Holly was a constant presence at rehearsals past a certain point, or maybe she'd been there all along. She was beautiful in the way that rich girls are: expensive clothes, skillful makeup, perfect teeth, a professional peroxide job on her hair. She sat, chain-smoking, in the back of the theater, next to the exit curtain, blowing smoke toward the curtain every time she exhaled.

"I guess she thinks the smoke's going outside," Sulynn commented.

The reason for her presence, it turned out, was Bobby, and he was dazzled. Lettie, bless her heart, had raised him right, according to her lights: cherchez the money. Holly sensed this and all but threw dollar bills at Bobby, showing up in her bright red Fiat, dressed to kill.

"She has cigarette holes in all her clothes," Sulynn observed. "And did you notice she wears makeup three shades darker than her skin?"

Holly modeled herself, loosely, on Holly Golightly in *Breakfast at Tiffany's* (her real name being Eloise). She wore little-girl clothes to try to hide that she was probably in her late twenties. At my age of twenty-one, this seemed really "up there" to me.

Fred had a ball imitating "Miz Holly," as he called her. Once during a rehearsal break, when Holly and Bobby went outside, he made a bandana out of his handkerchief and said to us, "'Oh, Miz Holly, 'scuse me. I know I'm only a lowly domestic and not fit to shine your shoes, because your family is from the House of Rothschild.'"

"You mean the House of Donuts, don't you?" Sulynn said.

Sulynn was wild with jealousy, and it showed. During one of the rehearsals, she had to slap Bobby, and she really slapped him, hitting him so hard he recoiled and put his hand over his ear in pain.

"Oh, I'm sorry," she said casually to Foss, "I was trying to get his cheek."

"THE HELL YOU WERE," Bobby screamed.

"WELL I WAS," she screamed back. "BUT YOU WERE IN THE WRONG PLACE. WHY DON'T YOU PAY ATTENTION, YOU ASSHOLE?"

"That's enough," Foss yelled. "Everybody take a five-minute break."

Sulynn left the stage as if shot by a cannon. I ran after her, Art following at a respectable pace. She sat sobbing with her head on the makeup table. Art stayed outside while I tried to console her.

"Bastard," she kept saying over and over. "I hope they'll be very happy together."

I let her cry it out for a while, then said, "Sulynn, we'll be gone from here in a few weeks, and she'll be history. You know Bobby — he never gets serious."

She lifted her head up. "Oh, that's right. Never is the word. And when am I going to accept that and forget about him?"

"I guess never." We both laughed. "Sulynn, I've suggested to you before that you should have it out with him. If you don't, this kind of thing is just going to keep happening."

"It's no use, and you know it's no use. Look at your own situation." My own situation was standing outside, undoubtedly straining his ears.

"We have to cut the cord, Sulynn."

"At least you act like you've cut it by seeing Chick. But you're not fooling me. You're not in love with him, anymore than I'm in love with any of these local bumpkins who want to take me out." She broke out in fresh tears. "Sometimes I wonder what we're going to do." She looked at herself in the mirror and started to pull herself together, using some of the makeup on the table. I left her there and went outside, where Art was leaning against the building, staring at the ground.

"Is she okay?" he asked.

"As okay as she can be."

"It's that Holly, isn't it." He stated it as a fact.

"No, it's that Bobby." Art wouldn't look at me. "Think about how she feels."

Turning, he walked away. "I don't have to think. I know how she feels."

I watched him. Then I called out, "You have a strange way of showing it." He didn't look back.

Rehearsals continued, with uneasy truces all around, and Miz Holly ever-present. Sulynn's troubles were far from over. We arrived at rehearsal one morning, and Sulynn went to the pay phone to call her parents, as she did every week. She came into rehearsal and sat on the opposite side of the theater, across from the rest of us.

When it was her turn on stage, she sang the first notes of her song, "Oh, Mother," and collapsed into tears.

"I can't sing this," she cried. "My mother's dying." Her mother had just learned she had a malignant stomach tumor. It didn't look good. "Oh, Mother" was a terribly sad song, since it was about Sulynn's character, Robin, breaking the symbolic umbilical cord with her mother.

Miss Fossey took the song away from her, and Tom rewrote like crazy. "Oh, Mother" was assigned to Amalia, and Sulynn got Amalia's song, "Don't Turn Back," a real showstopper in the right vocal cords. Amalia was ripping mad, but played along. The song was clearly not working the way Amalia was doing it. Chick transposed it into Sulynn's key, and when she sang it for the first time, the song came into its own at last.

The problem was, Sulynn's mother made a complete recovery and is still alive to this day. As time passed, and Sulynn's mother didn't die, Amalia threw a fit. "I thought your mother was dying," she snarled at Sulynn one day after "Don't Turn Back" got big applause from people watching the rehearsal. "Nice way to get my number, you bitch."

Then Art developed throat problems, which were diagnosed as "red throat" by a local doctor. Art turned into an opera singer, wrapping himself in scarves in the middle of August and drinking hot tea. He refused to sing at any of the subsequent rehearsals, doing what he called "marking." There is a special technique to marking, one Art never mastered. His idea of "marking" was to mouth the words rather than sing half-voice or an octave lower, and to exude absolutely no energy.

For our dress rehearsal, a nervous Foss, who thought we had something special but wasn't sure, invited all sorts of people. Zack Vincent was there with a group who came from New York. Tom Scardini was in attendance, as he had been through all the rehearsals, rewriting the script. Then there were Holly and her parents, President Lambini and his wife, all the apprentices, and local "regulars" who attended all the shows and hung around the theater. The little theater was SRO.

If the adage "bad dress rehearsal — good performance" is true, then we should have known immediately we had an unmitigated smash on our hands, because there has never been, and never will be, a worse dress rehearsal than the one for *Bloomin'*.

The first problem was the costumes, which weren't finished by dress rehearsal. Just before my entrances, I was pinned into each of mine. I had not been assigned a dresser — another grave error. In the show, I aged from thirteen to thirty and wore a variety of wigs, falls and costumes, more than anyone else in the show. During the dress rehearsal, I would run out an exit to change, or run into the dressing room. I managed along the way to lose all my props, wigs and costume parts. I was late for every entrance, since the right clothes were never at any exit waiting for me. Not only that, when I went to put on my dress for the third act, it had been altered incorrectly, and I couldn't get it over my head. Angry and frustrated, I went on stage in my slip, to make the point that I needed some help.

The costumes were put together with scotch tape, it seemed. Every time I was on stage wearing one (which, as the show progressed, was less and less often), another piece fell off; a sleeve on one, a panel of buttons on another. One dress opened so completely that I had a V all the way down my back. In order to keep that dress on, I backed up to Sulynn, sitting stage right, and stood in front of her while I sang. She buttoned me back up as best she could.

Then, Sulynn's Shirley Temple wig got caught on the buttons of one of my costumes. I went to walk away and started to pull her wig off. Her head was stuck to my chest, and we couldn't get away from each other. We couldn't sing, so no one sang the melody line of our ensemble. Bobby was on the other side of the stage, singing his one-note part all by himself while Art, laughing, tried to unhook us.

Costume and wig problems beset the chorus, too. During one of the big dance numbers, if they could be called "big" and "dance," one of the male dancers, a sophomore in the dance department, did a lift and, from complete stage fright, kept his partner up over his head for a good forty seconds more than he should have, thus missing two or three bars of music. In the process, his partner lost half her costume. The part she lost was a little skirt that she wore because her costume was too small underneath, and when the skirt fell off, she was, for all intents and purposes, nude from the waist down.

Miss Fossey's vision of Fred was that he should "look like Mike Jagger." "Mick Jagger," Fred corrected her. "Isn't his name Mike?" she frowned. When Fred arrived on stage in his Prince Valiant wig, which didn't look that different from his normal hairstyle anyway, the audience roared with laughter. "Somehow," he said after rehearsal, "I don't think I quite looked like *Mike* Jagger, do you?"

It went on and on. At one point, Sulynn was to offer Bobby chocolate. It was so hot that all the chocolate melted into a blob. When Bobby reached into the box, all he got was hot liquid. He cuffed his hand and pretended he was eating an actual piece, but it dripped on his shirt. More laughter.

Then there came the King of Marking, Art Gaines. His throat was bothering him, so he "marked" the dress rehearsal. After the rehearsal, the kind onlookers crowded around Sulynn, Bobby and me, lying to us and telling us how marvelous we'd been. Art stood off to the side with a puzzled and hurt look on his face. "I don't understand it," he said, "everyone is talking to you. Evidently, no one thinks I did well."

I cleared my throat. "What is it that you expect them to tell you — that you move your lips well? You can't have it both ways, you know, you're either singing full voice or you're marking."

Thus ended our brilliant dress rehearsal. Miss Fossey was in tears afterward as we gathered for notes. "We ought to be here all night," Bobby said.

Miss Fossey stood before us as composed as was possible, and said, "Well, I learned something tonight. I learned that this show isn't about performances, music or story. It's about props, wigs and costumes." We all laughed nervously.

Foss went into her notes, which filled an entire tablet. The first thing she did was assign me a dresser. Wearing my slip on stage had made an impression. We heard notes until 6:30 p.m. The dress rehearsal had started at one, and we were to perform *The New Moon* at eight. *Bloomin'* was due to open in two days, and it was in a sad state.

"I have to call another rehearsal tomorrow," she said. "Not the line-through we planned, but a walk-through. You can mark the songs" — she stole a look at Art, whose neck was wrapped in a scarf. "But we need to do the costume changes and the light cues."

Exhausted, we made our way to the dressing rooms and prepared for *The New Moon*. Grant Masters poked his head in. "Good job, girls. The show is great."

"I guess he wasn't there," Sulynn said. "God, I don't even think I can walk, let alone do a performance."

The moments until opening night of *Bloomin'* are a blur of tiredness. Somehow we crawled through *The New Moon* and yet another dress rehearsal of our show, which went much better.

My dresser, a local teenager named Mary, was fabulous, following me from place to place and helping me dress. She wrote furiously in her notebook where I dropped props, wigs and costumes, where my entrances were, and what I was supposed to be wearing for each scene. Chick called a music rehearsal. The costumer called for fittings. I don't remember sleeping; I don't remember eating.

Opening night. Sulynn, Amalia and I sat in our dressing room in concentrated silence. The stage manager, a local, knocked. "Ya decent?"

"Come in," I said.

He poked his head in. "Ladies, the joint is jumpin'. Lots of strangers. I didn't think this show would sell. They always do the old standards here. You'll be surprised when you see the audience."

I gave him a half-smile, and Sulynn ran past him, hand over her mouth. "She throws up when she's nervous," I told him.

"Oh, is that why?" said Amalia from the other side of the room. Then she murmured something unintelligible.

The stage manager made the peace sign and left. I said, "I didn't catch that, Amalia."

We looked at each other in our mirrors. "I said, I thought maybe she was worried about her *mother*."

I slammed my powder puff down, causing powder to fly in my face. "Amalia, I don't know what your problem is, other than that you think everybody's like you and would *fake* an illness to get something. I happen to like your song better."

"Which song? The one that was mine or the one I'm singing now?"

I continued lying, having learned that consistency in falsehood is important. "'Oh, Mother,' the song you're doing now, of course. Frankly, you do it much better than Sulynn did, because you're a better actress" — well, that part was at least true — "and I think 'Don't Turn Back' suits her just fine. 'Oh, Mother' is more poignant in your hands." Not as well sung, I said to myself, but poignant, and you were ruining "Don't Turn Back."

She didn't say anything, but I like to think I contributed to her mediocre, elevated from bad, performance that night.

The show went beautifully. We were like laser beams zeroing in on a target, high on adrenalin, our youthful bodies and voices unaffected by sleep and food deprivation. I could feel the audience with us in every scene, every song. At the end of the show, the audience stood and applauded us. Miss Fossey and Tom Scardini joined us on stage and, as she listened to shouts of "Bravi! Bravi!" tears streamed down her face.

We were a smash! I even hugged Amalia. Sulynn actually hugged

Bobby *and* Holly Morrison.

The cast party was held at a restaurant outside of Cofis. We had no idea who was paying for it, but Sulynn, Amalia and I left the dressing room in our best outfits and, meeting the guys, who were dressed in suits, followed the xeroxed directions to the restaurant. I was crowded into Grant's car with Art, Sulynn, Chick, Grant and Fred. Bobby drove with Holly.

A smiling Miss Fossey met us at the door. "It's back there," she pointed, and we went through the main, dimly-lit restaurant into a back room. Along the walls, there were banners that said, "CONGRATULATIONS BLOOMIN'" and balloons. There was a long table in the middle of the room, with several buckets of champagne.

"Who the hell sponsored *this*?" Art said.

There were already people seated around the table: Tom Scardini, who rose to shake our hands; Zack Vincent, who embraced the women and shook hands with the men; and a couple of total strangers. President Lambini and his wife arrived subsequently. *Bloomin'* was getting the royal treatment.

Bobby and Holly arrived after the Lambinis and made a sweeping entrance, Holly in a bright red low-cut dress. I grabbed Sulynn's hand. "It doesn't bother me anymore," she said. "Let's hit the appetizers before all the good stuff's gone." Art was already at the hors d'oeuvres table, filling up his plate.

"Open bar, folks," Zack announced. "Just give the waiter your drink order."

"Screw the hors d'oeuvres," Sulynn said, and waved to the waiter.

"We'll be carrying her home in a body bag," Art predicted. We sat at the table. "This is quite a bash," he continued. "I noticed Grant Masters yukking it up at the entrance with two men."

"There's something strange about all this," I told Art. "Something nobody is telling us." I kept my voice low. "Why does Lambini keep showing up? And who are these people?"

We were to find out soon enough. The evening continued with free drinks and a delicious buffet. Before dessert, Zack Vincent stood, and waiters appeared and poured champagne in our glasses.

"I would like first to congratulate each and every one of you on the wonderful debut of *Bloomin'*. I think anyone who was in the audience tonight will agree it was a magnificent production in every way."

Enthusiastic applause from assorted audience members and Fred, with four empty scotch glasses in front of him.

"I have great hopes for *Bloomin'*, and I'm not alone. I have known

Sandra Fossey for many years and admired her first as an actress, and later, when I heard the beautiful music she'd written, I asked her why she was wasting her time acting." Polite laughter from all but Fred, who laughed so hard he choked.

"I'd like to introduce to you some people who feel as I do about Sandra Fossey's work, and who enjoyed *Bloomin'* tonight and share my confidence in its future: MacKenzie Nathan, to my immediate right, is a New Yorker who has long been a patron of the arts, as have I. He has been a Broadway angel many times, although I don't think he's always gotten his investment back, have you, MacKenzie?" MacKenzie chuckled. Again, polite laughter. Fred fell off his chair. "Zack and Mack," he chortled. "Mack and Zack. Mack 'n' Zack."

The Zack of Zack 'n' Mack pretended not to hear. "But MacKenzie believes in the system anyway, and knows that in this country, it's the private investor who can make Broadway come alive. MacKenzie and I are going to put our money into *Bloomin'*. We have formed a limited partnership and intend to bring *Bloomin'*, hopefully, all the way to Broadway."

Fred stood and screamed. There was complete pandemonium in the room, most of it concerned with getting Fred back into his seat. The rest of the cast acted collectively stunned.

"Now, I want to say a few more things," Zack said, when it had quieted down. "The show needs work, that's number one. Number two, I want to make it clear that we are committed to this cast, which was hand-picked by Sandra. The third thing is, in return for our commitment to you, we would like your commitment to us.

"The process of bringing a show to Broadway or off-Broadway nowadays is long and hard. In order to work on the show, we want to set up a workshop situation in New York City and start performing it as a showcase. Working in front of an audience, we can change what needs to be changed and also, frankly, attract more investors. You may have noticed that neither Mackenzie's nor my last name is Rockefeller."

Grant put his hand over Fred's mouth.

"I realize the cast came from Boston. I'm hopeful that as many of you who can will consider coming to New York to work with us, and those of you who can't will let us know as soon as possible.

"Well, that's all I wanted to say. I'd now like to toast Sandra Fossey and Tom Scardini, and all of you."

I swilled my champagne down in one swallow and sat there comatose while others applauded.

"What do you think?" Art said.

"Wow! I don't know. Are you ready to move to New York?"

"Are you kidding? Am I ready to move to New York to go into a Broadway show? You bet I am. Do you realize what this could mean to you? You're the lead!"

I shook my head. "My God. Art, do you think he meant it? That they'll stick with this cast?"

"I don't know, but I think we should get it in writing."

Sulynn and Bobby came over to us and stood beside our chairs. "There goes the game plan," Bobby said.

"Yeah," I said, "looks like ready or not, here we come, New York."

"To us," said Art, and held up his champagne glass.

I poured more while Sulynn and Bobby grabbed their glasses.

"To *Bloomin'*," Art said.

"To *BLOOMIN'*," we yelled, and drank.

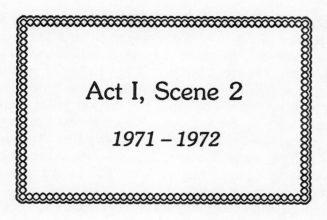

Act I, Scene 2

1971 – 1972

I was living at 75th and Broadway in New York by October of 1971, the first one of the *Bloomin'* cast to effect the move. I sold half my stock in Republic Steel, a graduation gift from my grandmother, in order to dole out the security deposit, the first month's rent and the phone deposit. Cindy, the Julie of *Showboat*, kindly let Sulynn and me stay in her apartment on West 86th Street during our visits, while we hunted for a place to live.

It wasn't easy. We soon abandoned looking in the newspapers — people bought *The New York Times* at 2 a.m. and signed their lease at 6 a.m. "If you're not first in New York, you're last," or at least that's how it seemed whenever one of us telephoned about an apartment.

The real estate agents wanted our first-born sons as payment, so we soon gave up on them, too. Then Cindy told us about the Clemency Hotel on Broadway and 75th Street. I had passed it every day, but thought it was a real hotel. "Oh, no," Cindy said. "There are plenty of hotels in New York that are actually apartment houses. Go in and talk to the manager. There are a lot of old people living there, so they might have vacancies."

As it happened, the Clemency Hotel had a furnished apartment just waiting for Sulynn and me, and we wasted no time grabbing it. The living room was very large, and the apartment had a small bedroom, kitchen and bath. The couch in the living room opened up into a bed.

I settled in first, and Sulynn's parents drove her in two weeks later. Chick helped me move, stayed for two nights, then visited the following weekend. It was apparent to me we weren't going to be able to keep our little romance going long-distance. I couldn't decide whether to let it die slowly or just cut it off. I decided to play it by ear. Chick planned to stay in Boston and work on his Masters, and from his complaints about the traffic and crowds in New York, I knew he wouldn't visit too often. I was right. Shortly after the weekend visit, Chick got a new girlfriend, and we broke up amicably over the phone.

"We're here! We're here! Far out!" Sulynn yelled out the first night in the new apartment, as she danced around the living room. "We made it — we're in New York. Groovy city." The night after Sulynn's arrival, we went to see *Company* — the ultimate New York show (standing room, of course). "That'll be us in a few months," Sulynn said, as the cast bowed.

I was happy, too, but also a wreck. Foss, Zack and Tom had met with the cast in Boston and asked us to sign contracts — which I was sure were absolutely worthless — for the *Bloomin'* "showcase." There was no money involved other than "transportation," i.e., subway fare, nor did we have any indication of a starting date for this showcase. It depended on when everybody got to New York.

The week after Sulynn arrived, Bobby and Art came into town with Lettie to find an apartment. Lettie loved the good life, so the three of them stayed at the Plaza. Sulynn and I wasted no time barreling over there. Lettie was out with some New York friends, but Bobby and Art were waiting for us with room service.

"We're going to need day jobs," I said. "Do any of us have enough to live on without them? Do you believe the prices?" The stock I had sold went entirely toward the apartment, so all I had left in the bank was the money Sulynn gave me for her share of the expenses, plus four hundred dollars I managed to save from singing. The rest had dwindled away over the summer, going for rent on the Boston apartment and extra expenses during the stock season. As I munched on room service at the Plaza, courtesy of Lettie's bank account, I realized I needed a job — soon.

I was excited by New York — everything thrilled me, even the decadence of Times Square. It was somehow a more alive city than Boston — Boston seemed like a small town compared with New York. There was a freedom and a sense of ever-present opportunities in New York, as well as danger. It was as if I was in a foreign country, such was my curiosity and my fascination with the people, the apartments, the offices, the stores.

After room service, the four of us went to Sylvia's, a jazz bar on East 62nd Street. Sitting at a window table, watching the people and listening to the music, seemed more romantic and thrilling than anything I'd ever done. Possibilities for my life seemed endless. I was in the most vital city in the world with my best friends, on my way to starring in a Broadway show. I looked at Bobby and Art and Sulynn, who were staring out the window as mesmerized as I was, and wondered what they felt. I never wanted the evening to end.

But it did, and on Monday, I was pounding the pavement looking for a job. I hit three temporary office services in one day and crawled back to the apartment with feet tired from walking and fingers sore from endless typing tests. But I had no problem getting work and soon realized that there was nothing particularly glamorous about a New York office; a typewriter, after all, was a typewriter.

Sulynn possessed no office skills, and her choice of job was on the strange side: corporate spy. Apparently, companies hired outside firms to infiltrate their employees and spy on them — for instance, if they suspected shoplifting or the selling of secrets, etc.

Art, holed up at the Plaza, thought it was the most revolting job he ever heard of and berated Sulynn for taking it. "You mean you pretend to *befriend* these people and all the time you're reporting them to management? How can you even consider doing such a thing?"

"I've got one for you," she said. "How do you like mooching off your mother, now that you're twenty-three years old?"

Sulynn's first assignment as a corporate spy was in a department store, where she actually worked as a store detective trying to spot shoplifters. This smacked less of actually spying on the employees, so to Art, at least, it was more palatable. "You can always spot the store detectives," she told me after her first day. "They wear raincoats and comfortable shoes."

Then she really was assigned a spy job, at a shoe factory in New Jersey, which meant she had to get up at 7 a.m. and take the Path train to New Jersey. Sulynn was physically incapable of getting up at 7 a.m. She set two alarm clocks plus a radio alarm and arranged for a wake-up call from her mother in Framingham — two rings. Each morning, I staggered into the living room, where she slept, and turned off the alarm clocks and the radio — none of which had roused her — and tried to wake her up myself. At last she'd get out of bed, but was consistently late for her job.

Art and Bobby rented a two-bedroom apartment on West 83rd Street, Art finding work at St. George's Hospital as a clerical worker, and Bobby, with his marvelous sense of direction, as a cab driver.

Lettie had sublet an apartment at the Ansonia Hotel so she could help her sons get settled, but stay out of their way. Each day, she made Bobby's lunch for him and stood outside on Broadway, hair wrapped in a scarf to hide the rollers, waiting for him to drive past. As I was walking on Broadway one day, I noticed her standing in front of a parked car on the street, a brown bag in her hand. I then saw a yellow cab slow down, cruise by her, then keep on going. The brown bag was gone. Art was furious with her for catering to Bobby in that way, but she felt it was her motherly duty.

The four of us signed up, separately, with the Broadway Bound Answering Service and dutifully reported such to Zack Vincent's law office at 30 Rockefeller Plaza. He called us in for a meeting on November 20th. Fred was not yet living in New York, although he planned to make the move, but Amalia was there and was first to reach the office. "Where are you living?" I asked her.

She picked up her ugly plaid pancho from her lap and began folding it so that I couldn't miss the huge diamond on her third finger, left hand. "Oh," she said, "I'm living on West 50th Street." She placed the coat on the chair next to her, flattening it, so again the ring was obvious. I didn't say anything.

Then she stood up and brushed non-existent lint from her skirt, making sure the ring caught the light. This failed to get my attention, so she fluffed the front of her hair with her left hand, facing me all the time. I still pretended not to notice. Finally, she couldn't take it any longer and stuck her hand in my face. "Notice anything?"

"Oh, how nice," I said. "Are you engaged?"

"Yes, to Hal."

So, she'd succeeded in stealing Winslow away from his wife. "Are you both in New York?" I asked.

"Well, no. I'm here, and Hal is going to teach one more year at the college, then get a job here."

Doing what, holding your used cough drops? I said to myself. Bobby, Art and Sulynn walked in just then. Zack's secretary escorted us into his wood-paneled office, which was loaded with antiques. If he'd sold his desk and given us the money, the four of us could have lived comfortably for a year. But as we were only getting subway fare for our participation in the *Bloomin'* showcase, I assumed he wasn't willing to part with his furniture.

"Well, I'm glad you all made it," he began. "I just called you here to update you. Our showcase is going to be done at the 16th St. Playhouse — it's already booked for performances beginning January 20, 1972, with a little over two weeks of rehearsal which start January 3rd. Really, those are just touch-up weeks with a few changes — the actual changes won't begin until we're actually in performance."

He picked up a letter from his desk. "I have here a note from

Federico Alfonso Corso. He returned his contract signed and states that he will be in New York by the time rehearsals begin. So we're all set. We'll be in touch shortly before rehearsal." He shook our hands, and the secretary escorted us to the door. We left the office in silence. Once in the hall, Art said, *"Federico Alfonso?"* and we doubled over in laughter.

I was cutting and pasting accounting textbooks at Peat Marwick when I met Reed Abel, an aspiring actor. We got to know each other sitting side by side at a long table as we put the books together and attempted to decipher the editing notes. He asked me out for drinks our third day on the job, and I accepted.

To me, Reed was a seasoned New Yorker who knew all the ins and outs of show business. And my waiting in the wings to walk onto a Broadway stage did not impress him.

"I don't want to hurt your feelings, Margo, but you know, all these damn showcases are supposedly going to Broadway. None of them ever get there."

I nodded, knowing he was right — the pit of my stomach assured me of it.

"I'll tell you one thing you can do," he continued. "While you're waiting to see what happens with it, why not earn more money than you're making as a temp?" He pulled out a business card. "Go see my agent, Harry Lasker. He and his wife Zelda are always looking for office people. I can't work for them, because then they'd never send me out on one audition if I did. But you could go, as long as you don't want Harry to represent you eventually. The money would be much better for you, and you'd learn a lot about the business."

I looked down at the card. It said, "The Lasker Agency" in the middle, with the address, 580 Madison Avenue, and the phone number. On the bottom, I read, left to right, "Harry Lasker" and "Zelda Lasker."

"What I just told you is important," he said with a knowing sigh. "Don't ever tell anybody who can hire you as an actress that you can do office work. Remember, they can always get an actress or actor, but a good typist — once they have one, they won't let go. And they'll never look at you as an actress again."

I gave Harry Lasker a lot of thought and talked it over with Sulynn, Bobby, Art and Lettie. "Get a job with him," Lettie advised.

Lettie, despite retiring from show business when she married, had, through friends in New York and voracious reading of the trade papers, kept her finger on the pulse of the business. I learned plenty from her that night about Harry Lasker, Agent to the Stars.

According to Lettie, Harry had been a big Hollywood agent in the old studio days, then married Zelda, a nightclub singer and sometime film actress, and moved to New York. Zelda quit the performing end of the business and became an agent. They had a very good client list, but inexplicably experienced a decline in fortune, which they put down to the fact that they had four children to feed, clothe and educate, plus a home to maintain.

The story of what had really happened to the Lasker earnings was famous in New York show business circles.

The Lasker office started out in the Paramount building, and in those days, Harry and Zelda shared the services of a secretary. Zelda was always tracking people down for quarters and complaining endlessly that she was broke. Her favorite trick was going to a fancy restaurant with a client, ordering one entrée and splitting it — a total class act. All of her clients knew she and Harry were in dire straits. If they didn't know it before dinner, they knew it by the time one cup of coffee was brought to the table.

One of her clients, a big Vegas comedian, said to her during one of her tirades, "I don't know, Zelda, you ought to ask your secretary for advice. Every time I go play Vegas, I see her at the tables." Zelda's secretary rushed out of the office every weekend, if not for Vegas, then to her house upstate.

No flies on Zelda. It only took her seventeen years, but she finally figured out that her secretary was an embezzler. An investigation indicated that in just the last eleven months of her employ, she bilked the agency out of $300,000 with her creative accounting.

Zelda pressed charges, but her secretary hired a cutthroat lawyer, while the nearly-destitute Zelda and Harry went to Legal Aid. Zelda, however, was philosophical. "At least now we'll get everything we earn," she told Harry.

"How could they have been so stupid?" I asked Lettie.

"Easy," Lettie said. "Harry was always out hustling and never paid any attention to money, and Zelda was busy hustling the clients — the male clients — in other ways." She rolled her eyes.

Art imitated Lettie's eye roll. "You know what that means," Art said.

I had my own reasons for wanting to work at the Lasker Agency. Supposing, I reasoned to Sulynn later that night — just supposing *Bloomin'* went nowhere, that we came to New York for nothing and wasted months not lining up any other work. If I were in an agent's office, maybe I could find a way to do some submissions of my own, or at least know what was being cast around town.

"I mean," I said, "if their secretary walked off with thousands, why can't I get myself and my friends in to see a few producers?" Sulynn agreed with my reasoning, and the next day, I called The Lasker Agency.

Harry Lasker himself got on the line. "So you've been working with Reed. Reed's a wonderful guy, good actor."

I can tell that by the office work he does, I said to myself.

Harry continued. "Yeah — I'm a little swamped — we go through secretarial help the way most people go through underwear. Hah! Hah!"

I faked a laugh.

"Tell you what," he said. "Meet me at the coffee shop on Madison and 48th Street — The Croesus — at three o'clock. I'll be wearing a white carnation. Hah! Hah!"

"Seriously, Mr. Lasker, how will I know you?"

"I look like Cary Grant," he said, and hung up.

There was no one in the post-lunch crowd at The Croesus who remotely resembled Cary Grant, but after I stood at the entrance looking bewildered for a time, a tall, balding man approached me.

"Are you Margo? I'm Harry Lasker," he said, and held out his hand. "And I do look like Cary Grant — but only in my dreams. Hah! Hah!" He escorted me to a back booth. "Eat something," he said. I really should order a big lunch, I thought, but instead I asked for coffee, as did he.

When the coffee arrived, I noticed Harry nearly put his face right into the coffee cup, as if reading tea leaves, and didn't look up as he talked. Finally, I said, "Excuse me. Is something wrong?"

"No," he replied. "I'm steaming my contact lenses." He continued to talk with his head in his cup. "I'll tell you what I need, Margo — I don't know how much Reed has told you about our set-up — I understand you're an actress?"

"Yes. I'm actually here to do a new show that starts rehearsals in January. It's only going to be a showcase, but there's some money behind it, and I think it's very good."

He couldn't have cared less. "Well, here's the deal. You can work whatever hours you want — if it's one thing I know it's actresses! Hah! Hah! I run the agency with my wife, Zelda — our actual office is here on Madison, but I work out of our apartment in town mostly, on West 73rd Street. I really need someone with me there."

I didn't like the sound of that. His face may have been in his coffee at that moment, but his eyes had run the length and width of me before we sat down.

"As a secretary?" I asked, swallowing.

He finished his steaming and raised his head. "More a personal assistant. Also a secretary. One thing I'm doing right now is writing my memoirs about my life in Hollywood. As a matter of fact, I'm having dinner with John Hawkworth — you know, of Hawkworth and Dale, the biggest public relations firm in Hollywood — this evening, and we'll be reminiscing about the old days — I need something to jog my memory. I'm not as young as I once was. Hah! Hah!

"So that's one thing I'll need, someone to type my book for me. Also, occasionally, you'll be working at the office here. Zelda and I are just coming out of a financial crisis..." I nodded in sympathy. "And thank God, now we have a whole staff of people. We used to do it all ourselves — with one secretary. Hah! Hah! Anyway, occasionally, Zelda will need someone at the office, so you'll go back and forth. How does that sound?"

"It sounds okay. I assume I'll be answering the phone and typing letters and filing and — uh, I guess mailing submissions, that sort of thing?" I tried not to make my voice sound too hopeful.

"Oh, yes," he said. "You'll have to be very good on the phone and deal with the casting people, and you'll send the submissions — all that kind of thing. Also, I do a workshop for young actors — you may have seen the ad in *Back Stage* — five weeks, called Being a Professional in the New York Theater. You'd be required to run the auditions, call the participants, collect the money."

"It sounds fine," I told him.

"Good. We pay seven dollars an hour." That also sounded fine. He stood. "Let me take you over to meet Zelda."

The frosted glass on the door said "The Lasker Agency." I hadn't been agent-hunting, but Reed told me New York agents did everything but house guard dogs to keep actors away. The Laskers' door was locked, and there was a speaker on the wall next to the buzzer. Over the mail slot was a sign, "Do not put résumés under the door."

Harry rang the bell, and a hostile voice said, "Yes?"

"Rosebud," Harry said. Then he turned to me. "That's the code word to get into the office. Don't give it to anyone."

He took me into a small outer office, where a receptionist sat. Behind the reception area was the main office, not much larger, where a secretary wearing a headset and operating a foot pedal sat in the corner, typing furiously. At the desk in the middle sat a woman who looked like Morticia.

Harry motioned to me. "Zelda, I'd like you to meet Margo Girard, who's going to be helping us out here."

Zelda came forward, unsmiling, and extended her hand. "Welcome. I hope you'll be very happy with us." She said it as if it were a death sentence.

Zelda Lasker was all in black, such that you almost couldn't tell where her long, pitch-black hair ended on her suit. Her skin looked embalmed. If Lettie's story was true, and Zelda Lasker was getting men to go to bed with her, I reflected, it was at the point of a gun.

The secretary stopped typing suddenly and ripped off her earphones. "Excuse me, Mrs. Lasker," she said. "But is motherfucker one word?"

"I prefer a dash in between," Zelda said.

At the same time I started working for Harry, I became a real aspiring New York actress and began taking classes. I soon learned one could become a professional class-goer, as there were so many, and it was all too easy to substitute classes for professional work. Bobby was taking three classes a day at Carnegie Dance Studio, and I registered for an intermediate ballet class two days a week and an intermediate jazz class once a week. Dance, of course, had been required study at the music college. According to Fossey, one was often required to dance at Broadway chorus calls.

I spoke to Harry about a good acting class. "You want scene study and cold reading. Actually, Margo, you and your friends should be in my class. It's the practical application you need."

"Sure, Harry," I agreed. I wasn't committing myself to anything before I got a look at these classes. However, my fellow dance students had taken it, some on a regular basis, and swore by both the classes and Harry.

Harry and Zelda's New York pied-à-terre on 73rd Street, where I worked, was a laugh riot. Both Harry and Zelda obviously used the place for trysts — I just wondered if they got together on scheduling or how they managed it.

My first weeks with Harry consisted of the boring job of organizing the folders in his house and catching up on back correspondence. At first, Harry dictated letters to me, but eventually let me write my own. I was amazed at the status of some of his personal clients, and the agency's — movie and stage stars, recording artists, comedians.

For excitement, every day I studied the casting lists to see what was going on and quickly learned who was who in the world of casting, producing and directing. My major job, however, consisted of typing up Harry's memoirs.

This posed two problems. The first was Harry's scribbles. The second was his inability to write a complete sentence. It wasn't long before I was rewriting as well as typing. Harry's memoirs weren't uninteresting. He told stories about Montgomery Clift, James Stewart, Lucille Ball, Frank Sinatra, Tab Hunter, Rock Hudson — it seemed he had known everyone, and I found the stories fascinating reading — when I could figure out what he was trying to write. There were times, however, even after a superhuman effort, when I could not decipher his handwriting. I would then call him at the other office and read him part of the sentence. "Do you think you were trying to say thus and so?" I'd ask, offering a suggestion of my own.

Harry's answer was always the same. "Possible." Well, I said to myself after one such conversation, what else could I expect from a man who spelled ad hoc "ad hock?"

Zelda's current boyfriend, whoever he was, left messages on the answering machine, which was intended for taking messages concerning Harry's class. These amorous messages were strictly stream of consciousness.

Because he was married, he called her from a pay phone. The messages went something like this: "Just when I think Zelda Lasker is a candidate for sainthood, you say something and bring me to earth, reminding me that you are indeed flesh and blood woman. I just want to make the point that I'm not affronted by anything you said. I think you asked probing questions and that your points were well-taken. I desperately need you to understand that you-know-who and I are going to be living peaceably quite soon..."

"Deposit five cents."

"Of course the situation upsets you — it upsets me, too, but bear in mind, please, it's only temporary. You know, I'm reading a marvelous book now, *The Grapes of Wrath* by John Steinbeck. I must say, it deals with some real life issues. I'm learning from it — I think you should read it. Last night, as I told you, was absolutely heaven for me."

"Deposit five cents," the recording said.

"I'm so thrilled we found each other. Do you believe in fate? I think there is such a thing as a guiding hand. I also believe in reincarnation. I believe we must have known each other in another life — perhaps we were brother and sister, or gay lovers, or married..."

He only stopped talking when the tape was completely finished.

The apartment was a pigsty, with parades of cleaning services and housekeepers cleaning it once, then quitting. Part of my job consisted of going through the yellow pages, hiring cleaning services and then replacing them.

Harry wasn't a well man, as evidenced by the rows of medicine bottles in the bathroom. He also dyed what was left of his hair — there were bottles of a shade called Iced Coffee all over the apartment, half used.

Harry wrote instructions in pencil on little scraps of paper and left them all over the place. They were always in a stream of consciousness mode, in the style of Zelda's mysterious boyfriend. "Shall we tell them about the lecture..." was one — he was giving a lecture at the New School on Breaking Into Show Business and wanted me to send announcements to his students and clients. Another penciled instruction he often wrote was "Send" with an arrow pointing to the right or the left. At the right or left of this scrap of paper was either nothing, or an entire deskful of junk, and it took psychic skills to figure out what he wanted sent and to whom.

I knew Harry was a frustrated producer and was negotiating to obtain the rights to a play called *Walnut Creek* — there were contracts and letters concerning it on every table in the apartment. One afternoon, he approached me as I sat at my desk, sorting out the usual stacks of papers.

"Margo, I need you to go to dinner with me tonight. I'm seeing a potential partner on this *Walnut Creek* deal and I need a witness. He's trying to cheat me. I want you to keep your ears open and take in everything he's saying, watch his body language, and I want your observations afterwards."

"Well, won't he be careful if there's somebody there?"

"You won't be there as my secretary, more like my date. Just act dumb and observe. Wear something short and low-cut."

It sounded interesting — kind of like Sulynn's corporate spy activities — so I agreed.

When we got to O'Neal's, the gentleman had not yet arrived. "He's five minutes late," Harry growled. "Order an appetizer. Let's make it look like we've been here waiting a long time. I'll be right back." He then disappeared, returning about five minutes later.

"How do I look?" he asked.

I didn't know what he meant. "You — you look fine."

"Yes, but do I look *okay*?" He continued to stand in front of the table.

"Uh — yes."

"Do I look *okay*?" At this point, he opened his suit jacket, and I saw the tape recorder. Harry closed his jacket and patted the place where the recorder was.

I assumed, then, he was asking me if the recorder could be seen. "You can't see it," I said.

The meeting went fine, as far as I could tell, but in the middle of it, of course, Harry jumped up, ostensibly to use the men's room, but in reality, to turn the tape over.

All I know is, he never did get the rights to *Walnut Creek*, and his ambitions as a producer were thwarted for the time being.

Every so often, I worked in the main office with Zelda and her group of lunatics. She employed several part-timers. Some were aspiring actors, some were felons, and there was one illegal alien. From what I could observe, none possessed any office skills.

I was friendliest with Elena, who was in the country illegally. Elena had difficulty with the switchboard and usually ended up cutting off super-big clients and putting through the smaller ones. So Zelda removed her from switchboard duties and had her sort mail, file and perform some messenger work.

Elena didn't like Harry — this dislike stemmed from his lack of attention to her problems with immigration. Her confusion concerning the English language especially came out when she talked about him. She said things like, "He's getting too big for his chair," "He doesn't want to climb up that tree," and "That is the back side of the coin." She was exotic-looking, with a gorgeous figure, which she kept that way with no effort. "I'm hungry," she'd complain. "I just ate some cookies and a piece of pizza, but it won't hold me till lunch."

The Lasker Agency, however, was a busy place, and Zelda often needed real help, i.e., people who could really type, really take dictation and actually run the modest phone system. Besides recruiting me, Zelda often called a temporary office service. She did so during the period of Christmas '71. Zelda and Harry were both working on Madison Avenue, negotiating like crazy, and a steady stream of clients paraded in and out of the office. A woman was brought in from a temp agency, and she went right to work, typing letters and contracts, while I was put on the phone system and served as receptionist to the clients in the tiny outer office. Elena served as general gofer.

The temp worker, Becca, was quiet and efficient, and for several weeks came in and out of the office without so much as a word. She was even given her own key, because she often started working before Zelda got there in the morning.

Right before Christmas, however, a soap opera actor dropped in to discuss a contract with Harry, a contract Harry had given Becca to type earlier in the day. Harry approached Becca for the completed contract.

Without warning, she shot out of her chair, screaming at Harry in an odd voice that didn't seem like it was from her body at all — something like Mercedes McCambridge's voice coming out of Linda Blair's body in *The Exorcist.* "I do the work of eight people in this office. I've been working all morning on your lousy letters," she snarled, and stormed through the outer office and out into the hall. Harry followed her as far as the reception area, then glanced at me, shrugged his shoulders, and went back to his desk.

Two minutes later, Becca came back into the office with a guitar, which she had retrieved from the coatroom in the hall. She sat at her desk and began to play and sing "I Never Promised You a Rose Garden." There was nothing for any of us to do but nod and smile and pretend to enjoy it — and change the lock on the office after she left.

Back Stage ran a chorus/small part call for *Bloomin'* two weeks before Christmas. They also ran an ad: MUSIC DIRECTOR WANTED for the show.

"Looks like it's really going to happen," Art said. He, Sulynn and I were walking on Broadway after seeing *A Touch of Song,* starring one of Harry's clients, Darla Jean Crane. Harry occasionally gave me free tickets to shows. I went backstage and introduced her to Art and Sulynn. Sulynn was not impressed.

"That'll be me in a year," she said, "greeting the nothings backstage."

"It won't be you as much as it will be Margo," Art reminded her. "Miss Margo is the *stah.*" He loved the New York accent and peppered his conversation with it. "Ask *heh.*" "*Cawfee.*" "*Cawlback.*"

I wanted to believe in a happy fate for *Bloomin'*, but I was afraid of disappointment, so I ignored their conversation.

"It feels like snow," I said.

Sulynn looked up at the time and temperature sign on the New York Bank for Savings. "Yeah, but it's not thirty-two degrees," she announced.

"It's twenty-seven degrees," Art said.

"I know, so it can't snow. It only snows if it's thirty-two degrees."

Art and I knew better than to say anything.

I left for Rochester December 22nd and returned the 29th, so I could spend New Year's Eve with Sulynn, Art and Bobby, who were all in Massachusetts, but came back to New York before the 31st. The day before I left, The Lasker Agency held their annual Christmas bash at the Madison Avenue office. Zelda gave everyone gifts. I got assorted jams, and Lance, her agent-in-training, got a tie which I'm sure Zelda stole out of Harry's closet. Elena got an ugly yellow scarf. "She's a cheap roller," Elena grumbled as we walked to the elevator. I assumed she meant "cheapskate," but didn't have the energy to explain it to her.

With my family in Rochester, I downplayed *Bloomin'*. Yes, rehearsals were due to start. Yes, anything could happen. I tried to adopt the same attitude once I was back in New York, but it wasn't easy, what with Bobby's New Year's toast "to fame" and Sulynn's proclamation that "this is our last year as unknowns."

The "party" to usher in 1972 was held at our apartment, and at 11:30 p.m., our buzzer rang.

"You have wonderful security in this building," Art noted. "They don't announce visitors anymore?"

"Who is it?" I called out.

"Your co-star, you bitch. On my way to Broadway with my booze and pills, like Neely O'Hara."

I threw open the door to Fred. "I made it!" Fred announced, somersaulting into the room. "I'm in New York — and my 'Mike' Jagger impression is going to make me a superstar!"

"Where are you staying?" Art asked him.

"I'm staying with a gentleman who has a huge apartment on Riverside Drive." I pushed a drink into his hand, and he sat on the floor, still wearing his coat. "I've got to find a job right away, although I know I won't need to work for long. I'll be making the Broadway salary soon enough. By the way, what is the Broadway salary?"

"People like us would get about four hundred a week," I replied. I hadn't been working for Harry and Zelda for nothing. I checked out every contract I could get my hands on.

"Not bad, not bad," said Bobby. "More than I get driving the old cab."

And so 1971 ended with a lot of dreams for 1972: an end to the "day jobs," superstardom on Broadway and the big bucks.

I sat on the floor and wondered what it would really bring.

January 3, 1972, Art, Sulynn, Bobby, Fred, Amalia Hayes, myself and four strangers gathered at our first *Bloomin'* rehearsal at the 16th St. Playhouse. The Playhouse reminded me of Cofis Summer Theater:

it was old and seedy. It was also dark, dirty and stuffy.

"No expense is being spared, I see," I remarked to Sulynn as we looked around.

"You'd think they'd buy something stronger than a twenty-five-watt bulb, at least," she said, dusting off a seat before sitting on it.

Foss stood on the stage, such as it was, with Zack Vincent and Tom Scardini, who announced he'd "done some rewrites." Mack the Moneyman was noticeably absent. We were introduced to the rest of the cast, all singer/dancers needed for the chorus and walk-ons: Tracy Friedman, pretty and auburn-haired; Marilyn Davis, a short brunette; Andy Kaufman, tall, blond and thin; and Jeff Archuretti, tall, brunette and thin.

Art ran over to sit next to me in the front row as soon as the introductions were completed. "Do you see a pattern emerging here?"

"I see heavy understudy fodder," I answered.

We each were given new scripts. "Sweet Times," one of my big numbers, was now in the middle of Act Two, and the show opened with an ensemble number called, appropriately, "Bloomin'." In the old show, "Bloomin'" was a quartet, begun by my character, Mandy Morgan. Now, the chorus sang it, too, and each solo was only one or two lines.

Sulynn still sang "Don't Turn Back," while Amalia kept "Oh, Mother." There were new scenes, scenes cut and relationships changed. Bobby's character, Ron, now became Mandy's love interest, whereas in the previous script, Keith, played by Art, had been her love interest.

The cast stretched across the front row and did a read-through of the script, without songs, since there was as yet no pianist-music director. "We're still interviewing," Foss announced.

"Hard to find someone to work for nothing," Bobby murmured.

"Do you think Mack Money dropped out?" I asked Bobby under my breath.

"What do you think?" he whispered back. "Look at this dump. Does this show seem Broadway-bound to you?"

I said, "Of course, we don't know how other Broadway shows started, or where."

"They didn't start here," Bobby snickered. "Unless we just don't know about it, because the casts died of depression after performing here."

I was determined to find out the real story. After the read-through, Foss announced rehearsal each night from seven to ten, Saturdays from eleven to four and Sundays as a free day. Then she dismissed us.

Working for Harry and Zelda, I had learned the direct approach. I waited until Amalia and the new people left, then approached Foss.

"Did you lose your backers?" I asked her, point-blank.

Sulynn, Bobby and Art decided not to bother straining their ears and joined us.

"We lost Mack," she admitted. "But, of course, Zack is still backing the show. And he's gotten some other people interested, but we must get the thing staged so they can see it. We're on a shoestring. Part of the money that Zack is investing has to go for rent here, a music director, advertising, copying, getting the piano tuned, paying transportation money — you have no idea what goes into just doing a show on a small scale. And the rest of his investment is being held for the eventual *big* production." She bit her lip, obviously fighting tears. "I'm sorry to tell you all this way. I didn't want to tell you at all. Because we're going to get more backers."

"Why did Mack drop out?" Bobby asked.

She sighed and shook her head. "It's long and involved — he had different ideas for the show than Tom, Zack and I have. That's all you need to know about it."

She half-smiled. "All of you — go home and get some rest. We have to make this show terrific. I made promises to you, and you've made a commitment to the show in return. I don't want to let you down and I won't. We will get backers."

It was a deflated bunch on the subway that night. "I wonder if Amalia caught on," Art yelled in my ear.

"I hope she did," I screamed back over the rumbling of the train, "because she'll never stay in it this way."

"I'm going to start doing some auditions," Bobby said when the train stopped at 42nd Street. "And if I get a job, I'm taking it."

"You can't," I said. "We've got to give the show a chance." The train started up again. I put my mouth against his ear. "At least wait and see what happens after we do the showcase." He didn't answer.

I was dejected when I went over to Harry's apartment the next day and even more dejected when I saw his pencil-scribbled note on the back of an envelope. "Set up auditions for this Saturday."

Part of my job was keeping a record of telephone calls from people requesting auditions for Harry's class. Periodically, he held auditions at the apartment. Since I'd started working for him, I'd run two such evenings and on both occasions, nearly quit.

I thought of Audition Night as Night From Hell. People either canceled at the last minute or didn't bother to show up or appeared even though no time was assigned to them. Auditions usually began at 7 p.m. — which meant I'd be in rehearsal from ten to four, then at Harry's by six to straighten out the apartment, get together the little forms the auditioners filled out and hunt up pens, since no one ever brought their own.

Sometimes, there was no one there to audition for huge gaps of time, then ten or twelve people would arrive at once. On Saturday night, I scheduled twelve people between seven and ten. To my surprise, only one person canceled. However, Harry scheduled an appointment at six at the apartment, and his meeting started late. At one point, he came into the den I used as an office.

"A girl with a Greek name might show up for a meeting with me at seven o'clock. If she does, I need to talk to her." This was typical of Harry, to schedule two or three things at once and not to even know the name of the person he was to see.

Shortly before seven, Zelda walked in. "We have auditions tonight," I reminded her. When I had told her earlier in the week, her reply was, "Oh, I won't be there." But she was there. "I'm going out to dinner with a potential partner," she told me. Zelda was branching out into the brassiere business, now that she and Harry, free of their embezzling secretary, were making some real money.

"I'm too exhausted to go out," she announced five minutes later and proceeded to sit at my desk and use my phone for half an hour.

I knew then it was going to be an interesting evening. As a former Hollywood nightclub singer and voice teacher, Zelda hated singers. I always had a great deal of trouble picturing Zelda as a glamorous chanteuse, especially with her horror show get-ups and her pack-a-day cigarette habit, which dried her face and voice out permanently.

Whenever Zelda came to the apartment, she was always "going out" and then she never quite went. I suspected her presence there was merely to keep an eye on Harry's extracurricular activities.

The Greek girl came for her appointment. I stuck her on the couch. Zelda got off the phone and took off her blouse. "Look at this bra," she said. "See how it gaps here? This woman gave it to me today after our meeting so I didn't turn it down. But can you believe she makes something like this?" She then took the bra off, revealing her pendulous, sagging breasts. I stole a glance at the Greek girl who was staring, red-faced.

"Look," Zelda held out the bra for my inspection. "You can't even fold it, it's so stiff." She then put on another bra — and, thankfully, her blouse — sat on one of the two facing couches and turned on the television — full blast — to a TV show starring David Janssen. "He used to be my client," she announced. "His real name was Meyers."

Harry got rid of the Greek girl, who I'm sure was happy to leave. My auditioners began filing in, filling out their forms, handing me their résumés, asking me where the bathroom was — which they couldn't possibly miss, since it was the first thing you saw, straight ahead, when you walked into the apartment — and asking for water. You also couldn't miss the kitchen at the right of the entrance. Every time the buzzer rang, Zelda said, "There's someone at the door." Thanks for the news flash, I felt like saying, and who do I look like — Jeeves?

Zelda spent the evening making sure everyone knew she sang at all the top clubs in L.A., made records, and, looking like a young Lauren Bacall, was signed to a personal contract by Samuel Goldwyn. And yes, a lot of her films were on television.

At one point, as Zelda held court, one of the auditioners, an actress named Kelly James asked me for water. I was on the phone at the time, taking dictation from Harry's accountant, and in the midst of that conversation, the doorbell rang (and Zelda said, "Someone's at the door"). I threw the phone down, ran to the door, and it was a courier — Harry's caretaker for his house upstate hadn't been paid in two months, because Harry kept forgetting she needed a check, so he was sending money by courier to keep her from quitting. When I returned to the den-waiting room, Kelly James was pointing to her throat — I'd forgotten her water. Evidently, at that point, I looked more like Gunga Din than Jeeves.

At nine o'clock, the doorbell rang, and after Zelda told me someone was at the door, I opened it, and there stood a blind girl with a beautiful golden retriever in harness.

It takes a very special person to live in New York as a disabled person, let alone actress, and Maxine was indeed special. I escorted her into the waiting room. Several of the people waiting knew her from her portrayal of Helen Keller in *The Miracle Worker* with a little theater company in New York. I began introducing her to the other auditioners, when I saw Zelda waving at me, indicating that she didn't want to be introduced.

Later, when I came back from escorting Maxine to the bathroom, Zelda said, "That girl was my voice student, and I threw her out. She's an aggressive, bitter little bitch. It's not my fault she's blind. I tried to get her to be realistic about singing — recitals, concerts — but she didn't want to hear any of it. I finally had to ask her to leave."

"Your secret's safe with me, Zelda," I said, thinking how mean-spirited she was. When I brought Maxine back, Zelda was alone in the room. Instead of being quiet, she mistakenly made a comment about David Janssen.

"I don't think we've met," Maxine said, realizing there was someone else there.

I froze. Zelda didn't reply.

"Excuse me," Maxine persisted, "have we met?"

Nothing.

"Margo?"

I pretended I hadn't heard her speaking previously.

"Yes?" I said in a jumpy voice, "I'm sorry, I was trying to figure out who this actress on television is."

"I haven't met this other person."

Finally, Zelda said, in a quasi-disguised speaking voice, "I'm Nadine. I'm visiting Mr. Lasker."

I then began chatting about David Janssen and how much I'd loved "The Fugitive," hopping up every thirty seconds to see why Harry was taking so long with the previous auditioner. I'm sure my nervousness was unnecessary; Maxine probably knew the quiet "Nadine" was Zelda.

It seemed as if Harry was giving the previous auditioner an hour instead of fifteen minutes. As it turned out, the actress he was auditioning was so neurotic that Harry was giving her a list of psychiatrists and doctors and trying to calm her down.

At last, at long last, it was Maxine's turn. I left her and her dog in the hall and ran in. "Your next appointment is blind, she's an ex-student of Zelda's, and Zelda doesn't want her to know she's here. So don't mention her." Just as I ushered Maxine in, Harry's phone rang. The volume on the answering machine was all the way up, and needless to say, the call was for Zelda. I'd never seen Harry move so fast in his life as he did to turn the volume down.

As I was leaving that evening, when the last song had been sung and the last monologue shouted, Zelda said to me, "You can be my bra model, Margo, and then you'll get your bras for free."

Then the evening was well worth it, I said to myself.

I decided my days with Harry were coming to a close. "God," I said out loud, as I walked out of the apartment. "Please make *Bloomin'* a hit."

The news on *Bloomin'* went from bad to worse. On the Monday following the thrilling "audition night" at Harry's, Foss held a meeting after rehearsal.

"As some of you know," Foss began, "one of our backers dropped out." Polite groans. "I don't like to discuss my personal life as a rule," she continued, "but you might as well have all of it. In order to work on *Bloomin'* with Tom and to be here in New York, I gave up my job at the music college as of this present term. Unfortunately, because I did that, we are not going to be able to use any of the costumes, wigs or set pieces from Cofis Summer Theater. I'm terribly sorry."

This time, the groans weren't so polite.

It was Tom Scardini's turn. "This means we're all going to have to pull together if we want the show to be a success," he said, sounding like a character in a Judy Garland-Mickey Rooney movie. "We need you to costume and wig yourselves, and we hope you'll be willing to do that."

"We" didn't feel there was much choice. "We" either stood up on stage looking like fools aging from thirteen to thirty in our own hairdos and bell bottoms, or "we" spent some money.

"Also," said Foss, "I'd like to ask Bobby to handle the choreography."

"That's no problem," Bobby said.

"We still don't have a stage manager or a music director," Miss Fossey continued. "And time is growing short. If any of you know one or the other or both, please ask them to get in touch with me immediately. Unfortunately, there's no money involved."

"We know a great stage manager," Art said. "And she'll work for free. Our mother."

"She's just sitting around all day anyway," Bobby said.

"Just sitting around making your lunch," I reminded him.

Foss lit up like a Christmas tree. "Oh, do you think she would do it?"

"We know she would," Art told her, "and I'll bet she can dig up someone to be music director, too. You should have told us the extent of the problem immediately."

Her eyes welled up with tears. "I've let you all down, and I was afraid to tell you."

Art stood up. "Look, we're here, and that's all there is to it. I say let's all pitch in and get the job done."

"Ditto," Fred yelled. "And don't anybody buy wigs till they see what I have first." Foss cried openly with gratitude.

Lettie agreed to stage manage and even owned a wig that Sulynn could wear in the first act. Once Lettie was brought into the "*Bloomin'* disaster," as we liked to call it, things took a turn for the better. Somehow she found us a music director, the son of a friend of hers. He was attending Hofstra as a music major, and he grabbed at the opportunity to play a "pre-Broadway" show.

Once Foss allowed her emotions to emerge, she cried at card tricks. When she saw the pianist, Greg, at his first rehearsal, she broke down totally and left the theater for a while. Then she tried to thank Lettie for stage managing, but her voice choked off in sobs. "That's okay, honey," Lettie said. "It's the least I can do. You're going to make my boys big stars."

At last, rehearsals were for real, and we weren't just going through the motions of saying our lines, then yelling the word "SONG" or "DANCE" and continuing, with our hearts not in any of it. Greg was an excellent musician who didn't just play through the music, but added to the arrangements. I thought Bobby's choreography was better than what we'd gotten from the local tap teacher in Cofis last summer, although, as he pointed out, that wasn't saying much.

There wasn't much time to get ready for the big opening, but then again, we principals had done the show quite recently, and the changes weren't so dramatic that we couldn't learn them quickly. It was the little chorus that needed work, and Foss was strict with them.

Opening night of our ten-performance run arrived, Friday, January 27th. Sulynn and I didn't work that day, choosing instead to lounge in our nightwear, watch daytime television and gorge ourselves on bagels and cream cheese. Shortly after noon, Art phoned from home — he had called in sick at the hospital where he was working.

"Is Sulynn with you?" he asked me.

"Yes."

"Go in the other room — and make sure she hangs up."

"I have to talk to Art about his vocal problems," I told Sulynn. "He's very touchy about anyone knowing. I'll take it in my room." I went into my bedroom and shut the door. After I heard the telltale "click" on the end of the line, I said, "Well?"

"Three guesses who's in town."

"Art, I have no idea."

"I'll give you a hint. Her rich father's here, too."

"Holly Morrison?"

"Real name Eloise Morrison. Yes, she's here, and she, her father, Bobby and my mother are at lunch right now. Is that far out or what?"

"Yikes. So the Queen of Cofis is in Gotham." I shuddered. "What are they doing here, besides trying to snare Bobby?"

"*Bloomin'*. Foss needs Big Daddy's bread."

"Wow. What do you think the chances are?"

"Don't know. I think good if Bobby plays along, which between you and me, he doesn't find difficult. He's slept with her, you know."

I didn't, but wouldn't admit it. "I figured," was all I said.

"I'm actually calling to find out what you think about Sulynn. Do we tell her before the show or let her spot that white-blonde hair in the audience? It's not that big a theater, and I'm afraid it will affect her performance." It was understood that Sulynn was no Bette Davis.

"I'll think about it," I said. "It could go either way."

He changed the subject. "Have you vocalized yet? My throat feels a little scratchy."

I advised him to gargle with salt and warm water and to keep drinking tea with honey and lemon, then hung up and returned to the living room/bedroom. Sulynn was stretched out on the coach, still in her bathrobe, watching "All My Children" and spreading cream cheese on a pumpernickel bagel.

I was in the kind of mess one only gets into when attempting to spare a friend's feelings. If I told Sulynn about Holly, she'd know that a) It was the subject of my conversation with Art and something Art didn't necessarily think she should know, and b) That Holly was with Bobby, otherwise, how would Art know Holly was in town?

So, I mused, as I watched Erica Kane go through her machinations, how could I tell her Holly was in town? Where did I get the information, if not from Art? And if I didn't tell her, what would happen at the theater when she discovered not only that Holly was in town, but that Bobby knew all about it?

My reverie was cut short by Sulynn. "Did Art tell you about Holly Morrison?" she asked me, her eyes still on the television.

"That Foss is trying to get Holly's father to back the show, yes, and that they're both here for it. How do you know about it?"

"Bobby told me last night at rehearsal. He said it was supposed to be a big secret, but I figured Art told you."

"Well, no matter that it was supposed to be a big secret, why didn't you tell *me*?"

She shrugged and sighed, "Somehow, it just didn't seem worth mentioning."

We arrived at the theater at 6:30, and it seemed colder inside than out. "I'll tell you the truth," Sulynn said as we watched our breath come out of our mouths in the dressing room. "I hope Bobby marries Holly, and her father gives us a million dollars. I'd about kill to get out of this dump."

"So would I. Let's hope Bobby continues to exhibit his famous lack of conscience."

Sulynn sat at her end of the table, her coat still buttoned. "Well, you know, he may love her."

"Did he tell you he does?"

"Margo, I only know he doesn't love me. And since I realized that, I've been okay. Really. I don't care what he does with Holly or anyone else. He might love her, or think he does. It doesn't matter. I'm free. I hope that if he doesn't love her, that he at least pretends he does."

"Of course," I said, plugging in my electric rollers, "we don't know that that's a condition for her father to invest. He might have to believe in the show."

Sulynn spread her makeup across her section of the table. "Then let me ask you a question. What's she doing here?"

I had no answer, and at that point, Amalia arrived. "You all ready to roast this turkey?" she asked us. "Hal is going to take notes from the audience. I wish he could have been at the dress rehearsal, but he taught until three o'clock this afternoon in Boston. He flew in, just for this. And guess who's here — that blonde from the summer — what's her name?"

"Holly Morrison," Sulynn and I droned together.

"Holly Morrison, that's it." Amalia snapped her fingers, then started jumping up and down in an attempt to get warm. "Boy, they're coming out of the woodwork for this one. It is freaky. You both have a lot of people coming?"

"Yes," we again answered at once.

Amalia threw off her coat and began doing toe-touches. "I've only got Hal here tonight," she panted. "Is that agent you work for coming?"

"No," I lied. Amalia Hayes was not going to be on the Lasker client list if I had anything to say about it. Harry and Zelda both promised to be in the audience, since I had threatened to quit if they weren't there. Elena and Lance were also coming from the office, as well as some students and clients of Harry's I'd met, but many of them were coming on other nights. In all, I'd sent out about fifty flyers, shocked that I already knew so many people in New York.

"What about you?" Amalia said to Sulynn. "Any of your fellow spies coming?"

"A few. To tell you the truth, Amalia, I don't feel much like talking, and I'd appreciate it if you'd keep quiet."

Amalia was finished exercising her chunky body, but not her big mouth. "If you don't want to talk, Reilly, then DON'T TALK. But DON'T TELL ME WHAT TO DO."

Art stuck his head through our curtain, which served as a door, not caring if we were dressed or not, since he didn't bother to announce himself first. There was no doubt that he heard what Amalia said. "Good show, girls," he said in his sweetest voice, then winked at me.

The little theater was filled to capacity. It didn't occur to me to be nervous until just before my entrance. Then I panicked. Foss stood behind me and squeezed my shoulder.

One thing that's good, I thought as I walked onto the stage, is that the lights blind you. In that respect, the Playhouse felt like a real live theater.

"We're all bloomin'," I sang. One by one, the rest of the cast came onto the stage and sang. From that point on, I was fine. As for the rest of the show, I was in too much of a concentrated daze to notice whether it went well or not.

When it came time for my curtain call, I bowed center, then to the right and left. When I turned back to the center, I saw Harry and Zelda, in a middle row, standing up. Harry was applauding with his hands over his head.

We ran back to the dressing room area. "We did it! We did it," we all kept saying over and over, hugging and kissing everyone in sight. Foss cried so hard she couldn't speak.

I pulled myself together and went into the lobby. There was no room in the backstage area for the audience, so anyone who wanted to see the cast waited in the narrow lobby. Harry and Zelda stood by the exit door, looking morose, and then Harry spotted me. He pushed people aside and rushed toward me, throwing his arms around me.

"You didn't tell me you could sing like that," he yelled. "What a voice! Hah! Hah!" Zelda, coming up behind him, even managed to crack a smile.

"You have an excellent talent, Margo," she said. "You didn't tell us about it."

"There's some good people in this show," Harry said, putting his arm around me. "That little brunette — Reilly?"

"Yes," I said. "She's my roommate."

"Have her come in and see me. And the blond boy — Bobby Gaines — that's some quality, hey, Zelda?"

"Absolutely," was all she replied.

"He reminds me of Jimmy Dean," Harry said. When he talked about the stars, he always used chummy nicknames: "Monty," "Frankie," "Betty." "Well, Margo, we'll talk on Monday," he promised me as I walked them to the door of the theater. "Boy," he continued, "I never had anyone like you work for me before. Can you imagine, Zelda, she sings like an angel and she's in a new show and we never hear a word about it, not till it's opening night? Hah! Hah!"

"That's me, Harry. Humble." I pushed the door open for him. "Beautiful job," a woman said to me as she went out. I was still holding the door open from the inside. "Excellent," her escort told me. He, too, took advantage of my doorman service.

I made it back to the dressing room. There was no sign of anyone else who promised to be part of the opening night crowd, so my hostess duties were over. Tom Scardini was pouring champagne into paper cups for us. I looked for Sulynn, but she wasn't in the dressing room. I noticed Bobby standing with the Morrisons, so I joined them.

"You were fabulous," Holly said, stamping out a cigarette with her foot.

Her father hugged me and almost broke my ribs. "Fantastic."

"Did you come all the way to New York just to see the show?" I asked him, extricating myself.

Mr. Morrison guffawed. "How can you ask me that when I have a grown daughter who loves to shop?" Everyone laughed the flattering, overly-hearty laughs of desperate people.

When the hilarity died down, he said, "Actually, we wanted to see how the show was going, especially since I heard from Sandra Fossey that she lost Mack as an angel. A real shame, too. It's such a marvelous show. With some great talent." His eyes rested on me, and I suddenly felt uncomfortable and wondered why Mrs. Morrison wasn't on the trip with the rest of her family.

I kept my voice casual. "Well, it's great seeing you both, and I imagine I'll see you at Foss's party later on. Talk to you then." I turned away, but not before I saw Bobby's mouth curl up in a smile. Or was it a smirk.

The cast party consisted of the chorus and their assorted mates, the principals, Fossey, Tom Scardini, Zack Vincent, Lettie, Greg, who played the piano for part of the evening's festivities, his girlfriend from college and the Morrisons. Foss's apartment in the West Village was small, so the place seemed packed. In addition, Fred brought his new boyfriend, Georgie, an albino.

"Here goes," Fred said, gulping his drink. "I overheard old man Morrison talking to Foss, and it looks like he's going to put some money into the show." I gasped, and he put a restraining hand on my arm. "The other thing is, Zack is saying something about backers' auditions. Art was standing with me when we heard that."

Rumors of all sorts continued to fly throughout the night. Art and I discussed the possibility — an idea of Lettie's — that Zack and Miss Fossey were involved romantically. We further formulated the theory that Mack, the investor, had been in love with Miss Fossey and, when rejected, dropped out as angel for the show. It was a nice soap opera plot. I doubted we could ever prove it and said so.

"My mother's never wrong about that type of thing," Art said. "She's pretty sure Holly's interested in Bobby for keeps, too."

"What does she think about Holly's father?" After giving me the fish eye, Mr. Morrison had moved on to Sulynn and then to Tracy. I heard him tell Tracy "her talent made the chorus."

"My mother said he definitely fools around," Art said.

"Perceptive. And what's this about backers' auditions?"

"Looks like we'll be doing them if not enough money people come to see the show."

I was to remember that remark as we did the performances. Not only did not enough money people come to see the show, not enough un-moneyed people came to see the show, either. On some nights, we were classical actors in the truest sense — i.e., there were more of us on stage than there were people in the audience.

Every night at intermission, Lettie went out into that pathetic excuse for a lobby — really, it was more like a hallway — with paper cups and bottles of regular and diet soda and sold drinks to earn extra money for the show. Sometimes she came back with as much as $1.50. "For the *Bloomin'* fund," she said.

All Fossey and Zack Vincent would say was that there were "plans in the making." But the size of the audience, and the fact that the show seemed to be falling apart again, made us start to lose hope.

What ailed the last few performances of *Bloomin'* at the 16th St. Playhouse could best be described as sophomore slump. That and just a touch of depression.

One night, Bobby did the unthinkable. There were four people in the audience. The show had dragged on, and it was evident that on this night, anyway, it was a pretty fair disaster, with a million little things going wrong. Bobby gave up somewhere in Act One, and stood on stage with his mustache half on and half off in Act Two. In the middle of my scene with him, he started offstage. The scene wasn't over. His lines weren't finished.

Still in character, but not saying lines from the script, I said, "Where are you going?"

Bobby's character was supposed to leave the stage angry — at the end of the scene. He turned to me and bellowed: "I'M GOING TO GET MORE SPIRIT GUM," and stormed away. The four people in the audience screamed with laughter, and for the first time that night, they were with us. The rest of the show went much better.

"Sometimes you have to take risks," Bobby said, deadpan, to a furious Foss after the show.

Sulynn, in the meantime, was making out like a bandit, thanks to *Bloomin'*. Harry wasn't quite willing to sign her, but he was willing to send her out on an audition for a soap opera, "A Bright Tomorrow." Sulynn was terribly excited, until he told her she needed to lose ten pounds. Then the death regime began: black coffee and half a grapefruit in the morning, no lunch, and two hardboiled eggs and a salad with half a tablespoon of oil on it at dinner.

Sulynn and I always got along well, and other than the fact that she refused to wake up in the morning, she was an agreeable roommate, and we were compatible — two slobs with good senses of humor, the same friends and the same interests.

However, Sulynn's darker side came to the fore when she embarked on her diet. She became alternately a sobbing, emotional wreck or a vicious, cruel monster. Once, she was so horrible to me that in apology, she brought me a beautiful bouquet of flowers. When I returned from Harry's later in the day, the flowers were destroyed and lying on the floor, and Sulynn was sobbing on the couch.

Frightened, I called Art at the hospital. He promised to come over after work, but called me back minutes later.

"Listen, Margo, I've been talking to a doctor here — he wants to know is Sulynn on anything. He said it sounds like she's taking diet pills."

This never occurred to me, nor had she mentioned it. "Hold on," I said, and went into the living room, where Sulynn now appeared to be asleep. I shook her awake. "Sulynn, are you taking any pills on this diet?"

Groggily she sat up and reached for her purse. She pulled out an unmarked bottle which contained some small green tablets. "Someone at work gave me these."

I took the bottle, left her there and went back to the phone. "Thank him for me, Art," I said. "I think I've just solved the problem." I flushed the pills down the toilet and very calmly went back to her. "Sulynn, if you get any more of those pills, don't bother coming back here. Either lose weight naturally or don't lose it. You're making us both insane."

Sulynn looked up at me, her face streaked with tears. "Oh, my God," she began to cry again, "do you think those pills were making me *sick*?"

"Oh, hell, no," I said. "You always rip flowers up and throw them all over the room."

Sulynn's audition was a success, and the casting director told

Harry he wanted to test her. This threw her into a panic. "I've never been in front of a camera before — I don't know anything about it." Consequently, Harry coached her.

"One of the things he told me," she informed Bobby before *Bloomin'* one night, "is that less is more."

"I wouldn't take that too much to heart, Miss Sulynn," Bobby warned her. "In your case, less might be less." Fortunately, the show started before they could break into a full battle.

To Bobby's (and, frankly, my own) surprise, Sulynn's test went very well, and lo and behold, the producers requested another test.

"It's getting serious," Art said. "We might end up with a serious breadwinner here."

Harry wasn't through with the *Bloomin'* cast as far as throwing a little luck our way, though. He treated me with new respect and asked a lot of questions about the show and the genesis of it. About a week after he saw *Bloomin'*, he asked me for Zack Vincent's phone number and also told me to have Bobby come in and see him. I hesitated on the latter, because I didn't want to hurt Art's feelings. I finally took Bobby aside at the theater and told him to see Harry, but to be discreet about it.

I was dying to know what Harry discussed with Zack, but there was no way I could find out for the present. I brought the show up to him, though, at every conceivable opportunity, hoping he'd say something. It was sometimes difficult to find ways to get *Bloomin'* into everyday conversation with him. One day he asked me to type something, and I said, "Oh, I can finish that next week, Harry, after the show's finished. Right now, I don't know what the next step will be, but I should be free for a while."

For a change, he didn't ignore the reference. "You're quite involved with this, aren't you?"

"Well, sure. I've been with it since the beginning, and I have the lead role. Don't you think I should be involved?" I gave him the innocent look I always used when auditioning for ingénue roles, not that I ever got the parts.

"I thought you were great, Margo, and it kills me to say it. I don't want to lose you. But no, I can't say as I blame you." End of discussion.

At the last performance, Foss asked us to stay afterward. After the six audience members had left the theater, she met the cast backstage.

"Don't be upset about the number of people in the audience after the first couple of nights. The show was a huge success from our point of view. And I'm pleased to tell you that we've had some people express an interest in backing the show. We're in the process of arranging some evening backers' auditions of selections from the show. These auditions will be held in various places — sometimes Zack's place, sometimes the prospective backer's place.

"I have to ask you to do this for us gratis. And, of course, Greg, who has so graciously consented to play the piano, will get a flat fee for doing the auditions."

"It just kills me how these pianists always make out," Amalia said.

"The backers' audition will be a cut version of the show which will involve only Margo, Bobby, Sulynn and Art, so we won't be needing the rest of you."

"Fine with me." Amalia again.

Foss ignored her. "We'll have a couple of rehearsals, and our first audition is February 15. Thanks, everybody."

"Another closing, another meeting — déjà vu," Bobby said, as soon as she left.

Sulynn grumbled. "We've heard it all before. Here's my question. When is this mother going to get *moving*?"

"I really don't know what the hell you're crying about," Bobby said to her as we walked outside. "You're about to become a soap opera queen."

Bobby's prediction became a reality (well, almost) the very next day. The good news was that Sulynn got a job on "A Bright Tomorrow." The bad news was that it wasn't the part she auditioned for, but a smaller role. "Lots of opportunity for growth," Harry told her. "If the viewers like you, no telling how big your part can get."

Sulynn typically was unhappy, demanding to know why she didn't get the larger part, who got it and what did that actress have that Sulynn didn't. Harry was very patient with her, but I could tell it wouldn't last long. I was at my desk in his apartment, while the two of them sat on the couch. I got up and ran into the living room, where there were phones for Harry's private and business lines. I picked up the business phone and called the private one, let it ring twice, then laid the receiver down on the piano, meanwhile hanging up the other phone.

I went back to the den. "You have a call from L.A. — John Hawkworth, Harry." That particular phone line wasn't in the den, so Harry went into the living room to get it.

I stood over Sulynn. "Tell him you want the part, for God's sake, and stop making trouble. Don't worry about the details."

Harry was back. "There was no one there. Try to get him back for me, will you, Margo?"

"After considering everything you've said, Mr. Lasker," Sulynn smiled, "I think it will be a wonderful part for me."

Sulynn left, and I said to him, "John Hawkworth's not in his office. I think he might have been calling you from somewhere else," and left it at that.

Sulynn's first day of taping on "A Bright Tomorrow," as "Cassie," the college-girl love-interest for one of the supporting actors, occurred the same day as our first backers' audition. Art, Bobby and I worked so much with Sulynn on her part that we hardly devoted any time to *Bloomin'*. "If she doesn't become a quicker study, she won't last," Art said. Not only couldn't she memorize her lines fast enough, she couldn't seem to remember where the important pauses in the lines were, which take place right before the commercials. "I'm just nervous," she promised us. "One or two days of this and I'll be fine."

The first *Bloomin'* backers' audition was held at Zack Vincent's apartment at 98th and Fifth.

We sat in folding chairs next to the piano, facing an audience of about twenty people. Zack's opening pitch was a revelation to all of us.

The first shock was that Harry had put money into the show, which made him, Zack and Mr. Morrison the show's three investors. The second shock was that the money was needed first to mount a pre-New York tour, followed by an Off-Broadway production. No mention of Broadway. Zack handed a budget sheet to each of the people there. By any standards, *Bloomin'* was considered a "small" show, not requiring nearly the money of *Follies* or *Company*.

Sulynn sat next to me half-asleep, and I kept elbowing her to keep her alert. After the audition, Art, Bobby and I mingled a little, drank some cocktails and ate hors d'oeuvres, while Sulynn made sure everyone in the room knew she was a working actress. Then the four of us departed en masse. When Sulynn and I got home, I dialed Fossey's number till I reached her.

"How'd we do?" I demanded to know.

"Well, we raised $20,000. It's a beginning."

"Twenty thousand! How many auditions will we have to do before we get all the money?"

"Oh, I don't know, Margo. These were actually small investors tonight. There'll be some bigger fish later on."

"Why didn't somebody tell us about Harry? He's my boss and Sulynn's agent, you know."

She laughed. "I thought he should tell you himself — I guess he didn't. I think he's interested in producing it, you know, with Zack.

It's exciting. But tell me, do you think we'll lose Sulynn now that she has this job?"

"I don't know if it's going to last," I said, "but if it does, I don't know why she can't do both. One is in the day and one is in the evening."

"Yes, but once we start touring... Well, we'll cross that bridge when we come to it. I'd hate to lose her. She *is* the character of Robin for me. Well, goodnight."

I hung up and got ready for bed. Sulynn was already asleep in the next room. I wasn't particularly tired, so I lay in bed listening to a Blood, Sweat and Tears retrospective on the radio.

I must have fallen asleep, because the next thing I knew, I heard a blood-curdling scream. I sat upright in the bed, too stunned to move. "Sulynn?" I called out, terrified.

"AHHHHHHHHHHHHHHHHHHHHHHHH," came the scream from the next room.

"Oh, my God," I said to myself, and got out of bed, scared out of my mind and not knowing what to do. There was silence. Blood, Sweat and Tears was over, and now "Pinball Wizard" played on the radio. Should I go into the other room?

Suddenly, the door crashed open and Sulynn fell in, crying and screaming. She dove into my bed, face in the pillow.

"My God!" I said, almost in tears myself. "What's wrong?" Since no rapist/attacker/robber followed her in, I found the courage to peek out into the living room. It was empty.

"Don't...go...in...there," she choked. "I...saw...a...m-m-mouse."

"WHAT?" I yelled, every bit as upset as she was. "Sulynn, where did you see it?"

"It...was...in...the...b-b-athroom..." She totally broke down.

Finally, we composed ourselves, and making plenty of noise, we ventured into the other room. We turned the volume up on the radio and blasted the television and sang out loud. "I'll just die if it's in my shoe," Sulynn said. "I'm afraid to pick it up." I took her hand, and together we walked over to the lone shoe, and I kicked it gingerly. Nothing happened. "It's safe," I assured her.

I woke up the superintendent, and he said he'd come in and put down traps and poison. "No traps," I said. Sulynn shuddered visibly at the word "traps." "How do we keep it from coming back?" I asked the super. "Can you find where it's coming in?"

"That's real hard, lady," he said. "The best thing to do is get a cat."

It was the obvious solution. I hadn't gotten a cat, because I never felt "settled," and more importantly, as long as Sulynn was my roommate, a cat was out of the question. She loved them but was allergic.

"Okay, Sulynn, this is it," I said. "We'll stay at Harry's apartment tonight — he and Zelda will be at their house this weekend. But either we move or you get allergy shots, because I think we're going to have to get a cat."

Art and Bobby brought Samson to us the next day. I absolutely refused to go to an animal shelter — I knew I would want every animal, and the whole scene would break my heart. I asked Art to go and find us an adult cat on death row.

Samson, or Sammy, as he came to be known, was about two years old when we got him and all black. We named him Samson because, when the shelter got him, he had been behind a restaurant stuck in glue, and the vet shaved off part of his fur.

"Let Sammy get the lay of the land, and if there's anything to catch, he'll catch it," Art said. "You two come over tonight. We've got something to show you."

"That sounds provocative," I told him. He didn't reply.

Sulynn and I arrived at the Gaines residence at eight o'clock with Chinese food and were greeted at the door by Art and a beautiful gray cat.

"Delilah," he introduced us. "In the death cell next to Samson."

It was a fun evening, playing with Delilah and gossiping about Sulynn's job and *Bloomin'*. Sulynn downed three glasses of wine, took two puffs of a joint and asked Bobby if he was going to marry Holly Morrison.

"Are you for real?" he laughed. "I'm not marrying anybody."

"I know you, Bobby Gaines," Sulynn said. "You're not marrying anybody, but you haven't told her that, right?"

"Oh, Sulynn, honey," Bobby answered, affecting a southern drawl. "You want to talk about bullshittin' people? Leadin' 'em on? Sugah, anythin' I learned, I learned from you. When your grades were at stake, you always found time to bat your baby blues at the teachers. There were guys you knew liked you, that you didn't give a damn 'bout — and don't say you did — that you sucked up to 'cause they were better in some subject or other. So don't go callin' the kettle black."

"You haven't answered my question," was all Sulynn said, and the three of us laughed.

Later, Delilah sat on Art's lap, and I sat next to him on the floor, leaning up against the wall in the hallway, petting the cat. "I can't believe I waited so long to get one," I said. "I love animals."

"We've always had cats in Yarmouth," he said. "My aunt's been staying at the house taking care of them while my mother's here. Has my mother talked to you at all about anything?"

"Your mother? About what?"

"Oh, I thought she might have talked about me to you."

I shook my head. "No." He was quiet. "Well, what about you?" I asked him.

"She asked me if we were serious."

I guffawed. "What did you say? What could you say?"

He shifted his position to face me, and Delilah jumped off his lap. "I didn't know what to say. I was pretty surprised when she asked me, but it's just this whole thing with Holly — see, my mother always thought Sulynn and Bobby would — I don't know. This business of Bobby and Holly, it's made me stop and look at things. I don't talk to Bobby about how he feels. He just tells me to be cool, and it's none of my business. But you don't have to be a psychiatrist to know that he and Sulynn could never be more than what they are to each other. They're alike in the wrong way — they're both kind of out for themselves — and then they're too different in what they should be alike in — you know, money, communicating."

I nodded in agreement.

He went on, and I was afraid to breathe, for fear his uncharacteristic soul-searching would stop. "I can admit now that I was jealous of you and Chick, but I really couldn't understand it. I told myself you were just my really good friend, so why was I so jealous? I convinced myself it was because I thought he was a little bit of a jerk, and you could do better.

"You know how it is with me. I've dated a lot but it's so casual, and the minute anyone gets serious with me I back off. I was seeing someone at the hospital, one of the secretaries. She saw the show twice, as a matter of fact, and now I feel pressured by her, so I haven't called her."

I groaned. "Don't do that to her. Take it from someone who's been on the other side of it — call her and at least explain where you're coming from, for God's sake."

"Yeah, I should. But — I've been asking myself, why can't I get serious with anyone? And I've come to the conclusion it's because I *am* serious with someone and afraid to do anything about it."

I didn't say anything. We just stared at one another, then he pulled me to him and began to kiss me, not tentatively, as in the past, but with a new passion. This went on for a time, until I pulled away.

"Don't mess with me," I warned him. "Don't pull this, then decide you don't want it. I'm not a secretary in your office — we're friends, and we have to work together. Let's make sure we know what we're doing."

"What does that mean? You need to think about it?"

"And you don't?"

"I — I *have* thought about it."

"Then maybe I should." I stood up. "We have to be sure, Art. It's no good otherwise. This is pretty sudden."

"Sudden? It's like *Gone with the Wind* — years in the making." He scowled.

"Well, I wasn't on the set during the shooting — I'm just being presented with the almost-finished film. And I don't know what the ending is. If it's going to be 'Frankly, my dear, I don't give a damn,' I'd rather not finish watching it." I could hear Bobby and Sulynn arguing about something in the living room. I left Art on the floor and walked in on them. "I'm leaving, Sulynn. I'm tired," I said, and grabbed my coat from the armchair.

"I'll go, too." I handed her her coat and we left, with a perfunctory good-bye to both Art and Bobby.

"What are you doing, running a race?" Sulynn yelled, when we were out on the street, and she was rushing to keep up with me. I apologized for walking so quickly.

"What's wrong?" she asked me.

"Nothing. I'm cold, that's all."

"Isn't that Bobby something?" she said, a little out of breath. "He's stringing Holly along for sure."

We stopped at a red light on 79th Street. "They like stringing people along." I told her about Art and his office romance, not wanting to go into my scene with him in the hallway.

Sulynn laughed. "Yeah, well, come the revolution and they'll be digging ditches. There are some awfully cute guys on this soap. Wait'll you meet a couple of them."

"Straight?"

"Most of them seem to be. And sharp dressers. I haven't had time to really check them out, but once I do, we'll have our pick."

When we arrived at our apartment, there was a dead mouse in the middle of the floor.

The backers' auditions continued through March and April. The potential number of "angels" present varied from five to as many as twenty-five people. Lettie attended one of them and put in five thousand dollars. "Just take care of my boys, that's all I ask," she told

Zack Vincent, handing him the check.

Holly became an occasional visitor to New York, staying with Bobby and Art — in Bobby's room, of course — when she was in town. There was no further discussion — or action — between Art and me regarding any romance.

Sulynn, in the meantime, began to date one of the soap actors, Clark Davidson, who played Matt on "A Bright Tomorrow." He was gorgeous in an all-American way, and Sulynn wore him like a Phi Beta Kappa key. "You know which one he is on the show, Bobby," she said, "the really handsome one. Tell him, Margo, tell Bobby how handsome he is."

"He's short, fat and has a shaved head," I said with a straight face.

"Hmm. Match made in heaven," Bobby said.

Sulynn and Clark had been dating about two weeks when she stopped coming home most nights, which left just me and Sammy. Together, he and I watched Sulynn on the soap most afternoons at three o'clock.

Without Sulynn, I was suddenly lonely and glad for little Sammy's company. Bobby spent a lot of time with Holly, and Art and I were avoiding each other, although we never would have admitted it. Lettie was going back to Yarmouth soon, and Art spent a lot of time with her and used that as an excuse. It was fine with me.

Living alone was a new experience, and I wasn't sure I liked it. Was it true loneliness, I asked myself, or just an uneasy feeling that there was something wrong with my life? Everyone seemed to be pairing off. Fred had Georgie, Sulynn had Clark, and Bobby had Holly. Art, for all I knew, had the secretary in his office. I had Sammy the cat.

The night after an April 25th backers' audition, Zack Vincent invited us to dinner at his apartment for the following evening. Sulynn was furious because she had to be up the next morning for a taping. After dinner, Zack announced, "Last night was it, folks. We've got the money."

Pandemonium. When the screaming, hugging and kissing stopped, Sulynn whined, "What am I gonna do? Do I have to give up my soap job?"

Foss put her arms around her. "Sulynn, we're not going on tour right away. Maybe Harry can come to some agreement with them, to write you out for a time or whatever. In the meantime just go on as you are. You know we want you, but it's going to have to be your decision."

In the weeks that followed, we learned the tour was due to start in mid-July, due to Harry's unbelievable wheeling and dealing. Another show due to go on the summer stock circuit failed to make the Equity bond, and Harry moved right in with *Bloomin'* as a replacement, posting the bond himself long before the money was raised.

"Can you beat it?" Art said. "He was taking a helluva chance."

We all signed contracts and were told to go join the union. Actors Equity — the actor's ultimate goal. Tear-stained with the emotion of the moment, I went to the Equity office. (Sulynn was already a member through the sister union, AFTRA, that she had joined in order to do "A Bright Tomorrow.") I was just about to write out my check for the fee when the Equity rep stopped me. Harry, in his inimitable style, had given us all out-of-date-contracts, and the union refused to accept my check.

I called Art at the hospital. "Don't bother to go to the union to join," I said. "Harry gave us contracts from 1965, and they're no good." I searched the Madison Avenue office high and low until I found the right ones and typed them all up myself.

Harry submitted Bobby for several jobs around the time the final money was raised, and Bobby landed the role of Patrick in *Mame* in, of all places, Las Vegas, to begin rehearsals mid-May and play through June 15th.

Sulynn and I invited the whole gang over to dinner on May 12th as a combination celebration of *Bloomin'* and a farewell to Bobby. Clark was there, and Fred brought Georgie, Bobby brought Holly, and Art brought Lettie. Bobby told us about the show.

"It's a cut version they're doing at The Vegas Palace," Bobby said, "starring Neda Palanz."

"Neda Palanz!" I exclaimed. "One of her movies was on television just last night."

Bobby said, "What year was it made — 1934? I'll probably have to carry her on stage."

"She might have a portrait in her closet like Grant Masters did," Fred said. "You know, *The Portrait of Neda Palanz.*"

"So Sulynn and Bobby are taken care of. That leaves Fred and you and me, Art," I said, as Sulynn brought in a tray of food from the kitchen. "I'll have to hit Harry up to get us all jobs."

The room fell silent. I looked at everyone sitting at the table, and each one of them stared back at me. "What's wrong?" I asked.

Art stood behind my chair. "Unfortunately, Margo — or perhaps fortunately — you and I won't be able to take jobs right away."

My face felt hot. "Why not?" I asked in a small voice.

His hand was now in front of my face and there, in between his thumb and forefinger, was a diamond ring. "Because I hope we're going to be on our honeymoon," he answered.

I didn't move an inch. Everyone's eyes bore through me. I heard the steady tick-tick-tick of Art's watch and Joni Mitchell singing "All I Want" from the stereo.

I slapped my hands to my face and burst into tears.

"Is that a 'yes?'" Sulynn demanded.

I nodded.

"Jesus Christ," Bobby said.

CURTAIN — ACT I

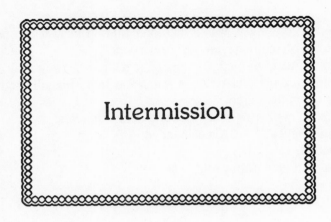

Intermission

I was due to become Margo Girard Gaines on June 15, 1972, at St. Mark's Chapel in Las Vegas, Nevada. Bobby couldn't leave *Mame*, so we would go to Bobby. Invited to the wedding were my parents, my brother Paul and his wife Kathy, Lettie, Sulynn, who was my maid of honor, and Bobby, the best man.

My engagement to Art seemed to be a signal for many of my friends to officially become couples. Art stayed over with me at the apartment the night we became engaged and basically never left, moving most of his clothes in the next day. Sulynn decided it was as good a time as any to move in with Clark, and did so. Holly came to New York to visit every weekend, since Bobby had the place to himself.

I allowed myself to be in love, discovering it to be a strange, exciting and wretched experience. The transition from friend to lover is awkward. "Sex shouldn't make such a difference," Art said, after we made love the first time. "But it does." I found myself self-conscious, tentative and much more feminine than I had ever been with him before. He, in turn, was painfully considerate and deferential.

The humor, for a time, went out of our relationship, and our new meaning to each other made us uncomfortable around our friends and vice versa. Lettie, whom I had always thought of as a surrogate mother and friend, was now soon to be my mother-in-law and somehow became threatening.

After a week or so of unbearable tension, I said to Art. "Maybe this isn't such a good idea. Everything's changed, and I'm not sure for the better."

He breathed a huge sigh. "I feel the same way," he admitted. "I tried to think about what it would be like, but I never came up with this scenario. Do you want to become unengaged?"

I wasn't sure, but I said, "Do you?"

He was quiet for a time. Then he said, "No, but I think we have to figure out what's wrong and fix it."

"I know what's wrong. We're not acting like ourselves. We're tiptoeing around each other and being weird with our friends. I can't figure out why."

"I know why I'm acting weird. I'm embarrassed that everyone knows we're sleeping together."

I burst out laughing. "I am, too!" I screamed. He joined in the laughter, then took me in his arms and kissed me. "Let's get over ourselves," he said. "You kick me when I'm acting crazy, and I'll kick you."

Sulynn let herself in just then. Half her things were at Clark's, half at the apartment, and she was constantly traveling back and forth between the two places.

"We're normal now, Sulynn," I announced.

"Well, thank God for something," she replied.

My mother was thrilled that I was getting married, naturally, but not thrilled about Las Vegas. My father, on the other hand, couldn't wait to get there and immediately booked a suite at the Galaxy Hotel.

Art, Lettie and I arrived on June 13, with Sulynn due to arrive the next day for the weekend, and my brother and his wife flying in on the actual morning of the wedding. The day after the wedding, Art and I would be en route to Puerto Vallarta, Mexico, for our honeymoon.

Back in New York, Clark, now Sulynn's slave, was seeing to Delilah and also taking care of Sammy, who was the subject of a bitter custody battle. Art and I wanted to have Samson and Delilah in our new apartment. Sulynn wanted to take Sammy with her to Clark's. "You're allergic," I reminded her. "And besides, the mouse problem is in *this* apartment, and until Art and I can afford to move, we're stuck here." But of course, I didn't want to keep Sammy just because there might be mice.

"I'm used to Sammy," she replied stubbornly. "And besides, I outgrew my allergy. I just hadn't been around cats enough to know it."

The situation was still unresolved when Art and I left for Vegas. Lettie had booked a suite at the Galaxy as a wedding gift for us. Lettie and Art were going to stay in it, though, until after the wedding, and in the meantime, I would stay with my parents. "I know you think it's hypocritical," Lettie cut me off before I could say anything, "but do it anyway. Not all parents are as *liberal* as I am!"

Our plane was late, and we didn't arrive at the hotel until 11 p.m. Bobby's show was just ending, so we would see it the next night. When Art, Lettie and I walked into the hotel, the first thing we saw was my mother, wearing sneakers and a skirt and blouse, standing in the lobby with a Tupperware container of nickels in her hand. She greeted us warmly, then took us into the gambling casino, where my father was in the midst of a blackjack game.

We gambled for hours. One lost all track of time in Vegas. I played the one-armed bandit until my arm hurt, winning some and losing more, then went in search of Lettie, while Art and my mother stayed at the machines.

Lettie was playing some game which required rolling dice. I could hear her screaming, "Baby needs a new pair of shoes," even before I saw her. I watched her raking it in for a while. "My son's getting married," she told people around the table. "I'm going to give him and his new wife my winnings."

Finally, I couldn't keep my eyes open any longer. My mother yanked my father away from his blackjack game, and Art walked us up to the suite. He and I were a little ahead of my parents, so he took my key and attempted to insert it in the lock. He stopped and flexed his hand a few times, then tried again. Then he used his left hand and the door swung open.

"What's wrong with your right hand?" I asked him.

"Too much one-armed bandit," he said, shaking his fingers in the air.

"No, do this," my father said. He took Art's hand and manipulated it back and forth. "Now pretend you're using the one-armed bandit," he ordered. "Go ahead. Isn't that better?"

Art was impressed. "It is better."

"Oh, great," I said, "now you can go down and lose another thousand dollars."

He kissed me lightly on the lips. "No, I'll let my mother do the losing. Good night, everybody."

I woke up the next morning at 11 a.m. and went down to breakfast with my mother, my father having hit the tables hours earlier. Lettie and Art were in the restaurant with Bobby. Lettie held up a stack of bills and waved them at us. "Look what I won!" she yelled.

"How much is it?" I said, leaning over so Bobby could kiss my cheek.

"$3000."

I didn't sit next to Art so much as fall into my chair. My mother looked faint. "Lettie," I said. "You won $3000? How? Do you have a system?"

"Jesus is the only system I need," she declared, talking a mile a minute. "I just say, 'Jesus, you know me. You know my boys. Art's a good boy, and he's marrying a wonderful girl. I want this money for them!'" She held the bills up again. "See?"

"You're a wonder, mother," Bobby said. "I wish I could get the same divine intervention. I need it."

"Do you gamble much?" my mother asked him.

"You can't help it," he told us. "The machines are everywhere — they're backstage at the hotel where I do the show. They're even at the airport. I suppose I've broken even."

"You don't know the right people," my mother said.

"Jesus will never let you down," Lettie said solemnly, digging into her breakfast. "I'm giving you kids this money, and I want you to use it for your honeymoon or anything you want."

Art and I protested. Not very hard, but we protested. My parents had given me money for the honeymoon, as had Harry as a wedding gift. Art and I had not a cent of our own with which to get a new apartment. We didn't want to live in my place, which Art lovingly referred to as "Mouse House." We looked at each other. This was our way out.

"Thank you, Mother," Art said. "We're happy to take it, but I'm sure Margo will agree that it's just a loan until we get on our feet."

I nodded. "Absolutely. It's your money, you won it fair and square." (Although I had my doubts, Jesus to the contrary.) "And you've already given us the hotel suite. I'd rather it just be a loan, too."

She shrugged, "Well, we can work that out later," and handed Art the money. Bobby was drooling.

"If I ever get married," he announced, "it'll be here in Vegas, and mother, you'll be a guest."

After breakfast, Art and I took a cab to the church, fully expecting to see a slot machine on the lawn. We met with the priest, and he went over the simple ceremony with us and gave me the organist's phone number. My mother had arranged to have the church decorated with flowers, and for the reception, we were all going to dinner.

I knew my mother wasn't entirely happy about the arrangements. I, after all, was her only daughter, and Vegas wasn't exactly an ideal spot for a church wedding. My parents were disappointed that I wasn't getting married in Rochester — although my father seemed to have recovered from that blow — and that it wasn't going to be a big wedding. I explained that there wasn't a lot of time and that it was important for Bobby to be there, so the wedding had to be in Vegas.

My mother didn't ask me why I didn't wait until, for instance, *Bloomin'* finished its tour. I knew she wondered about it, probably deciding it was because Art and I wanted to live together on the tour, as if not being married would have stopped us.

Although I didn't go into it with her, I felt big weddings were a waste of money, energy and time, and I never could understand the reason for them. Except, I supposed, if you weren't an actress with lots of opening nights, your wedding day was probably the most glamorous and attention-grabbing day of your life.

Sulynn had checked in by the time we got back to the hotel, so Art and I went to her suite. She was in a terrible mood.

"Does this freak you out or what?" she said, slamming a suitcase on the bed. "Harry says I have to fly first class and take a SUITE, thank you very much, because I'm on television now and have to act like a STAR. I don't notice him GIVING me any money, just TAKING his lousy ten percent. Then he says I need a manager and a SECRETARY to answer FAN MAIL. And who, may I ask, is paying for THAT?" She stopped her harangue long enough to give both of us a hug, then said, "Fred dropped off a gift for you, but I didn't bring it. It was too heavy." She was surrounded by suitcases.

Art poked one of the bags with his foot. "Sulynn, you're here for two days. What's in the bags?"

Deeply offended, she replied, "Clothes, makeup, shoes — what are we, camping out? Besides, don't forget, I'm on television. I have to LOOK LIKE A STAR." Removing her platform shoes, she flung them across the room.

"You must be planning to change clothes every five minutes," I observed.

"It's not that. I wasn't sure what to bring. In all the movies, the women at the gambling tables are all dressed up in gowns. Remember what the gangster's girlfriends always looked like on "Mission: Impossible?" So I bought a few gowns. But it looked like a real bowling alley crowd going into that casino when I came in."

"We're not in Caesar's Palace, Sulynn," Art laughed. "Besides, you don't think women are wearing gowns here in the middle of the day, do you?"

"Boy, I'm glad it's Margo who's getting stuck with you," was all she said.

That evening the entire group went to The Vegas Palace for the dinner show, *Mame*, starring Bobby and, as the card at the table said, "The Incomparable Neda Palanz."

"Who is she, anyway?" Sulynn asked, squinting to read the display card. "Neda Pal*anz*."

"It's Neda *Pal*anz," my mother said. "She's from my day. Actually, a little bit earlier."

Sulynn was still stuck on Neda's name. "Why is it Neda *Pal*anz and Jack Pal*ance*? And are they related? Maybe his family changed his name when they came to this country and hers didn't."

My father laughed, almost spitting out his drink. "Isn't Jack Pal*ance* part American Indian?" he asked.

Art said, "I don't know if he's an Indian. I think sometimes people do say Jack Pal*ance*. I don't think they're related."

"If they're related," Sulynn persisted, "it should be Neda *Pal*anz. And I've *never* heard *anyone* say Jack Pal*ance*. You're getting him mixed up with Richard Boone."

This statement was followed by a perplexed silence at the table. I knew I was the only one who could unravel this. Sulynn would lose her temper at Art and annoy my parents and Lettie to distraction if any of them tried. "Okay, I'll bite, Sulynn. Why do you say Art has Jack Pal*ance* mixed up with Richard Boone?"

"Because Richard Boone played *Pal*adin," Sulynn explained. "He's thinking of *Pal*adin."

The lights went out, and the orchestra started a drum roll. Art took a chance Sulynn wouldn't have time to answer him back. "It was Pala*din*," he snapped, as the overture started full blast. We saw Sulynn's mouth move, but couldn't hear her.

Neda *Pal*anz was incomparable, all right, and it was a good thing — you wouldn't want two like her in the world. "She's got plaster of Paris on her face," Lettie announced two minutes after Neda's entrance.

"I think her bones are pinned together," Art said. "Look at the way she walks."

Neda couldn't sing a note. Even wearing a microphone, the show seemed like *Mame* for the deaf when she "sang." She led a mediocre, I'll-phone-in-my-part cast, with the exception of Bobby, who was like a breath of fresh air on that stage. At intermission, I asked Lettie if Bobby had said anything about his famous co-star.

Lettie shook her head. "You know Bobby, he never says anything about anybody. But, as his mother, I can tell he's not finding this a pleasant experience, and he's glad it's only two weeks."

At that moment, two women came over to the table. One of them asked Sulynn, "Aren't you Cassie on 'A Bright Tomorrow?' Can we have your autograph?"

Sulynn beamed and autographed two cocktail napkins with a flourish. She hunched her shoulders together. "Oooh — isn't that exciting? Maybe I should get a secretary after all. I might be getting pretty popular."

My dad brought her to earth. "What are you going to do when your show starts touring?"

"It looks like they're letting me stay in the show and just writing me out for six weeks. Harry's handling all that." Art and I exchanged glances. Harry went from being the big bad thief to her father protector in a matter of hours.

We endured the rest of the show. When it was over, I said, "I'm going backstage to see if I can get a look at Neda closeup. Anyone want to come along?" Since my father had just ordered another round of drinks, everyone declined.

I found the backstage area easily enough, and the shouting directed me to Bobby. He was in the middle of a large room, stripped to the waist, cold cream all over his face, standing directly opposite an old woman I assumed was Neda *Palanz*, recognizable only by her last scene costume. There were chorus people surrounding them, and I realized I must be in the chorus dressing room. What Bobby and Neda were doing in there, I didn't know.

Neda seemed to have plenty of volume now that she was off stage. "I have asked you time and again NOT TO STEP ON MY LINE at that point!"

"I wasn't stepping on your line, Neda," Bobby answered with no attempt at politeness. "It's just that audiences don't like to wait five minutes for the next line."

"What do you mean, five minutes? You constantly STEP ON MY LINES — not just that scene, all the scenes!"

"Neda, you don't know what pacing and tempo are. This show would take seven hours if you had your way."

"Don't you talk to me that way," she hissed. "You — you HITLER JUGEND!"

In five years of being Bobby's close friend, I had never seen him so furious. "WHAT DID YOU CALL ME? WHY? BECAUSE I MAKE YOU LOOK LIKE SHIT UP THERE? IS THAT IT, YOU OLD BAG?"

A small chorus girl flung herself towards them and grabbed a wrist from each of them. Crying, she said, "Wait. Wait. Please." A hush fell over the room. "Can't we be friends here? Can't we just have peace and joy and love in our world?"

Bobby yanked his wrist away and, backing up, extended his arms outward, like a holy card picture of Jesus. "Great, great. Let's all go to a hilltop in Italy and sing a fucking Coca Cola commercial, for Christ's sake. Stay away from me, Neda. JUST STAY AWAY." The chorus girl held onto Neda and led her out of the room, past me. As Bobby watched them leave, he spotted me. Without speaking, he sat at a small table with a mirror in front of it, grabbed some tissues and attacked his face.

I approached him. "Is this your dressing room or the chorus dressing room?"

"Oh, I have to be in here because that fucking bitch took TWO ROOMS. It's in her contract. One room is for her FUCKING GOWNS. We had to draw straws for the rest of the rooms, and I lost."

"Bobby, just remember not to call her names in front of my mother or yours."

"Oh, I'll call her anything I want, that cunt." He rose with such force that he knocked over his folding chair. "Did you hear what she called me? What do you suppose my mother would think of that — calling me a Hitler youth! Me!" He went to the door and screamed at the top of his lungs: "MY FAMILY LOST PEOPLE IN THE HOLOCAUST, YOU GODDAMN BITCH. DON'T YOU CALL ME NAZI NAMES." He kicked the doorway. The stage manager arrived at that moment. "What's going on?" he demanded to know.

Bobby grabbed his shirt off the rack next to the door. "Ask her. Ask the COLLABORATOR. ASK THE NAZI COLLABORATOR." He left, and I ran after him. As he passed the door with NEDA PALANZ written on it, he hollered, "Oh, Neda, I heard your FAN left in the middle of the first act."

Once with the rest of the group, he was quiet and, in between straight scotches, had very little to say about the show or Neda, except, "It's like being on stage with a corpse. An embalmed corpse."

After separating and playing the slot machines for a while, the six of us went back to the Galaxy, leaving Bobby at the Palace elevator. I was in my parents' room for a few minutes when the phone rang. It was Art. "Meet me in the bar to the right of the elevators," he said, and hung up.

"Did Bobby say anything to you backstage?" he asked as soon as I found him in the bar. "He cornered me at one of those slot machines and asked me if I had any dope.. That's not like him when he's performing."

I told him what happened. "Well," Art said when I finished, "the job is almost over. And it must help him some that we're here."

"I suppose. Are you ready for tomorrow? The big day?"

He laughed a little. "I still can't believe it. Can you?"

"I really can't. It'll seem strange, after knowing you for so long."

"Do you still want to go through with it?"

"Yes, of course. Do you?"

"I do, but — have you wondered what it will be like?"

"What?"

"You know, married life."

I ordered a Tom Collins, and Art ordered a scotch. "We've already gotten a taste of married life," I said.

"Yes, but it's never the same, you know, once you're actually married. And are you going to miss not having a big wedding?"

"You know how I feel about that. I think this works out best. We can have a honeymoon before the tour starts. Otherwise, who knows when we'd be free?"

He nodded. "My mother was concerned, you know. She felt we had too much to think about with the show touring and then going on Broadway, that it was all going to be too much adjustment to be newlyweds, too."

The waitress brought the drinks, and I raised my glass. "We won't know till we try," I said, and our glasses touched.

Art said, "I feel like this is the first time we've been alone in months."

"This business of separate rooms to keep up a pretense. I guess our parents' generation is really into that."

"They are, but you're not as unconventional as you'd like people to think. If I had my own room, I bet you wouldn't stay with me tonight."

"Yeah, you're probably right."

After we left the bar, we strolled outside. "This city is totally alive twenty-four hours a day," Art said as we walked. "I heard if you drive up and down by the casinos, people are selling their cars and jewels to get gambling money." We stopped, and he kissed me, pushing me up against the hotel.

"Where's your dad's rental car parked?" he asked, his voice husky. "Tell him we want to go for a drive and get the keys."

"I'm not having sex in a car the night before my wedding," I told him. "I guess you were right when you said I wasn't unconventional.

Come on, let's go back." I took his hand, dragging him toward the hotel.

"Killjoy. You can't turn me down once we're married."

"Oh, yeah? Where'd you read that, *Playboy*? Forget it."

"So now you're not only going to be conventional, but frigid."

We were at the elevators. "Right," I said, "and I say *Pala*din instead of Pala*din*."

"Well, since I pronounce *Pala*nce like Pal*ance*, we should just call it all off."

The ceremony was set to take place the next day at 1 p.m. It began at 1:30, because my parents and I had to wait for Sulynn to finish dressing. She finally emerged like Queen Elizabeth from the elevator at 1:15, instead of the agreed-upon 12:30.

"It's not your wedding, you know," I chastised her. "No one cares how you look."

"You can be late for my wedding," she promised. "And you still look better than I do, so don't worry about it."

My stomach was in knots. "This is worse than any performance I've ever done," I lamented as we drove over. "I'm so nervous. And Art's going to think I stood him up. Do you think they'll still be there?" Bobby had taken a cab from his hotel and picked up Art and Lettie at the Galaxy earlier.

"Where can they go that we can't find them?" my father said.

"Do you think my dress will wrinkle too much?" I was afraid to put my rear end on the car seat and was sitting with my hips mid-air.

"You look lovely," my mother assured me. "Your dress will not wrinkle." It was a scoop-necked, ice-blue empire-waist dress, on the short side (my mother said). I had on white stockings, and my shoes were dyed to match the dress. My mother and I had our traditional brassiere argument. She claimed, as usual, that I was not wearing the right bra. She believed most of my life's problems could be solved by wearing either the right bra or the right girdle, and I wore neither.

My father became weepy when he saw me, and said, "With your long hair, you look like a Madonna." When my mother saw he was crying, she decided she couldn't hold back any longer and opened the floodgates. I had just finished putting on my makeup, but seeing both of them cry, I joined in, which meant that both my mother and I had to reapply our mascara.

When we arrived at the church, Bobby, in a suit, stood in the lobby with my brother, his wife and Lettie. "Sulynn was late, right?" Bobby sneered as we walked in. He looked at Lettie. "What did I tell you?"

Sulynn breezed by him. "Shut up. You've never been on time for anything in your life."

"I was on time for this!" he shot back.

Lettie intervened. "This is a happy day, no bickering."

"Right, Sulynn," Bobby said. "They'll be doing plenty of that *after* they're married." Bobby and Sulynn thought that was funny.

My dad, Sulynn and I stood at the church entrance as the rest of the crowd proceeded into the church.

"I have one thing to say," my father began. "If he's a bum, get rid of him." The organ music began. We started down the aisle. I could see a pale Art in the distance next to Bobby and the priest.

It was over as soon as it started. Lettie and my parents wept out loud all during the short ceremony, so much so that Bobby, Art, Sulynn and I got the giggles, and when it came time for me to say, "I will," I nearly didn't get the words out. The priest gave me a dirty look.

After he pronounced us man and wife, Art and I turned to each other. "I don't believe it," he said.

I replied, "Neither do I." We kissed and paraded out of the church. The photographer my dad hired clicked a mile a minute. Bobby raced out ahead of us with Lettie, and when we got outside, we were plummeted with confetti.

My parents had reserved a section of a fabulous restaurant just outside of town, and the reception was just what I wanted: simple decorations, a lovely dinner and a lot of fun, cut short only when Bobby had to leave for the theater. "It was perfect," I told my parents. I think they were pleased, too, even though it wasn't exactly what they'd envisioned originally.

We partied well into the night, gambling and drinking back at the hotel. Bobby joined us after the show.

Art and I went to our suite on the fourteenth floor at 3 a.m. Lettie was now on the eleventh floor, but she left us a bottle of champagne.

"Well, let's see," Art said. "We leave for Puerto Vallarta tomorrow at 1 a.m. That means we have to leave for the airport at about eleven tomorrow."

"Which means if we fell asleep right now and got up at ten, we'd only get seven hours sleep."

Still fully clothed, he jumped on top of me and together, we fell onto the bed. "But we're not going to sleep now, Mrs. Gaines," he said, and kissed me.

We were packed by 10:00 and in the restaurant with my entire family, plus Lettie and Sulynn, at 10:05. Everyone was leaving at different times, so afterward, Art and I said our good-byes and piled our luggage into the airport van.

I was thrilled about going to Puerto Vallarta. I had never been to Mexico, while Art, on the other hand, was a world traveler and considered himself an expert on every country. In between sneaking kisses and feels on the two different planes that we took to arrive there, I got a run-down of Puerto Vallarta as compared with Cancun and La Paz, and got my instructions: don't drink the water and be sure to haggle with the vendors.

Art had a travel agent friend who arranged our entire trip. The hotel, the Gran Oro, was in the middle of town. I was wearing a white dress, which, thanks to the dust blowing in the street, was somewhat the worse for wear when I walked into the hotel lobby.

The hotel looked good, but left a lot to be desired. Other guests at the hotel included the San Pietro, California, "Dons," a high school drum and bugle corps which reveled in staying up all night singing "Ay-yi-yi-yi" and "La Cucaracha" in the halls and in the street outside the hotel. Unfortunately, our room was on the street side of the hotel. The teen-aged "dons" walked around wearing oversized sombreros and fake guitars, symbol of Ugly Americans, making utter fools of themselves and making anyone they came into contact with miserable. Art very carefully got the name of their group, intending to write a letter of complaint to their school district as soon as we got back to the States.

"I'm so glad you have a friend in the travel agent business," I told him after our first night of ai-yi-yi-yis, loud music, brawling and screaming in the street below. "Are you sure it's a friend?"

His travel agent "friend" also failed to mention that the hotel and the street outside were under reconstruction. The drilling outside the hotel began at 7 a.m. each day and was incessant.

"It's so considerate of them to start then," I said to Art. "Everyone on vacation wants to be up at 7 a.m. — I know I do." Sleep not being an option, we were up and out of the room early each day and spent our time shopping or lying on the beach, where we were bothered by a constant parade of vendors who would not take no for an answer.

All the shops sold the same merchandise: silver and turquoise jewelry; boxes; money clips. After a few days, all this merchandise could be spotted on every tourist. If I bought a pair of earrings, the woman next to me at dinner inevitably had on the same pair. If I bought a tote bag that said "Vallarta" on it, by the last day, every person in the hotel carried the same tote.

The room was never cleaned when we returned to it each day at

4 p.m. for a much-needed nap. "There's lots of that mañana bullshit around here," Art said. He was on the phone complaining every five minutes about something, but it never did any good.

Despite the fact that he never drank the water, on the last day Art got Montezuma's revenge anyway. Thus ended our lovely Mexican honeymoon.

On July 1st, we were back in New York and ready to begin rehearsals for *Bloomin'* under a new director, Len Magnuson, a man with an excellent Broadway track record.

Sulynn and Bobby had put a JUST MARRIED sign on the door of the Clemency Hotel apartment and hung a sign inside that said, CONGRATULATIONS, NEWLYWEDS, over a table laden with wedding gifts.

Art carried me across the threshold, where we were greeted by Sammy and Delilah. We spent our first day back unpacking and opening gifts. Art had moved most of his belongings in before we left for Vegas. Sulynn called at four o'clock, from Clark's. "How's married life?" she asked. "I got your postcard. The place isn't all it's cracked up to be, huh?"

"Let's just say the hotel wasn't and leave it at that," I replied. "And married life so far is okay. You should try it."

"Oh, who knows, maybe I will. Now, here's what I want to know. What about Sammy? I talked with Clark, and he agrees with you two and Bobby that Sammy should be with Delilah, provided they get along, and he said he'd take them here while we're all on tour. And he promised that as soon as we get back, we'll get our own cat."

"Sounds good to me." If Clark hadn't suggested it, we were going to bring the cats to Lettie in Yarmouth. Bobby was planning on getting another cat also.

"Next thing," she said, as if going down a list. "What's the story on the apartment?"

"We're putting everything into storage before we leave on tour and getting our own place as soon as we get back. Can we stay with you and Clark until we find a place?" They had more room than Bobby.

"Yes, that was coming out of my mouth next. So everything is set."

"No, it isn't. I have to write thank you notes, and I don't know what half these things are and neither does Art. Can you come over and help me identify some of them?"

"I'm terrible at that, but I'll be over tonight. It's ten past four now — how's six?"

"Great — come at six." At that moment, I felt something wet on my neck — Art's lips. They traveled up toward my ear. "Make it seven, Sulynn," I said, before dropping the phone.

I should have been nervous the first day of *Bloomin'* rehearsals. After all, we were a bunch of unknowns about to be directed by the great Len Magnuson. Instead, I was so calm that my serenity was the thing making me nervous.

Art and I were the first of the cast to arrive at the rehearsal room in the Minskoff theater, and Miss Fossey, sitting with Tom Scardini, two other men and a big woman, jumped up to greet us. "Margo, you look beautiful!" she exclaimed. "Married life really agrees with you."

I hugged her. "Thank you, and thank you for your gift..." I panicked, not remembering what it was.

"It's such a beautiful frame," Art said smoothly. "We're going to put our wedding picture in it."

"Wonderful! Come over, and you can meet Len and Bertha, our new stage manager."

Len Magnuson was tall, even taller than Art, who was 6'2". He looked as if he had slept in his clothes and hadn't bothered to comb his hair, perhaps trying to give the impression of a Jimmy Stewart-type country boy. I didn't buy his corn-pone act.

Then Art and I met Morty Showalter, the music director, another one with a lot of Broadway credits under his belt. Greg, out of college for the summer, was working as our rehearsal pianist and came in a few minutes later, carrying a take-out coffee cup.

By 10 a.m., Sulynn, Bobby and the chorus had arrived, followed closely by Amalia, lugging a large scrapbook and sporting a wedding ring. "I'm Amalia Hayes-Winslow," I heard her say to Len Magnuson.

"She was *damned* if you were going to have one up on her," Bobby commented.

A young black man and woman came in just then, and Len yelled out, "Finally! Get in here, you two. Now we can get started."

"Where's Fred?" I said out loud, to no one in particular.

"That's Fred," Sulynn whispered, looking at the handsome black man across the room. Art took my hand. "No one wanted to say anything to you and spoil the honeymoon, honey, but Fred was replaced. Harry and Zack had a meeting with Foss, Tom and this new director, and they decided to make some changes and do rewrites that would make the show better. Foss wrote the show to be interracial — it's just there were no black upperclassmen at Cofis the summer she did the show."

"But how's Fred taking it?"

"He took it pretty hard. But you know, Fred has that spiritual side to him or whatever it is, and now he's in the flow of the universe."

"I can't believe no one told me. And you knew?" I asked Art.

"I only found out from Bobby last night."

"Okay, let's start," Bertha barked. She read a long statement, as required by Actors Equity at the beginning of the first Equity rehearsal, of which I heard not one word. Doing the show without Fred — I couldn't conceive of it.

"The next thing," Len said, after introducing Morty and Greg to the group, "I'd like to introduce you generally to your new cast members, and you can introduce yourselves personally later. Everyone, this is Beverly Reed, who is going to play the new role of Karlene, as you'll see in your scripts, and Howard Lane, who will play the part of Larry."

"That's Howard Lane?" Bobby muttered. "He was just kicked out of *Porgy and Bess* for starting a fight with the Porgy on stage and making the Porgy so angry he stood up."

"Oh, swell," I groaned. I still couldn't believe no one had told me anything.

We did a read-through, including music. The new people had already learned their music and had more than a nodding acquaintance with their lines. "I'd love to know when they were cast," I said to Art out in the hallway during a break. "It must have been a while ago."

Foss joined us just then. "It isn't fair," I said to her. "Fred stuck with this show from the beginning. He moved to New York to do it, joined the union to stay with it, went through all that crap at the 16th St. Playhouse. He worked as a busboy, for God's sake. I don't know how you could have been so cruel." I walked further away from the rehearsal room, over toward the elevators, without giving her a chance to speak.

My anger had been building up since the read-through began. Everyone was acting very blasé about what I considered to be an utter betrayal. "It's no wonder no one told me," I said to Art when he caught up with me. "I'm the only one who seems to care."

He put a consoling arm around my waist. Out of the corner of my eye, I saw Sulynn and Bobby standing in the hallway, watching every move we made. "Honey, everybody is as upset as you are, but it was presented as a fait accompli, and there was nothing anybody could do. You, me and Bobby were out of town, and Sulynn found out about it after it was over, from Fred."

Tears stung my eyes. "Margo." It was Miss Fossey, Sulynn and

Bobby on her heels. "Margo, please talk to me."

"There's nothing to talk about. Do all of you know what this means?" I asked, turning to face them, hoping the new cast members weren't right around the corner. "This means all of us — after everything we've suffered through doing this show — can be kicked out at any time."

Miss Fossey broke in, "Margo, that's simply not true."

"You're right, Miss Fossey," I said, "it isn't true. Bobby and Art can't be kicked out because people close to them have money in the show. Maybe if I'm lucky my marriage will hold my part for me, but it might not. And Sulynn hasn't got a leg to stand on, and neither has Amalia." I didn't add that Amalia's precarious position didn't bother me in the least.

Miss Fossey tried to speak, but I didn't give her the chance. Lowering my voice a little, I said, "I can understand the need to have a more integrated cast, but if you could create a part for one of them, why couldn't you have found a way to keep Fred in the show?"

Miss Fossey looked as frustrated as I felt. "It wasn't in the budget, Margo. That's all I can tell you. It was a money decision."

"What about Fred's money decisions — coming to New York, getting an apartment, doing the showcase for nothing, providing his own costumes..." I threw my arms up in disgust. "You mess with people's lives, and then you say it was a money decision. You were an actress once. Think how you would have felt."

"Break's over," Bertha stuck her head around the corner. I followed Bertha back into the room, the others, strangely quiet, straggling behind me. Beverly and Howard were already back in the rehearsal room. I smiled at them. It wasn't their fault that Fred was out of the show.

For the rest of the rehearsal period, I kept my distance from Foss and Tom. The new script was better, we all agreed, and the addition of the character of Karlene was a good move. But it didn't excuse the callousness of our producers and the lack of backbone on the part of Foss.

I decided against letting my wrath loose on Harry. He, after all, was in charge of the money, and Fred was no more to him than any actor trying to figure out a way to get his picture and résumé through Harry's blocked mail slot. But for the present, anyway, I couldn't forgive Foss, who should have spoken for all of us.

Len was a great director to work with, and the show was in excellent shape by the time we left on tour, July 10th, 1972.

The itinerary consisted of six towns, from Kentucky to

Pennsylvania, in as many weeks.

"We should know something about the show after this tour," Art said, as we looked over the itinerary that night.

I had a funny feeling about it.

"If we're still alive," I said.

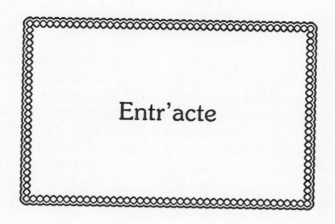

Entr'acte

The *Bloomin'* tour officially began on July 10th, when we took off by plane for the Richmond airport. There we were picked up by patrons of the arts and driven to Muskeegee, Virginia, home of the Lake Theater.

There wasn't much to do in Muskeegee, we soon learned, and the cast was split up, staying in different homes. Art and I were with a lovely old couple in a small house within walking distance of the theater. Sulynn, on the other hand, was not within walking distance and refused to rent a car. Instead, she prevailed upon the woman she was staying with — fortunately, "A Bright Tomorrow" fan — to drive her to the theater every time she needed to be there. Bobby, Beverly and Howard were together in another house and rented a car.

The show got wonderful reviews in Muskeegee, and the audiences, small the first night, but growing larger and larger each night after that, loved it. Len did not accompany us on tour, but Bertha gave us notes, and Tom and Foss were along.

If the rest of the tour had been like Muskeegee, all would have been well. But Muskeegee turned out to be the exception rather than the rule for *Bloomin'* during its fateful tour. My "funny feeling" about going on the road was justified.

Berkeley, Kentucky, was our next stop, and it was there that things began to take their strange turn, and the tour began to be known, among us, as the Twilight Zone Tour. Each time we arrived in a new town, after Berkeley, Art would mimick Rod Serling: "Actors — on the road performing a show called *Bloomin'* — but really acting in the theater of THE TWILIGHT ZONE," and Bobby, Sulynn and I would hum the "Twilight Zone" theme "do-do-do-do...do-do-do-do."

Each performance situation, of course, was different. The Jefferson Davis Theater in Berkeley, Kentucky, was small — much too small for our new and expensive set, so the crew hung a lot of the set pieces on black netting that they stretched across the stage.

In our new staging of *Bloomin'*, Len had us begin the first song, which was now "Bloomin'" and not "Sweet Times," from the back of the audience and walk on stage. After the number, we all exited stage left and were squished together, waiting to make our entrances through a narrow opening. Bobby went out first. His buttons got caught on the netting. He tried to go on stage, but bounced back as the netting yanked him in.

Bobby said his lines with just his head stuck out sideways. None of us could get by him, and there was no other way to get on stage. So we all did our lines by sticking our heads out around him.

In order to resolve the situation, Bertha came out with a pair of scissors and cut Bobby loose. Everyone then fell onto the stage.

After the last performance in Berkeley, I was back in the dressing room, when I heard a familiar voice. "Doesn't that sound like...?" Sulynn and I stared at each other. "FRED," we shouted, and ran out, half-dressed.

It was Fred, flanked by Bobby, Art, the chorus and Miss Fossey. "Fred, what are you doing here?" I said, hugging him.

"I'm a swing. And do want to know something? I had a sign about it before Foss called me. Like the night Diana Ross left the Supremes, and my poster of them fell off the wall. I've got a gift. The night before I heard from Foss, I dreamt she called me and said, 'Fred, we need a swing dancer and understudy.' The next day, it happened!"

"How did you — swing — this?" I asked Foss, as we stood off on the side.

"I made a good case for it, and we found the money."

"You must be very persuasive," I said.

She smiled. "I can be, when I assert myself."

I chuckled. "I can't wait to see him dance."

"The thing is, if one of the male dancers had to go on for any of you, we'd be short a dancer. So we really need someone, and what you said that day in rehearsal meant something to me, it really did. As it is, we're short a woman, too, but we can't do anything about that for a while. But I wanted to get another male in here as soon as possible."

"Why as soon as possible?"

"I think Bobby might be coming down with something." She

poked me in the arm. "Newlywed. You're not noticing much these days. Bobby's lost a lot of weight, and his color isn't good."

I hadn't noticed, and I was sure Art hadn't, or he would have said something. My eyes fell on Bobby, drinking a soda and talking with Fred.

"He has lost weight," I said. "Did you say anything to him?"

"Yes, and he said he feels fine and that he often loses weight when he does a lot of dancing over the summer."

"Well, that's true. And as far as his color, he never goes in the sun, because his skin is so sensitive. But anyway, I'm glad Fred's here."

The next day, we left for Elvira, Ohio. "The name of the theater there is The Show Tent," Art said. "Sounds like a carnival." We drove to Elvira in rented cars, and it took an eternity for our vehicle to get there. My conversation with Fossey proved prophetic; one of our cast had a delayed trip.

I was in a car with Fred, Art and Bobby, and after what seemed like hours of driving, we were slaphappy and stopped at a 7-Eleven, since Bobby had complained he was thirsty and the rest of us just wanted a break. We wandered up and down the aisles — going to stores and checking out the merchandise was the ultimate Tour Activity.

Art, Fred and I wandered to the junk food aisle and began to read ingredients. We found out, for instance, that the creamy center of my favorite cupcake is sugar and lard. Appalled, we moved on and read other shocking ingredients. Then Fred picked up a bottle of Marshmallow Fluff.

"I don't believe this," he said, in total seriousness. "Do you realize there's not even any *marshmallow* in this?"

Art and I, giddy to begin with, erupted in uproarious laughter. "What do you think?" Art said. "That marshmallow is an ingredient that grows on *trees*?"

"I must have purah mahshmahlo," I said, imitating a dowager.

Still laughing, we went to find Bobby and saw that he was sitting in the car, drinking from a large bottle of water. We climbed back into the car and continued our drive. Bobby was quiet, even for Bobby.

Bertha had given each driver a clear map to Elvira — but as clear as it might have been, I couldn't decipher it, so I passed it back to Bobby. "Keep us on track," I said.

"You do it, Fred," he said, passing it over to Fred. "The names are too small for me to see them."

"You going blind?" I asked him, wondering if he was too vain to wear glasses, like Sulynn was.

He didn't answer, and then I heard Fred say, "Art, pull over."

Fred sounded truly alarmed, so Art didn't even question him and just pulled off the highway. Bobby sat in the back seat, crying, his shirt soaked with sweat. I thought the back seat must really be warm. It was hot out, but with the breeze coming into the car, I didn't feel it.

"Bobby, what's wrong?" Art demanded.

I said, "Is it what I said to you about going blind? I was only kidding. Are you really worried about it?" He nodded, unable to speak. "Honey," I continued, "you need to see a doctor, that's all. Are you afraid a doctor's going to make you wear glasses, is that it?"

He swallowed and tried to talk. "I think I'm really sick," was all he could say.

"Okay, that's it." Art's voice was sharp and authoritative. He yanked the car back onto the highway. "Watch for hospital signs," he snapped at me.

"No, Art," Bobby choked.

"I don't want to hear another word about it," Art said. He pulled into a gas station and got directions to the nearest hospital. A half hour later, we found ourselves in an emergency room somewhere in Ohio.

Art's face was pinched with concern. Bobby was taken into an examining room immediately, and an hour later, a doctor emerged and called, "Who's with the Gaines patient, please?" We all ran over to him.

"Are any of you family?" he asked,

"I am," Art said.

"Okay, I'm Dr. Marshall. Your brother was almost in diabetic shock when he got here. We have him more under control now, but he'll have to stay in the hospital."

"You mean he's a diabetic?" Art groped for my hand.

"Yes, he is. It was almost too late, you know. According to what he told me, he's been having symptoms for months."

Art burst into tears. "I should have known there was something wrong with him, I should have known."

The doctor patted him on the back. "You're not a doctor, Mr. Gaines. There's no way you would connect his symptoms, even if you lived with him."

"What are the symptoms?" Fred asked.

"Excessive thirst, which in this heat would never be noticed, weight loss — he's a dancer, so weight loss probably isn't unusual — irritability..."

I thought back to Las Vegas and Neda Palanz.

"...and vision problems," the doctor finished. "He'll be here for a while. Do you want to see him before we take him to his room?"

The three of us went into Bobby's cubicle. He was lying there with an IV tube in his arm, but he managed a smile.

"I'll call mom," Art told him. "God, Bobby, I didn't know you didn't feel well. Why didn't you say something?"

"I didn't know what it was," he groaned. "Now that I know, I'm sorry I came in."

"Don't be ridiculous," I said. "It's a controllable disease."

"Yeah, and you can't fool around with it," Fred said. "Your days of drinking and junk food are over."

"Don't worry," Bobby said. "I'll dance on all your graves with my wooden leg. And even with a wooden leg, I'll dance better than you, Fred."

When we finally arrived in Elvira and told Bertha and Miss Fossey what had happened, all hell broke loose. Foss paced frantically, saying, "I knew it, I knew it." The dance captain corralled Fred and attempted to show him the steps, while Andy, the understudy whom Fred would replace in the chorus, began work with Bertha on Bobby's part. He had had only one rehearsal in Bobby's role, right before we left New York.

The cast was housed in a bungalow colony right near the performance tent, and as soon as we were settled, Art called Lettie from the pay phone on the grounds. I could hear her screaming from where I stood. After hanging up, he said, "She keeps saying there's no diabetes in the family. I don't know what that's got to do with anything. He's got it. Anyway, she's flying into Cleveland tomorrow morning, renting a car and going right to the hospital. She said she'd ask at the hospital to recommend a place to stay. And she'll come to the show tomorrow night."

We went back to our room, and Art collapsed on the bed, staring at the ceiling.

"You blame yourself, don't you?" I asked him.

He covered his face with his hands and cried as if his heart was broken. I felt terrible, too, but was determined not to let him see it. I sat on the bed. "It's not your fault. Does Lettie think it is?" I put a box of tissues on his chest. He sat up, yanked a bunch of tissues, and blew his nose. "You're supposed to notice when someone you love is in trouble," he said. "And then one day, you don't."

"If you'd realized it, do you think this would have ended any differently? Do you honestly think you'd have gotten him to go to a doctor?"

"I guess not."

I lay next to him on the bed, and we held each other. I could feel the tension in his body lessening, when there was a banging knock at the door.

I swung my legs around the side of the bed. "Come in, Sulynn," I called out, knowing full well who it was.

She threw the door open. "WHAT is going on?" she demanded, standing at the entrance of our room.

I said, "You're letting flies in. Come in and close the door."

She paced in front of the bed. "I can't believe it. It can't be true. He can't be sick. How could he be that sick and none of us have known about it? How bad is it? Will he have to take shots? Will he have to stop dancing? Where's Lettie? Did anybody call her? What did she say? How come he got it?"

Neither Art nor I said a word. Finally, she stamped her foot. "Well, doesn't anybody know anything yet?"

I shook my head. "Not really." I told her all I could. "The big thing will be getting Andy into the show."

"Pathetic, pathetic," she groaned. "And God knows how long we'll be stuck with him."

Art fell asleep after Sulynn left, and I went to the pay phone to call Holly. It occurred to me, as I waited for the Morrison housekeeper to bring her to the phone, that I hadn't exchanged more than a sentence with Holly since meeting her the previous summer. It also occurred to me that Bobby played things so close to his chest, that I really had no idea of the present status of their relationship.

I told her about Bobby and could tell by her voice how much it upset her. "Do you think I should be there?" she asked.

"Why don't you call him tomorrow and see how he feels?" I suggested. I gave her the name of the hospital. "I'm sure he'll have a phone in his room, and the switchboard can put you through."

Her voice shook. "I can at least send flowers for now. I — I can't tell you how much I appreciate that you called me, Margo."

I just hope I did the right thing, I said to myself as I hung up. Well, if not, I'd hear about it soon enough.

A rehearsal was called for 10 a.m. the next day, and the task began of pulling the show together without Bobby and with a non-dancer as a member of the dancing chorus. Before the rehearsal, the dance captain collected money for flowers. Art and I had sent flowers, so we didn't contribute. Sulynn put in a few dollars, saying, "He still owes me for a Coke." When she saw Art and I staring at her, she said, "I was only kidding."

If no one realized Bobby's contribution to the show before, they certainly realized it watching Andy's attempts to step into his shoes. On the other hand, Andy's contribution as a member of the chorus had been great, and we certainly appreciated it as we watched Fred trip and hobble all over the stage, lifting, then dropping his partner mid-air and consistently starting dance numbers on the wrong foot.

But we made it through, and the audience, who were told a dramatic sob story before the performance, loved it. Lettie, looking drawn, came backstage. "Bobby's room is full of flowers," she announced, kissing me. "Everyone has sent such beautiful flowers."

"We spoke to him just before you got there," I said. "How is he?"

"Depressed. He has to learn how to give himself insulin and how to test himself and what to eat. A whole new way of life. It's going to be very hard for him. Holly's coming, did you know that?"

Art, Sulynn and I saw Bobby the next day. He was already looking better, although his spirits weren't exactly elevated. Holly appeared at the hospital in the late afternoon, and from then on was a permanent fixture on the tour.

By the time Bobby rejoined the tour, we were in Scarma, Pennsylvania, renamed by Art and me, Berserka, Pennsylvania.

Bobby was now with Holly in her car, so instead of Bobby as a passenger along with Fred, Art and I inherited Tracy, one of the chorus people. Since there was now an extra car and one less person riding in the rented *Bloomin'* cars, I couldn't figure out why we had to take Tracy in our car. Until I spent five minutes with her.

It seemed that while we were in Virginia and Kentucky, Tracy had found the Lord and, according to Bobby's understudy, had even gone through total-immersion-baptism at one of the churches. With her newly found zeal for the Bible, Tracy had thrown all her booze, pills and grass down the toilet, to the utter horror of her roommate, the other chorus girl. Tracy then went around stamping the back of people's hands with a stamp that said, "Jesus loves you," as if admitting them into a Bible Belt dance.

I couldn't remember hearing anything about her behavior, and Art and I hadn't been around during the stamping ceremony. So, when a position opened up in our car, in Tracy went.

The five hours we spent in the car with Tracy were torture. Rather than avoiding a discussion about Tracy's religious beliefs, Fred and Art provoked her the entire trip. As Fred put it, he had nothing to lose in a discussion, because as a homosexual, he was a "doomed man."

He wasn't alone. Everything Art did, according to Tracy, was the work of the devil because he didn't tithe ten percent of his salary for the church. Tracy announced that she couldn't find it in her heart to claim him for Jesus. This meant he certainly was going to hell. Then she started on me. I said, "I am not going to get into a discussion about this. But I refuse to be separated from my husband, even in death, so if he's going to hell, I guess I'll just have to go, too."

"I'll be there, Margo," Fred said, from the back seat. "We'll have a ball while Tracy here is holy rolling her way across heaven."

"You're an infidel," she snapped.

"Good, good," he said. "I've got something to look forward to — an eternity WITHOUT YOU."

We arrived, hot and irritable, in Scarma. We were all to meet in, of all places, a church, so that housing assignments could be given out. After spending time with Tracy, a church was the last place I wanted to be.

Two of the cars got lost, so we ended up sitting there for two hours, while some of the town patrons extolled the virtues of Scarma and of performing at their wonderful summer theater that came complete with orchestra, our first one of the summer.

At last, everyone was gathered together, and Bertha gave out the assignments. When she got to Art and me, she said, "Well, there could be a problem with your housing assignment, because the woman you're supposed to stay with — she's just been taken away. So we might have to find another place for you to stay.

We sat there, shell-shocked. "Taken away?" Art asked. "What exactly does that mean?"

Bertha was uncharacteristically vague. "Well, she's old. I guess she has some health problems." She scribbled on a piece of paper.

"Okay, just go to the house. Here's the address, and the place should be open. If there's a problem, call the person who set up the housing for us. I wrote his number down along with the directions."

When we arrived, there was a young, thin man standing out on the lawn, and two women in their late forties-early fifties screaming at each other, looking as if they were going to start pulling each other's hair out any minute.

The young man stopped me before I could get to the house. "Can you tell me who you are?" he demanded.

"My husband and I are supposed to be staying here," I said, as calmly as I could.

He brought me into the house. He explained that both the women were "health caretakers" of the absent old lady, and each one was trying to get rid of the other as caretaker. The old woman who owned the house was eighty-odd years old and had been temporarily sent to a nursing home. It was no wonder, with these two taking care of her.

According to this fellow, who did not introduce himself, one of the women, whom I'll call Earth Mother, had taken two days off from her caretaking duties, and on her return, the other woman — I'll call her Mass Murderer — had taken Earth Mother's stuff and moved it out of the house. The guy went on to say that Mass Murderer had already "killed off" three husbands, as he put it, and was a force to be reckoned with.

Art and I were told before arriving in Scarma that we'd have this entire house to ourselves. We now had Earth Mother and this man, whom I'll call Alien, a twenty-three-year-old astrologer from England who was in the country illegally.

I called the housing director from the old woman's house and asked, with exceeding politeness, if there was any place else we could stay.

The housing director sounded to me as though he was over the edge and just keeping up a semblance of sanity as he told me that no, we were assigned to the old lady's house, we were to move in there at once, there was no place else to stay at the present time.

Art and I soon learned we couldn't keep any groceries in the house. According to Alien and Earth Mother, they only ate the absolute essentials of natural food. However, they continually wiped out all our lemonade and anything else that had sugar or preservatives. At night, we'd go to bed at 1:00 or 2:00, and by 10 a.m., when we got up, the food would be gone. Alien and E.M. went to bed at 3:00 and got up at 6:00. The phone was in our room, and people began calling the house at 6 a.m. just to chat.

Tom Scardini gave us massive rewrites the night we opened in Scarma. I wondered if the show would ever be "set" and realized it would not be, until we actually opened on Broadway.

The script changes meant rehearsal, and our domicile was not exactly convenient to the rehearsal space, a mere twenty-five miles away. Well, that's where Art's rehearsal space was. Mine was twelve miles south of that — thirty-seven miles away. I could have stayed in New York and commuted just as easily. And had more sleep.

The day after we opened, E.M. and Alien were out preparing for the return of the Grand Dame, who was due to be released from the home any day. While they were out clipping hedges and buying health food, five members of the Theater Board came to the house at 8 a.m. Art and I were both in our pajamas.

"We are here to count the silver and all the valuables," one of them, an older man, declared. He hastened to add, "We just don't want anyone to accuse you of taking anything since you're staying here by yourselves."

They then decided they had to change the locks on all the doors. This was evidently to keep Mass Murderer, who was on the outs, it seemed, from breaking in and stealing things. One of the Board members told me the Earth Mother's brother was a locksmith. The locksmith, however, made all of the locks fit one key. In order to do this, he had to saw new holes in all the doors. When Art came home from rehearsal in the middle of the day, he was greeted by one room after another with wood shavings on the floor.

"Before you leave," the locksmith told him, as if Art was the lawn man, "clean up the wood shavings."

Later that day, as we were getting ready to leave for the theater, there was an incessant stream of people coming in and out and arguments about who could have keys and who couldn't.

Then it started with the old woman's insane daughter, Jessica, who owned the house next door.

Jessica's first husband had deserted her, leaving her to care for their three children. She later became engaged, and as the story went, she either watched her fiancé be killed before her eyes or she killed him. I never did find out which. Either way, she saw it happen and went over the edge.

The cast was asked to do a fund-raiser at Jessica's house. At the last minute, she decided it was going to be an outside garden party. The piano, however, was inside the house behind sliding glass doors that did not open. We had to make our entrances from a porch, so when your name was announced, you ran from inside the house, all the way around it, and out onto the porch in order to stand outside. To signal the accompanist to start playing the piano, the singer had to leap and wave his or her arms.

Bobby started the gala fund-raiser off by singing "All I Need is the Girl." I was inside the house, in the study, vocalizing. Over the fireplace was a huge portrait of the head of the Theater Company which hadn't been there an hour earlier. The room was a good distance from the audience, but I could still hear Bobby.

The door to the room was open, but suddenly, it closed. Jessica was behind it, holding a huge butcher knife.

"I've got a great idea," she said, eyes shining. "Run to the window that looks out over the concert and sing out the window while he's singing."

"He's singing a solo."

"Make it into a duet."

Given the fact that she was holding a knife, I was willing to sing just about anything. But I smiled sweetly and said, "I don't think it would be appropriate. We haven't rehearsed it that way." I then ran past her.

Jessica then started breaking into her mother's house on a regular basis. While we were at rehearsal, she would go into the house and stay all day long, playing the stereo and leaving the needle on the moving turntable with no record on it. She would then take all the knives out of the drawers, all the food out of the refrigerator, put all the lights on, go through all the drawers and take out all her mother's silver. She broke into a steel file cabinet and threw all the papers on the floor. Where the caretaker and the illegal alien were during all this, nobody seemed to know. At some point, they both had taken off and seemed to be gone most of the time.

One night, after a performance, the cast was invited back to Bobby and Holly's. I was too exhausted to go along, so I took the car and went back to our house. No one was going to be there. The Alien and Earth Mother were off someplace, and I figured Jessica would be at her own house.

When I walked into the living room, I noticed the phone wire was cut. I then heard the phone in the kitchen ring. I answered, "Hello?"

It was Jessica. "How did you answer the phone? I thought I took care of all of them there."

"There was an extra one I found, and I plugged it in," I lied.

"I don't want any phones in that house. There's something wrong with the phones. They don't work."

I decided I wasn't taking any chances. I made sure every entrance to the house was locked. I put a chair and bureau in front of my bedroom door. At 1:30 a.m. — Art still wasn't back — she was throwing her body up against it. She was gone by the time Art got home, at 2 a.m.

I decided against saying anything to Art about this particular incident, knowing his temper. I told myself we were only there for a few more days. I had about fifteen minutes sleep that night.

The next night, when we returned from the theater, I went into the kitchen to get a cold drink while Art was in the shower, and when I returned to the front of the house, I noticed a police car out the window. I thought, uh-oh, Jessica must have done something. Suddenly, there was a big searchlight on the house. The police were standing in front of the car.

I opened the door a crack. "Can I help you?" I yelled.

"Yes, would you please come out with your hands above your head and identify yourself."

The police had been informed — they never said by whom — that no one was to be in the house.

"We've been staying here," I said, and began to tell my story.

They explained to me there was an injunction against Jessica, who, it turned out, owned the house we were staying in as well as the one next door. The injunction stated that she was not allowed into the house, and she could be arrested if she even went into the backyard. They told us to report to them if Jessica came near the place.

By now, Art, in his bathrobe, had joined us on the lawn. He said, "I don't understand how you can have a restraining order on someone when they own the house."

"I value my life," I said. "I am not calling you if she comes over here."

The police told me she had already been arrested once for slapping a policeman. Recently, her family had had her arrested, and she had talked the fifteen-year-old son of a friend of hers into driving from Scranton, which was twenty-five miles away, with bail money. He had to bring his sister, because he only had a learner's permit.

"We're supposed to be here doing goddamn performances," I complained to Art, "and instead we're remaking *The Snake Pit*. In any other country, artists are treated like high mucky-mucks."

Meanwhile, the show must go on. And it did, with an absolutely fried star, since I gave the Performances of Death — barely able to walk, I was so exhausted. Appeals to Bertha, to Fossey, to Tom Scardini, did no good. There simply wasn't any place else for us to stay.

Not that the theater was a haven of serenity either. Scarma didn't earn the name Berserka only because of my experience with Jessica, Mass Murderer and Earth Mother.

During one performance, Bobby had a diabetic reaction and needed to give himself insulin. He was sharing a dressing room with Art, who had made it abundantly clear that he had no stomach for watching Bobby test his blood or give himself injections.

Rather than do the sensible thing, which would have been to go into the men's room down the hall, Bobby ducked into the dressing room I shared with Sulynn and Amalia, knowing we were all on stage. What he forgot was that Sulynn's character left the scene, and Sulynn returned to the dressing room, did a costume change and went back on stage. When Sulynn opened the door of the dressing room, she was greeted with the sight of Bobby injecting a hypodermic of insulin into his thigh. She promptly became light-headed and sank to the floor.

When Sulynn did not return to the stage to finish our scene, Amalia and I improvised until Bertha had no choice but to bring down the curtain in the middle of the scene. Bobby had informed her that Sulynn was in a dead heap in the basement.

Miss Fossey ran out and explained to the audience that there had been an accident and that the show would continue in ten minutes. Fortunately, Bertha, as an experienced stage manager, kept a supply of smelling salts. Sulynn came around and weakly continued the show.

The production was not designed for a raked stage, and the Scarma Summer Theater had a raked stage. One night, when they brought Howard, who played Larry, out on a hospital gurney after his bad acid trip, the brakes wouldn't work and the thing headed for the orchestra. Art caught it in the nick of time.

Another raked-stage disaster occurred during one of my big numbers. There was a set piece that came in and out by means of a hand crank. The tech person was an ex-computer wizard who decided mid-stream to go into theater. She couldn't remember which way was forward and which was backward on the hand crank.

The stage was a completely open one, so that one could also see backstage. It wasn't that the theater was of any new modern design, it was just that it wasn't finished, because they had run out of money. I had just completed my very poignant song, "Dusk," one of the highlights of the show. I finished the song sitting in a chair. The lights were supposed to dim, and in this particular theater, the area I was on was to be backed off the stage, by means of this hand crank, so that another piece could be flown in.

However, the chair was not backed off — it was sent forward. I could see that the piece flying in was going to whack me on the head when it dropped. Luckily, the tech person was so uncoordinated that the piece wasn't dropping in very quickly. I leaned forward to avoid it. I kept leaning and leaning as my area of the stage headed toward the orchestra. The conductor threw himself to the ground, and I jumped off into the pit. But not before Bertha could be heard yelling "BACK UP, GODDAMN IT, BACK UP!"

After nights like these, Art and I longed for some peace. We were doomed to disappointment and counted the days until Scarma was history.

Finally, one night, Jessica became furious with the telephone company, because her phone didn't seem to be working to her specifications (Jessica had a real problem with phones). She ran out of the house, carrying her famous butcher knife and yelling, "I'm going to get some service whether anybody likes it or not, or someone's going to get it soon." She continued yelling and ran into her mother's house, through the kitchen and out the back door.

That's when Art and I decided it was time to move, even if we had to sleep at the theater. After packing as fast as we could and cleaning the house as fast as we could, we left a big note and felt we had fulfilled our responsibilities.

Art and I ended up in a beautiful motel for the weekend. It cost more than our per diems, but we decided it was worth it.

Jessica was finally arrested again and put into psychiatric care, after being taken away in a straitjacket.

Jessica's mother moved back into her home right after we moved out, and Miss Fossey strongly suggested that I pay a social call. "The theater company needs the housing," she explained. "So it's important to keep up good will. And remember, the old lady didn't do anything to you. It was her daughter, and she's in an institution."

I called the house to talk to the old woman, and Jessica's sister Norma answered the phone.

"Well," she hissed, "aren't *we* feeling guilty, finally calling? Aren't *you* just the most *responsible* person, moving *out* in the middle of the night?"

I went over to the house. I totally snowed the old lady, and she wanted to give me a gift. "Oh, don't give that to *her*," Norma said. "What did she ever do for you?" She took me into the kitchen and said, "Don't take those things from my mother. She doesn't know what she's doing, and I don't think it would be a very gracious thing for you to do, to take a gift from an old lady. My mother has some old nightgowns she can't use anymore. They have a lot of medicine down the front of them and stuff." This seemed to be to be a total non sequitur, but having dealt with Jessica, I just wrote it off to the family genes and didn't comment. I went back to the old lady, and as soon as Norma left the room, I took the gifts and stuck them in my duffel bag.

As I was leaving, Norma accosted me again. "I don't understand why you moved out in the middle of the night. How irresponsible can you be?"

"Well," I answered, "I decided when your sister ran through your mother's kitchen with a butcher knife, it was time to go."

When I got into my car, there were two unwashed nightgowns in the front seat.

Rondot, Pennsylvania, Art and I reasoned, was bound to be better.

There was a student performance for inner city kids who went to special day camps. They threw nails and pennies at the orchestra. The first violinist refused to play, and the performance was called.

None of us ever believed it would happen, but at long last we hit the final city of the tour: Berwick, New York. By this time, we were candidates for a production of *Night of the Living Dead.*

When we reached final performance, Harry, Zelda and some money men were in attendance to assess the show. The second act entr'acte had started. I was looking at it on the backstage monitor, when I saw the conductor run from the pit. Then I heard a crash, as the whole set fell forward toward the audience. It took twenty minutes to reassemble.

New York never looked so good.

While the powers-that-be decided what to do with *Bloomin'*, the cast got on with the business of living. The first thing everyone did was regroup. Holly moved in with Bobby. Sulynn officially moved in with Clark. Fred moved in with Howard, his own replacement in the show. Beverly, our new actress, moved in with a trumpet player.

Art and I began to look in earnest for a new apartment, finally finding a one-bedroom on West 89th Street.

Harry and his investor friends were not enamored of what they saw at the last performance of *Bloomin'* on the road. But the show was booked into an off-Broadway house, and if it did well and got favorable reviews, it would move to Broadway. "I'll believe it when I see it," Art sighed.

More rewrites, more rehearsals. And now that *Bloomin'* was headed for a New York opening, our director was brutal. The show was set to open on November 18, 1972, at the Commedia Theater, in Greenwich Village.

Fred was now permanently out of the show, which he knew would happen as soon as we returned to New York. He didn't seem to mind at all. "I was sent there for a reason," he said mystically. "To replace Bobby and meet Howard."

"New York critics. New York critics," Len chanted every time one of us made a mistake. "You do that, and John Simon will make you wish you'd never been born." Harry was a constant presence at rehearsal and, at one point, asked me if I wouldn't mind doing some work on his memoirs. "I've never found anyone who could read my handwriting like you can," he told me.

"I'm flattered, Harry, but I'm getting ready for my New York debut, and I'm a little busy."

"Maybe after the show opens," he said.

We posed for pictures, from which came the official *Bloomin'* poster ultimately defaced at every subway stop: Bobby and me from the waist up, in profile, our hands on each other's shoulders. Over our heads it said, "BLOOMIN'," and on the left side, "The musical symbol of a generation," and then the name of the theater, etc. Somehow, seeing people's faces marked up on other posters never bothered me. Seeing my own face and the face of my friend covered with black magic marker and swear words scrawled across our foreheads gave me a different feeling.

"New York audiences. New York audiences," Len said during his final pep talk. "Not unsophisticated summer-stock crowds, but discerning audiences shelling out their money. Not because they have nothing better to do, but because they want to see something. Give them something. Give them honesty, give them picked-up cues and on-pitch singing, give them a tight, professional show, and you won't disappoint them."

We filled the first night audience with as many of our friends as we could. My parents, brother and sister-in-law flew in, as did Lettie. Even my old boyfriend Chick came from Boston with his new girlfriend.

Given the preponderance of supporters in the audience and the fact that it was an opening night, which always has a special energy, it was difficult to assess the true impact of *Bloomin'* on people who didn't know the cast and had never seen the show. Harry threw an opening night party for us at his apartment, and there we waited for the reviews.

Fred and Howard went out and got the papers at 2 a.m. and rushed back with them. The consensus was the same — *Bloomin'* was a "sweet" show, with "pretty" music and, as *The Daily News* put it, "An attractive cast led by Margo Gaines and Bobby Gaines, who, according to the program notes, are in-laws."

The Post said: "*Bloomin'* has many funny and poignant moments, lacking only true excitement."

The New York Times said, "The music by Sandra Fossey is lyrical, and most of it will eventually appear on albums by Judy Collins and James Taylor."

"Okay," said Harry. "This means we're going to sell tickets and have a run."

Success!

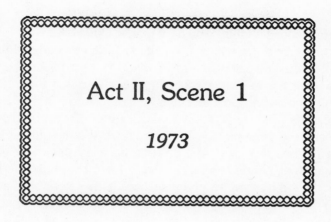

Act II, Scene 1

1973

New York, I discovered, was fun if one was working in one's chosen profession. I came to New York to be an actress and singer, and that was precisely what I was. I looked around me and knew it wouldn't last, but I decided to enjoy it. In show business, only a tiny percentage of performers are fortunate enough to have full-time employment.

Once Art and I were settled in our new apartment and no longer involved with touring, rehearsing, Bobby's diabetes, and dodging scenery and butcher knives, the honeymoon came to an abrupt end.

First of all, there was the problem of my housekeeping. Art had always known, as I pointed out to no avail, that my domestic talents were non-existent. I had embraced feminism in the cradle. Art married me, aware that cooking, for me, consisted of a trip to the deli; doing laundry meant I brought it across the street to be done by someone else; ironing consisted of hanging the piece of clothing in the shower; and hanging up clothes entailed a trip to the nearest chair.

It didn't sit well. Art and Bobby had been raised by Lettie, who waited on them hand and foot, and since they were the Polish princes of their family, the rest of their female relatives followed Lettie's example.

Art hated living with Bobby, because Bobby was a slob and did not share in the chores. He thought sex would help him tolerate my domestic similarities to Bobby. It didn't.

"I don't care what men say before they're married," I told Sulynn over lunch. "When they get married, they want a wife. A real wife. And I'm not one. I need one, as a matter of fact."

Sulynn nodded. "I think you have one, if I know Art."

"Yes, but he's not happy about it, and we've been fighting. He wants his shirts ironed. Well, I solve that. I just send them out. But he doesn't want me to send the laundry out. He doesn't want anyone doing his underwear. So I told him he can just do it himself. We go out to eat after the show, so that takes care of dinner, but he moans and groans about the money. Well, my God. We're both working — it's not like we're broke. And does he honestly think I'm going to cook something before or after the show? I don't see him offering."

"He *can't* think you're going to cook either before or after the show. You can't cook." She put the rest of her sandwich on her plate. "I'm taping this afternoon. I shouldn't have eaten what I did." She asked the waitress to wrap the remainder of her sandwich. "Clark *hires* somebody to come in two mornings a week and clean. It's fine with me. He's paying for it."

"I don't know why you and Art didn't get married," I lamented. "I'm not bad with money, but I guess I never realized he was so *frugal.*"

"You should have lived with him first. If I marry Clark, I'll know exactly what I'm getting into."

"I did live with him. A little."

"Doesn't count. Those first couple of weeks are all sex. He couldn't do enough for you. It's after that time that you really get to know a person."

We ordered coffee. "I'll tell you something else," I said. "Lettie is driving me nuts."

Sulynn laughed out loud. "Boy, I knew that one was coming. But I thought you'd be safe because she was back in Yarmouth. Too bad about Bobby's diabetes. You'll never get rid of her now."

"I love Lettie, but when she's in town, or even when I talk with her on the phone, she practically runs down a list: have I done this for Art? Have I cooked that? That's his favorite, blah, blah, blah. Till I want to scream. I don't get it, Sulynn. Why didn't I see any of this before?"

She poured a half-and-half into her coffee. "What is it they say? Love is blind? By the way, are you going to Amalia's party?"

I narrowed my eyes. "I'm taking a survey. Did she invite you?"

"No. I guess she didn't invite you, either?"

"No, but guess what? She borrowed the punchbowl Art and I got as a wedding present."

"What balls! She borrows your punchbowl and then doesn't invite you." An old woman approached the table and Sulynn gave her an autograph. "I'm on the cover of *Soap Digest* next month," she announced, Amalia's party a distant memory. "It should be good publicity for *Bloomin'*, too."

"You're the closest thing we have to a star," I admitted.

NOT CLOSE ENOUGH, as I learned the next day.

Harry now acted as my agent. Also as Bobby's and Sulynn's (another sore spot between Art and me). He occasionally sent me out on commercial auditions, and the morning after my lunch with Sulynn, he told me to pick up some commercial copy at the Madison Avenue office.

When I arrived, the copy wasn't at the front desk, so while I waited for Zelda to get off the phone, I sat in the little reception room reading *Variety*, where I spotted the following item:

> "Producers Harry Lasker and Zack Vincent, who are planning to bring their flower-child musical, *Bloomin'*, to Broadway in the fall, have approached folksinger Dani Cluny about taking a possible part in the production. Cluny's representative at William Morris, Maurice Kaufman, confirmed that Cluny has a script of the musical, now playing off-Broadway, but declined to comment further."

There could only be one "possible part" Dani Cluny, with her long hair and guitar, could play, and that was my role, Mandy Morgan. I tore out of the office without seeing Zelda, flagged a cab and was at Harry's door, opening it with the key I still had, in ten minutes.

Harry wasn't there, but came in with a blonde as I was writing him an outraged letter in my old office. "Margo, what are you doing here?" he said from the hall, a little nervously, his eyes shifting toward the blonde. It was the old, "Get lost, Margo." I wasn't having any.

"I need to speak to you, Harry," and there was no mistaking the tone of my voice.

"Wait for me in there," Harry said to the blonde, directing her toward the living room. He closed the curtain over the den entrance. I threw *Variety* at him.

He glanced down at the paper laying at his feet. "What's this about? It's missing a section? Hah! Hah!"

"Don't pretend you don't know what's in there. You're trying to replace me with Dani Cluny. What happened? Did Judy Collins turn you down?"

"Calm down, Margo. Your face is so red you look like you're

gonna blow up. Hah! Hah!"

"I'm going to do more than that. I want to know what's happening, Harry, and I want to know now. Am I going to be replaced when this show goes to Broadway?"

"Well..." He sat down on the arm of the sofa. "You won't be out of the show, of course. You'd be understudying the role of Mandy."

I couldn't believe my ears. "UNDERSTUDYING? MY OWN PART? THE PART I CREATED?" I burst into tears. "You don't think I'm good, is that it?"

"Margo, baby. Baby..." I backed away as he came toward me. "Margo, I think you're fabulous, but we need a draw when the show gets to Broadway."

"Then replace somebody else," I snapped. "Get a black rock star to play Howard's part. Get Leslie Uggams to play Beverly's part. Make one of their parts bigger and replace them. But you're not replacing me."

He flapped his arms in the air. "There you go again, Margo. You wanna be in the big time, but you don't want you or your friends to have to pay the price. It's okay for Howard and Beverly to pay the price but not you."

"DAMN STRAIGHT!" I screamed. God only knows what his afternoon trick thinks, I said to myself. "We started with this show when it was NOTHING. Howard and Beverly are great in the show, and they're wonderful people, but damn it, they didn't start with it. We did. And we deserve something for that. We're the ORIGINAL CAST."

"Margo, I can't help it. Some of the people interested in putting up money love the show but they want a *star*. You're not a *star*."

I sobbed, "Then make me one. You can't take this part away from me. I won't let you." I ran out of the room, crying, "I won't let you."

I took the stairs down to the next floor and sat on the steps, licking my wounds. After an indeterminate time, I went home. Art was in the apartment, reading.

"Zelda called," he said, without looking up. "She's got some copy for you." He saw me then and jumped up, poor Delilah landing on the floor. "Jesus, what happened?"

I told him.

"It's impossible," he said. "Have you talked to Foss or Tom or Len, or anyone else?"

I shook my head.

By evening, the whole cast, artistic staff and crew of *Bloomin'* knew, either from the paper or via the telephone. I didn't speak to anyone, preferring to sit in my bathrobe watching television and petting the cats. We had a performance the next night, and I had no idea how I was going to get through it if my present state continued.

The next morning, Art and I were awakened by our door buzzer. Art rolled out of bed to answer it. "It's Bobby and Holly," he called into our room. I stayed in bed, and a few minutes later, Bobby and Holly stood over me.

"We brought breakfast, Margo," Holly said, holding up a white bag. "Croissants."

"And coffee." Bobby held up his bag.

I sat up. "What time is it? Why are you up so early?" Bobby was an inveterate noon riser who napped at 4 p.m.

Bobby winced. "I have to take insulin every morning at dawn. So I get up."

Art brought in plates. He sat on the bed, and Holly and Bobby sat on the floor, Sammy and Delilah crawling all over them.

"They smell Circe," Holly said, referring to their new white cat, fresh from the ASPCA death row.

"Holly talked to her father last night," Bobby said, biting into a croissant which most definitely was not part of his diet.

"My father is supposed to give *Bloomin'* extra money to go to Broadway, and he brought in another investor," Holly told us. "But he called Zack last night and said that if you leave the show, he's withdrawing his money, and he has convinced the new investor to do the same."

My jaw dropped. "You're kidding," I said. "How much money are we talking about?" Because, I reasoned, Harry would just go and dig up someone else. I never trusted him, but now my mistrust had taken on a new dimension.

Holly sipped her coffee, then smiled, flashing her perfect teeth at me. "$500,000."

Everyone laughed as I sat there, not quite taking in the information at first. "Do you think it will work?" I asked.

"Definitely," Holly said. "My dad's prepared to go to the other investors and raise hell. Not money, hell. You don't realize this, but the main reason my father invested in *Bloomin'* was your performance. He thinks you hold that whole show together. The reviews support that."

"Yes," I said, "but with the opportunity to get someone like Dani Cluny..."

"But Margo," Holly broke in, "the original investors didn't put money into the show because it had stars in it. They invested in the show and the cast they saw. From what my dad said, getting Dani Cluny was Harry's idea."

Foss was at the theater that night, for the first time in a while. "I understand we might have a mutiny on our hands," she said to me. "A lot of people are very unhappy."

"Do you want Dani Cluny in this show?" I asked her.

"No. Loyalty aside, she can't sing the music. I wrote more than folk songs for Mandy. I wrote for a belt voice. Your belt voice. And I just don't see her pulling it off. I also think it throws the show off-balance considerably if there's a star. Mandy is the biggest role, but the piece is an ensemble piece. I think Zack understands that."

"I'm glad someone understands something." We headed for the wings. "Harry never ceases to amaze me."

"Harry made a big mistake, Margo. He put his own money into the show. A producer should never do that. Now he's scared. Don't be too hard on Harry. He's seen them come and he's seen them go. I don't think he views anything but money with too much importance. You, Dani Cluny — it's all the same if they can make him a buck."

"You say that, knowing for years he didn't have a dime because he wasn't paying attention to his own business? I don't know what makes Harry tick. He's probably sleeping with Dani Cluny."

She giggled, then pointed to a cup of water behind the first act set. "You know, every time I'm backstage, I see these little glasses of water all over the place. What are they?"

Bertha happened by at that moment and heard her. "They're Amalia's. She leaves them everywhere. One of these days, I'm going to put rat poison in one of them and just *let her go*." The three of us were roaring with laughter as the overture began and Amalia ran into the wings and took a sip of water.

I went out and gave it everything I had, especially knowing there might be a potential investor or two lurking in the audience.

Although I heard nothing further about Dani Cluny, I was aware of a variety of internal problems concerning the *Bloomin'* powers-that-be. There were always strange people backstage staring at the cast and speaking in low voices with Zack, Harry, Foss and Len Magnuson. The show continued to run to excellent houses, with no closing notice posted or news in the trades as to when or if it would move.

I decided, as far as *Bloomin'* was concerned, to take each day as it came, and to forget what Harry was attempting to do to me. He was a good agent, willing to send me out on potentially lucrative casting calls. I knew it was time to "toughen up" as far as show business was concerned. We would all be replaced if it suited our producers, and there was nothing any of us could do about it.

Besides, *Bloomin'* was the least of my problems. I was married to Art Gaines.

You could cut the tension in our apartment with a knife. I stopped telling Art when Harry sent me out for a casting call, although it was obvious when I left the apartment dressed in my best clothes that I wasn't going to the grocery store.

Art made no attempt to find an agent, expecting that someone would see the show and offer to sign him. It didn't happen, although Bobby and I were bombarded with offers from agents and, pressured by Harry, ultimately signed with The Lasker Agency. I pointed out to Art that his role wasn't as showy, that the fact that he was in an off-Broadway show was a good inducement for agents to interview him and see more of what he could do, but that he needed to contact the agents. He refused and spent his days cleaning, cooking and ironing — reminding me every second that those were really my jobs. In between those chores he read and watched television.

Our physical relationship dwindled to an occasional peck on the lips, and whenever I tried to interest him further, he said he was tired or not in the mood. One night he accused me of being "too aggressive." That did it.

"Art, we can't go on like this," I said, fighting tears. "We haven't even been married a year yet, and you won't come near me. What have I done? Can't we at least talk?"

He was sitting up in bed and grabbed for a cigarette. Lately, cigarette smoking had become more and more a habit, as had marijuana smoking. In the past, he had only indulged occasionally.

"It seems to me that everything in this place is switched around," he began. "I do housework, and you tell me when it's time to make love."

"I didn't ask you to do housework, and I don't see why you're the only one who can call the shots as far as sex is concerned. Maybe if you 'called the shots' more often, I wouldn't have to. What's really bothering you?"

"Everything is bothering me." He didn't elaborate, and we sat silently for some time.

Finally, I said, "I feel like you've changed, like everything we had between us is gone. Getting married was a big mistake. I don't know what you wanted, but I'm not it. You don't even seem to *like* me anymore, let alone love me or want me. You act resentful of me, like it's my fault that I have a good part in *Bloomin'*, my fault I'm hooked up with Harry. It's not my fault. And why is my career a bad thing?"

He continued to stare at the sheets.

"Art, you knew when you married me I didn't have a domestic bone in my body. My God, we joked about it every time you came over here. And I'll be honest with you. I'm not willing to even try to do any better with housework and cooking. And you know why? Nothing I do around here will ever be good enough for you, so why should I bother? You'll just criticize me and do it over, like you always do. It hurts me. It hurts me a lot. So I've just let you do everything to your own satisfaction."

I couldn't keep the tears back any longer and let loose with a lot of pent-up pain and emotion. "I can't live like this."

"Do you want me to move out?"

"That's what you call a solution? Just giving up when we haven't even started?"

He pulverized his cigarette into the ashtray. "I think I need some time to think," he said at last. "Maybe I should just stay with Bobby for a few days and clear my head."

I called Sulynn at two in the morning and took a cab over to her place. Although she was taping the next morning, she stayed up with me until four, consoling me. She called Bobby the next day and found out Art was there, bag and baggage, so I went home.

Doing *Bloomin'* for the next week was hell. Art and I were not speaking. Everyone was pussyfooting around us. Then, in the midst of our marital riff, the closing notice for *Bloomin'* was posted. Backstage became a funeral parlor.

I left the dressing room one night during the second-to-last week of our run and found Art outside the door. "Let's talk," he said. We went to the Riviera Cafe on Seventh and got a window table.

"It's too bad about the show," he began. "Have you heard anything about plans for it?"

I shook my head, not trusting myself to speak or look at him.

Art lit a cigarette. "Margo, I've been an asshole. I've been jealous and taking all my career resentments out on you. To tell you the truth, I'm not sure I want to be an actor. It was kind of a family thing, you know? My mother always assumed we'd be involved in the theater. It was her first love. But Bobby was always the one with the real talent and ambition."

"You have a lot of talent," I broke in.

"We haven't been in New York that long, Margo, but you know how little talent means. It takes something else to really make it, and I don't think I have it. I'm not sorry about it, but I just haven't known what to do with myself. I love doing the show, but now that's ending, and where do I go from here?"

We gave our order to the waitress, and when she left, Art said, "Everything's all mapped out for you. It always has been. You're pretty and you have an amazing voice, and you're just offbeat enough, without being weird, so that you have a special quality. And you have the drive to continue."

He paused for a minute, watching the passersby through the window. "I think what I've been angry at is how you never apologize for anything. You are who you are, no pretense. See, I feel like all I do is pretend. I pretend to be an actor, pretend to be a good son, a good brother. Truth to tell, I don't quite live up to what everybody thinks I am. You don't clean house, you don't cook and you don't pretend you can, and you don't care whether I like it or not. I admire that."

For the first time in two weeks, I laughed. "That's not the impression I got."

He leaned toward me. "I want to try again. I want you to give me another chance."

"I'm not the one giving out the chances. I didn't ask you to leave, and if you hadn't been so unhappy, I never would have been, either."

The waitress brought our omelettes. Art's voice was shaky. "I still love you."

That night, we made love for the first time in a long time. We woke up with Samson and Delilah curled up together at the foot of the bed. Except for the fact that Art and I would soon be unemployed, life was good again.

Then, in the week that followed my reconciliation with Art and the posting of the closing notice, everything happened at once.

First, rumors flew around the dressing rooms that the show was moving to Broadway, a rumor that no one — Foss, Harry, Tom, Len — would verify. Even Holly, with the pipeline to her dad, couldn't get any information. I took a trip to the Equity office to see if *Bloomin'* was listed on any future production schedules — nothing.

Two nights before our June 1st closing, we got the word: *Bloomin'* was getting a major overhaul and moving to Broadway in October of 1973.

None of us knew whether to be happy or not, since we didn't know if we were going with it. As Zack put it, "No decisions have been made regarding casting as yet, because the show is going to be changed drastically. Some of you may need to audition again. Everyone will be notified when casting and a rehearsal schedule are set. Rehearsals should start in mid-September."

"Well," Bobby said as he left the theater that night, "his days of begging us to move to New York and making a commitment to the show are over."

"Yeah," I agreed. "They don't need us anymore, that's for sure."

In the years to come, original casts would be protected by their contracts and at least get a financial settlement if the producers decided not to move them with a production. But all that would be too late for the *Bloomin'* cast, and to us, it felt like we had been used up and were about to be bagged and thrown away.

In the time before the show closed, the cast scrambled like mad to get other work. Bobby was off to do Cornelius in a tour of *Hello, Dolly*. Art didn't look, deciding to go on unemployment and take time to "regroup and think about life," and I was kept from looking for work by an announcement from my ex-roommate, Sulynn Reilly, known now to her television fans and theater audiences as "Susan Reilly."

"To hell with all of it," Sulynn proclaimed. "Clark and I talked to the soap producers, and they're going to let us off to get married in August. It's fine with me that there's no show."

Sulynn's proclamation, followed by her notification that she'd need me to help with the wedding every step of the way, threw me into a tailspin. I had hoped that Harry could line me up at least a last-minute summer stock job. But I didn't know how I could be involved with Sulynn's wedding and work at the same time.

I had two commercials on the air by this time, one for soap and one for pudding, and I was collecting residuals. I'd been tested for limited-run roles on two soap operas, but didn't get either part. Now I was free to do something out of town, and I would: Sulynn's wedding. It wasn't quite what I had in mind.

Art and I discussed our current situation at length.

"We can make it." Art said, "We have our savings and your residuals, and if we both draw unemployment, except for the weeks you get a residual check, that should hold us until we find out about *Bloomin'*. And it will give me time to make a decision."

"I don't want to spend the summer in New York," I said. "I asked Harry to try and get me something like a guest artist contract for one show. You know, sometimes people get cast in something and get a better job and drop out. This is the time to get that type of job. It would be great if it were around here or New England. Then you could visit, and it would be easier to help with this wedding. I think we should sublet our apartment like Bobby and Holly did, and you can go to Yarmouth with Sammy and Delilah."

"Nice of you to work all this out without consulting me," he said. "Do you think you could *act* married once in a while? Don't I have a say?"

Blew it again, I said to myself. "I'm sorry. I'm just talking out loud. Nothing's decided. Of course, I want to hear what your ideas are."

"You're not just talking out loud, Margo. You said you already talked to Harry about a job. When was I going to find out about it? While you were packing?"

"I would never take a job without discussing it with you. He hasn't even gotten me an audition yet, so why discuss it? Art, I don't want to fight. Tell me what you have in mind, and let's go from there."

He scowled while I waited for him to say something. It was a long wait. At last, he said, "I would like us to stay together this summer. I'd rather you didn't go off and work someplace. I thought it might be nice if we enjoyed the summer together and worked on our marriage a little." The implication being, I heard in his voice and words, that I was only interested in my career.

"Honey, that sounds great," I said. "I just don't know if it's practical as far as money. If I got a job, why couldn't you come with me?"

He exploded. "I'm not interested in hanging out with working actors all summer, thanks, and I'm also not interested in that merry-go-round that happens out of town. You don't seem to understand, do you? I need time to sort things out. I've asked you to help me. If you don't want to, fine. Go off on your own." With that, he left the apartment.

"Well, Sammy," I said, picking him up. "It was a short but sweet reconciliation."

I needed expert advice. It was time to take my marital problems out of the closet. I called Lettie in Yarmouth.

I told her as much as I comfortably could. While it was true that I often felt she was overseeing my good-wifeliness, she also was an ex-performer and had given me good advice in the past. Besides, she knew Art better than anyone. Certainly better than I did, even after being married to him a year.

When I was through, she said, with her usual rapid-fire delivery, "Margo, I'm going to talk to you like your own mother, or as your friend Lettie, not as your mother-in-law.

"My mother-in-law advice to you would be to do whatever Art wants. But the advice I'm giving you is to take a sheet of paper and make two columns. Head the column on the left, What's Best For Me. And also head the column on the right, What's Best For Me. And that will make your decision for you.

"You young girls aren't like young girls of my generation. In my day, everything had to be the husband: what the husband wanted, at all costs. That's not going to work for you. And to tell you the truth, Margo, it didn't work for me either, and the boys suffered for it. I spoiled them. They became my whole life.

"I love my Art with my whole heart and soul, but I love you, too. I'll help you in any way I can, but you know that in the end, you two have to work this out. And let me tell you something else. Marriage is all compromise."

I wondered if it wasn't so much compromise as the female giving in every step of the way, as I'd always seen my mother do. In the end, I honored the age-old tradition. I told Harry not to send me out on any auditions, so Art and I could spend the summer together.

A few days later, I got a call from *Soap Stars* magazine. The wedding of Sulynn and Clark was going to be the cover story for their September issue. If they sent a photographer, would I take $1000 for an eyewitness account of the ceremony and reception, as written by a fellow actress-friend?

"Don't worry about the actual writing," the editor told me. "Just write down everything you see. All about it. And someone here will work it up into an article with your byline." As if a rough-draft effort by me wouldn't look like John Steinbeck compared to the drivel that appeared in *Soap Stars* magazine.

"I'll write it as an article," I replied. "You make whatever changes you have to." I had been an A student in composition all the way through school.

When I told Sulynn, she said, "You know why they did that? They wanted to send one of their own writers. I said, get real, I'm not having any strangers nosing around my wedding. It was like something out of that *Philadelphia Lawyers* movie we saw with Katharine Hepburn."

"*The Philadelphia Story*. But they are sending a photographer, Sulynn."

"I told them they could if I could have all his pictures for free. That way, I don't have to hire a photographer. You know what they want for wedding pictures?"

All the angles covered. As usual.

Plans for the Wedding of the Century began in earnest and continued throughout the summer. To accommodate Bobby's *Hello,*

Dolly and Beverly's *Two Gentlemen* schedules, the date was set for August 22nd in Framingham. Sulynn invited everyone from *Bloomin'* with the exception of Amalia and her husband, the hated Winslow. Howard was doing *Showboat* in Europe and would not be able to attend. Harry and Zelda sent a silver tray, but said they'd be in L.A. during the wedding.

Sulynn's parents planned to have the reception catered at their home, as an outdoor garden party. This meant preparing the house for possible rain-out. I didn't envy them.

Art, Bobby and Fred were among the ushers. I was matron of honor, and Sulynn decided to hold the bridesmaids down to ten of her nearest and dearest. One thing about Sulynn, she was stingy with her own money and profligate with everybody else's. My gown cost a fortune. Sulynn's sister, cut from the same cloth as Sulynn, flatly refused to buy her bridesmaid's dress.

Art was as involved with the wedding as I was, which was good for our relationship. He also shared, with the rest of the *Bloomin'* cast, curiosity about the show, and each week we scoured the trades and worked on Harry and Foss for information. But none was forthcoming. Tom and Foss were busy reworking the show.

"The show got great reviews," I said to Harry. "Why does it have to be changed?"

"Because we want it to run," he said. "And when you're doing a show like this, you have to be sure it doesn't date itself and go out of fashion the way *Damn Yankees* did. When was the last time anybody did *Damn Yankees*?

"There's nothing wrong with the story of *Bloomin'*. The songs are pretty. But there's too much folk music. It needs more pop stuff, more up tunes to offset the folk music, not change the quality of the entire score. And some of the topical references need to come out of the script. Otherwise, it's lucky if it squeezes out a year. And if a show goes kaput because of being dated, there go the royalties for summer stock and dinner theater."

I asked Art if he would stay with *Bloomin'* if he was offered a contract. "Sure," he said. "But whether or not I'm going to pursue a career further, I don't know right now." Sometimes he acted less tense and unhappy, other times he was moody and pugnacious. I couldn't get a handle on what would set him off, so I tried instead to be around as much as possible when he was in a good frame of mind and stay away when he wasn't. Any woman would have envied the way he treated me on our anniversary: flowers, dinner, champagne — he was a fantasy husband. But an anniversary is only once a year.

I played a social worker on "The Doctors" for a week, made another commercial, and also typed more of Harry's memoirs, in between helping Sulynn with the wedding invitations, choosing her gown, throwing a shower for her, writing down each gift and helping her write the thank you notes. Art went with Clark and helped him choose a beautiful suit. The four of us took a trip to Long Island to see Bobby in *Hello, Dolly.*

On August 2nd, Art and I got our new contracts for *Bloomin'*. I excitedly called Sulynn and Bobby. We were all in the new production and called for rehearsal September 6th. I was ecstatic.

On August 18th, Art and I put Sammy and Deli in the hands of a cat-sitting service and left for Boston for a short vacation — although we'd basically been on vacation all summer — before heading to Framingham for what we now called "The Zefferelli Production," Sulynn's wedding. We decided to take the ferry to Provincetown, have lunch, then rent a car, spend the night with Lettie in Yarmouth and go to Framingham.

We spent the 18th recapturing our lost youth in Boston, then on the morning of the 19th got the ferry to Provincetown for what Art thought was going to be a romantic trip.

"It's a little rough out there today," the woman taking the tickets warned us as we boarded. About twenty minutes into the rocky ride, I began to feel sick. Art, of course, was fine. I staggered up to the woman running the concession stand. "I'm so nauseous," I said, "do you have any suggestions?"

"Yes," she told me. "Go out onto the deck and breathe in the fresh air. You'll find it helps." Waving to Art, I lurched outside. The air helped a little, but I felt faint, so I sat, and finally reclined, on the deck bench. As I lay there, the boat tilted to one side — the side I was on — and I was engulfed in a wave.

Now soaked as well nauseous, I made my way back to Art. He wrapped me in his jacket and helped to dry me off as best he could with napkins. I sat at the table, shivering and sick. He got me huge, empty popcorn containers from the concession stand so I could throw up, then disposed of them as I filled them. Everyone was using them. After I had been throwing up for a while, I leaned against the wall and moaned. The woman at the concession stand thought I was going to throw up again and held up an empty popcorn container, as if to say, do you need this?

Eventually I went into the ladies' room, where people were lying on the floor, face down, holding onto the pipes underneath the sink. One non-prone woman said to me, "The piano on deck tipped over."

"My God," I said. "Then what happened?"

"The band stopped playing," she said.

By the time we got to Provincetown, I had lost interest in lunch.

Sulynn's family and friends poured into Framingham, as did Clark's, filling up the little motel across from the church where she was to be married, where Art, Lettie and I were staying. There were also members of the two families in a motel across town.

Most of what happened did not appear in my write-up in *Soap Stars* magazine.

Clark arrived the day before the wedding and forgot to bring his new suit, bringing instead an atrocious bell-bottomed baggy number that looked like it belonged in a Red Skelton skit. One would never have known the guy was a daytime TV star.

"You should see this thing," I complained to Sulynn's sister, Peggy. "It hangs off of him and has these huge pockets."

Sulynn piped up in a defensive tone. "The pockets aren't that big."

"All he needs is a ring of keys and his name would be Captain Kangaroo," I said. "Big enough for you?"

The day of the wedding, I worked like a total slave at the church, seeing that bows were put on the pews, the carpet put down, the flowers arranged, although none of this was my forté. I did this work alone, not because I wanted to, but because no living soul offered to help. The stag party had left Art comatose. After the party, Bobby, driving himself and Clark back to their motel in Sulynn's car, plowed the car into a pole, and Clark had to unpry it. So I wasn't inclined to call Bobby and Holly either.

I was running way behind schedule. Not only had I not done Sulynn's hair and makeup, but I wasn't dressed myself. Into the church sauntered one of Sulynn's cousins from the motel across the street, where everyone was relaxing and having a wonderful time, I presumed, while I was killing myself.

"The family wants to know when they can come over," she whined. "We're all hot. It's so hot over there in the motel."

"Ariella, I want you to give the family a message for me." I was dead calm. "I want you to tell the family to go fuck themselves."

"Okay," she said, with equal calm, and left.

Disgusted, I followed her over to the motel. Sulynn was getting ready in her cousin Christine's room, so that I could be at the church and help her simultaneously. At about the time I was starting Sulynn's hair and makeup, the family went over to the church. "Sulynn, you're not ready," Ariella said.

"I can be late for my own wedding if I want to. It's my right," Sulynn snapped.

I gave Ariella a flower arrangement to put on the altar. Wrapped around the basket was a yellow plastic bag with a red Manhattan skyline, from the Red Apple Supermarket, held on by rubber bands.

Ariella had two brain cells, and one was on vacation. She must have thought the arrangement looked nice with the bag around it, because that's how she put it on the altar. By the time I got back to the church, after slopping through Sulynn's hair and makeup, perfuming myself, throwing on my dress and hat, and then slapping on lipstick, there was no way to remove the offending bag. I didn't see it until I was on my way down the aisle. In the pictures of the ceremony, one's eye is immediately drawn to the lovely red Manhattan skyline, crossed with rubber bands. The *Soap Stars* photographer spent a lot of time cropping out the offensive item for the magazine story.

I sat in a room off the main entrance with Sulynn and her father and watched the arrival of the bridesmaids. The dresses had a Scarlett O'Hara motif: big pink skirts with hoops. Sulynn's bridesmaids consisted of *Bloomin'*'s own Beverly, two friends from the soap opera, and the other seven were cousins and Sulynn's sister. Beverly and the soap people handled the skirts beautifully, but the hoop of one of the cousins didn't quite leave the car with her, getting stuck inside, and she slipped out of it and landed on the sidewalk with her dress up around her neck. The photographer clicked away. I was glad Sulynn hadn't seen it.

The group that gathered at the back of the church waiting to be seated looked right out of the Sermon-on-the-Mount scene from *King of Kings* — a mob. One of Sulynn's cousins was an usher out of jail on parole and considered his ushering duties sacred (the night before going to prison, he ushered at a Billy Graham crusade and found God). He escorted people down the aisle as if he were walking them to the electric chair, taking his sweet time about it and talking with them. When it came time for him to usher Tracy, the cast's resident Jesus freak, he basically stopped ushering and sat with her in the pew and talked.

Fred didn't take his own ushering duties seriously and kept poking his head into the foyer off the church entrance, gossiping about the guests.

"Come here and look at that VPL," he said to me during one trip, pointing to a woman in the foyer.

This was a new one. "VPL?" I asked.

"Visible panty line."

Even though he was hung over, Art was the only one with any efficiency. Finally, everyone was seated, the church was filled to capacity, and we were ready to roll.

Despite the Red Apple bag around the flowers and Clark's "Captain Kangaroo" suit, the wedding itself went off without a hitch. Sulynn looked like a doll, and if the wedding did have the scope of a De Mille film, rather than intimacy, it was at least sumptuous and beautiful. Clark's best man, a Swede named Lars Andersen, was so handsome, he deflected some of the focus from Clark, which was all to the good. "The press is having a field day!" Fred joked as we watched the photographer nearly tripping Sulynn and Clark on their way out of the church.

We rode in limousines to the reception at the home of Sulynn's parents. The yard was magnificently decorated with flowered arches and a canopy. There was even a string quartet.

"Wish you'd had all this?" It was Lettie behind me.

"Oh, no, Lettie. I would have lost my mind. This isn't even my wedding, and I nearly went crazy as it was."

The high point of the afternoon for me was the arrival of Sulynn's Aunt Bronwyn. Bronwyn had bright red hair and once worked in the garment district in New York, as a model, then as a designer. Then she married money and left New York. Bronwyn was a raving beauty, but very wild. She loved to drink, and she loved to crash weddings. She and her brother, Sulynn's father, had been on the outs for years, but Bronwyn showed up at Sulynn's wedding anyway.

She came in wearing a designer outfit, looking absolutely drop-dead chic, flirting with everyone's husband and drinking incessantly. I was standing in the house with Art when she went upstairs to the bathroom, and as she was coming back downstairs, she toppled and went flying down the whole staircase.

Unruffled, she stood up and smoothed her dress. Then she swore at the staircase, "Cheap carpeting!" and went back outside.

The wedding did something to Art. Maybe it was the hangover, or the continuous champagne. He was openly affectionate with me, which was rare, and we danced most dances together. "You know," he said, "I think the dresses Sulynn picked out are hideous. But you look beautiful in yours."

"I hardly had time to get ready. It's sweet of you not to notice."

"You look prettier than Sulynn."

"I hardly had any time to get her ready either," I said, "so that isn't surprising either. She spent more time on her hair and makeup for dates with guys she never saw again."

He kissed my neck. "I got a little jealous watching you with that best man. He looks like he came from Central Casting." His voice vibrated against my ear. "I wish we could go back to the motel now. How long do we have to stay?"

"Till Sulynn and Clark leave, silly." Sulynn and Clark were flying to Europe the next morning for ten days, having gotten, as Sulynn put it, "a great deal." "Sulynn has to throw her bouquet, and Clark throws the garter — all that stuff we didn't want."

His lips were up against my cheek. "I only wish I'd seen you in a wedding dress."

Sulynn and Clark took off at about six, after Tracy caught the bouquet, and the Billy Graham usher caught the garter. From then on, it was chaos. The food served at the wedding was excellent, but I have to admit that Sulynn's family shocked me a bit, pulling out their Reynolds Wrap and taking everything home with them. What I was going to write for *Soap Stars* magazine, I had no idea.

Art and I went back to the motel with Lettie. I was exhausted, but Art had other things on his mind besides sleep. We rolled around on the bed for a while, then I grabbed my diaphragm kit.

He took it out of my hand. "Don't," he said, and threw the plastic case on the floor, kissing me.

I squirmed away. "You're crazy. I have to." I was half on and half off the bed, reaching for it.

He pulled me back toward him, laughing. "Just once, can't we be spontaneous? Do you always have to break things up to put that thing in?"

I did a quick calculation, then decided I just couldn't take the chance. "Yes," I said. This time he didn't argue. I found the diaphragm as big a nuisance as he did, but I didn't want to be on the Pill.

At about 1 a.m., I was almost asleep when I heard him say:

"Let's have a baby."

I thought I was just dozing off, but it seemed I was asleep and dreaming. I opened my eyes. No, I really heard that. I turned over. "Art?"

"Did you hear me?" he said, facing me. "Let's have a baby."

I sat up and turned on the light. "What brought this on?"

"Don't you think it's time?"

"No-o-o. I'm about to star in a Broadway show. Your timing is a little strange. I thought we were going to wait."

"I don't know what we're waiting for anymore."

"You don't?"

"No. Supposing the show runs for a long time?"

"Supposing it does? Isn't that the idea?"

Now sitting up, he lit a cigarette. "I just mean, it seems like there'll always be a reason for you not to get pregnant. Now it's because the show is opening. Then it'll be because the show is into its run. Then your career will start to take off and you won't want to. Do you want children?"

"How can you ask me that? You know I do. But not now. I don't know what you're thinking of sometimes, I really don't. I've put so much of my heart and soul into *Bloomin'*. We all have. You want me to give up a chance to make some real money and get some real exposure because you don't want to wait a year or two to start a family? If I got pregnant now, I'd have to quit right after the show opened."

I was used to the silences that followed any kind of altercation we had, normally followed by Art leaving the premises. But since he wasn't dressed, there was no danger of that tonight.

"You're looking for something," I said. "You think fatherhood is your answer. I don't think it is. And I'm not saying that because it's in my own interest. I know where this is coming from, and a baby is not the solution."

He exhaled deeply, puffing his cheeks out as he did so. "But you agree there's something missing."

"From your life? Or from our life? I think there's something missing from our marriage, because there's something missing from your life. I don't know what that is. God knows, I've tried to help you figure it out. I thought that's what this summer was all about."

"It was, and I've been giving my life a lot of thought. I didn't think *Bloomin'* would keep me on, so I figured I'd be job hunting soon. One thing I might like to do is hang around at the production office. That end of the business has a lot of appeal for me."

"What would you do there?"

He crushed his cigarette out without finishing it. "I don't know. Just watch and look at what's going on. It'll be hard once we're in rehearsal, but the office is on the next block. I can start going over there as soon as we get back to New York. Maybe they'll even give me something to do." The *Bloomin'* Company had set up a hole in the wall on 44th Street. Zack originally tried to set up a corner of his office for the production work, but it interfered with his regular business.

I was pleased. "It sounds like a great idea." I kissed him and put my head against his chest. "Let's wait a little longer to have a baby, okay?"

He stroked my hair. "Okay."

We went back to New York the next day, and true to his word, Art began to spend time at the office. They were happy for his help and used him for clerical work, messenger work and phone work. He was like a new man.

I, in the meantime, tried to write the story of Sulynn's wedding as a fairy-tale romance, sans parolee ushers, an unkempt groom, a nearly-nude bridesmaid, a drunken aunt and vultures with packages of Reynolds Wrap inside their jackets. The photographer played along, and when the article finally appeared, it looked and sounded like the Wedding of the Year.

The day before rehearsals were due to begin, Sulynn called. "Hey, how was the honeymoon?" I asked her.

"It was wonderful, except for the flight over. Clark's dad is in the service, so we got an army flight to some outpost in Germany for only ten dollars per person. Sounds good, right?"

"It sounds unbelievable. What was the catch?"

"Ready for this one? Our seats were in the very last row of the plane — up against the wall, so they didn't recline, and right next to the bathroom. So not only no sleep, but constant traffic and smell."

"Leave it to you to complain about a ten-dollar flight to Europe."

"I'm not through. In the middle of the flight, the attendant passed out barf bags because the plane went into maneuvers. Did you ever see those stunt planes? That's what happened! The plane starts turning upside down and dropping ten thousand feet in two seconds. Well, everybody started throwing up, except for Clark. He slept right through it. And get this. He wanted to fly back that way! I said, forget it!"

"It must have been horrible, for you to say that. How was the rest of the trip?"

"It was gorgeous. Paris was my favorite. It was so romantic. You and Art should go sometime. Things any better?"

I flopped into our blue bean bag chair, and we talked for a while. I told her everything, as usual. Just as I was about to hang up, she said, "Oh, by the way, I've got to write some thank you notes..." Her voice got suddenly more baby-like. "Do you think you could help me?"

"You know," I said, "here I am, about to embark on a fabulous Broadway career, and I have a husband who wants me to get pregnant, an agent who wants me to type his memoirs and a best friend who wants me to identify soup tureens. By the way, are you still using that planter as a doorstop?"

"A planter! Is that what it is?"

"I give up," I said.

Act II, Scene 2

1973 – 1974

This was success, as measured by the world. Or at least by unemployed New York actors.

Bloomin' no longer resembled the *Bloomin'* of Cofis Summer Theater, the *Bloomin'* of a showcase, the *Bloomin'* of summer stock, or the *Bloomin'* of off-Broadway. The new *Bloomin'* was less about flower children and more about relationships; less about protest and more about romance; less about Vietnam and more about the music business.

In retrospect, it was a good thing. The old *Bloomin'* was almost past its prime by the time we got the go-ahead for Broadway.

Bobby, Sulynn, Art, Amalia and I made our way through these changes in the show and in our characters, many times finding it painful. But a lot of the pain dissipated when we discovered ourselves one Sunday on the front of the Arts and Leisure Section in *The New York Times*. The article was called "Moving a Production to Broadway in Uncertain Times." You couldn't pay for that kind of publicity.

Despite this, we almost lost Bobby, on whom the show heavily depended. More than any of us, Bobby did not like the changes in *Bloomin'*, even though his part was now almost equal to mine.

"Hey," Sulynn said to me one day. "Did you hear Bobby was offered a new production of *Threepenny Opera* and that he might take it?"

"No," I answered, disturbed. "Are you sure?"

"Yes. Holly told me about it. They want him for the Jack the Knife role."

"Sulynn," I sighed. "It's Mack the Knife."

"Mack the Knife. Why am I thinking about Jack the Ripper?"

I didn't bother to answer, as it was useless anyway. It was typical of Bobby not to mention *Threepenny Opera*. Art and I went over to see him that evening. Holly was back in Cofis visiting, and he was alone, except for their cat, Circe.

"So what's the story?" I confronted him. "Are you going to give your notice before we even open?"

"I'm not happy with the show," he said, not asking me where I'd heard about his offer.

"What does Harry say?" Art asked.

I didn't give Bobby a chance to answer. "Are you kidding? It's more money, or he wouldn't have sent Bobby in to audition."

Art said, "Harry's just thinking about the money, Bobby, but you've got to think about your reputation. It doesn't look good for you to walk out now. Once *Bloomin'* opens, there will be all kinds of job offers for you, and you can leave as soon as your contract is up. You know what this show is going to do for you."

"There wouldn't be any *Bloomin'* without you, Bobby," I said. "I know you've never made a pretense of being particularly loyal, but I hope you'll give this some serious thought. We need you, and we've been through a lot."

"I know. But I think we'd have been better off staying off-Broadway. To pour all this money into it and put such crap into the script, so it'll appeal to blue-haired ladies on Long Island. It makes me sick."

"I still think it's a good show, and that it says something," I said. Art went into the kitchen.

"What does it say? Almost all the political stuff is gone, and that was what Ron was about."

"Okay, the focus has changed," I admitted, taking a beer from Art. "It doesn't make it a bad show. I like the new music. Give it a chance."

"I'll think about it," he promised.

On the way home, I asked Art, "What do you think he'll do?"

He chuckled. "Don't ask me to second-guess my brother. That's a lost cause. You see what he's like. Holly's hanging around and hanging around, and he's not going to do anything about her. One day she'll put too much pressure on him, and he'll throw her out. Maybe that's how he sees *Bloomin'* now, as a commitment he can't make all the way, so it's time for it to go. All I know is, if they cut my part any more, I'll be an offstage voice."

But we both knew that really didn't bother him. Art had become very involved in the production end of *Bloomin'*, to the point of getting a title, Production Coordinator, and some extra money in his weekly paycheck. The back office was now much more interesting to him than what happened on stage.

Bloomin' began previews the following week in its new theater, the Avery, which, by Broadway standards, was a small house. Lettie was on hand taking notes in the audience. She saw the show six times before it opened. Each night something was cut, added, switched. I often went on stage and, in the middle of a scene, broke into a sweat, not sure if the line I was about to say or the song I was to sing was still in the show.

Compared to the rest of us, Howard and Beverly were newcomers, but they found the going as rough as we did. Howard, if the story about the Porgy-Who-Stood-Up was true, had never been one to keep his thoughts to himself. During one performance, in the middle of a scene, he announced, "This is ridiculous. I have no idea where I am," left the stage and returned with his script which lay off stage right. The audience laughed and applauded, while Sulynn, Beverly and I stood on stage, trying to keep in character.

"Okay," he announced. "It's the next scene that's cut, girls. But I guess I don't sing my song now."

"You're going to get fined for this," Bertha told him after the show. But he just shrugged.

Art, Bobby and I went to Joe Allen's with Howard and Fred after the performance, and Howard told us where he got his nerve. "I started in opera," he said, "and I was told the best thing to do was to get a job in Europe. So I did. I went to Europe, and I got a job in a little opera house. My first role was singing Sarastro in *The Magic Flute.*

"What everyone failed to tell me was that in Europe, the opera directors feel the only way they can make a name for themselves is by causing a scandal with a production. So the production was set in 1944 Germany.

"So opening night, here I am, a black American, and I have to walk on a German stage in 1966 wearing a Nazi uniform. I knew if I could survive that, I could survive anything. Believe me, I haven't been afraid to speak up since."

"Is it true? About *Porgy and Bess*, I mean," I asked him, when the laughter subsided.

"That's a long story, and one I'd rather not rehash." He changed the subject and said, "I think in spite of everything, this show is going to be a hit." I stole a look at Fred.

"It doesn't bother me," Fred assured me. "I believe in fate. If I hadn't been replaced by Howard, we never would have met. See? There's a reason for everything."

"What I want to know," Howard said, poking a French fry into the ketchup on his plate, "is, if the Younger Gaines is going to stay."

"At least for this contract period, he will," I said, relieved. We hadn't discussed it further, nor had Bobby given his notice.

"The guy's good," Howard said. "And you're dynamite."

Five days before we opened, I woke up, a bundle of fizzled dynamite.

I couldn't talk, let alone sing. My throat wasn't sore, but when I opened my mouth, nothing came out. I went to the famous Dr. Jahren, throat doctor to the stars.

Besides heat treatments in his office, Dr. Jahren gave me pills, a schedule for gargling and drinking tea, a throat spray, and above all, orders that I wasn't to talk or sing. "Your focal corts are seferely svollen," he told me.

The cortisone spray looked like it grew off my hand. I was never without it. Art waited on me hand and foot, making me tea, preparing my gargle and buying me boxes of Kleenex, so I could cry with security.

I sat in the audience during previews alternately sobbing and spraying, as my understudy played Mandy. I tried to concentrate on what the show looked like, now that I had an opportunity to actually see it, and to gauge the audience reaction close-up.

There was no way I could be objective. I thought my understudy was awful. I looked past her and watched the rest of the show.

Without me, it looked like the Bobby Gaines Show, which was fine. The audience couldn't get enough of him. Amalia was not good. Or was it that I was in no position to judge? Sulynn was adorable, and Art was excellent. Just days earlier, his part had been restored to its former size.

In the transition to Broadway, the chorus grew from four to eight, and the new choreographer gave the dances a jazz rather than ballet orientation, and they were terrific. Of the old chorus from the 16th St. Playhouse and summer stock tour, only Tracy, now engaged to Sulynn's criminal usher/cousin, and Marilyn, my understudy, remained. The swing was doing Marilyn's chorus assignments while I was out sick, and she was a better dancer than Marilyn ever dreamed of being. As the swing, she had to know the routines of each chorus woman.

All in all, I liked *Bloomin'* and mingled in the lobby at intermission to see what the audience had to say about it. "I think it'll run," I heard one man say to his wife.

"The music is gorgeous," a woman said, fanning herself with her program.

"I hate coming to a show and seeing understudies," grumbled another.

"I could do without that rock singer," a man said, referring to Howard.

"I see that girl on my soap opera. She just got married in real life," one woman told another.

"Hi, Margo. Eavesdropping?"

I looked up to see the new Mr. Sulynn and the best man, Lars Andersen. I had two words to describe Lars: "hubba-hubba."

I mouthed, "Hello, Clark. Hello, Lars," and pointed to my throat. Then I threw my head back and sprayed my vocal cords with my trusty cortisone spray.

"Yes, hello," Lars said, kissing my hand. "I hope that you will be well for the opening. If you need anything" — Lars was a doctor at an East Side hospital — "please call on me."

I pantomimed "Thank you." Then I pointed into the theater and to my head.

"What did I think of the show?" Lars asked. "I think it is magnificent. Very American. I like it."

"It's going great," Clark assured me. "But not nearly what it's like when you're up there. It's amazing how the dynamics change with just one cast change. Wait until you hear Margo sing, Lars. Her voice is wonderful."

I smiled in thanks and fervently hoped Lars, and everyone else who saw *Bloomin'* after it opened, would have a chance to hear me.

Backstage, as I was congratulating the cast, a petite, beautifully dressed brunette of about twenty-eight approached me.

"Margo Gaines, I've been waiting to meet you," she pumped my hand. "I'm Corinne Goodwin. I'm doing publicity for the show."

I pointed to my throat and shook her hand.

"I know, I know," she laughed. "I hope you're going to recover soon. As soon as you can talk, I want to get together with you and arrange some interviews with the press, that kind of thing. Can I call you?"

I nodded, and wondered if there would be any reason to be involved in *Bloomin'* publicity.

But Dr. Jahren wasn't a famous doctor for nothing. I followed his orders to the letter, with Art's help, and the day before our official opening, the doctor told me I would be able to sing the performance.

I went home immediately and vocalized very carefully, easing myself through the vocalization slowly and lightly. On one hand, I didn't want my voice to be stiff, so I needed to vocalize and also to talk; on the other, I didn't want to strain myself.

My parents, my brother, his wife, and a bunch of aunts, uncles and cousins arrived in town the day before the opening. Art kept everyone at bay, he and Lettie going to dinner not only with my family, but also with Sulynn's parents.

"How are you feeling?" he asked when he got home.

"Good." I was still jittery about talking and did so self-consciously, every word a test.

"Talk a little more," he said. "You have to know you can do it."

He made tea, and as we relaxed on the couch, he talked about his evening with "the families." I forced myself to speak in a normal tone of voice. Then I sang a scale. "I think I'll be fine tomorrow," I said. "But I don't want to talk any more."

He leaned forward and kissed me. "Then don't. We'll do something else instead."

The next morning, Wednesday, October 31st, 1973, the day of our opening, Art brought me breakfast in bed. "Star treatment," he announced. At eleven o'clock, I did yoga exercises and vocalized for the first time. My voice was there. I did my monologues full voice.

"I'm going out," Art yelled from the next room. "Want anything?"

"No," I answered.

"Take a nap if you can," he called back.

"Taking a nap on the day of an opening. Remember Eve in *All About Eve*? I don't think I've got what it takes."

I kept telling myself this was my opening night on Broadway, but it didn't register. I read part of an Agatha Christie story, went out for a walk, came back, sang some more, lay down in the dark, got up and started to pack my things for the theater.

Art didn't get home till nearly six. "Where have you been?" I asked him. "We should be leaving soon."

"I wanted to give you a chance to rest," he said. He stood behind me in the bedroom and rubbed my neck and shoulders. It was very relaxing. I faced him, and he took me in his arms.

"Is sex good or bad before a performance?" I asked, tugging at his belt.

"There are different theories." He put his hands over mine and removed them. "But it can't hurt afterwards. I think it might wipe us out now."

I sighed. "You're right."

We fed Sammy and Deli and set off for the theater. "Well, Art, we made it," I said as we climbed into a cab. "Tonight we open on Broadway. I thought it was going to feel like something, but it doesn't."

"That's because we haven't done it yet. It's gotta feel like *something.*"

The nerves didn't hit me until I saw the theater. Suddenly, it was real. Art and I looked at the marquee, which we'd seen a million times.

"It's starting to feel like something," I told him. "And I'm not sure I like it."

My dressing room was filled with flowers: red roses from Harry and Zelda; a basket of flowers from my brother; roses from my parents. There were cards and telegrams all over my mirror and wall from Foss, Tom, Zack, Fred, clients and employees of Harry and Zelda's, people from Rochester, college friends.

I sat in my dressing room, pouring tea from the thermos Art had prepared for me, and quietly panicked. Suppose my voice gave out in the middle of the show, suppose I couldn't make my high notes, suppose I couldn't keep the changes straight. I grabbed for my script and thumbed through it.

Outside my door, I could hear the cast and crew assembling, and fragments of their conversation drifted into my room. "Break a leg, everybody." "Good show." "In bocca." "What the hell's 'in bocca?'" "Something about delivering you from the mouth of a wolf."

I had opening night gifts for the cast, crew and production staff. As a calming exercise, I took each wrapped gift out of the shopping bag and piled them up on the card table in my dressing room. I wasn't any calmer. I vocalized.

There was a knock at the door, and Sulynn poked her head in. "You sound great, honey. Break a leg." She ran in, and we hugged each other.

"Are you nervous?" I asked her.

"Nah. What's there to be nervous about? We've done it a trillion times." We stared at each other. "BROADWAY," we yelped, then clung to each other. "If I forget any lines," she said as she left, "cover for me, okay? You're so good at improvising."

As I put on my makeup, nearly everyone connected with the show knocked on my door with encouragement, hope, luck, broken limbs, wolves-in-mouths, "toi-toi-toi" from Howard, and from Bertha, "half hour," followed by "fifteen minutes", followed by "five minutes."

I grabbed my guitar as Art opened the door. "Ready?" he asked.

"As ready as I'll ever be. I wouldn't be here tonight without you."

It wasn't a summer stock audience, an off-Broadway audience or a preview audience anymore. *Bloomin'* had made it to the big time, and I couldn't let it down.

I stood in the wings with my eyes closed and listened to the overture, using the music to center myself and concentrate.

The music stopped. Applause. The theater sounded packed. I heard the curtain. I saw my spotlight.

I walked to stage left with my guitar and sat on the stool.

"We're all bloomin'," I began. "Flowers starting to rise..."

Bobby's spot hit stage right. "New in the sun, just opening our eyes..."

Sulynn was next, upstage center. "Feeling the warm, learning the day..."

Art sat down center. "Bloomin', and hopin' to stay..."

In every performer's life, there is only one Broadway debut, if you're lucky enough to get there. Mine remains a fog to this day. I had no sense of anything other than being Mandy Morgan, a sweet young thing who sings her way through becoming a revolutionary. Once I knew my voice wouldn't leave me, I let loose and within what seemed like minutes, I stood off stage left, waiting for my curtain call.

My co-actors were kissing me and slapping me on the back, but I was numb. I watched the chorus bow. Beverly was next, to very appreciative applause. She broke to the right, and Howard came out to enthusiastic yells. He threw his arms out, then collapsed his entire upper body towards his knees. Howard was always "Live to you from Las Vegas."

Next was Amalia. Was it my imagination, or did the applause let up — a lot? There was a lone "brava" from the audience.

"I guess her husband's here," Sulynn said.

Then Art. And there was no doubt, if there had been an applause meter, it would have gone all the way up.

Sulynn turned to me, excited. "They liked him," she squeaked, as she ran out for her bow. The audience loved her.

Bobby, handsome and sweaty, ran out on stage, and at that point, I started crying. "Bravo," I heard voices in the audience cheer, and I saw some people stand. Oh, swell, I said to myself. They're leaving, and the curtain calls aren't even over.

Bobby looked stage left and indicated me with his hand, lining up next to Sulynn as he did so. Out I went, tears making the walk a little difficult. To my utter amazement, most of the people in the theater stood up, and instead of some intermittent cheering throughout the theater, the whole audience seemed to be yelling.

The principals formed a line and bowed, then I went to the side and brought out our conductor-musical director, plus Len, Foss and Tom, to tumultuous applause.

The curtain fell, then zipped right back up again, and the principals walked forward and bowed again, three more times. The audience was still applauding.

"EVERYBODY CLEAR THE STAGE!" screamed Bertha as she ran over to us. These were the "in case" bows, but the cast was so dazed, we hadn't realized they were needed. Bertha scattered the rest of the cast, got Bobby and me in a half nelson, and shoved us forward as the curtain went up for a fourth time. We smiled at each other and took a sight cue off each other to bow in sync. Curtain. Continued applause.

"BOBBY GAINES!" Bertha roared. "MARGO — CLEAR OUT!"
Bobby took another bow.

"MARGO!" she howled. "ENTIRE COMPANY — GET READY!"

After my bow and a last company bow, it was over. Art swooped me up and swung me around. "You were right," I said, still crying. "It did feel like something."

"We've done it!" he yelled, kissing me.

Once the reviews were out, there was no stopping *Bloomin'*. All the television stations gave us raves. *The Post* headline said, "A Family of Stars," and underneath — "The Gaines clan lights up *Bloomin'*." *The Daily News* called us "an uplifting evening" and *The New York Times*: "Bright, intimate and beautifully sung," but went on to say: "The production was better served off-Broadway."

Despite all the fantasies young performers indulge in, I was unprepared for what success in a Broadway show really meant. I had visions of sleeping until noon, drinking mint juleps on the veranda and rolling into the theater eight times a week with shopping bags stuffed with my day's purchases.

Instead, there were interviews, benefits and understudy rehearsals. I worked with both a voice teacher and a vocal coach to keep my voice in shape. Sulynn and I joined a gym.

The publicist, Corinne, saw that our names were in the paper for every little thing. The glamour couple, of course, was Clark and Sulynn, and their names were always appearing in one gossip column or another for the most inane things, mostly fabricated. "Pert Susan

Reilly, who appears by day in 'A Bright Tomorrow' and by night in the hit musical, *Bloomin'*, burns her candle not only at both ends but in the middle. In private life, she is Mrs. Clark Davidson. He's the handsome Matt Jamison of 'A Bright Tomorrow.' I asked her how she juggles all her duties, and she laughed merrily. 'Easy. I never sleep!'"

The columnists must have been desperate. "Pretty Margo Gaines and hubby Art Gaines were at Joe Allen's last night, along with Margo's agent, Harry Lasker, and it looked like they were all pretty cozy with an executive from Columbia Records. Could there be a platter in silver-voiced Margo's future?"

No such meeting took place, but a record company, evidently as a result of this item, did contact Harry and ask if I'd signed any contract yet.

Although Art was approached by several agents seeking to represent him, he eschewed pursuing a performance career and instead became my manager. Before I knew it, I was rehearsing a late-night cabaret act, produced by Art, which opened at the Ballroom at midnight, March 9th, 1974. Of course, I kept having to add new material.

So much for the mint juleps and the shopping trips.

The dumb luck of the situation was not lost on any of us. Had it not been for the happenstance of *Bloomin'*, and my going to work for Harry Lasker — Bobby, Art, Sulynn and I would probably have been, at the time of the 1973 Broadway opening, just arriving in New York, clutching our savings account passbooks. It was heady stuff, and all of us tried to handle it as best we could. But sometimes, it was overwhelming.

Harry was bombarded with offers for Bobby from the TV and movie crowd, and as a result, he refused to allow Bobby to do any commercials. "Pie in the sky, pie in the sky," Bobby complained to him one night at the theater. "All they want to do is test me for this garbage. No one's actually offered me anything. I have a chance to make real money, and you won't let me."

"It just seems like it happens overnight, Bobby," Harry reminded him. "But it really doesn't."

I still have a photograph of myself, taken for *Vogue* magazine, up on my wall. It's a picture of me standing in profile, wearing a black evening gown slit all the way up my leg. My head is tilted back, and I'm blowing soap bubbles. The caption reads, "Margo Gaines, floating to success in a bubble named *Bloomin'*."

My bubble burst.

It burst at the most peculiar time, when I was at the pinnacle of my success with the show. My contract had just been renegotiated, and Bobby's name and mine were now above the title. I was doing my cabaret act at midnight on Friday and Saturday nights, and I received wonderful reviews. I was sent original material by a brilliant young songwriter, and Art was negotiating with two record companies for me to record some of the music. Bobby, Sulynn and I were named Theater Award Winners for 1974. *Bloomin'* was nominated for a Tony in the Best Musical category. Bobby and I each received nominations, and one of the ensemble numbers, "Up the Establishment," was opening the Tony Award ceremonies. In the midst of this, disaster.

I was in my dressing room taking off my makeup one Thursday night about seven months into the run, when Sulynn crashed in without knocking. Every night without fail, once all the nominations and awards had been announced, Sulynn came in and discussed what we would wear to both the Theater World ceremonies and to the Tony Awards.

I could see Sulynn in the mirror. Her face looked as if she had been assaulted by twenty squirting lemons.

"What's the matter with you?" I asked, ripping off my false eyelashes. "You look awful."

"Not as awful as you're going to look." She dragged a chair across the room and sat next to me. "Margo Girard Gaines, you get your head out of the clouds right now."

There was a knot in my stomach. I knew this tone of voice only too well. "What's wrong?"

"What's wrong? Where have you been? Oh, don't tell me. I've known you too long. What's wrong? What in hell is going on between Art and that publicity woman, that Corinne or whatever her name is?"

"I don't know what you mean."

She stood up and crossed her arms in front of her chest. "Did you know it's *all over the company* that they're fooling around?"

If she'd thrown a medicine ball at my stomach, she couldn't have stunned me more. "Sulynn," I began, "you're crazy. Where did you hear such a thing?"

"At Tracy's engagement shower. And if you'd been there, I never would have known about it at all, naturally. Apparently it's been going on *for months*. Since *before we opened.* Goddamn it, *everybody* knows."

"Wait a minute, wait a minute. Who's everybody? Who told you this?"

She took a deep breath. "I walked in on Tracy and Marilyn in the kitchen, and they were saying something about Art and Corinne. They shut up as soon as they saw me, but I wouldn't let them leave until they told me everything.

"According to them, it's common knowledge. Before *Bloomin'* even opened, some of the guys in the chorus went to a restaurant and they saw Art and Corinne inside. As it was put to me, they looked 'real cozy,' so the guys went somewhere else. Another time, Marilyn and Tracy went to the same place, and when they got to the door, the same thing happened — Art and Corinne — so they left. Now it's gotten to be a big game, tiptoeing by this joint. Evidently they're always there. It's been going on all along."

I shook my head. "This is crazy. For one thing, Art and Corinne work together..."

Sulynn abruptly grabbed my shoulders and shook me. "Margo, wake up! Does he tell you that he hangs out with her while you're singing your club act? Does he? Where does he say he is? What does he do during the day?"

"Sulynn —" I broke away from her. "I don't keep tabs on Art. Why should I? Look, there's an explanation for this. I just wish someone had come to me before."

"Margo, you listen to me. I won't have you humiliated any further. Now, I told Tracy and Marilyn they were wrong and they were to tell the other kids it's not true, but I want you to talk to Art and find out what's going on."

"Do you seriously think Art is cheating on me?"

She studied me long and hard. "I'll tell you this. I think, as usual, you don't know one day from another. Your head has been in nirvana since the day I met you. You never pick up on a damn thing until it hits you in the face. I know you've had problems with Art in the past, and while I admit he's not the unfaithful type, I also know he's a Gaines. That means he's screwed up. My advice to you is to confront him with this, and if it's not true, fine. But find out."

"Do you think Bobby's heard about it?"

"If he has, he'd never say anything, and you know it."

"Sulynn, if this were true, I'd know."

"No, you wouldn't. How's the sex between you? And how often?"

I could feel myself getting defensive. "It's fine. You know what my schedule is like, what all our schedules are like. On the nights I do my act, I don't get home till two." My mind was racing.

"Get with it, Margo," Sulynn said. "Find out what's going on. He's already left the theater. Where did he say he was going?"

"He said he was meeting some record people who saw the show, and that he'd be home in a couple of hours."

Without definitely formulating any thoughts, I ran past her and banged on Howard's dressing room door. Fred was with him.

"Howard," I said. "I need a favor. Go talk to some of the chorus people..."

Howard's eyes lit up before I could finish. "Good girl!" he said, punching my arm. "We want the One O'Clock Café on Ninth Avenue. Get your bag, Margo. We'll go with you."

I sank into a chair. "So everybody thinks they know something but me," I said, unable to look at them. Fred didn't answer, but hugged me.

The One O'Clock Café was off the beaten track of after-theater places, with good reason. It was an all-night dive that looked like a truck stop.

"I used to come here years ago when I did a showcase around the corner," Howard said. "They have good food and plenty of it, cheap. It's a great place for young actors."

I felt relieved. So far, there was no sign of Art and Corinne. We sat in a corner booth. I faced away from the door.

Fred looked at me with concern. "Waitress," he called out. "Do you serve any alcohol?" He massaged my hand and ordered me white wine.

"How long have you known about this?" I asked them.

Fred leaned forward. "Margo, honest to God, we didn't want to say anything before we could prove it, I swear to you. Howard's been staking Art out while I'm at work during the day. Anything to find out what's going on. He's followed him."

I was stunned. "You've been *tailing* him? How is it he hasn't seen you?" Howard was not exactly non-descript. A six-foot black man with an Afro that made the actor from "Mod Squad" look like Telly Savalas.

"I've seen my share of Bogart movies," he said, grinning. "Believe me, he hasn't noticed a thing."

"We tried to follow them from here one night," Fred said. "But he got her a cab here and then went off alone."

"I don't believe you guys."

Howard continued, "Well, the latest is, I've followed Art a few times to an apartment house on West 76th Street, but Corinne's name isn't on any mail box or buzzer. She's not in the phone book."

I was stubborn. "It still wouldn't have meant anything. I don't know what everyone's so excited about. Art would not cheat on me. And even if he did, he wouldn't be so stupid as to get mixed up with someone involved in the show."

"Look, Margo." Fred shook his head slowly from side to side. "I grew up with Bobby and Art, and I love them like brothers. But if I were married to one of them, or even going with one of them, I wouldn't trust them from here to the door. It all looks real glistening and gleaming, to hear Lettie talk, but she's a con artist from way back. Those kids got messed up early on, especially Art.

"Now, when you married Art, I said okay, if anyone can make it work, it's Margo. And then I started hearing this shit. I'm not married to him, so I don't have stars in my eyes."

"Well, hold onto your hats," Howard muttered, "because here they come."

I held my breath, not daring to turn around. Howard covered himself and Fred with a menu.

"Is he with her?" I whispered.

"Yes," I heard Fred say from behind the menu.

"Oh, God, what do I do now?" I said, putting my elbows on the table and hiding my face with my hands.

"You guys were great," I heard a voice say. There was a man standing on my left. "Wonderful show."

Howard lowered the menu. "Thank you," we said. The man left. I kept eyes forward. "Where are they? Have they seen you?"

Howard's head met mine in the middle of the table. "They still haven't seen us, believe it or not. They're way over in the corner."

"I'm going to faint," I announced.

"Don't faint," Howard said, through his teeth. "We need to get their reaction to seeing us here."

"How are they acting?"

Fred wasn't pulling any punches. "They came in holding hands."

I put my hand over my mouth as if I were going to throw up. "We're not ready yet," Fred snapped at the waitress who was trying to take our order.

I could feel myself getting angry. "Fred, change places with me. Now!" He came around to my side of the table as I scooted past him and sat next to Howard. I looked at Art and Corinne. It was no wonder they hadn't seen us. They were sitting side by side, gazing into each other's eyes.

"They must think this is Sardi's," I said. "It's the only place I've ever been where they sit you next to each other on the same side of a normal table."

"Good, good, keep your humor." Fred patted his sweating forehead with a handkerchief. Spy work didn't agree with him.

I stared and stared, until Art looked over toward us.

The look on his face was one of sheer terror. First he turned chalk white, then red. He casually said something to Corinne. I saw her eyes wander over my way, then her body jerk in a sharp intake of breath.

Suddenly, I felt in control. I smiled my biggest smile at the waitress. "We're ready to order now," I said. "But first, do you think it's possible to bring us a large pitcher of water?"

"Margo, what are you doing?" Fred asked me.

"I'm thirsty," I said. I busied myself studying the menu. The restaurant was slowly filling up.

The waitress brought the water, and I poured everyone half a glass. I ordered what I usually did after the show: a Swiss cheese omelet, toast and coffee. Fred and Howard ordered. I had no idea what was going on across the room. "Keep cool," I reminded them. Then I laughed out loud, to keep up pretenses. Under my breath, I said, "I have no doubt from the look on his face that something's going on. Do you?" I nudged Howard.

"No," said Howard.

"How did he look?" Fred asked. "I wish I could turn around."

"Don't," I warned him. I laughed again, louder.

Howard joined in the laughter, then lowered his voice. "He looked like she caught them fucking," he said. "He wishes he were dead."

I smiled. "He will be."

"He can't stand the heat, so he's getting out of Hell's kitchen," Howard said. "They're leaving."

"He'll stop by here first," I said, as the waitress brought our coffee. "He has to."

Sure enough, Art and Corinne, having decided on a story, no doubt, walked over to our table. Art's attempts at a casual smile told the world why he was quitting his acting career. He couldn't pull it off.

"Hey, you guys," he said. "Out slumming?"

I beamed. "One might ask the same of you," I said. "Where are my record producers?"

"Oh, Bertha took a phone message saying they couldn't make it, and on my way out, I ran into Corinne here..."

She grinned. "Trying to get some good dish from the chorus boys to plant in one of the columns..."

"And I asked her if she wanted to get something to eat."

"I guess she didn't," I said, "since you're leaving. But maybe you're both thirsty." With that, I doused them with the pitcher of water. Unfortunately, it also splashed a woman at the table directly behind them.

I took my purse, walked between a dazed and wet Art and Corinne and approached the table, where the woman sat, her blouse stuck to her back and the bottom of her hair soaking wet. Her escort was frantically handing her napkins, as were people at the other tables, and she was half-moaning, half-crying.

"I'm TERRIBLY sorry," I said at the top of my lungs. "I just caught my husband with a woman he's been screwing for about seven months. I'm SURE you understand. I'm VERY upset." I pulled some money from my bag and gave it to the waitress. "Do you think you could help this woman?" I asked her. "Take her in back, dry her off. Maybe you've got a sweater or something." I threw money on the table. "This should cover your meal." As I walked out of the restaurant, some people applauded me.

The phone was ringing as I entered the apartment — probably Howard and Fred. I let it ring, intending to call them as soon as I was finished with the next task. I was like a robot, mechanical and unfeeling. Making sure Sammy and Deli were in the living room, I closed the bedroom door, then threw open the window. I emptied all of Art's belongings out into the street — underwear, socks, T-shirts, suits, dress shirts, ties, shoes — the works. I watched them land on 89th Street.

My apartment building soon took on the aura of a garage sale, as pedestrians picked through Art's things and held them up against their companions. Satisfied, I closed the window.

I called Howard and Fred's place. No answer. I called their service and left my name and a message: "Thank you." Then I called Sulynn, who must have been sitting next to the phone. She picked it up on the first half-ring.

"What happened?"

"It was true," I said. "I just threw all his stuff out the window."

"Do you want to come over and stay?"

"No. He wouldn't dare come back here tonight. I'm going to chain-lock the door anyway."

"I'll be right there." She hung up before I could protest.

Sulynn and Clark only lived three blocks away. She buzzed me from downstairs ten minutes later. As I let her into the apartment, she said, "It looks like a fire sale down there. I'm not sure you should have done that."

I didn't answer. Collapsing into the bean bag chair, I picked up the glass of wine beside it. Joanie Mitchell's *Blue* album, the one that was playing on the stereo the night Art and I became engaged, again resounded throughout the apartment. Sulynn turned it off.

"What's that scene you always loved?" she said. "You know — *All About Eve*, when they hear that German thing on the radio?"

"Something about hating sentiment."

"Yes. Don't indulge in it now, of all times." I noticed she had an overnight bag with her that she put into the bedroom. "Margo, can you talk about it at all?" She curled up on the couch.

For the first time, the tears came, in a flood of self-recrimination, embarrassment, anger and fear. "It's like he's dead," I sobbed. "Like somebody just told me he died."

"You should be so lucky."

"But how is it that I didn't *know*? How could I have not seen it, how could he have fooled me?"

She dragged me over to the couch and put her arms around me as I cried on her shoulder. "Margo, so much has been going on with you, with all of us. You're not going to like this, but I think he got you mixed up in that club act and the demo record and everything else to keep you in the dark."

That threw me into fresh hysteria. "You're not describing Art. You're describing a person I don't even know. A monster. That's what hurts most of all. I thought he loved me."

"Margo, I'm sure Art does love you. But Art's like everybody else in this world. He takes the easy, convenient road. And if you're really honest, you'll admit you're not any different. Why did the two of you get married when you did? It was easy and convenient. Everyone was pairing up, and it seemed like the thing to do, an easy solution to the roommate situation. I'm not trying to be mean about it, but it was too damn quick.

"And I think it was easy for you not to see what was going on right in front of you. All this domestic stuff gets in the way of your performing, Margo, and you're the first to admit that. You played right into Art's hands. This babe probably doesn't mean anything to him, but Art's an insecure man with a Broadway star for a wife. I'm sure Corinne knew just how to play him."

It was 3 a.m. before we went to bed, Sulynn on the couch, sleeping over at her own insistence. My head weighed a ton, and three aspirins hadn't helped. I lay in bed exhausted, but unable to do anything but cry.

I heard the door, stopped from opening completely by the inside chain.

"Margo?" It was Art, and his voice sounded pained.

"Get out of here, Art." Sulynn. I went into the living room.

"Margo, please, I've got to talk to you."

"Art, you're drunk," Sulynn said. She turned to me. "Go back to bed, Margo. I'll take care of him." I held my ground, trembling.

"Go away, Art," she said, going toward the door. "Margo can't talk to you now. Just go."

He banged on the door. "MARGO," he yelled. "MARGO."

Sulynn's voice pitch matched his. "Art, if you don't clear out, I'm calling the police."

He continued to bang on the door, calling my name. My neighbor from across the hall, a man who was always telling our landlord, "Just because I'm home doesn't mean I'm in," now got into the act.

"What's going on?" he yelled.

"Call the police," Sulynn yelled back, trying to push the door shut.

We heard Art run down the stairs. "Do you think he'll go to Corinne's apartment?" I sobbed.

"Margo, don't think about where he'll go. Just get back to bed."

At that moment, a rock came flying through the window. Had Sulynn been standing two inches to the right, it would have creamed her. I looked out the window and saw Art running up the block, carrying a pile of his clothes (those rejected by the pedestrians). The police knocked at the door a few minutes later.

We probably got two hours sleep. At 8 a.m. Sulynn went out for croissants and came back with *The Post*. The front page had my publicity photo, next to the headline "BROADWAY STAR IN MARITAL BRAWL...story on page 6." The story reported only what happened at the apartment. However, the man who had congratulated me in the restaurant then called the newspaper and told them about *that* incident, thus giving *The Post* a second day of what they called "The Gaines Feud."

Sulynn took the phone off the hook, got someone to fix the window, had the lock changed on my door and went so far as to find out about the service exit for the building. I had a long day ahead of me. Not only *Bloomin'*, where I would be on stage with Art, but my act afterward. I was dreading it, physically and emotionally. A nap was out of the question, but Sulynn made me stay in the bedroom and try to rest anyway. At 5 p.m., we made our way out the back of the building and got a cab to the theater. "No one will hang around the stage door till around six," she reasoned. "This will give you a chance to lock yourself in your dressing room before Art gets there."

Sulynn acted like a Secret Service agent, belying her petite appearance. She left me inside the stage door, while she went ahead and made sure there was no one I didn't want to see hanging around. Then she led me to my dressing room, locked me in and made two trips in order to move everything from her dressing room to mine. "You'll need someone to answer the door for you," she reasoned. I pitied anyone trying to get past her.

And a lot of them tried. Sulynn got rid of Harry, Zack and Foss by saying I'd call each of them when I felt better. She let in Howard and Fred, "But only for a few minutes," she warned. They brought me flowers. When I started to cry, Sulynn said, "I knew this was a bad idea. Look, guys, give her a couple of days," and they left. When Holly appeared at the door, Sulynn went into the hall to speak with her.

"Did Holly say where Art is staying?" I asked Sulynn when she returned.

"Holly doesn't know a damn thing."

"Then that means he's staying with Corinne."

"Margo, you can't brood about this right now." Sulynn began to apply her makeup. "Just get through these next couple of days of doing this show and your club act. Then you've got a day and a half to figure things out. But you've got to hold yourself together till then."

She was right. But it didn't keep me from listening for Art or Bobby at the door. Neither of them knocked.

At half hour, Sulynn left the dressing room and returned a few minutes later, letting herself in with my key. "Art's going on," she said. "Can you handle it?"

"I have to."

Over the next weeks, I learned about the wonderful mechanism performers have to shut off their real emotions and turn on fake ones, and have them seem just as real. Doing *Bloomin'* face to face with Art was a breeze. And being on stage was the only peace and happiness I knew.

Offstage, there was only misery. No one was speaking to anybody else, and I all but crawled in and out of the theater to avoid everyone involved in *Bloomin'*.

Especially crushing to me was the feeling of loss. Art put letters under my door, and I ripped them up and threw them away without reading them. At home, I convinced Sulynn after two days that she could move back to her own place. I kept the phone off the hook. Every time I called the answering service, there were at least four messages from Art. I cried myself to sleep every night and wondered when I would run out of tears.

Eventually, with Sulynn's help, I packed the rest of Art's things, and Clark and Sulynn delivered them to Bobby's apartment in their new car. Sulynn was not speaking to Bobby, so she sat inside while Clark carried up box after box. According to Holly, Art wasn't staying there. Bobby avoided me like the plague offstage, so what little information I got came from her.

Dealing with my parents was another unpleasant part of the break-up. My mother blamed me, that was evident. My father, on the other hand, wanted to have a contract put out on Art. Every time I talked to them (which was as little as possible), my father got on the phone and said, "It's times like this I wish I knew some people. I'd have him taken care of."

Corinne was fired, for the simple reason that she was not the person to handle my divorce publicity, and it seemed to me the producers were planning on getting a lot of mileage from the situation. Zack hired someone else and also put me in touch with a divorce lawyer. I delayed going to see him.

I wasn't ready to talk to Lettie, but she sent me flowers and a card that said, "You're still a member of my family. Love, Lettie." I wrote her a note thanking her, and promised I'd get in touch as soon as I could. But I didn't know when that would be.

When it came time for the Tony Awards, Sulynn insisted that Lars, the handsome doctor, escort me. I flatly refused, even though I realized Art would probably be there with Corinne. As it turned out, Art did the opening number with the rest of the cast, then left before the ceremony.

Neither I, Bobby, nor *Bloomin'* won anything. It was just as well. Despite the best efforts of Sulynn to convince me to take an interest in my appearance, I looked awful. No sleep will do that to you.

I looked past Art on stage and eliminated him from my life, but when it came time to proceed with the divorce, I knew there was no putting off a meeting any longer. Harry let me use his apartment as neutral territory.

I hadn't looked Art straight in the eye in almost a month by the time of our meeting. As I let him into the apartment, I realized he'd lost weight from his normally robust frame and looked as haggard as I did.

We sat in the living room, he on the couch, I in a chair across from him. There was no small talk.

"I guess you know why I asked you to see me," I began. "I'm

getting a divorce."

He studied his fingers. "Margo, I wish you'd just listen to me first."

"I don't really want to. Your actions have spoken very well for you."

"It's not what you think. None of it is. Please. If we're going to have a meeting, let's really meet. This business of not talking is absurd."

"I have a question for you, then," I said. "It's something that's really been bothering me. The night that *Bloomin'* officially opened, I remember that you were gone all afternoon and that when you came back, I wanted to make love and you said no, it wasn't good for the energy level. What I want to know is, were you with Corinne that afternoon?"

"Margo..." His face was flushed, and he continued to look at his fingers.

"I want an answer, Art."

He sighed, but said nothing.

"Okay, then I have my answer. And I was right. There is no reason to talk."

"We never should have gotten married," he said in a rush. "We don't want the same things. When I realized that — after the show took off and I saw how it was taking you with it — I knew it was going to end up like this."

It appeared we were going to talk, whether I wanted to or not. "My understanding of your little fling was that it started before we opened. And as far as me 'taking off' with the show, you aided and abetted me every step of the way."

"I wanted you to have what you cared about. And, well, I felt guilty, so I helped you any way I could. As far as anything beginning before the show, Corinne was a sympathetic ear, nothing more. That's how it started. You don't know what you can be like, Margo. You were so involved in rehearsals. My part was getting smaller and smaller. You just got real distracted. Every time I turned around, Corinne was there. She acted interested in what I was saying, in what I wanted to do. I don't know, she was just *around*."

For the first time, our eyes met. "Margo, I don't love Corinne, I never have. You're all I wanted. You've been all I wanted since practically the day I met you. But I'm an oaf. I can't express myself, and when I do, I get scared.

"I wanted to marry you, I really did. But it was a mistake. I stopped believing in myself. The better you got, the worse I got. The more successful Bobby was, the more diminished I felt. I started hating myself. I was jealous of both of you, and I had nothing, nothing of my own.

"When it was evident that we weren't going to want the same things, I decided to make the best of it. Hell, I didn't want a divorce." His head back hit the back of the couch. "I kept thinking, okay, I'll ride it out. She's hot, the show's hot. She'll get it out of her system, and I'll get myself set up in production or whatever I'm gonna do, and we can get through this and come out the other side. We'll be ourselves again. We'll have a family."

I broke into his monologue. "And you thought the way to achieve this was to have an affair."

"*No*. But I was *lonely*. I guess you can't understand that, can you? Because you're not lonely. You're never lonely, as long as you have your voice and an audience."

"I don't think that's fair, Art, or even true. But one thing you said is correct. We never should have gotten married." I stood. "I guess you'll be sent the papers. I hope you'll sign them, and then we can get on with our lives." I started toward the door, and he followed me into the dark hall.

"Do you even care? Do you even care that I was with someone else, or is it just your pride that's hurt?"

I swirled around to face him. "Were you trying to hurt me? Are you disappointed that I'm not more devastated? Gee, I'm sorry." I opened the door. "Get out."

"A typical gesture," he said, passing me, "throwing me out of a place that's not even yours. That about sums you up, Margo. Massive ego." I slammed the door so hard the wall shook. I stood in the hall, trembling and crying. "I won't let him do this to me," I said under my breath, clenching my fists. "I won't let him upset me, I won't, I won't." I ran back into the living room and shut the paneled doors, so he wouldn't hear me crying.

I went to see the lawyer Zack Vincent had recommended. After listening to him for half an hour, I knew I couldn't go through with it, and told him so.

"There's one other option," he said. "You can get a fast Mexican divorce. If you're interested, come back next Thursday with $1500." He went on to say the $1500 covered his fee, fare to Mexico and the Mexican lawyer. My only additional expenses would be any food I ate and the one night expense of staying at the Holiday Inn in El Paso: $11.50.

I took vacation days from *Bloomin'*, and on Thursday, I arrived at the lawyer's office. There were ten other clients there to pick up their air tickets. "Be careful," the lawyer warned me before I left for the airport. "Everyone will know why you're there. That makes you vulnerable, so don't talk to anyone."

When I arrived in El Paso, I checked in at the motel and spent the night watching television. I called Sulynn to let her know I'd arrived and find out how the show was without me. The next morning, as per instructions, I left my room, and at 10 a.m., a Mexican lawyer and someone else arrived, each driving a station wagon. The potential divorcees piled in and were driven to the lawyer's office in Juarez.

Here, we were told what to expect in court and what to say. Then, back into the wagons. We headed for the courthouse, where dozens of other lawyers also transported their clients, so that there were about three hundred people awaiting divorces. I waited for my name to be called. Then I signed a paper, and in Mexico, the scene of my honeymoon, I became divorced.

We piled back into the station wagons. The trip on the way back included a stop at the local gift shop before crossing the border. I bought ten key rings in the form of miniature sombreros, assorted colors. Back at the hotel, I got my luggage, checked out and headed to the airport with the rest of the clients.

On the plane, I sat between two older men. One cried the entire trip back and the other kept saying, "Sweet Jesus, I'm free. Sweet Jesus, I'm free." I thought back to my lawyer's warning and allowed myself a chuckle. So much for being the sexual prey of lonely men.

Back in New York, I went through the motions of *Bloomin'* and reflected that all the fun had gone out of it. Art was out of my life and with him, apparently, went Bobby — I hadn't spoken to him since the break-up with Art. Sulynn had totally dropped both Art and Bobby from her list of friends.

A few days after I got the divorce, Bobby appeared at my dressing room door. I was surprised as well as pleased, and invited him in. There was a problem with the air-conditioning, so he propped open the door with a wooden block before sitting down.

He was uncomfortable. "I'm real sorry about you and Art," he said.

I burst into tears. He put his arms around me and squeezed me, but didn't say anything else.

"Well, if it isn't the Gaines family." Amalia stood in the hallway. She glared at me. "You've brought disgrace on this production!" she cried, and ran down the hallway.

I stopped crying and looked up at Bobby. He threw his head back and laughed. I laughed with him. He let go of me and doubled over, tears streaming down his face. When Bertha came to announce half hour, we were still laughing.

Art and Bobby went on vacation three weeks later, to Poland with Lettie and some of her relatives. Their understudies took over their roles.

"When are you taking your vacation?" Sulynn asked me after the show one night. We were in her apartment, and Clark was already asleep.

"I hadn't thought about it. I'm already two days down because of Mexico."

"I think you need one."

I was alarmed. "Do you think I'm lousy on stage?"

"No, but you've been through a lot. You ought to start doing something besides singing, for God's sake. Have you, for instance, thought of dating?"

"I have not. Haven't you heard? I'm all ego, and I don't need anyone. Besides, no one's interested."

"What about Lars?"

Sulynn was leading up to something.

"Has he said he's interested in me? I thought the Tony Awards were your idea."

"Not entirely. But I'll tell you something about him I'm sure you don't know. He's gay."

I tried not to act surprised. "I thought he might be."

Sulynn giggled. "No, you didn't, Margo. You always leave these things up to me. You had no idea. Actually, he *might* be bisexual. To tell you the truth, he's pretty uptight about the whole thing."

I broke a Mint Milano cookie in half. "I've never been clear about his friendship with Clark."

"Lars was an exchange student at Clark's high school. When he came back to the States, he looked up Clark. They're always talking about going into business together. You know Clark, he works with so many gays on the soap, he couldn't care less. He's the one that told me about Lars. Lars pretends to be totally straight around me.

"Anyway, here's my point. He's handsome, he's debonair, he's got an accent — a huge advantage in this town — and he's a doctor. You're not looking to get involved with anyone after what you've suffered. Why not see him from time to time? Why not have him pick you up at the theater occasionally?"

"You mean so Art will see him."

Sulynn slammed her hand down on the mahogany table. "Well,

why shouldn't he think you're dating some catch? Don't you think he deserves it? He embarrassed you, and as far as I'm concerned, you're taking it *lying down*. All you've done so far is fight him for the cats. Big deal. He paraded that tramp in front of the company, and all you can do is get misty-eyed so everyone knows how upset and hurt you are."

"But what about Bobby?"

"What about Bobby? You don't honestly care what he thinks, do you?"

"I mean he'd certainly tell Art that Lars was gay."

"How's he going to find out? I, for sure, am not going to tell him, and neither are you. He doesn't tell you his business. Why should you tell him yours? I've never understood what goes on between you two."

"Friendship," I said.

"Oh, please." Sulynn bit into her fourth cookie. "Are there violins playing? I know I carry a grudge, and I had no business being mad at him because Art cheated on you, I admit that. But do you have to be so goody-goody and peace and love all the time? You don't have to tell him everything. Go out with this guy for a while. Let Corinne's replacement get you in the gossip columns. Then tell Bobby about it."

Lars called the next day and invited me to dinner. I couldn't help but marvel at his timing. I also couldn't help but notice that he inexplicably was unable to see me on my day off; he would have to pick me up at the theater. Sulynn's doing.

Lars certainly was impressive-looking, and my stock went right up with the company when they saw him waiting for me several nights a week, after the show. There was no way that Art, once he returned from his vacation, could miss what was apparently going on, but I had no idea what his reaction was.

It was nice to be taken to dinner at the best restaurants, and fun to keep up the illusion that there was something fabulous going on. Lars played the game like a master, giving no indication of his true sexual preference, flirting and being as charming and flattering as a man could be. Had Sulynn not tipped me off, I would have been completely snowed.

Snowed, but not smitten. The hurt was too new and too deep. Lars was an interlude that was fooling the world, but not me. Each evening, when he left me off at my apartment, it was just Sammy, Deli and me inside, and that's how I preferred it. I knew Art was living in an apartment on West 78th Street, but I didn't know if he lived alone. Besides the show, I didn't know what else he was doing, and I tried not to ever think about him. We never spoke at the theater, nor did we even look at each other. It was tense for the rest of the cast at first, but now everyone seemed used to it.

Of course, I was tempted to ask Bobby about Art, but there was an unspoken understanding between us that Art would not be mentioned. The situation was strange. When Art and I split up, Bobby began to hang around me, waiting for me at the stage door on nights I didn't see Lars, often having dinner with me and showing up at the apartment on our day off. There were two possibilities: either he was trying to get information out of me to tell Art, or he was having problems with Holly and was using the traumatized me as an excuse not to go home.

I knew Bobby. Marital squabbles weren't his bag. Even if Art had begged him to "spy," he would have refused. Not only that, he never asked me about Lars, apparently deciding it was better to keep in the dark about the whole thing. So that meant there were problems with Holly. I approached the subject gently.

"I haven't seen Holly at the theater lately. Is she back in Cofis or something?"

Bobby was lying on my living room floor with his legs on a chair in an attempt to rest his back. "No, she's here. As a matter of fact, she's looking for a job. She's never worked a day in her life."

"Did her dad cut her off?"

"I don't think so. Not yet, anyway."

"Doesn't she want to get married?"

"Oh, Margo, that's all she wants. She's on me about it day and night. I'm so sick of it I could scream."

"Well, why don't you break up with her?"

"I don't want to break up with her. But I don't want to marry her, either. I don't believe in marriage. This alternate life-style business suits me just fine. It used to suit her, too, until we started living together. And it's not just her, it's her parents into the act now."

"I think her parents have always been in the act. I think that's why her dad was interested in *Bloomin'*. Don't you think he was trying to woo you for her?"

Bobby massaged his temples and closed his eyes. "I guess so. I just ignored all of it. You know how good I am at that. But I told Holly how I felt, and she went along. Now she's pressuring me. And her father's really pressuring me — you know, offering to buy us an apartment as a wedding gift, that type of thing. Rich people use money as emotional leverage and to keep their kids in line. They've been buying Holly off for years. She tried to move away from Cofis when she graduated from college, and they kept her there by threatening to cut her off if she left town. Now they're threatening to cut her off if she keeps living with me. I told her, go ahead, let them. But she's terrified. I guess that's why she's looking for a job."

I raised my eyebrows. "You've changed, Bobby Gaines. It's not like you to tell someone to throw away the family fortune for love."

He grunted. "Love. What the hell is it? I don't even know. I'll bet you don't either, any more."

"You're right there."

"Do you call what Sulynn and Clark have love? The way she orders him around? Maybe he loves her, but I wonder about Sulynn. Sulynn is big on means-to-an-end thinking. I know something about that."

I smiled. "I think Sulynn loves him as much as she's capable. They both have a lot of idiosyncrasies, and yet they're really compatible. Sulynn's never been one for a lot of romance. She's too practical. I, on the other hand..." I didn't finish. "I feel sorry for Holly, I have to tell you. I hope the two of you can work it out."

He did a leg lift with his legs, swung to his left and sat up. "I'd better get going." He kissed my cheek, and after petting Sammy and Deli, left.

Sulynn soon usurped me for the Misery Award. In September of '74, Clark was killed off "A Bright Tomorrow." Sulynn was livid. They had just purchased a home in Greenwich, Connecticut, and Sulynn was trying to get pregnant. The timing couldn't have been worse.

"Three people asked him for autographs while he stood in the unemployment line today," she fumed to me backstage.

"Is his agent lining anything up for him?"

"Oh, who knows. So far he hasn't. And here's the worst part. Clark isn't sure he wants another job. He's talking about going into the restaurant business with Lars in Connecticut. Have you ever heard anything more absurd? I want you to tell Lars that all restaurants in this country fail, fail big. Clark is not squandering what's left of our money — soon to be only *my* money — on some business deal."

I was used to Sulynn's tirades and took them in stride. I had been listening to her stories about trying to get pregnant for months.

"He'd better start shooting with real bullets," she'd say. "Big stud. And now he's out of town at my most fertile time." Soap stars often had to make public appearances in shopping malls.

The cancellation of Clark's contract meant that he was home all the time, and by November, Sulynn was pregnant. Instead of being happy, she was frantic.

"He's still talking about doing this restaurant thing with Lars," she complained. "And he's not going out on any auditions. He sits around all day preparing budgets. We don't have that kind of money, not with a new house and a baby coming."

On our casual dates, Lars never discussed money. He just seemed to have plenty of it, and he was very secretive about business. However, to help Sulynn out, I broached the subject of his partnership with Clark one evening while we ate at Tavern on the Green.

"I understand you and Clark might go into the restaurant business," I said, hoping my discomfort didn't show.

"Yes, we were. But unfortunately, it is not looking good."

"Oh, really? What a shame."

"It is. We have a lovely place we were intending to buy in Greenwich —" he pronounced it "Green-vitch" — "but it is looking instead as I must return to Sweden."

It was difficult for me to tell if this would leave Clark in the financial lurch or, if indeed, things hadn't progressed very far. "You don't have to go back for a bad reason, I hope," I said.

"It is a matter of opinion, Margo. I like it here very much. But one does not work here indefinitely. My visa will expire very soon."

"I didn't realize that. Can't you renew it?"

"Not without a job. It does not appear as if I will be at the hospital much longer. But please, I do not wish to discuss this. When I am with you, I like to be happy."

I called Sulynn as soon as I got home and told her all I knew. She almost had apoplexy. "I'm sure Clark doesn't know any of this," she whispered into the phone. "I'm going to have to take matters into my own hands, that's obvious."

I heard nothing else for several weeks. I continued to see Lars for dinner a few nights a week. He never mentioned the hospital or his imminent return to Sweden. We talked, as usual, about *Bloomin'*, my singing, New York, other shows he'd seen, Sweden, New York, "A Bright Tomorrow," which he always watched in the hospital lounge, politics. A whole range of impersonal topics.

Sulynn invited me over to her apartment for dinner on the first Monday in December. When I got there, I was surprised that it was just going to be the two of us. Clark was out drinking with Lars.

The meal was light — soup, quiche, salad — but the conversation was not.

"I'm going to tell you everything I know," she said. "I did some nosing around, phone calls and stuff, like when I was a corporate spy.

Lars was fired from his position at the hospital, but I can't find out why. Whatever it is, he's not able to get another job as a doctor so he can't hold onto his visa."

"Do you think he killed someone?" I asked her.

Sulynn took a gulp of milk. "I wouldn't put it past him. He's probably not even a real doctor. And I'll bet anything he saw this coming and tried to cover himself with this restaurant thing, you know, like an escape hatch. But he and Clark have had a lot of trouble with the seller and getting the budget right, one thing after another. I tell you, I've been going nuts.

"I told Clark what you found out, and the two of us went to work on Lars the other night."

"You didn't let on I'd told you anything, did you?"

"Of course not. Clark started trying to pin him down about the restaurant, and, of course, he had to tell us that he's going back to Sweden. He told us the only way he can stay is if he marries an American citizen."

"Well," I said, "he'd better hope they legalize gays marrying in this country real soon."

"He won't even admit he's gay, so how is it that you think he'd up and marry one? I mean, it took everything Clark and I had to keep from laughing in his face. But then he said he's got access to many more funds than he was originally willing to put into the restaurant, and he'd put everything he had into the restaurant and push the deal through if somehow we could arrange for him to stay here."

In my life, I'd been called dazed and distracted. I'd been accused of living in nirvana, in fantasy land. True to form, I did not see the train coming this time either.

I took another bite of quiche and shook my head. "I don't know how you're going to do that. I remember Harry trying to help a girl who worked in his office. Immigration's tough, even if you know someone who works there. Do you? If not, maybe I could ask Harry for advice. This girl Elena still works for him, so something must have happened."

She put her hand on my wrist. "Margo, Harry can't help Lars, and he can't help us. But you could."

"Sulynn, how can I help the guy? Short of marrying him." I slid my fork under a small piece of quiche left in the pie plate. I was just about to lift it out when I realized what Sulynn wanted me to do. My arm froze in mid-air. Then I let the quiche drop back onto the plate.

I stared at Sulynn. "Woman, have you lost your mind?"

Her grip on my wrist tightened. "Margo, stay calm and just hear what I've got to say. He'll drop a huge amount of money on you. And it will set Clark up in this business, and with all this money behind it, they'll make a go of it. Then you can get divorced."

"Honest to God, Sulynn, I really think you've gone off the deep end. I'm already divorced. I most certainly am not marrying some gay guy so he can stay in the country. I don't care how much money's involved. How could you even ask me to do it?"

She was facedown on the table, still holding my wrist. "I'd do it for you."

"Get real, Sulynn. You would not marry someone you didn't love, someone you couldn't have a real relationship with."

"To help you out, I would do it. You can't doubt that."

"I doubt it totally. Have you thought this through? What about my parents? They'll kill me if I get married again."

She lifted her head up. "Your PARENTS! What in hell do you care what your parents say? You're twenty-five years old. Besides, they don't have to know anything."

"No, but what will they think when I'm divorced a second time?"

She laughed. "You don't *have* to *ever* get divorced, you know. Unless you meet someone you want to marry. And that's not going to happen, and you know why as well as I do. You're still in love with Art. So I say, marry this guy and take the money and have affairs. You could do worse than be known as Mrs. Dr. Lars Andersen. Lots worse." She studied me for signs of capitulation. Failing to see any, she continued. "You're not worried about what your parents will say. You're worried about Art. You're being really stupid."

I knew every tone of Sulynn's voice, and this one said she knew something she wasn't telling me. I didn't want to talk about Art.

"Even if I agreed to do this, which I'm not going to do, what about Lars? Is this what he wants? And if he does, why doesn't he ask me himself? What are you, his procurer?"

She made a face. "He asked me if you'd be interested, that's all. If I tell him you are, of course, he'll discuss it with you. But I think he was afraid you'd turn him down."

"That isn't it. He doesn't like to get his hands dirty and talk about uncouth things like money. He's a big phony."

Sulynn started to clear the dishes. "All I ask is that you think it over. And remember, Art isn't worth wasting your time worrying about. Believe me."

I followed her into the kitchen. "I can see I'm not going to get out of here until you tell me the latest gossip about him, so let's get it over with now. Is he marrying Corinne? Is that it?"

She hesitated. "I wouldn't tell you ordinarily, but it's obvious from this conversation you're still hung up on him, and you've got to get on with your life."

"By marrying a homosexual so your husband can open a restaurant. Thanks for the concern. What about Art?"

The words tumbled out, "He has a new girlfriend, and they're living together."

I returned to the dinner table and let the news penetrate. "He didn't waste any time," I said after a few minutes. "Of course, he didn't think I wasted any time either."

"Don't kid yourself, Margo." She plunked two coffee mugs on the table. "He doesn't care what you do, or what you think, and the sooner you understand that, the better off you'll be." She left and came back with a pot of coffee. "You can hate me for being selfish, Margo, but no matter what you do, admit to yourself you've got to let go of Art."

I didn't know how to let go. All the time Art and I were together, I thought I had him, and in reality, he was already gone. I'd been happy, and he'd been miserable. Even knowing that, I couldn't truly let go, and I'd divorced him out of anger and hurt pride.

Art told me before our divorce that he didn't love Corinne, that she was "just there." I realized as I walked home from Sulynn's that not only had I believed him, but I'd clung to the fact that he didn't love her. Somewhere in my subconscious, which I had been unwilling to confront, lurked the thought that he'd be back.

Hearing about this new girlfriend brought the realization that he wouldn't be back. And with that, another realization: I just didn't care about anything anymore. Not about my love life, not about my career. Nothing.

On New Year's Eve 1974, I became Mrs. Lars Andersen.

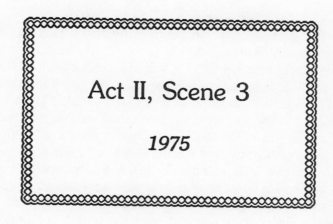

Act II, Scene 3

1975

Rochester *Democrat and Chronicle*, January 3, 1975, "Rochesterians Out of Town" column:

> "Broadway star-cabaret performer MARGO GAINES, (née Girard), whose parents live at 43 Wynand Lane in Brighton, has followed in the steps of former Rochester resident INGRID BERGMAN and married a Swedish doctor.

> "Remember in the 1940s, when Ingrid and her husband, Dr. Lindstrom, lived here?

> "Margo's husband is DR. LARS-ERIK ANDERSEN, and he's not only a doctor, but a Connecticut restauranteur. Our warmest congratulations, Margo and Lars-Erik."

I've often been asked how Sulynn could call herself my best friend and then "sell me down the river," as it's been put to me many times. According to Sulynn's lights, she was doing what was best for all of us. It's true that Sulynn's primary interest in life has always been Sulynn. It is also true that her protective nature and fierce loyalty know no bounds.

In convincing me to marry Lars, Sulynn appealed to me through a way she knew would win me over: her desperate situation. However, Sulynn had a hidden agenda: revenge on Art. She felt he had made a fool of me and, with his new girlfriend, was about to make a fool of me again. She blamed my humiliation on the fact that I wore my heart on my sleeve, and she was furious with me for still caring about him.

If I wasn't going to show Art I didn't care on my own, she would be puppeteer to my limp puppet.

The sadness I carried with me was like a sack of stones. There was no more old college gang. I didn't speak to Art out of fear that Sulynn would kill me. If I wanted to forgive him, I couldn't allow myself to think about it for fear it would just cause another rift. Fred never spoke to Art, his childhood friend, choosing to "side" with me. No more pizza gatherings after the show. No more late-night suppers at Joe Allen's. Everyone trailed off in different directions.

So this is what happens when you grow up, I thought. Your friends stop hanging out together and wounds get too deep to heal, and you start lying. Everywhere I went, I heard the song "Lies." Art's lies — my lies.

My life was a lie to all but Sulynn, Clark and Lars — and Fred, I found out later, who pegged Lars as gay at the wedding. I couldn't tell Bobby that my marriage was a sham. I couldn't tell anybody, or Lars would have been deported.

What amazed me most of all was how, to the world, I had everything: a lead role in a Broadway show, a handsome doctor husband, no money worries. The whole ball of wax.

The guilt ate me alive. If I hadn't married Art, I told myself, we'd all still be friends. He wouldn't be persona non grata and beat it out of the theater every night, living a life apart from the rest of the cast. I would have married someone else, and when Lars Andersen came along, I would have been unavailable.

Sulynn had no idea what she was getting me into, and neither did I. She couldn't foresee my emotional turmoil, nor just what it took to marry someone so he could stay in this country. Lying to one's friends was one thing. Lying to immigration was something else.

I lived through my interviews, and, thanks to my status in the community and the little bit of publicity Lars and I had attracted while dating, the officials bought it hook, line and sinker. However, they did drop in on us to make sure we were living together. The whole thing made me sick.

Before we were married, I laid down the ground rules to Lars. He had an apartment in Washington Heights and wanted me to move there. I explained that this was out of the question — it was too far away. He agreed to move in with me. He was in no position to fight me on anything.

Then I said to him, "Look, Lars, another thing. You can't bring any boyfriends here, and I expect you to be the soul of discretion on the outside, if not for your own reputation or mine, then because of immigration. They can't get any idea this was arranged." I knew he had to be a practicing homosexual, homophobe or not. Up to this point, he'd done a good job of keeping it quiet, but it would be just my luck that his activities would change now that he was married to me.

He was deeply offended. "Margo, how can you even say these words to me? I would not bring disgrace on you in any form."

"Good," I said. "As long as we understand each other."

Several days after my marriage, I was packing my bag after the performance, when I heard a voice at my dressing room door.

"I understand congratulations are in order." It was Art. I didn't look up, nor did I say anything.

"Sulynn didn't waste any time, I see," he continued. If I were paranoid, I would have assumed that he knew the real story. But he only knew what everyone had been told, that Sulynn had brought us together (a partial truth).

I knew he was trying to bait me, so I said, "I think I'll let that worm dangle, thanks." Realizing I wasn't going to speak with him further, he left.

Art's life was a mystery to me. I knew from Sulynn there was a girlfriend, and that was it. Most of the company sided with me, and his name was never mentioned, except when someone commented that it was strange he stayed with *Bloomin'*. I understood why he stayed. The situation was no less resolved for him than for me. The only hope of resolving it was to stick around on the odd chance that some of my pain and his anger would subside, and that we might actually talk.

I played the game all the way, even taking vacation time in March of 1975 to bring Lars to Rochester. My parents weren't happy, and this was my way of smoothing things over. My mother wasn't remotely fooled. "Why did you marry him?" she asked me. "You're not in love with him." Acting onstage was one thing. When it extended to offstage, I wasn't very good.

"I was lonely."

"You can't be over Art already, and over what happened. I don't understand how you can be so foolhardy, rushing into these things. First Art, and now Lars. And I don't understand why you and Art didn't try to save your marriage. Not at all."

"There wasn't anything to save. And I'm sorry if you don't approve of my marriage to Lars, but I didn't ask you to approve it."

"That's right," she said quietly.

She was disappointed in me. I could only imagine her feelings if she knew the true story. I shuddered just thinking about it.

My father, on the other hand, was impressed with Lars. "I never liked Art," he confided in me, as Lars and I left for New York. "I didn't want you to marry an actor."

A gay doctor on the lam from immigration is much better, I agreed silently, as we waved good-bye and boarded the plane.

The only amusing part of the whole thing was that the first time Lars and I slept in the same bed was in my parents house and, to my utter shock, we had sex.

Given the circumstances, this was totally unexpected. Like any woman, I was attracted to Lars. But after Art, the sexual part of me, it seemed, had ceased to exist. I was almost glad Lars was gay while I was "dating" him. I wasn't ready for anything else.

Sulynn had said she thought Lars "might be bisexual," but I had never questioned him about it. I didn't care. I set him up on the sofa bed in the living room, and that was it. Our relationship the first three months of marriage was polite and sterile, each of us going our own direction, except when we occasionally got together with Clark and Sulynn. I saw Bobby and Holly on my own, still a little wary that, if they spent too much time with Lars, they'd see through him. I usually made the excuse that he was working late with Clark on plans for the restaurant.

When we got to my parents' home, my mother put us in my brother's old room. When I saw the double bed, I almost said something, then remembered I was supposed to be Lars's "wife" in more than name.

Lars found our predicament hilarious. "So — which side do you sleep on?" he laughed.

"I'm glad you think this is funny."

"Perhaps you would like for me to sleep on the floor?" he offered.

"Never mind." I got ready for bed and, in my high-necked nightgown, crawled under the covers. Knowing I wouldn't sleep no matter what, I considered trying the floor myself, but decided if I was going to lie awake all night, I might as well have a level of comfort.

Lars had a magnificent body, which I'd seen a million times, living with the man, and he always slept in jockey shorts. I watched him come out of the bathroom and walk around to the other side of the bed and felt a twinge. Having this sun god next to me wasn't going to be as easy as I thought.

I lay in the dark, acutely aware of him, when I felt a hand on my stomach. I involuntarily jumped. Then the hand tightened around my waist, and he pulled me toward him and kissed me.

Off guard, I said, "Hey, what is this?" and struggled against his chest.

"I am kissing my wife," he murmured, and kissed me again. I was getting excited and angry at the same time. After indulging in some amazing tongue action in my ear, he massaged my scalp as he kissed me. "I like women sometimes."

I tried to get out from underneath him, but it was no use. "Since when?" I asked.

"Since always, Margo." He put my hand in his crotch. "See?"

"Oh, Jesus," I gasped as I felt him. He released my hand. I kept it where it was.

It was a night I'll never forget.

After that incident, which was repeated once a month or so, the situation seemed less of a sham. When I told Sulynn, she shrugged. "See? I told you he has tendencies," she said. "But once a month isn't enough. I think you ought to look around for somebody else."

Sulynn was by then four months pregnant and, because of the way she was carrying the baby, looked fat rather than pregnant. "My whole family's this way," she told me. "My mother worked until the day before she had me, and nobody even knew she was expecting." So Sulynn stayed with the show and planned to stay with it until she was bodily ousted from the production. "We need every cent we can lay our hands on," she said. The soap opera kept her on also, shooting her while she was sitting down, hiding behind furniture, or in close-up, as her character was still that of a virginal college co-ed.

Lars saw *Bloomin'* one night and reported that at intermission, a woman said, "I liked the girl playing Robin," and another one said, "Oh, you mean the pregnant one." Like it or not, Sulynn's days with *Bloomin'* were numbered.

The end came during a Sunday matinée in April. As soon as Sulynn sang the first note, I realized there was no way she would get through the performance. She was having some trouble breathing and couldn't sing.

After the first scene, Bertha sent Sulynn's cousin-in-law/understudy, Tracy, into the pit to sing Sulynn's music and put the swing in Tracy's place on stage. By the end of the act, Sulynn knew she couldn't finish the show and was hysterical. Tracy was told to get into costume.

I stood in Sulynn's dressing room while she sobbed and got out of her costume, her pregnant stomach hanging over her underwear. I helped her dress and get a cab, then waited in the wings to begin Act II. Bertha went out on stage, announcing:

"Due to the illness of Susan Reilly, her understudy, Tracy Norris, will replace her for the rest of the performance."

After the entr'acte, we all headed out for the Act II opening. Tracy sang her first line. I heard someone in the audience scream, "BRING BACK THE SICK LADY."

Bloomin', however, couldn't be kept down. Understudies, divorces, pregnancies — nothing could stop it. It was a small show in a small theater and probably would have worked better off-Broadway, but still, *Bloomin'* found, and kept, its audience.

Broadway was changing. The choreographer was becoming God, and I wondered what a performer like myself would do when *Bloomin'* ended. Bobby Gaines was another story. All the new shows wanted him, but Bobby wasn't interested. He continued in *Bloomin'*, using it as a home base, telling Harry he was interested in "big money" jobs, i.e., television and film. At the time Sulynn left the show, Bobby was in Hollywood doing his first film, while his understudy replaced him on Broadway. It was a small part, but great money.

Bobby returned from his film-making stint around his birthday, in April, and I wanted to have a party for him. But there was, as usual, the problem of Art. I missed the family feeling, long gone. I was divorced from Art, Sulynn was out of the show, Bobby in and out, and Fred was doing Tarot card readings in Washington Heights. Then there was my "marriage" and the fear that someone might inspect it too closely.

I went to Greenwich after the first Sunday matinee in April, to stay over at Sulynn and Clark's new house. I often did this, and Lars spent a good part of every week there, working on the restaurant.

I broached the subject of Art with Sulynn. She let me get half a sentence out. "Don't you crawl back to him," she said. "What are you leading up to?"

"Sulynn, I can't continue like this. None of us can. I've got to at least have a truce with him. All the fun has gone out of doing the show, and everyone is uncomfortable."

She bit into an apple. "Can you tell me why that bastard doesn't quit? He was supposed to."

"You mean as far as you're concerned, he was supposed to."

"Well, wouldn't you? After what he did? His wife's the star of the show. I can't believe Zack didn't pressure him to leave. He doesn't add anything. Tell you the truth, I think his understudy what's-his-face does the part better." Suddenly, she put my hand on her stomach. "Can you feel that? She's moving."

"She can tell you're excited. Well, Sulynn, whether you like it or not, I have to do something."

"I don't like it, and let me tell you another thing. You're trying to rekindle something that's gone. We're not in college anymore, Margo. Everyone has their own lives now. So what if you get on some sort of speaking basis with that wife-cheater? The four of us aren't going to be hanging out anymore. And no matter what you do, I'm finished with Arthur Gaines. If I were you, I'd concentrate on getting your husband to lay you more than once a month."

I called Fred for a chat when I got back to the city on Tuesday afternoon. Since my break-up with Art, he hardly ever came by the theater. "Come up and have a reading," he invited. "I've got some new Tarot cards — they're herbal." I passed for the time being. "I want to have a party when Bobby gets back," I said. "I'll be in touch soon." I hung up, reflecting there really didn't seem to be anyone to talk to about my dilemma.

At the theater, I slipped a note under Art's door. "Please see me after the show. Margo." Trembling, I ran back to my dressing room.

But he did appear at my door after the last curtain call. Without speaking, I indicated a chair. He sat, waiting.

"Now that you're here," I said, looking at the tip of my right shoe, "I'm not sure what to say." He didn't respond. I cleared my throat. "I guess I just wish we could be on slightly better terms. I mean, couldn't we at least talk?"

"I guess we could."

I tried to remember what I rehearsed in my mind, but it was gone. "We made a mistake," I began. "We shouldn't have gotten married, but we had a friendship before that. It's like you've fallen off the face of the earth, and it's making the situation harder. I feel like everything and everybody are gone now."

"It's the same for me," he replied, in a voice so low I could hardly hear him. "But I don't agree with you. I don't think we made a mistake getting married. I think I made the mistake." His words hung in the air between us. "Margo, do you love this man?"

I bit down on my lip so hard it nearly bled. "I can't discuss that with you," I said. Boy, is that the truth, I thought. "I had a fun idea for a party as soon as Bobby gets back. I'd like to invite you. What I'm saying is, I want to feel we can at least be civil to each other."

It might have been my imagination, but he seemed disappointed. "Okay," he agreed. "It wasn't my idea not to speak to you in the first place. The divorce wasn't my idea either."

When I opened the door, Lars was outside. Without missing a beat,

I said, "Lars, do you remember meeting Art at Sulynn's wedding? Art, this is my husband, Lars Andersen." I held my breath as they shook hands. "Goodnight, Art," I said. "And thank you."

"'night," he called out, going down the hall.

I flung myself into planning the party: invitations, catering — the works. I contacted Holly out in California and told her about the arrangements. The party was to be an elaborate practical joke on Bobby.

The party was held the night after Bobby's return to *Bloomin'*, a Sunday night. The party had to be held on Sunday, not only because of the day off the next day, but also because I told Bobby it was a costume party. Had the party been held after an evening performance, he would have noticed that everyone else leaving the theater was in street clothes, and he was the only one in costume.

Holly played along and was coming in costume also. However, she had a change of clothes stashed in my closet.

I invited the entire cast and crew of *Bloomin'*, the production staff, Foss, Tom, Fred — everyone. Sulynn came in early from Connecticut to help me get ready. I was a wreck. I needed to get through Art coming in the door with his new girlfriend, and then I'd be fine. Sulynn knew this without my telling her.

"Just stick to Lars like glue," she said. "And remember, as far as anyone knows, things are as they seem."

The party was set to begin at 8:00, with Bobby not due to arrive until 9:30. Every time the buzzer rang, my heart did flip-flops. At 8:45, Art entered with a tiny, vapid blonde, introduced to me as Brownie. My heart stopped doing flip-flops. Instead, it sank. I smiled my biggest show biz smile and greeted both of them with sickening effervescence. I could see Sulynn, afraid that I'd give my true emotions away, watching me from the other side of the room. She agreed, as a favor to me, to speak to Art, and when she approached them, I made myself scarce.

Sulynn found me in the kitchen some time later, discussing with the caterers which canapés to put out first.

She pulled me aside. "You okay?" she asked.

I replied, "I'm fine, so long as he stays on the other side of the room, and I can pretend he's not here."

"It was your idea."

"I know, and I guess I'm glad I talked to him. It's just..."

She didn't let me finish. "You're a sap, Margo. You felt sorry for him. I hope you don't live to regret it."

Bobby, the guest of honor, arrived as the world's tallest Peter Pan, in a green cap and tunic, green tights and elf slippers. When he walked in, we screamed, "Welcome back," as he looked at all of us, normally dressed.

"Well," he said, "I guess no one told you fools it's a costume party. Don't you all feel stupid?"

But Bobby had a big surprise for us. When the party was in full swing, he and Holly stood on adjoining chairs. "We have an announcement," he said. "We're married."

Holly and Bobby found themselves thrown onto the shoulders of Howard and Fred and paraded through the room, as we pummeled them with shredded napkins.

The party was a smashing success and didn't break up until 2 a.m. Everyone bet on the date and weight of Sulynn and Clark's baby and, on their way out of the apartment, put one dollar and their bet in a large pink box designed by Fred.

I not only didn't see Art and Brownie leave, I didn't say good night to them. When I told Sulynn, she said, "How polite of them to say good night to the hostess and thank her for a lovely evening. Trash." She and Clark decided to spend the night at their apartment, instead of driving back to Connecticut.

Bobby and Holly were the last to leave. "The pictures of the party are going to be a scream," I said to him, "with you in your Peter Pan outfit surrounded by people out of costume."

"Yes," he said, keeping his cool. "I really don't know what was the matter with everyone. It *was* a costume party. You were foolish to change, Holly. You shouldn't have been intimidated."

Holly looked like a new woman. "Thank you, Margo. It was a beautiful party." She actually glowed. I could remember looking like that once myself.

"It would have been a reception for you if I'd known."

"A costume reception," Bobby corrected me. I giggled.

Lars came out of the kitchen just then. "Coffee, anyone?"

"We have to leave," Bobby said, propelling himself off the couch. "It was fabulous, Margo." He hugged me. I walked the newlyweds out to the elevator.

"Lars is so charming," Holly said. "This is the first time I've really gotten to talk to him."

Bobby didn't comment, only stared at me as we stood at the elevator bank.

"You look like Dracula going for my jugular vein," I said. When the elevator arrived, the mood suddenly shifted back to its former levity with hugs and good-byes.

Lars was lying on the sofa when I returned to the apartment. "Did you talk to Bobby much?" I asked him.

"A little. Mostly to the new bride. Her mother's Swedish, did you know that?"

"No." He put his hand out to me, and I sat next to him. "It was a good party," he said, and kissed me. He was clearly drunk.

"I'm tired, Lars. I'm going to bed."

"Very well. Good night, then."

I went into the bedroom and shut the door. Instead of being happy, I was jittery and couldn't put my finger on why.

Foss called me two days later and asked to meet me after the show. I met her at the Dancers bar.

"Margo, I'll get right to the point," she said, as soon as we had our drinks. "Tom and I are working on a new show. Are you interested?"

"Wow!" I said. "Tell me about it."

"Well, it's a musical version of *As You Like It*. I'd like you to hear a tape of the music. A lot of people have expressed interest in producing another show of ours, and Tom and I are excited about this."

"Gee," I said. "I don't know. Leave *Bloomin'*? It's like home to me at this point."

"It can't possibly feel the same as it once did."

"You mean because of Art."

"No, I mean because Sulynn isn't in it for now, and Bobby's not always there. Lots of changes."

"I'd have to think about it. Harry's offered to send me out to audition for other shows, but somehow the parts are never as good or as big, and the feeling isn't the same. I don't know how to describe it. Basically, I've done things like my cabaret show and commercials, because I can do the show at the same time."

"But Margo, much as I love *Bloomin'*, it won't last forever. Have you thought about what direction you'd like to go in when it closes? Recordings? Films? Clubs?"

"You sound like Harry. He says I've gotten complacent and lost my focus. He wants me to be more like Bobby. It's funny. I used to be. It's what wrecked my marriage."

Later, I gave a lot of thought to what Foss said about putting me into her new show. I thought about where my career was headed and what I wanted out of it. I loved doing *Bloomin'* and hoped it would go on forever, and I had no reason to think it wouldn't continue at least a while longer.

My ambition had gone the way of my feelings — into a ball of numbness in the pit of my stomach. I stopped doing my cabaret act after New Year's Eve 1975, and there was no record deal forthcoming that I could see. "You're losing your momentum," Harry warned one day. But in reality, my momentum was already long gone.

Part of what I loved about performing was the team spirit. I thought back to college, summer stock and the beginning days of *Bloomin'*. My party had been great, but it was a "blast from the past," not a portent of things to come.

So, for the time being, I decided to do nothing but stay with the show, save my money and hope for the return of some emotion, some drive, some impetus. The irony was, had I still been married to Art, it would have been the perfect time to have that baby. But would I feel this way if Art and I hadn't divorced? I had no answers.

Meanwhile, plans for the restaurant — imaginatively called "Clark's" — continued, but something else was finished first: Nicole Susan Davidson, born July 3rd, 1975, in Greenwich, Connecticut.

Sulynn was in labor for twenty-four hours, and right before the last scene of *Bloomin'*, Bertha, grinning from ear to ear, handed me a note: "You're an aunt. Nicole, born 9:05 p.m., seven pounds, four ounces. Clark." After the first set of bows, I came out in front of the curtain and made the announcement to the audience, and it was the first the cast heard of it, too. One of the chorus kids won fifty dollars in the pool.

The next day, I drove out to the hospital with Lars. Clark escorted us to the nursery, where I had no trouble picking out Nicole. She looked exactly like Sulynn.

Instead of being a jubilant mother, Sulynn was in a horrendous mood, not to mention exhausted and in pain. "Take my advice, Margo," she said as soon as Lars and Clark left the room. "When it's your turn, forget natural childbirth. Have the anesthetic."

"Rough, huh?"

"ROUGH? And here's what I love. The way they threaten you. You know what that doctor had the nerve to tell me? That if I didn't cooperate — that was his word — he was going to have a perform a caesarean. He said it as though he was going to have to shoot me. I said to him, "SO WHAT? GO AHEAD."

I laughed. "Well, she looks like she was worth the agony."

"Oh, I guess she was. If only I could figure out this nursing thing. She can't seem to hold on to my nipple. Well, I guess that's my fault. You're supposed to prepare them in a certain way, and I didn't do it.

A nurse was just here trying to show me what to do. It was embarrassing, this nurse grabbing at my nipple. The baby screams every time I try to nurse her, because she's not getting any milk. But you know, Margo, can you see me whipping it out on some bus or something? I'm not the type. Big earth mother. The baby's on formula, and I told Clark to buy some for her when we leave. He said, 'Thank God.' He's already sick of listening to her scream."

I went out to Connecticut on Sunday night and stayed until Tuesday afternoon. Sulynn's mother was there, too. Sulynn required an entire staff to take care of both her and the baby. At one point, she handed me a bottle she had very helpfully heated for the baby. I let Nicole suck on the bottle for a bit, then I removed it, thinking she needed to breathe or swallow. Nicole bellowed.

"Don't do that," Sulynn said. "Let her keep the bottle. She's very demanding."

"But how will I know when to take it away?"

"When she starts choking."

"Oh, honey," I said, "please be sure I submit your name for Mother of the Year, will you?"

"Well, I can't help it. She cries and cries if you don't let her have the bottle every second!"

"Crying is part of having a baby, Sulynn. Get over it." The road signs were clear. Here was another "Veda," Mildred Pierce's overindulged, dreadful daughter, in the making.

Lars and I were Nicole's godparents, and I reflected at the christening that for a fake husband and wife, we sure did a lot of normal things: we lived together, indulged in sex occasionally, had the same best friends. If only I were in love with him, and he weren't gay, we'd be the perfect couple.

The restaurant was at long last ready for its grand opening in September of 1975. A Sunday night was chosen, so the cast and crew could be part of the festivities (and sing a few numbers free of charge). Art was invited, but bowed out at the last minute, still keeping his distance. He sent Sulynn and Clark congratulatory flowers, though, and Sulynn put them on a special table right at the entrance.

"Clark's" was situated on a main drag, at the far end of a huge shopping mall. Clark and Lars had purchased the building and then renovated both the interior and exterior. And despite a huge investment by both Clark and Lars, they had to borrow a big chunk of money. However, the place was a good risk, not only because of the location, but also because of the spacious interior, which allowed them to accommodate throngs of people. They had taken pains with every detail of the furnishings, lighting, music, menu, and they had hired a top staff.

If the "oohs" and "ahs" of the patrons that first night were any indication, the investment was going to pay off handsomely. Lars and Clark greeted the customers at the door. I stood near the entrance for a time, talking with Sulynn, and we watched with amusement as the female patrons drooled over Lars and Clark.

"I have a feeling it's not going to matter what the food is like," I said.

"It had better matter, with what that chef is costing," Sulynn grumbled.

The chef was worth his high salary, and as far as the actual first-night patrons were concerned, the opening was a huge success.

I was seated next to Bobby, at a long table with a lot of the *Bloomin'* crowd. Since his welcome-back bash, Bobby had acted strangely toward me, at times even avoiding me. At first I put it down to perhaps a difficult adjustment to married life. A few times, I asked him if there was something wrong, and he assured me there wasn't. But I didn't believe him. On this particular night, though, he was more like his usual self, joking with me about Sulynn being a new mother and gossiping about Harry and Zelda.

After the restaurant closed that night, the friends and families of Sulynn and Clark stayed, singing, drinking and having an overall great time. Clark and Lars bellied up to the bar and caught up with everyone else, drinking as fast as the bartender could make drinks.

It didn't take Lars long to get sloshed. And he hung on me as if attached by velcro. Bobby was walking around the restaurant, so Lars sat next to me, with Holly on the other side of him, and appeared to all the world as an attentive, if smashed, husband. At some point, I felt the pressure on my shoulder let up, and he left the main dining room.

Approximately ten minutes later, the merriment was stopped cold by the sound of smashing glass — lots of it — in the area of the kitchen.

"That's some clumsy waiter," Howard said.

"The waiters have gone home," I said. Then I heard screaming. I jumped up. "That's Sulynn." Several of us ran into the kitchen. I pushed the swinging doors open and recoiled with such force that Holly ran into me and nearly fell over.

Bobby and Lars looked like they were killing each other. An entire steel counter top had been cleared of glasses — by someone's body, from the look of the floor. Lars was lying on the counter, and Bobby was straddling him, punching him. Bobby's dress shirt was ripped wide open.

Sulynn stood in the corner, screaming her lungs out. Howard, Fred and Clark rushed forward and, with a great deal of difficulty, got Bobby off of Lars.

Lars staggered to his feet, a total mess.

"You keep away from me," Bobby yelled at him, breathing hard and fighting the grip Howard and Clark had on him. "You rotten bastard."

Lars leaned against the counter, doubled over. "Everyone, please go outside," I said, turning to the crowd that had gathered. "Please." Bewildered, they did as I asked, leaving me, Clark, Sulynn, Holly, Bobby and Lars in the kitchen. Clark still had Bobby by the arm.

Sulynn was crying. "Look at all this," she sobbed. "What in hell is the matter with you two? Are you both crazy?"

"This is some husband you've got, Margo." Bobby panted, ripping his arm away from Clark. "I told him at your party to stay away from me, but he just won't take no for an answer." He focused his anger on me, rather than Lars. "I don't know what the story is, but the next time he comes near me, I'm going to kill him." With that, he crashed out, Holly at his heels.

"Oh, my GOD!" It was Sulynn, out of control. "After everything Margo's done for you, you turn around and do this to her? You promised her. You promised US."

Clark took her in his arms and escorted her out of the kitchen, leaving me alone with Lars.

I didn't want to stay in the kitchen with him, but the prospect of facing my friends was even more horrible. I didn't know what Bobby had told them on his way out — not the truth, I was sure of that — but I certainly didn't want to see any of them.

Sulynn read my mind and sent Clark back with my purse and coat. "I'll take you back into the city," Clark offered in a low voice. I'd come out in a van with the rest of the cast. "Lars can stay here. I'm so sorry, Margo."

"It's okay. We'll both go back to New York in Lars's car." There was no way Sulynn would let Lars into the house. "Could you ask Sulynn to meet me outside, Clark?"

In order to get out the back, I had to walk by Lars. He was sitting on the counter now, holding a cold cloth over his right eye. "I'll meet you at the car in five minutes," I told him. "I'll drive." He only nodded.

Sulynn, still crying, met me in the parking lot, holding a pile of Kleenex. I attempted to console her, but she cried harder. "When I think of all you did for Clark and me, when I think what I made you do. I never dreamed he was such an asshole, Margo, honestly I didn't. And of all people — Bobby." This seemed most upsetting to her. "What the hell has Bobby got anyway?" At which point, I had to laugh, and she laughed with me, crying at the same time.

"Sulynn, you didn't make me do anything. I knew what I was getting into, and I'll deal with it, don't worry. You can't let this spoil everything."

"I wish Clark could buy him out." She blew her nose into a bunch of Kleenex.

"Look, Sulynn, he got drunk. He can't be criticized for being gay, just for being indiscreet. You know if he'd been sober, it wouldn't have happened. So forget about it." I didn't exactly feel that way, but it was important to me that I do a convincing acting job for her and Clark.

Lars lunged out of the back entrance. "I'll call you tomorrow, Sulynn. Don't worry," I said, and got into the car. Lars and I exchanged not one word on the trip back to New York. We parked the car in the garage Lars used two blocks from the apartment, then proceeded home in silence.

When we got home, I fed the cats, while Lars disappeared into the bathroom. When he emerged, washed and bandaged, I was waiting for him.

"Pack your stuff," I said. "You're out of here tomorrow."

"Margo, no," he pleaded. "Immigration will find out."

"You should have thought about that before you made a pass at Bobby. I'm not discussing it, Lars."

"Are you going to divorce me?"

"Probably."

"You cannot. Margo, you know you cannot. I will be deported for certain then. We must wait at least two-and-a-half years. What about the restaurant? I am needed there. It's partly mine."

"Hey, Lars, like I said, you should have thought all this through."

"Margo, I can give you more money than I promised..."

"Don't you dare bring money into this. This isn't about money and you know it. I kept my part of the bargain. You didn't keep yours."

"If you divorce me, you will not keep your bargain."

"I'm going to bed," I said. "When I get up tomorrow, you had better be gone."

I had no intention of divorcing him, but I wasn't going to tell him that. I couldn't face a divorce and the stigma of two super-short marriages, couldn't face people finding out it was a marriage of convenience, couldn't face people finding out I had a gay husband, and I couldn't face my parents, who this time would kill me for sure.

Lars didn't wait till the next day to move. He left that night. In the morning, I called Sulynn and explained that no matter what Lars said, I wasn't going to divorce him, and she and Clark shouldn't listen to him. "I'll let him stew plenty," she promised. "I hope he's terrified."

Then there was the matter of Bobby. I took a deep breath and dialed his number. He answered the phone himself.

"How do you feel?" I asked.

"Okay." As usual, his voice told me nothing.

"Can we get together?"

Silence. "Yeah."

I met him at the Pizza Joint on Broadway. I told him the whole story, from beginning to end. I left nothing out, including my unresolved feelings for Art. He shook his head in disbelief.

"So Art was right," he said. "It was Sulynn's idea all along. He knew you weren't in love with that guy and that Sulynn put you up to marrying him. Of course, he doesn't know about the rest of it."

"Is he going to?"

"Margo, I don't want to get mixed up in it. He already heard about the fight and called me. I just said Lars was drunk and picked a fight with me."

I opened my mouth to thank him, but he continued before I could say anything. "I'll tell you why I punched him out, and it wasn't because he made a pass at me. Guys have been doing that since I started in dancing school. It was because I was angry that your own husband had so little regard for you."

"I don't know why that should surprise you. My last husband had no regard for me either."

"Don't talk about Art like that, Margo. That isn't true. Start taking some responsibility for your marriage breaking up."

I concentrated on my salad, in an attempt to hide my tears. "I do take responsibility. But I can't tell you I fully understand what happened. I thought I knew Art so well, and it turned out I didn't know him at all. He always seemed so confident to me. It came as a shock that he's very insecure and seems to need someone so..." I groped for the word as I pictured his latest girlfriend. "...well, fluttery — weak — around him."

"Art has very romantic ideas about love and marriage, and he's old-fashioned about the husband's role. A lot of that is from his relationship with our mother, because he was the man of the house."

"You marry someone, thinking you understand what makes them tick..." I sighed.

"You tend to take things on such face value, and I was furious that you didn't know Lars was gay. I don't know what it is with you. I sometimes deliberately don't see things the way they are because it's easier. I don't think you do that, but the end result is the same."

"I'm trying to sort out a lot of things now," I said, "so let's just drop the whole topic of me. Are you happy now that you're married?"

He thought a minute. "I don't feel any different. I was happy with the way things were. I think Holly's happier, though."

After lunch, he walked me over to Harry's apartment, where I had to pick up some commercial copy. I found the courage to ask him if he thought Art would marry "this Brownie."

"Art's not happy either, Margo. If you weren't on another planet, that would be obvious to you."

We separated at the corner of 73rd and Columbus. Going up in the elevator, I felt the first twinges of a good mood, as I thought about what Bobby said. I was glad Art wasn't happy, and not guilty about feeling that way.

Harry was home. "Ah, just the person I want to see," he greeted me. "Margo, how'd you like a part in a movie?"

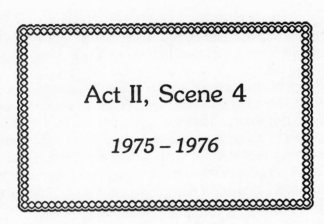

Act II, Scene 4

1975 – 1976

"Me? A movie? What is it? I'd love it."

He picked up a script that lay on his desk and tossed it to me. "This is your copy. It's called *Blind Murder*. It's about a has-been movie star who gets involved in a murder. Todd Lang is starring."

I nodded. "Good casting."

Todd Lang appeared occasionally on television, and I could remember my brother watching some western series of his that hadn't lasted too long. I had a vague memory of him from some late-night films. Real vague.

I paged through the script. "What would my role be? Do I have to test for it?"

"It's a good role. You play Todd's girlfriend. It's not a co-starring role, but it's a supporting one. And no, I don't think you'll have to test. The producers know who you are from *Bloomin'*."

I felt some of my old excitement returning. But as I looked up from the script, I noticed a strained look on Harry's face. I put the script back on the desk. "Okay, what's the catch?"

He cleared his throat (a bad sign). "Here's the deal, Margo. Todd Lang is in rough shape. He's been making movies in Europe for the last ten years, and frankly, he's ready to come home now, and this script is his chance to get back into the mainstream.

"Todd was my first client. I don't know how much you know about him. He hit it big when you were in baby clothes. It was all set up for him to be a major star, but it went sour."

"Why?"

He shrugged. "Long story, but one of the main problems was that

Todd could never play the Hollywood game with any comfort, and Roger Carew could. When Roger showed up at the studio, the brass sort of forgot about Todd. Todd could have changed that, but instead he started boozing it up. One thing led to another — bad choices, bad roles — and he hit the skids."

"I'll say he could have changed it," I said. "Roger Carew is the worst actor I've ever seen." Roger "Mr. Hollywood" Carew, thanks to a couple of major TV series, was a multimillionaire, always in the gossip columns and on the award shows dressed to kill, but he still couldn't act his way out of a phone booth with the door wide open.

"Roger knew how to play the game. And Todd was no match for him." He took a deep breath. "I feel responsible for him in a way, especially since Zelda sued him for $50,000 in back commissions last year. It hasn't helped his situation."

"Well, I'm sorry for him, Harry, but what has all this to do with me?"

He drummed his fingers on his desk. "The producers are ambivalent about him, but one of them knew Todd in the old days and wants to give him a chance. But he's a big risk. First, he's been out of it for years; secondly, he's a known alcoholic; and third, he's associated with sandal and sword pictures."

I snapped my fingers. "Todd Lang! He was Nero!"

"Right, and try not to mention it, Margo, when you meet him."

Nero was supposed to have been one of the all-time-great Hollywood costume productions, but for a variety of reasons became instead somewhat of a joke. It had, however, attained a certain popularity and was on television at least every week. I giggled. Harry glowered at me.

"Okay, Margo. The producers are interested in you for this picture. Filming starts February 5th. But I need a personal favor from you. Just keep an eye on Todd. No big deal, just let me know immediately if he starts showing up to the set late, drinking, that sort of thing."

"Spy on him?"

"Mmm, I wouldn't call it spying. Just watching out for my interests. See, he's not insurable, so I had to guarantee him with my own money."

"Yuk. You're taking a helluva chance, Harry. Also, what will happen on days when I'm not on the set?"

"Naturally, I'll be dropping by, and it wouldn't hurt you to learn a little something about the film business and observe on your own during your free days. Hah! Hah!"

"I don't know, Harry. I want to do the film, but I don't know how

I'd feel. You need Sulynn for this. She's the spy."

"Stop using that word. At least think about it. You've got the part no matter what. But remember, if he can't finish the film, you're off the big screen, too. There's every chance they'll just scrap it rather than start over with another actor. Before you go, let me show you something." He opened his right-hand drawer and took out a framed photo. It was Todd Lang, around the age of twenty, dazzlingly handsome. The inscription said, "To Harry — Thanks for everything. Onward and upward. Todd Lang, 3/8/54."

I held the frame in my hand. "Does he still look like this?"

"A somewhat older version. Margo, he's the sweetest and gentlest man I've ever known. You can see that just by looking at his face. Whatever passed for his dreams were long ago drowned in alcohol. I'm asking you, as a personal favor, to help him get another chance."

Tears stung my eyes. I'd never heard Harry talk like that about anyone. But then, the thought of losing a fortune if Todd didn't finish the film was cause enough for him to wax poetic.

"I will think about it, Harry, I promise. And I'll let you know in a couple of days, if that's okay."

I walked to the Billy Rose Library and accessed their files on Todd Lang. Real name, Samuel Spivak, born 1932 in Des Moines, Iowa. Married and divorced from actress Linda Wolfe, one child, Samuel Spivak, Jr., born 1954. There were two other ex-wives listed and a lot of film and TV credits. Most of the films, with the exception of two or three early ones, were of little consequence. The film that brought him to prominence was a classic, though: *The Misbegotten*. So he'd been off to a great start.

Todd Lang was a major heartthrob in the '50s, with good reason. However, once his downhill slide began, around the time of *Nero* and his second divorce, he kept sliding and didn't stop until he hit the center of the earth. In recent years, he had been living in Spain, making what the trade termed "sausage films," i.e., low-budget quickies.

I was mainly interested in the newspaper items, which included reviews: the headline for one read, "Nero Fizzles While Hollywood Burns."

Another item concerned a 1965 arrest as a result of an altercation with a cab driver. According to the story, Todd got into a cab while drunk. He gave the driver a location, but when he got there, he refused to pay the driver, claiming that he didn't know where he was. The driver turned him over to the police. The police were unable to find out whether or not Todd had a previous record because of some sort of system shut-down in Sacramento, and consequently, he spent forty-eight hours in jail.

In February of 1966, he was arrested for driving into a coffee shop. Fortunately, it was closed. However, a janitor "sustained minor injuries." Later that year — evidently no one had figured out yet that he was a road menace — Todd was arrested for backing his car into a hotel lobby. This time, somebody got smart and revoked his license. So, in early 1967, he was caught driving without a license, while intoxicated. "...While intoxicated" was the operative phrase in every article.

There was a lot of coverage of his second divorce, a pretty vicious event, in 1965. I only scanned these clippings. I'd read enough. Todd Lang was a real winner.

Nevertheless, he was a movie star of sorts, and I was intrigued. Partly it was that angel face that stared up at me from every clipping.

I signed my contract for the film a few days later, and the *Bloomin'* publicity person planted items in all the trades. Everyone congratulated me.

Todd Lang had quite a following in the gay community, and *Nero* was some sort of cult film, to judge by the reactions of both Howard and Fred. "Good God," Fred sighed, "you're going to be doing a film with *Nero*? First Lars and now him — you sure do get a parade of gorgeous guys around you. So how come nobody has any fun?"

"Just lucky, I guess," I said.

"Todd Lang — oooh," Howard said. "I used to have pictures of him in a pair of white trunks. See if he still has them, will you? And if so, call me."

"Will do," I promised.

"Oh, *him*," Sulynn said. "He did a lot of westerns and war movies, didn't he? Blue eyes, right? Does Art know?"

"I'm hiring a skywriter tonight," I said.

"Todd Lang," Bobby repeated. "Todd Lang. Was he Jesus?"

"Nero," I said.

All the excitement centered around Todd Lang, and everyone, myself included, seemed to forget I had a part in a movie. But I registered for a course in film acting. With all the commercials I'd done, I still flew by the seat of my pants whenever I got up in front of a camera. I intended to give this film role everything I had and justify being cast.

Sulynn returned to *Bloomin'* in October, but her character in "A Bright Tomorrow" was soon killed off in a car crash. There was no way Sulynn could do both jobs and have Nicole know who she was.

She chose *Bloomin'* so that she could spend most days with the baby. Naturally, she put pressure on me from the day she got back to bring Todd Lang out to the restaurant. I assured her I would, if only to scare Lars into thinking divorce was imminent. He still called me daily to find out my plans. I never gave him an answer.

The hunt was on to spot Todd Lang movies being broadcast on television. Each day, almost the entire cast pored over the newspaper. I stayed up until 4 a.m. on more than one occasion to watch him. The films I saw were all pre-*Nero* and showed me that, with good direction, Todd Lang was an excellent actor. Unfortunately, he didn't always have good direction. What he suffered from most of all was terminal juvenilism; he could only pull off a leading man role if he was surrounded by younger, weak performers. Of course, compared to Roger Carew, with whom he made several films, Lang seemed like Gregory Peck.

When I think of Todd, I think of a line in the James Taylor song, "Only a Dream in Rio:" "often as not it's rotten inside, and the mask soon slips away." That was Todd — an incredibly beautiful mask hiding a rotted soul.

The night Todd hit town, in January, Harry brought him to *Bloomin'*, and they came backstage afterward. Years of debauchery had not marred his looks, though it had aged him.

I'm not sure when I fell in love with him, whether it was the day I saw the photograph of young Todd in Harry's office, or when I came face to face with him backstage and looked into those maddening blue eyes. At any rate, I was a goner, and I think Harry knew it and wasn't unhappy about it.

Todd's smile lit up the universe. "You were fabulous," he said softly, taking my hand. "You have such a beautiful voice."

My face was on fire. "Thank you. It's nice to meet you." Then we just stared at each other. His hair was gray at the temples, just enough to make him devastating.

Harry spoke up. "Are you ready, Margo? Todd hasn't had dinner yet, and you must be hungry, too."

We went to Joe Allen's. Everybody was looking at Todd, and a couple of middle-aged women asked him for autographs. "I was in your fan club when I was a teenager," one of them said. I was impressed by his graciousness to her. I was impressed by him, period, and could feel myself sinking fast. It wasn't that unpleasant a sensation, either.

Reluctant to talk about himself, he asked about me and the show, skillfully changing the subject every time I tried to find out something about him. Harry, for a change, kept his mouth shut.

Afterward, Harry dropped Todd off at the Mayflower Hotel and helped to carry Todd's luggage. I got out of the car to stretch my legs and noticed there were only two large suitcases. "Light traveler," I commented.

"I was robbed before I left Spain," Todd said. When I started to ask him more about it, Harry broke in. "Come on up with us, Margo. You'll freeze down here."

I wasn't through trying to make conversation, however. "Where do you normally live?" I asked him as we stepped into the elevator. "Do you have a place in Hollywood?"

"I guess I live here now." He smiled that magical smile of his at me.

I adopted a breezy air once Harry was driving me home. "He's a nice guy," I said. "Nothing like his publicity."

"I told you," he said.

"Well, I feel better having met him," I admitted to Harry, as he parked in front of my building. "He seems to have straightened himself out. I think your money's safe." And, I said to myself, I won't have to report drunken binges to you.

The first day of filming took place a week later in Washington Square Park, in the freezing cold. I met Harry on the set. "Why can't we do interiors?" I asked him.

"They always do interiors last, Margo. They save them in case the weather is inclement."

I jumped up and down in a vain attempt to get warm. It was 7 a.m. and well below zero. "The weather's inclement now, as far as I'm concerned."

Todd emerged from the makeup trailer, and for a few seconds, I forgot my frozen body and concentrated on the view. "He looks great," Harry observed.

I didn't want to gush too much, so I just said, "Yes. He's handsome."

"That he is," Harry agreed. "Handsomer than all of them, I always thought."

The atmosphere on the film set was "hurry up and wait." I didn't know how people made movies full-time. The waiting around for set-ups drove me nuts. For the entire day, Todd and I did one scene: a mere twenty takes. I left for the theater at six. I was so cold I was numb.

"What a drag," I complained to Bobby. "Do you like film work?"

"I'll be honest," Bobby said. "I prefer the stage, and I agree, the standing around is endless. But you can't beat the money."

It wasn't long before the freezing weather began to match the atmosphere on the set. Todd Lang kept sober enough, but had a tough time of it. For reasons I didn't understand, I became the object of a lot of his bad humor. I decided he resented having an inexperienced unknown in the cast, seeing it as another sign of his fallen star.

At any rate, the lovely man I'd met backstage at *Bloomin'* vanished. I couldn't do anything right. Every time the director called for another take, Todd acted as if it were my fault. My acting got more and more uptight.

I kept telling myself his nastiness had to do with problems in his personal life, problems which were broadcast throughout the set whenever he called one of his ex-wives from his trailer. The words, "YOU BLACKMAILING SLUT," often wafted through the air. Call it my dumb luck, but these conversations usually preceded the filming of a scene with me. Todd would barge out of the trailer, nostrils flaring and look at me with murder in his heart.

Needless to say, I couldn't wait to film our love scenes.

I thought I had a stay of execution, since the love scenes were scheduled for the end of the three-month filming schedule. But a blizzard hit the city in late February, and one of our bedroom scenes found its way into the shoot schedule. Our scene took place in the bedroom of an apartment in Washington Square, which had been rented for the interior scenes. Todd and I were to wake up and begin making love, which would be interrupted by the doorbell. That couldn't happen fast enough for me — the entire thing scared me out of my wits. I dutifully did my yoga, and Fred even came on the set and did some sort of mind control exercise with me. If it was cosmic, Fred was into it.

"You have to come to grips with what's making you so nervous," he said, after our meditation.

"That's easy," I replied, as he rubbed my temples. "Todd Lang."

"Think of it like doing a love scene with Bobby. You do one every night."

"But he's not Bobby. He's a man who doesn't like me. And on-stage, I'm not in bed with Bobby. I've never done anything like this before, and I thought I'd have more time to get ready for it."

"You have to become one with the universe," Fred told me. "There is no embarrassment, no negative thought, no hatred in infinite mind. Todd Lang's hatred of you is only a perception of mortal mind. See him as he really is: a loving creation of the universal force, as we all are."

I didn't understand one word he said, but I was as ready as I was going to be. I got into bed wearing a strapless, one-piece, flesh-colored leotard, so my shoulders and the top of my chest would be bare. Todd walked in, wearing only boxer shorts. I almost laughed, remembering Howard's comments about Todd's white trunks. He did, however, look pretty yummy.

Todd didn't even say hello, just crawled into bed with me.

Be professional, I kept telling myself. This is a scene in a film. You are a pro. And please, God, don't let my face turn red.

Love scenes aren't as they appear on screen. The director talked through every single motion with us, and someone else had Todd get on top of me while he measured the distance between us with a tape measure. Incredibly romantic.

"Okay," the director said. "Let's try it."

"ACTION."

I opened my eyes and turned toward Todd, who lay on his back. I stroked his chest with my hand.

"CUT. We're picking up the top of her leotard."

"Lower your leotard, Margo," the director said.

"I don't understand why she's wearing it," Todd said. He gave me a mocking smile. "Nervous?"

I didn't answer, but self-consciously rolled the leotard down to the middle of my breasts, cutting off the blood supply to my head. I lowered myself further under the covers.

Another take. This time, we got as far as Todd moving on top of me and kissing me. We really got into it, so much so that we were tongue-kissing before I knew what was happening.

"CUT, CUT, CUT. HOW MANY TIMES DO I HAVE TO SAY IT?" Todd rolled off of me. The scene had shaken me up. Todd, on the other hand, seemed bored. The director stood over us. "Get that blasted leotard off. It looks like you've got a push-up bra on. Roll it down to your waist."

I pulled the covers up. "I didn't agree to nudity."

Todd guffawed. "You be quiet," I growled at him.

Sitting on the bed, the director used his most patronizing tone on me. "Sweetie, you won't be nude as far as the camera is concerned, you'll just be nude under the covers. We're all professionals here. You can handle that, can't you?" My face felt as it if was burning off. "Yes," I mumbled. "I'm sorry. I didn't understand you." I understood just fine — Todd Lang would be putting his bare chest on mine. Margo Gaines, you don't have a professional bone in your body, I scolded myself.

There was no getting around it, but it turned out I was a pro after all. My in-control mechanism miraculously returned as it always did, and I became totally businesslike. The scene came off beautifully. Todd gave me a strange look when it was over. If he was searching for further ammunition against me, I hadn't given him any with my uninhibited performance.

This, however, didn't stop him. Todd began to refer to me (behind my back, but loud enough so I could hear) as "The Ice Princess," to the delight of some of the female assistants and extras on the set. I ignored him.

I had no idea what Todd wanted. The implication of "The Ice Princess" was that I had rejected him. The truth of the matter was, he hated my guts and did everything possible to make sure I hated his. He deliberately gave people who worked on the film a mistaken impression, but I didn't know why he bothered.

I only knew I desperately needed *Blind Murder* to be over, and for Todd Lang to be out of my life. "And to think I was so enchanted with him when I met him," I said to Sulynn. "My antennae never miss, do they?"

Also, while making a movie had sounded good, making a movie and doing a Broadway show was a wipe-out. Getting home from a performance at 11 p.m., falling asleep at 2 a.m. and getting up for a 7 a.m. call, to go into a torture chamber atmosphere, was wearing me down.

One Tuesday night I finished the show and, arriving home, found Todd Lang in my doorway.

"Hi," he said. Can I come up for a few minutes?"

"Sure," I said, mystified. He followed me upstairs, and I let us both into the apartment.

"This is a little awkward," he began. "I can't go back to my hotel. My ex-wife is trying to get more money from me, and a process-server showed up on the set today. I got away from him, but he's sure to be waiting for me at the hotel. I called Harry at his house upstate — he said I could use his apartment and that you could give me the keys."

"Okay. Uh, would you like some coffee or something?" There was something so lost about him off the set. It was the same quality he had exhibited the first night I met him.

"That would be great." I took Todd's coat and invited him to sit down. When I brought a mug of coffee out to him, Sammy was sitting on his lap. "What's the cat's name?" he asked.

I started to say "Sammy," then realized Todd's real name was

Samuel. "Samson, and that's Delilah over there."

"They're beautiful." He accepted the coffee from me. What a Jekyll and Hyde, I thought, as I sat on the opposite side of the sofa. "I guess I've been pretty shitty to you," he said. "I'd like to apologize."

I didn't know if I should admit his ugly attitude toward me bothered me or not. "You've just acted very differently from when I first met you. Different from the way you are now, as a matter of fact."

"I don't know what my problem is. I haven't worked on a decent film in a long time. This isn't the biggest budget in the world, but it's back in the States, anyway, and I have a lot riding on it. I guess you know I have a tendency to drink too much. I've been trying to stop, but it hasn't been easy."

"I think I can understand that. But I have one question. What's this 'ice princess' business?"

"I'm sorry," he said. "I was trying to get friendly with some of the crew and extras. It was just something to say."

"Hell of a thing to say."

Talk about getting lost in a person's eyes. His eyes hypnotized me. "Why are you here?" I asked him finally.

"I told you. There's a process-server at my hotel." He put his coffee down on the table.

"You could have gone to another hotel."

In response, he pulled me to him and kissed me.

The next morning, my entire life had changed.

I was in love again, but it was different than it had been with Art. This promised to be much more dangerous. I felt totally lost in this man, dizzy with desire and willing to give up my soul for him. Married to Art, I retained a great deal of independence. Too much, according to him. With Todd, I melted into him and didn't know my own mind anymore.

Todd retained his hotel suite, but basically moved in with me. That was more discreet than to have me going in and out of the hotel. But more importantly, he was desperate for a sense of home. There really was a process-server, so I took his key and packed a suitcase for him. Having him with me in the apartment, making love to him, was as natural to me as breathing.

The change in me did not go unnoticed, and soon the joke around the theater became "*Bloomin'*? What's *Bloomin'*? What show? On stage? Where?" as I became more and more addlebrained. "Margo's got a new fella," Howard teased. "Does he wear the white trunks for you? How does that big dick of his feel?" He waited to put that question to me as the entire cast filed past us in the dressing room hallway.

"What do you know about it?" I asked him.

"Oh, come on. I've seen that long, big thumb of his."

. This intrigued Sulynn. "Is that how you tell?"

"Sure, and Nero's got a nice one. Tell us about it, Margo."

"I'm not telling you anything, but I thought nothing could compare to you black boys."

"Hi, everybody." It was Art. I was too mortified to say anything. He rushed past.

Sulynn ducked into her dressing room, a hand over her mouth. Howard let out a hoot and closed his door.

I met Sulynn in the wings after Bertha called "places." "Is what Howard said true?" she whispered.

"About what?"

"You know." She stood on her toes and got as close to my ear as she could. "About Todd's dick."

The overture started. "He's hung like Man of War. Is that what you want me to say?"

"Don't say anything unless it's fact, baby," advised Bobby, standing directly behind me. He and Sulynn roared with laughter. I then had to go out to begin the touching opening number. I could have cheerfully killed both of them.

Art obviously knew what was going on. Considering that in his eyes I was "cheating" on Lars, which I'm sure was a rumor throughout the rest of the company, he must have found it infuriating after I had thrown him out for infidelity. And legally, his supposition was correct.

Todd and I couldn't become a public "item" for several reasons. Despite my threat to divorce Lars, we were still married, and if I appeared in the press with Todd Lang, Lars would soon find himself escorted to Port Authority by two gun-totin' lugs from Immigration. I couldn't do that to Sulynn and Clark, since Lars would surely want his money out of the restaurant. In Todd's case, he was in the middle of a court battle with his most recent ex-wife over increasing her alimony and didn't want to give her any ammunition. She apparently had plenty as it was.

We played it cool on the set, but at night, after the show, I got home at breakneck speed so that we could be together. Twice he actually came to the theater and saw *Bloomin'*, and as I stood on stage, my knees nearly buckled at the mere thought of him being there.

I found him incredibly romantic and tender, and very experienced, bringing me to a level of feeling I never knew existed. I didn't care about his drinking. I didn't care about his ex-wives. I only wanted to be with him for all time, even if it meant giving up my career and going to Spain with him, or wherever, when *Blind Murder* wrapped.

One Saturday, I got to the theater for the matinée and learned Art's understudy was going on for him. "Where's Art?" I asked Bertha.

"Don't know," she said, and rushed away, scribbling on her clipboard.

I intercepted his understudy running down the hall. "Is Art sick?"

"Don't know," he said. "I've got to get ready. Talk to you later."

Bobby and Sulynn weren't at the theater yet. I got into makeup and costume, and when Bertha called places, I went into the wings. "Where's Art?" I asked Bobby and Sulynn.

"He called in sick," Bobby answered. "I don't think it's anything serious."

He was lying. I knew it.

After the performance, Bobby came to my dressing room with Sulynn.

Bobby said, "Art and Brownie got married this morning."

I — and they — expected a bad reaction. But I surprised all of us. I waited for the blow to the pit of my stomach. It didn't come. I waited for tears. No tears. I looked at them in wonderment. Then I smiled.

"I'm okay," I said, shocked. They threw their arms around me, and we had a group hug. "I think I'm really happy for him," I told them.

"Bring Todd out to the restaurant tomorrow," Sulynn said. "Bobby and Holly are coming." Clark's was a safe place for Todd and me to appear in public. "Rub Lars's nose in it a little," she said.

"Okay," I agreed. "How's Lettie doing with this?" I asked Bobby.

"She's all right. I think she likes Brownie, but she loves you."

After they left, I sat in the quiet of my dressing room for a while. I felt good. Thanks to Todd, the pain was gone.

Lars attached himself to me the minute Todd, Bobby, Holly and I entered Clark's on Sunday.

"Margo, Margo? Have you made up your mind yet?" he panted, the divorce hanging over his head like the sword of Damocles.

"No, not yet." I brushed by him.

All eyes zeroed in on Todd, resplendent as usual. Clark placed us at a prominent table. A few minutes later, I saw him at the bar with a bucket of champagne. Sulynn stopped him before he could bring it over to us.

I waved to Sulynn to join us, and I'd never seen her move so fast to seat herself next to Todd. Initially, she was speechless (another first). Todd focused his brilliant blues on her, and as if in a trance, she answered his questions about the restaurant. Bobby and I exchanged grins.

Bobby had a few questions of his own. "So, Todd, what made you decide to play Nero?"

Todd groaned. "Money, the all-star cast, the big budget, the publicity. I was twenty-eight years old and waiting for that pivotal 'breakthrough' role. My first big role was in *The Misbegotten* in the late '50s. That got me to one level, but you know how the business works. You have to keep moving up. I thought *Nero* would do that for me. It might have, but we filmed in Italy, and when we got back to the States, something had happened to the sound. I had to dub my entire role in a recording studio. You're an actor, and you can imagine what that meant as far as my acting. As a career decision, it backfired."

"How can you say that?" Bobby asked. "It's what everybody knows you for."

"But it type-cast me."

I knew that was all an excuse for what really happened: alcohol. But I held my tongue. According to Todd's list of credits, after *Nero*, he was involved in some very different types of roles. In truth, he just boozed away his momentum and sank.

Over antipasto, Sulynn found her personality. "Actually, Mr. Lang, Margo and I are of the television generation."

"Right," I said. "'Route 66' and 'Dr. Kildare.'"

He smiled. "There was a Dr. Kildare in my generation, too, Lew Ayres."

"I belonged to the Richard Chamberlain Fan Club under an assumed name," I admitted. "Debby Arnold. And I had an intern shirt. I wore it open at the neck."

"I had a 45 of him singing Dr. Kildare's theme song," Sulynn said. The four of us sang it for Todd.

"He went into movies after that show," Todd said.

Sulynn shook her head. "I wasn't allowed to go to his movies. Margo, were you?"

"Of course not. The Legion of Decency rated them B."

Sulynn and I recited together, "Morally objectionable in whole or part for all."

"I used to love the Hardy Boys on the 'Mickey Mouse Club,'" Bobby remembered.

"My son was photographed with the Mousketeers," Todd said, wistfully. He played with his fork, then abruptly stood up. "Excuse me." His hand touched my shoulder. "I'll be back in a second."

Sulynn nudged me. "Shouldn't you go with him, in case he takes a snort in the men's room?"

"Do I look like I've had a sex change? Besides, I've learned the hard way. If he's determined to drink, he'll find some way to do it."

"Clark almost helped him along. Everything I say to him goes in one ear and out the other. I told him a thousand times, no liquor at this table."

Bobby groaned. "So what does that mean? We're all on the wagon because of him?"

"Please," I begged, "as a favor to me, Bobby. Just for today? Get tanked up later."

Holly put her arm through Bobby's. "Can't you see, Bobby? Margo's ga-ga over this guy."

He was disgusted. "Can't I see? Margo's *been* ga-ga for weeks."

On his way back to the table, Todd stopped and talked to the bartender. "I ordered something special for you," he said, when he sat down. "I want you to try it. A pousse-café."

"What is it?"

"It's layers of liqueur, each a different color and density so one stays on top of the other." A waitress put it in front of me. "It's pretty," I said, sipping it. It nearly burned my tongue off.

Attempting to hide the fact that it was god-awful, I handed it to Bobby. "Here, taste it." He did so, then said, "If you hold it on your tongue it tastes like gasoline." Todd threw his head back and laughed.

Holly took it from Bobby. "I love pousse-café, if nobody else does."

Todd tickled the back of my neck. "You didn't like it, Margo?"

Whenever he touched me, I tingled from head to toe, which was fine in private. I forced myself to breathe evenly. "Not really," I said. "Let's dance." The lounge had a singer-pianist Sunday afternoons.

Lars stood by the entrance, lips set in a straight line as he watched us dance to "When You Fall Asleep."

"You're a very powerful young lady," Todd murmured, pulling me closer. "I may be getting into some difficulty here."

"I'm trying to control myself. You'll have to do the same." But I could barely talk, I was so excited. I tried to snap out of it. "This song could have been in *Bloomin'*." I sang softly, "They don't have the right to say/They've never loved this way/They don't know how I feel when you fall asleep in my arms."

Todd moved his lips through my hair. "Todd, don't," I said. "We have to be careful, we really do."

Our eyes met. "I wish it were warm out," he said softly, his eyes never leaving my face. "Do you know what I'd do if it was?"

I sucked in a breath, my entire body on fire. I must have looked like a giant stop light. "I can't handle this. We have to sit down."

He tightened his grip around my waist. "We stay right here."

"I feel like everybody's watching us."

"Fuck 'em."

"Do they think that I'd cause you harm?" the song continued. "They don't know how I feel when you fall asleep in my arms." Gently, Todd pulsated his pelvis against mine. Never had a dance seemed so long, yet so short and frustrating.

The rest of the afternoon was complete agony. "We have to get back," I told Bobby as soon as I dared. "Todd and I have an early call tomorrow."

Since it was Holly's car, she drove, and Todd and I again had the back seat. The winter night was pitch black. "Are you warm in that?" he asked me, unbuttoning first my coat, then my dress down to the waist, then unhooking my bra from the front. I wondered if Holly and Bobby knew what was going on. As uncomfortable as the situation made me, I felt unable — and unwilling — to stop him.

By the time we reached the apartment, I was half-crazy, and we ripped each other's clothes off before we were entirely through the door. Neither of us slept the entire night and reported for work in Greenwich Village the next morning at 7 a.m.

"Do you have a rash?" the makeup artist asked me, touching my face.

"Ow," I said, suffering from horrendous beard burn. Todd's face felt smooth enough, until he went over me like sandpaper about five hundred times.

"Your lips are purple," she said.

"I was in severe winds," I answered.

"Your eyes are bloodshot," she said. "I've got my work cut out for me today. Put this on first." She handed me a jar of cream.

It was my longest session to date with her. When she was finished, I stood up and started out of the trailer. "You're walking a little funny," she said. "Are you sore?"

"I fell while I was skiing over the weekend."

When the director yelled "print it," after my scene, he said, "Margo, we won't try for your close-up today. You either, Todd."

I wondered if my biography in the *Bloomin'* playbill shouldn't have a line added: "Her favorite activities include sex with Todd Lang."

I had acting class Monday night, and Todd asked if he could come with me. The teacher was thrilled and invited him to critique.

Todd watched a scene from *The Big Knife.* "You threw away one of the lines," he told the actress playing Dixie. "You accuse him of not knowing what Hollywood producers are capable of. You kind of tossed the line off. There was nothing underneath it." He smiled a little, and that smile spoke twenty years of bitter memories and abuse. "See," he said, his voice very quiet, "you really don't know what they're capable of."

"Can you give us an example?" the teacher asked.

"The studio heads could tell you who to date — even who to marry, and when to marry them. In the old days, the studios controlled everything: the fan magazines, the police, everything. If you didn't play ball with the studio, your career was over. It's important to bring that idea into this scene. Remember, this actress later has an 'accident' and is killed, because she poses a threat to the studio."

After class, the students mobbed him.

"Thanks for taking me with you," he said later, almost shyly, taking me into his arms. "It was fun."

I kissed him. "Todd, what's going to happen when filming's over?"

"How do you mean?"

"Us."

He pulled me down on the couch with him. "Margo, let's not think that far ahead. Let's just enjoy what we have now."

"Do you think you'll go back to Spain?"

"I won't go back to Spain. Are you kidding?"

"Why not?"

His voice hardened. "I just won't, that's all." He pushed me aside. "Don't start making demands on me, Margo. You'll only be sorry, and I don't want to see you hurt."

I had a heart-to-heart with Sulynn at the theater. "Here you go again with these problem children," she said. "Not that I blame you in this case. But he's trouble."

"I'm in over my head," I told her. "I'm in love with him."

"You'd better get un-in love with him real quick. What are you planning on doing, taking care of him the rest of your life? You know how that will end up."

I knew she was right, but it was too late for me.

Art was back in the show after his long weekend honeymoon. I made a point of congratulating him. "What's happening with you?" he asked me point-blank. "I've been hearing some weird things."

"Such as?"

"Such as you're not living with the Swede anymore, that you only married him so he could become a citizen, and that you're shacking up with that drunk Lang."

Every time Art and I tried to be polite to each other, it ended badly. "Mind your own business," I snapped, and angrily left his dressing room.

The *Bloomin'* audiences were markedly smaller than a month or two earlier. Although the closing notice was inevitable, it wasn't something I could face. While the rest of the cast made plans for the rest of their careers, I refused to think about the end of *Bloomin'*.

Harry wasn't interested in my fantasy life. "Time to get in gear, Margo. I want to send you out for some other musicals, even some plays."

"Any chance of me doing the movie of *Bloomin'*?" If Todd wasn't going back to Spain, then he would probably head for Hollywood.

"I've submitted Bobby and Sulynn. The thing is, they're interested in Travolta for Bobby's part. They'll cast a star in your part. So there are two possibilities for you. One is, I could probably get you a test for Amalia's part. The other is, depending on who they get to play Mandy, you could dub the voice."

"No, thanks. I might be interested in doing another film, though. What's the reaction to my work in this one?" The film had another six weeks to shoot, but my scenes were almost finished.

He nodded. "You could get cast in more film. But I'll be honest, there's more work for you in musicals. I also think you should pick up your club act again."

"I'll consider it. Could you get me bookings on the West Coast?"

He studied me from his position on the couch. "Does this shilly-shallying have something to do with Todd?"

I shifted in my chair. "He's not sure of his plans."

"Your plans shouldn't include him. Margo, I've been lecturing you since I met you about growing up and getting some savvy. An affair between actors while they're working together isn't unusual, but it's nuts for you to expect it to continue once the film ends. I never made any bones about what a fuck-up he is, and you've been living with the guy. You can see it firsthand. Even so, there's a lot you don't know about him. Take my advice and go back to the Swede." As I was leaving, he said, "There's something else to consider. When the hell are you going to get off your rear and do something about your career? Are you planning to have *Bloomin'* on your tombstone or what?"

I brooded over Harry's words for weeks afterward, as I watched Todd's attitude toward me change, subtly at first, then in a more pronounced manner. A clear division between Todd in and out of bed emerged, as I began to feel more and more like a back street mistress. Although we were never publicly lovers, we had been publicly friends. But gradually, this changed.

One afternoon, while I was vocalizing, Todd interrupted me. "I might not be here tonight when you get home. I'm going to dinner with Rock Hudson."

"Well, excuse me for breathing the same air. Thanks for the kind invitation."

"What are you talking about? You're performing tonight."

"I'm not performing all night."

Flustered, he said, "Well, I didn't think you'd be interested."

"I can well understand that," I said, stomping into the bedroom. "Why in God's name would I be interested in meeting Rock Hudson?"

He followed me. "Margo, you're being ridiculous. I don't really even know him that well. I haven't seen him in years. He was really a friend of my ex-wife's, from when they were at Universal together."

Oh, and hasn't she just had a fabulous career, I said to myself. "I don't suppose it occurred to you to bring him to the show. But then, you probably didn't think he'd be interested in the show anymore than I'd be interested in meeting him. Do you think there's something wrong with the show? It was good enough for Lauren Bacall and Richard Chamberlain and Elizabeth Taylor and..."

"That's enough, Margo!" he yelled. "Stop throwing celebrities in my face and reminding me that I'm not one of them. Harry arranged this dinner with Rock, and I'm going. If you think it's going to be any treat for me to discuss the old days, and then hear about how well he and Roger Carew are doing, you're dead wrong. And if I don't want to introduce you to him, you might think about how I feel, for a change."

I felt about six inches tall, but kept my voice even. "I was every bit as excited about meeting you as I would be if you told me I was going to meet Rock Hudson. This comparison business is all in your head. I think you're a better actor and better-looking. Your careers just went in different directions, that's all." An understatement.

"Yeah. Different directions. I played Nero, and he made a fortune with Doris Day."

"Hey, Todd, that's life. It doesn't make him better." Smarter, maybe. Luckier, less self-destructive career-wise, able to take advice.

"Leave two tickets at the box office," he sighed, disappearing into the bedroom. "I'll see what I can do."

Lately, we'd had more and more fights like that, and any small victory for me always left a bitter taste in my mouth. I didn't care about meeting Rock Hudson. I cared that he didn't want anyone to know we were lovers.

Several weeks after this incident, the film wrapped on schedule, April 12th. There was an enormous "wrap party" at the Algonquin Hotel, and I was told to invite anyone I wanted. I asked Bobby, Holly, Fred, Howard, Sulynn and Clark, but only Bobby and Holly could make it.

Despite the fact that I worked on *Blind Murder*, I really knew very few people at this party and was shy about talking to those I did know. They all seemed busy with important types. I knew Bobby, of course, but as Harry had slept with practically every woman at this party, he informally assigned Bobby to keep them all apart, not mentioning that it was probably more a task for the Red Army than for one individual. Bobby was, therefore, too busy to talk to me.

I had attended several functions with Todd in the past. He never felt compelled to talk to me or introduce me to anyone. This particular evening, as usual, he disappeared, and I slumped in a chair by myself. I did spot a female producer I'd just sung for, with my slip showing about three inches, which Harry told me about after the audition. I lowered myself in my seat.

Harry brought over a woman named Gloria, who was from Rochester. "Oh, hello, Mary." She called me Mary all night, reminding me of the time I went to a party with Todd and was introduced as Mary Churchill to Edward Albee and Tony Richardson. "Are you having a good time, Mary?" she asked.

Everyone stood around talking about their careers, and I continued to sit in the chair, wolfing down food and drink.

Eventually, I found Todd and informed him that I was leaving. "I've been here for four hours, and I've talked to two people," I said. "Good-bye." He decided to leave with me, since he was staying in my apartment and knew from my mood that the chain was going across the door before he got on the other side of it. He flagged a cab.

When we got into the cab, I let him have it for leaving me alone the entire evening, for not speaking to me. It was a totally one-sided conversation. I stopped talking in the middle of a sentence. "I'm not sure I feel very well," I said, and threw up all over the backseat.

The cab driver had us blockaded, except for the money slot. Todd banged on the window. "Stop the cab," he demanded. The cab driver slammed on the brakes. I crawled across Todd, threw open the door and started to walk. Todd gave the cabbie an extra ten dollars, which I'm sure the driver was thrilled about, not realizing someone had just ruined his cab.

Todd and I fought on the street and on into the apartment. I had either the flu or food poisoning. I'd never been so sick, and it seemed to come from nowhere. I got into my nightgown, then went into the bathroom and threw up. I took my nightgown off and threw it in the corner. At 6 a.m., I woke up, naked, face down on the cold bathroom floor. Todd slept in the living room, so he wouldn't have to listen to me barfing, and as far as I know, never checked on me once.

Our relationship was deteriorating by leaps and bounds, but he had a maddening way of convincing me every horrid thing he did was a momentary aberration. Sort of like a wife-beater does, only these beatings were emotional. I held on with the same compulsion as an abused wife. I was about to lose *Bloomin'* and see my friends scatter. I couldn't lose Todd, too.

He had nowhere to go after *Blind Murder*, so he continued to live with me and waited for Harry to line up something else for him.

On April 30th, I walked into the theater and saw the notice: the show was closing May 14th. I stared at the notice, and as I did so, was surrounded by Sulynn, Bobby and Art. It reminded me of the old days around the school bulletin board, studying the casting lists. But in those days, the news was usually good.

"I guess that's it," I said.

"Two-and-a-half years. That's not a bad run," Bobby said.

"I wonder if I'll ever work again," Sulynn said.

Art didn't say anything. I took Sulynn's hand on one side and Bobby's on the other and squeezed. "I'll miss it," I told them.

"We'll all miss it," Art replied, and walked away.

The final performance was sold out. Lettie, my parents, Sulynn's family, Fred, Foss, Harry, Zelda and the rest of the investors, Holly's dad included, and Todd piled into the theater with the rest of the closing night audience. I had to invite Lars, since my parents were there. If my mother even had an inkling about Todd... I shuddered just thinking about it.

The press was there in full force. It was an event for another reason: it was the first performance in ages for which the entire "original cast" had assembled. The joke around the company was that

Bobby and Howard used the show as a rest stop.

I got through my last performance of *Bloomin'* without breaking down, until the last song, the reprise of "Bloomin'." We stood across the stage — myself, Bobby, Sulynn and Art, and I began, "We're all bloomin'..." My voice shook. "Flowers starting to rise..."

"New in the sun," Bobby sang. "Just opening..." I heard him take a breath. "Our eyes," he spoke.

Then there was nothing from Sulynn. The orchestra continued. Finally, she said in a tear-laden voice, "Feeling the warm, learning the day..."

"Bloomin', and hopin' to stay..." croaked Art.

The chorus and other principals slowly joined us on stage, and we found our voices. "We're bloomin'," we sang with all our hearts. "Bloomin' with life."

The curtain came down to deafening applause.

We bowed before a constant, cheering standing ovation. The cast got into the act, applauding one another. When it was my turn, everyone on stage hooted and hollered loudest of all. Zack and Harry brought flowers out to me, Sulynn, Amalia and Beverly. Foss and Tom Scardini — no one had seen him for two-and-a-half years — joined us on the stage, which was by now wet with tears. Balloons floated down on us, flashbulbs popped, and the curtain closed for the last time.

We remained on stage, without exception, sobbing and hugging. "You held it together, Margo," Harry cried, holding me. "Be in our new show, Margo, please," Foss begged, handkerchief over her mouth.

I made my way to Sulynn, and we collapsed in each other's arms, unable to speak. I saw Art standing with Amalia, and I went over to them. I hugged and kissed Amalia, then faced Art, tears dripping off my chin, and he put his arms around me.

There was nothing to say, so he kissed me, a kiss loaded with memories and old feelings for both of us. I smiled and backed away, running smack into Bobby, who buried his head in my shoulder and cried like a baby.

I finally made it to my dressing room. I'd been clearing it out little by little, and tonight, I packed the rest of two-and-a-half years of accumulated garbage. "Management" had invited the entire cast, crew, and assorted relatives and lovers to Tavern on the Green. I put on my new blue dress and tried to fix my face. It was pretty hopeless.

I gave my little home away from home a last look and opened the door. Sulynn, Bobby and Art were waiting, all looking as messed up as I did.

"We thought we'd have a drink together first," Bobby said.

"I'd love it," I told them. Linking arms, like Dorothy and friends in *The Wizard of Oz*, we started up the yellow brick road into our futures.

CURTAIN — ACT II

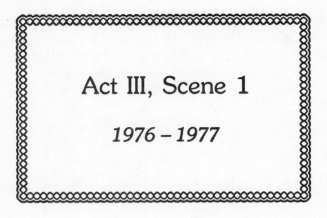

Act III, Scene 1

1976 – 1977

The first thing I did was cut off my hair. The '70s were almost over, and I hadn't been in them yet, thanks to *Bloomin'*. And no, I told the hairdresser, I do not want the Farrah Fawcett-Majors look. No, I don't want any streaks. Just cut it.

He gave me a "blunt cut" that fell right below the chin, and I left the Act II Hair Salon a new woman. I wondered what Todd would say. He loved my long hair, loved to watch it move, to touch it and to have me tickle his chest with it.

He was furious. "Is that all I am to you, long hair?" I accused him, and he backed off. "I'll get used to it," he said, but he didn't sound sure.

Bobby was the only one of us cast in the film of *Bloomin'*, but Art got a job as an assistant producer — read, glorified secretary. In July, they and their respective spouses and animals left for Los Angeles. "I'll call you from Valentino's old house," Bobby promised.

Todd had to turn over his entire fee for *Blind Murder* to his ex-wife. Not eager to go to Los Angeles with no money and no place to live, he did some guest spots on TV shows that filmed in New York throughout the summer. I collected unemployment and did my old cabaret act a few times.

Despite Foss's pleas, I turned down her musical version of *As You Like It*, selling out for love. I began preparation for my club act, backed by some of the old *Bloomin'* investors. It was to be an expensive proposition: arrangements, pianist, choreographer, gowns. But Harry secured me a lot of bookings in L.A., San Francisco and Vegas, and also lined up some television work for Todd on the coast.

"I hope you know what you're doing," Sulynn grumbled. She felt deserted and stuck in Connecticut with a baby and no acting work. Not that she'd tried. The restaurant was doing well, and for all her moaning, she seemed content to be a full-time wife and mother. But I could tell she missed the excitement.

I didn't know what I was doing, and Sulynn knew it. But I couldn't bear to be separated from Todd.

But I was, anyway, despite my best efforts. Todd received an offer to do another film in Spain in October, and though reluctant to go back, he couldn't turn down the money. Although I was in the midst of meetings with my pianist-arranger and gathering material for my act, I wanted to go with him.

He was firm. "No, it's better if you don't come along."

"But why?" I had concerns about his drinking, among other things. Todd's life in Spain held an aura of mystery.

"Look, Margo. I'm trying to pull myself out of a lot of garbage over there. I don't want you to be a part of it."

He was gone for three weeks and, during that time, telephoned me once. I spent the days biting my nails off, crying, and no matter what I told myself about not caring about his past, I tortured myself about other women and his boozing. Surrendering to complete insecurity, I wondered if he would even come back.

The three weeks dragged on and on, even though I tried to fill the hours. Finally, they were over, and Todd called me from Kennedy Airport to say he was in New York. Our reunion erased all my doubts. He couldn't wait to get me into bed, dispelling my fears about another woman. And he looked good, which told me he hadn't been drinking heavily.

Before we left for L.A. in November, I took a good, hard look at our finances. Almost everything Todd made went to his ex-wives. He gave me half the rent and paid the rest of his living expenses, but there didn't seem much left over when he was finished.

There had always been something incredibly fishy about Todd's whole financial predicament, and I was unable to get to the bottom of it, as he was extremely touchy on the subject of money. The settlement he had made with his last wife was exorbitant, so huge, in fact, that he had to go back to court to get it cut. Why had he agreed to it in the first place? Also, if Zelda Lasker had been able to sue Todd for $50,000 in back commissions, that meant Todd earned $500,000 at some point. So Todd Lang was still earning good money; however, he didn't have any.

I adored Todd. I would do whatever was necessary to help him, but

I had a fail-safe mechanism where my hard-earned cash was concerned — probably from all that time living with Sulynn. I had saved and invested a lot of money during the run of *Bloomin'*, leaving aside a good portion to live on in times of no work. Actors have to think of these things. Todd and I would need money for an apartment in L.A., a car....my mind ran down the list.

Lars couldn't be found at his apartment in Washington Heights, so I hopped the train to Greenwich. Sulynn and baby Nicole picked me up at the station and drove me to the restaurant.

My marriage to Lars was to include a "generous" financial arrangement, but other than half the living expenses, I'd never seen a penny. I faced him now. "I'm going to Los Angeles, and I need some money."

"How much?"

"Let me put it another way. We had an agreement. I'd like the money you promised me: $3,000."

"I no longer have that money. Everything I have is involved in Clark's, you know that."

"No, I don't. I know Clark's is doing well. And I know you didn't sink all your money into it, not you. Since you're not understanding me today unless I say things over and over, try this: we have another year to go before I can safely divorce you. If I don't get my money, I'll just divorce you now. And if you think it's only a threat this time, try me."

He gave me the money.

Sulynn, Clark and Nicole saw us off at the airport. "You're not going to live out there for good, are you?" Sulynn asked.

"I don't know right now. I sublet the apartment for a year. We'll see what happens."

Sulynn glanced over at Todd, seated near the check-in counter, talking to Clark. "Don't get screwed up, Margo," she warned me. "Just don't get screwed up."

Sulynn said good-bye to us on one coast, and Bobby greeted us on the other. Holly had insisted that, rather than go to a hotel, we stay with them. "We've got a spare room," she told me over the phone. "Lettie just left and got a place on Park La Brea."

"We're like a traveling carnival act," I said to her. "Where does Art live?"

"He's about five minutes from us."

Bobby and Holly lived on Sunset Boulevard, in an old house that had been converted into separate apartments. On the drive over, never having been to Los Angeles, I stuck my head out the window to take in everything. Todd wasn't happy about being back. Sammy and Deli were unhappy as well, now that the vet's tranquilizer had worn off, and were screaming in their carrier.

I must say, I was disappointed with Los Angeles. The entire city looked like Ridge Road in Rochester, except for the palm trees. It was all cleaners, fast-food places and mini-malls. But I liked the lightness of it — the sun on the beautiful Spanish-style buildings and the wide-openness of everything.

I couldn't get over the space Holly and Bobby had. For the same rent I paid in New York, they had triple the area and more light than I'd seen in any New York apartment. "You can use my car until you get your own," Holly offered, releasing Sammy and Deli from their carrier to get reacquainted with Holly and Bobby's cat. "It's not a stick shift, so you'll be able to drive it." She'd hired somebody to drive her car out there when she and Bobby moved, and Bobby bought his own car in L.A., a stick-shift, which nearly everybody out there seemed to drive.

Todd disappeared into the bedroom. "I'd better go in and see how he is," I said. "Being here is a little tough for him."

He was lying on the bed, and I lay down next to him and put my head on his chest. "Everything's going to be great, you know," I said. "Especially when *Blind Murder* comes out."

He idly stroked my hair with his fingers. "You can't think I like any of this, Margo. Not having any money, staying with your friends. I used to be somebody here. I'm on the Walk of Fame, but I don't have the bus fare to get over there and see my piece of sidewalk."

I kissed him. "It's all just temporary. Now that you're back, there will be plenty of work, and you're not always going to owe back alimony. Are you going to see your son?"

"Yeah. I'll call him a little later." Sammy, Jr. was working at a public relations firm. Todd hadn't seen him in over a year, but he talked to him on a regular basis.

He undressed me. I tensed. Bobby and Holly were in the next room. "We'll be quiet," he whispered. "But I need you now." As always, I gave in to him.

We spent the next two days apartment-hunting and found a nice, airy one-bedroom in Westwood. It was the not the nightmare hunt for empty rooms I'd anticipated after living in New York. Todd had furniture in storage from a between-divorce existence, and soon it looked like a home. I leased a car, and we were on our way.

Todd went to work on an episode of "Columbo" — with a limousine picking him up every morning, because his license had been revoked. And I rehearsed with the pianist for my first show, also spending time on the set of *Bloomin'* when Bobby's scenes were being filmed. *Bloomin'* as a film was totally different than it had been on Broadway; it even had two new songs (which Foss did not write). Bobby's part was cut down to a supporting role, but he danced more than in the original show. I thought he was wonderful and that the part was going to be a fabulous showcase for him.

I realized I was prejudiced as far as the rest of the cast, but I didn't care for any of them, especially, of course, not for Amy Hamilton, the star playing Mandy Morgan. However, as I reminded Bobby, I'd never liked her before she stole my part in *Bloomin'* either. With the exception of the very top notes, which were dubbed by somebody else, she did her own singing, which was a shame for the audience.

I visited the set only when Bobby had something important to do. Art was ever-present in his assistant job, as was Lettie, who sat in a chair with thermos bottles and liniment. Nothing thrilled her more than the belief that Art and I had parted friends. We let her think it. Every time she spotted me anywhere near Art, I could see her mouthing, "Thank you, Jesus." Art and I were on good terms, although it was an unspoken rule that we never discussed anything remotely personal. Not only that, but in talking with Bobby, Holly or Lettie, Art's wife never came up in conversation.

I still carried a lot of guilt about my marriage to Lars, and dealing with my parents on the subject was no picnic. My mother knew Lars wasn't going on the trip to Los Angeles, and once I got there and was settled in my own apartment, she said to me, "You're separated, aren't you?"

"Yes."

Silence, followed by muffled sobs. It wasn't enough that *I* felt guilty, my mother had to join in and share the guilt. "This is my fault somehow. Two failed marriages. It has something to do with the way I raised you. I don't understand. Your brother Paul is perfectly happy."

I debated whether it was better for her to think I had two failed marriages, or know that I had married Lars so he could stay in the country, and then lied my face off to her about it. It was a toss-up.

"Well, Mother, if you must know..." I gulped. "Lars is actually a dear, dear friend. And I married him so he could get citizenship. But I couldn't tell a soul, or else he would have gotten into terrible trouble."

Now her sobs were convulsive. "Mother, a lot of people do it. It was purely platonic, and when enough time has passed, we'll get a divorce."

"And what am I supposed to say to people?" was all she could eek out.

"It's no one's business. And besides, I'm an actress. People expect bizarre behavior from me. You'd better face facts, Mother. Paul did all the safe, conservative things, and I'm just not that way." After an hour on the phone, I managed to calm her down a little bit. I figured once she got used to the idea, it would sit better than Margo Gaines, Sex Temptress.

I was always happiest when I was working or rehearsing, and now, although I missed *Bloomin'*, I had triple reason to be happy. Not only was I working on a new project, but Todd was working and staying reasonably sober. We were together where the weather was beautiful, and some of my friends were here, too.

There was so much about Los Angeles that needed getting used to. The silent law that said "no walking" bothered me. I walked everywhere in New York. Where Todd and I lived in Westwood, one could walk without being stared at, but as Bobby put it to me, "only the weirdos walk in L.A." I also found it difficult to adjust to the hours. I was a night person, as are most stage performers. It was nothing for me to go to bed at two or three in the morning, provided I could sleep till ten. Even while Todd worked in New York television, I stayed in the living room till the wee hours while he slept.

Los Angeles, or at least the people in it, shut down at 9 or 10 p.m. It drove me nuts. I couldn't imagine Bobby adjusting to this, but he had, and so had Holly.

"You want to go shopping tomorrow?" she asked me one day.

"Sure," I said. "I'll know my schedule for tomorrow when I see my arranger later tonight."

"Okay, call me at seven."

"I won't know by then."

"Seven tomorrow morning, Margo."

It was a whole new clock.

My first booking took place in early December at the chic Chez Robaire supper club. For my opening, I had a cheering section composed of Todd, Lettie, Bobby, Holly and some of their new friends. Sulynn and Clark sent gorgeous flowers. The audience was great, and I would have been on top of the world except for one thing.

I had asked Todd to invite Sammy, Jr. to my opening, as I had asked him time and time again to invite Sammy for dinner. But there it was again, his complete refusal to bring me into the mainstream of his life.

I kept my disappointment to myself until we got home from the club. Once we were alone, Todd was loving and romantic. I wasn't having any. "I take it you don't want your son to meet me," I said. "Why didn't he come to the show tonight?"

"Margo, please don't start with this."

"Are you ashamed of me? I'm here so we can be together, and you shut me out. Do you want me to go back to New York?"

He spoke gently. "You know that I don't. You also know that my life is very complicated."

"I'm sick of hearing that. All I get from you is a lot of innuendo and secrets. When we make love, I feel like I know you totally. But it's all a sham. I really know so little about you. You don't confide in me about anything. What do you intend to do about me?"

"Do you mean marriage?"

I flopped down on the sofa, not very easily. My beautiful blue gown was designed for standing in front of a microphone and almost ripped when I sat. "Todd, I don't need to be married to you to be part of your life. I don't need to have flashbulbs going off in my face or be linked with you in the newspaper. But I feel as if I've made a commitment to you and that you're ashamed of me. I didn't have to come to Los Angeles, you know. I'm here to be with you, and I'm not."

He kissed my bare shoulder. "Margo, Sammy's been through a lot with me. Two stepmothers, plus his own mother's been married twice. You have to let me do this my way."

I was full of my own unhappiness. Sammy Spivak, Jr. was only a name and a picture on a bureau. "He's an adult, isn't he?"

"He's an adult with a lot of problems like his old man's. He's been in some trouble with drugs." He took my face in his hands. "Margo, I don't think you understand what you mean to me, and that's my fault. It's true that I've kept you out of my life. I don't want my life to touch you or what we have, that's why. What you interpret as an insult is actually the highest compliment I could pay you. You represent sanity to me, a haven, happiness. Maybe I think you'd be out that door in two minutes if I involved you in my mess, and I can't risk it.

"I told you a long time ago not to get serious about me. And I also know we can't really control what happens with our feelings. I can't promise not to hurt you, Margo, but I'm trying not to, I really am." He kissed me, unzipping the back of my dress. I'd lost another battle.

Los Angeles was much more isolated than New York. It was harder to meet people, and the impression I got was that "friendships" were based on "you scratch my back, and I'll scratch yours." When the back-scratching stopped or didn't happen, "friends" drifted away. I was glad for the friendship of Holly and Bobby, and that Todd liked them. Bobby called one afternoon and invited us to a salsa club the following evening, Friday. "It'll be fun," he said. "Lots of dancing." It wasn't enough for Bobby to dance all day. He was like a machine. Todd was working on an episode of "Barnaby Jones," and I was sure he wouldn't want to go, but to my surprise, he agreed.

Todd and I got to the club at 8 p.m. Bobby and Holly were already there, and with the exception of three men who sat in the middle of the club, the place was empty. I noticed these three men were all wearing gray suits and red ties.

"Was there a sale on those suits?" I said to Bobby.

Todd howled with laughter. "That's the band, Margo!" Unlike the rest of L.A., the crowd that inhabited this club got rolling more on a New York schedule. The place started jumping an hour later, so much so that the heat in the club became almost unbearable. As a result, we drank like fish. Todd drank too much, but I'd never seen him have so much fun. The band spoke only Spanish, of course, and he interpreted for us, and we danced on the packed dance floor for hours.

Other men asked both Holly and me to dance, and we accepted. The men we danced with only spoke Spanish. The place had a neighborhood feel to it. Young girls went there alone or with others, and sat very politely at a table until they were asked to dance. It didn't seem to be a pick-up place at all. Some girls were even accompanied by their mothers! There was something very sweet to me about the old-fashioned values I saw in this place, and for the first time, I felt more at home in Los Angeles.

I didn't even mind, too much, celebrating Christmas where there was no snow. The day started out fabulously, with Todd and I making love and spending a leisurely morning together. Under our tree — white with blue ornaments — typical California — were piles of gifts from my parents, my brother, Todd's parents, plus my gifts for the Gaines family and Todd's presents for Sammy, as well as our own to each other.

There were a bunch of small gifts for me from Todd, and one large gift leaning up against the wall. I ripped it open, to find a beautiful charcoal portrait of Todd. There were three poses: one as Nero, one in his role in *The Misbegotten* and a large center portrait of Todd circa 1954. It was gorgeous.

"That was done for me about ten years ago," he said, drawing me to him. "Do you like it?"

"It's beautiful. Are you sure you want me to have it?"

"No one else." He kissed me.

I didn't want the idyllic morning to end, but it did. Todd was picked up by cab to go have dinner with Sammy, Jr. I took a deep breath and headed for Christmas dinner at Bobby and Holly's, where there would also be Art and Brownie.

Lettie made a huge fuss over me, to cover the strangulating tension in the room. Art sat on the couch playing with a glass of ice, while I stood at the arched entrance talking with Holly and Lettie about the nice weather. There was no Brownie in view.

Bobby shoved a drink into my hand. I headed for the couch and sat opposite Art. "What do you think of this? No snow at Christmas," I said.

"I kind of like it," he answered. "How do you like it?"

Rather than dreading an uncomfortable day, I said to myself, I might rather have worried about dying from boredom before the afternoon was finished. "I'm not really crazy about snow," I said, already sick of talking about the weather, "but I do like snow at Christmas. Where's your wife?"

"Back East with her family. I need a refill. Do you want me to freshen your drink?"

As my glass was full, I said, "No, thanks." I met the laughing gazes of Bobby and Holly across the room and waved to Bobby to come over to me.

"Why isn't his wife here?" I whispered. I saw Lettie knit her brow, trying to hear us.

"They're not getting along," he hissed in my ear. "Don't say anything. My mother doesn't know."

Well, it wouldn't be the first time Bobby and Art had taken her for a fool. She sure did know, and it accounted for a lot of her forced cheerfulness.

We finally managed to get off the topic of the weather, and the rest of the afternoon centered on the filming of *Bloomin'*. Art smoked a pack of cigarettes, drank a quart of scotch, didn't say much and left early, kissing me on the cheek as he departed.

Once he was gone, Lettie disappeared, crying, into the kitchen, and Bobby followed her. "One big happy family," I observed to Holly.

"She's upset about Art."

"He seems miserable." I didn't know that I was too unhappy about it, either. As much as I thought I was over my bad feelings, I still got a certain thrill at the sight of his moroseness.

"He is miserable." Holly sat cross-legged on the floor, petting

Circe. "He never should have married Brownie."

"Then why did he?"

"My understanding is she put a lot of pressure on him, and he gave in before he was really sure. Also, he wants a family."

"Yeah, I know." I downed the rest of my drink. I really did feel sorry for him, I decided, but there wasn't much I could do about it.

Abruptly, she asked me, "Are you going to marry Todd?"

"Todd can't afford to get married again. I can't imagine him even considering it. I don't think about a future with Todd. I just take each day as it comes. I guess that was the problem with Art and me. He kept looking at the big picture while I was just slogging along day by day. His way is supposed to be the mature way to live, but it doesn't seem to have brought him much joy."

Lettie and Bobby emerged from the bedroom, Lettie red-eyed, but composed and smiling. "Christmas is a hard time of year," she said, by way of explanation, as if I hadn't spent the afternoon there.

We exchanged gifts now that Art was gone, and I said my good-byes.

Todd was polluted, in front of the television in a semi-stupor when I got home. Dizzy with anger, I turned off the television, left him where he was and went to bed.

He was still there the next morning. I shook him awake, and groggily, with my support, he made his way into the bathroom, where I opened the shower curtain and pushed him into the tub. I turned the cold shower on full blast and left, shutting the door behind me. I made coffee to the percussion of his curses.

Later, he appeared at the kitchen entrance, a towel wrapped around him. "What do you think you're doing?"

"Making coffee."

"You know what I mean."

I faced him. "Todd, you and I both know you're not supposed to be drinking. You promised me you wouldn't. You know my terms. I can't stay with you if you drink." I burst into tears. "You ruined Christmas. Everything was going so well, and you wrecked it."

He disappeared from my view. When I came out of our kitchenette, he was in the living room, the towel still around him.

"Things didn't go too well with Sammy," was all he said.

"Did you fight?"

"I wish we had fought. We have nothing to say to each other. We're strangers. Except that when I look at him, I see all my own problems. And his problems are my fault."

I rubbed his shoulders. "You're out here now. There'll be lots of time to spend with him. But Todd, drinking isn't going to help your relationship with Sammy."

"I know. I just — I got depressed."

In February, I left for a San Francisco engagement. I hoped Todd could come with me, but unable to get a film offer, he was by then working on an episode of "Cannon." "Episodic television, the lowest of the low," he groaned. Harry, like all New York agents, had a Los Angeles office, and Todd was on the telephone to the contact person there every day. "Get me a TV movie," he'd say. "Get me anything but this blasted one-shot guest star crap."

It was in this charming frame of mind that I left him for San Francisco. My nails had grown back from our first separation. Now I could chew them anew.

The 4 a.m. phone calls from Spain started shortly after my return three weeks later. With the phone right next to the bed, these weren't exactly welcome. Todd never seemed to hear the phone, so after twenty rings or so, I usually had to answer and wake him. He'd stumble into the living room to take the call in there, waiting till I hung up before talking.

It was always the same woman, and through the bedroom door, I could hear Todd yelling at her in Spanish. I had studied Spanish in high school, but it wasn't any help at all, unfortunately.

I knew it was a lover calling him. So, despite his ardor, there had been another woman in Spain. I decided not to make a scene and waited for him to say something. The morning after the fifth call, he finally did. "I think I owe you an explanation for those phone calls."

I found this business of acting like I didn't care, while my heart was breaking, tough going, but I did the best I could. "I'm only interested in what it would take for you to answer the phone on the first ring. Or better yet, when this person is going to stop calling at four in the morning."

He sipped his coffee. "Well, see, it's my secretary. She's pregnant."

"By you?"

"She says so. I don't believe her, so I won't pay for an abortion. I don't have any money anyway. What she really wants is for me to marry her, and I can't do that either."

He told me this as if he was announcing he didn't separate his white laundry from his colored. It threw me off balance. "What are you going to do?"

"I don't know."

"Here's another one. How did she get this number?"

"She had the New York number." There was a recording on it now, which gave the new number. "I was thinking, maybe we could just take the phones off the hook from now on."

Well, of course, this was the perfect solution — I couldn't believe I hadn't thought of it. I took a deep breath. "We can't do that. Supposing there's an emergency and my family or friends need to reach me? Or someone needs to reach you?"

"All right. I'll figure out something."

"Is she in love with you? Or does she want money?"

"That's hard to say. I think she wants money for the abortion."

"Todd, you were in Spain in October. It's too late for her to get an abortion now."

He flushed and slammed his empty coffee cup on the table, smashing the cup into large pieces. "Dammit! I told you it isn't mine!"

"DON'T YOU SCREAM AT ME." I jumped to avoid the flying pieces. "You have no right to lose your temper at ME. As far as this baby not being yours — she still must be four months pregnant, or else she couldn't say it was yours. And how do you know it isn't? Are you now going to tell me you didn't sleep with her?"

Methodically, he picked up the pieces of the cup and threw them, one by one, into the waste basket. When he finished, he took a napkin and slid the slivers of dead cup into the palm of his hand.

"Todd, what are you going to do?"

He took my hand and pulled me onto his lap. "I did sleep with her," he began, and my heart fell into my stomach. "But just once. And I was drunk and I couldn't — I couldn't come. There's no way she's pregnant by me. But she thinks I've got more money than whoever the father is."

"Did you have an affair with her before?"

"Yes. She's bitter because I didn't bring her back to the States, and because I didn't marry her after my divorce was final."

"Todd, if the baby isn't yours, she's got no hold on you."

"It doesn't matter. She can make a lot of trouble for me. Even if she lost a paternity suit, she could still bring one against me."

"Back to my question. Can she be bought off? And for how much?"

"I think she could. But I don't know for how much. Or where to get it."

"It's time to call Harry," I said. "If there's anyone who'll know what to do, it's Harry."

Todd spent an hour and a half on the telephone to New York, and in the end, Harry advanced Todd a ton of money, arranged for a detective to fly to Spain to give it to her and put the fear of God into her at the same time. My sense was she could be bought off pretty cheaply, but with the detective and the air fare and hotel, Todd was going to owe Harry a bundle.

Harry was no fool. He called in some markers, and before Todd knew it, he had that TV movie he'd been trying to get since returning to Los Angeles. *Blind Murder* wasn't due out until Christmas of 1977. If the film and Todd got good reviews, things would be easier for him.

I told myself from the beginning: all that mattered was that Todd and I were together, and that I was in love with him. I could not control what he did when we were apart, and I couldn't reach into his past and change anything.

Faced with the reality of this new problem, I asked myself, did he not care for me at all, that the minute he got away from me, he hopped into bed with someone else? Did I just think we had something special because I was dazzled by the sex? And wasn't it obvious that Todd knew that I would not leave him under any circumstances, no matter what I said, so that he felt he could not only do just about anything, but confess it to me as well?

"Margo, you're crazy," Sulynn said on the phone to me later. "All you are to that guy is a good time and a chauffeur service. Don't old men do this — take up with young girls so they can feel young again?"

"Todd's not old, Sulynn. He's forty-four."

"He's getting up there. And that's just the time they have these crises." Sulynn was doing a lot of meaningful reading in her spare time and had become an expert on every facet of pop psychology. "What if this baby's his? What do you think about him just throwing some money at her as if that's going to solve anything?"

On this, I was firm. "It's not his baby. I believe him, Sulynn. If he had any doubt at all, he wouldn't handle it this way."

I left April 5th for Las Vegas, scene of my marriage to Art. One thing I liked about California, I had no unhappy memories — yet. Todd couldn't stay with me, because at that point, he was filming an episode of "Quincy." However, he came for the weekend with Bobby and Holly. *Bloomin'* had wrapped by this time, and Bobby, like Todd, was doing the TV circuit while trying to get another film.

After Vegas, I went to Lake Tahoe. After a week there, I rushed home to Todd, only to find a stranger in the apartment having a drink with him, and it looked like many drinks had preceded the one I saw in Todd's hand. "Margo, meet my friend from Madrid, Dr. Gustavo Ochoa."

I hated this man on sight and didn't want him in the apartment. Every bone in my body told me he was trouble. Never had I had such a strong reaction against someone, but there it was. He was a short, small man with graying hair and bloodshot, half-opened eyes. Every inch of him spelled "bum," "doctor" or not.

I greeted him politely, telling myself I'd seen too many old movies where Gustavo would have been type-cast as a swindler or cold-blooded killer. I asked Todd if I could speak to him privately.

"Who is this guy?" I demanded to know as soon as we got into the bedroom. "You knew I was coming back tonight. What's he doing here?"

"I just told you. He's a doctor friend of mine from Spain. He was the doctor on the set for a lot of my films. What's wrong?"

I bit my lip. "I don't know. I missed you, and it just threw me..."

He cupped my face in his hands and kissed me. "He's an old friend, Margo. I couldn't tell him not to come over. He'll be leaving in a little while."

"Fine, but if he's your friend and a doctor, he should know you shouldn't drink." I hadn't wanted to say that was what I found so upsetting, but at that moment, I felt out of control.

He turned on his heel and went back to Gustavo.

I made no attempt to be polite to Gustavo. I stayed in the bedroom and eventually went to bed. They were still laughing and talking at 2 a.m. Welcome home, I said to myself.

Gustavo, a man I began to refer to as The Angel of Death, hung around Todd on a regular basis after that, driving him around, showing up for dinner, even visiting him on sets when he filmed. Nothing about him that surfaced made me change my original opinion. From what I could gather, he had the bizarre idea of renting X-ray equipment and running some kind of clinic in his apartment. It didn't appear that he was licensed to practice medicine in this country, but evidently he didn't feel that was a barrier. I also found out that he had originally studied for the priesthood, but according to Todd, was thrown out of the seminary for writing letters to his dentist's receptionist. Two points for the Catholic church; they'd seen the error of their ways.

Todd very often wasn't home now when I returned from rehearsals or performances, and more and more he turned up drunk at 1 or 2 a.m. Or, worse, I'd call Todd from my pianist's and find out Gustavo was at the apartment. I'd then end up at Bobby and Holly's for the evening. This meant more often than not, I'd run into Art, trying to get away from his wife. It was getting so there was no place I could go.

Finally, I decided, if you can't beat them, join them. It was actually Bobby's suggestion. Perhaps he was just sick of running group therapy sessions in his apartment.

"If you don't like the influence this guy has on Todd, why don't you hang out with them and exert your own influence?" he said. "Fight him a little bit instead of just giving in." He was right, of course.

So I became a third wheel and organized a trip to Disneyland for us, when what I really wanted to do was avoid Gustavo like the Black Hole of Calcutta.

We picked Gustavo up from his digs in East Los Angeles at 10 a.m., and it was obvious he was already stoned. As we walked through Disneyland, he continued to dope himself up, eating five hash brownies. The alcohol I knew about; the drugs were a revelation.

On the spaceship ride, he opened a vial of amyl nitrate and spilled it. When we got to Tom Sawyer's Island, we stopped at the Bayou restaurant. By this time, Gustavo was so out of it, the waiter asked if he should call a doctor. "I am one," Gustavo answered. He then proceeded to pass out at the table. The paramedics arrived and put him on a stretcher. "I'm a doctor," he told them. They took him to the clinic behind the Big Bear Jamboree. We accompanied him. "Let me go — I'm a doctor," he said.

When Todd and I got home, I told him it was either me or Gustavo. I was not at all sure who he'd pick.

"Stay out of this, Margo," Todd snapped at me. "He's leaving for Santa Fe soon."

"This guy's some sort of Dr. Feelgood. You're crazy to even spend time with him."

"I told you, Margo, he's an old friend. I'm not turning my back on him just because he's having problems."

"PROBLEMS? What about our problems?" But I was talking to myself by that point. Todd had left the room.

Then Todd got another TV movie, and Gustavo came by every morning to take him to the studio. I was a zombie from worry. Todd was back to his old tricks — keeping himself together while filming during the day and getting loaded at night. In the past, this kind of behavior had always caught up with him.

If it caught up with him now, it would be curtains. I decided to become a fixture on that set. Harry's office arranged for a pass for me, and I arrived at 11 a.m. on the third day of filming.

When it came to booze, Todd was a master of deception. I marveled at how un-drunk he could act when it was necessary. On the set, Gustavo acted as a kind of majordomo for Todd. At three o'clock, Todd asked him for juice, which he brought to Todd in a plastic container. When he asked for second and third cups, I intervened.

"I want to see this juice," I said, blocking Gustavo's exit from Todd's Winnebago.

"It's just orange juice." He held it out. I brushed by him and conducted a search of the trailer. Under the bed, I found a case of Pernod. I also saw an open can of coffee with a spoon beside it. Todd was back to eating coffee grains to mask the booze on his breath.

"You're not to give him any more liquor," I told Gustavo. The guy scared me to death, and standing up to him was no easy feat. "Not one drop, or I'll tell the director." I emptied the bottles into the toilet.

I poured a glass of pure juice and brought it out to Todd. "Taste this," I said. "It's my own recipe."

He drank some, screwed up his face, and then glared at me. "That's all you're getting from now on, Todd, so get used to it. No arguments." There was nothing he could say.

When filming ended for the day, I said to Gustavo, "I have my car, and I'm going to be here from now on. I'll see that Todd gets home and gets to the studio in the morning."

Todd was in his trailer, and I saw Gustavo eyeing the door. "I'll say good-bye for you." I held my ground. Gustavo left.

Ripping mad, Todd let me have it as I negotiated the freeway. "You had no business going through my trailer like that," he growled. "You had no business being on the set like some — some nurse or something."

I couldn't argue with him and drive at the same time, so I said nothing until I maneuvered into the parking lot of El Coyote, where we often had dinner, and slammed on the brakes. "Yes, I did. I had every right. Why am I the villain? Because I love you, and because so far, you've been doing so well out here? Because you look wonderful, and your acting is great? Because this is a whole new beginning for you, and I don't want to see you spoil it? I see someone out to absolutely destroy you and I step in. And I'm the bad guy. I gave you a choice, Todd. It seems to me you've made it."

He sighed. "There's no way I can make you understand." He turned to me with sad eyes. "You're a kid, after all. Someday you'll realize, Margo, that no one can destroy me, and that there aren't any new beginnings. You can't hurt or resurrect the dead."

Tears fell on the steering wheel, which I gripped with all my might. "What are you saying? How can you talk like this?"

"Let's go home," was all he said.

That night, when he tried to make love to me, he couldn't, and collapsed in tears on top of me.

"Please, Todd," I begged him. "Talk to me — please." I felt like his hands were on my heart, and he was yanking it out of my body.

But he closed me out totally. The next day, I drove him to the studio. "I'm not coming with you," I said. "Get a studio limousine to bring you home. Baby-sitting you is useless." I stared out the windshield at the guard station. "It's your life, Todd. Do what you want with it." Without another word, he got out of the car.

Holly was at home when I banged on her door. I lay down on the floor of the living room, sun pouring on top of me, curled up in a fetal position and sobbed. Poor Holly didn't know what to do, so she called Lettie. Lettie had never learned to drive, so she took a bus to the apartment.

I don't know what I said to them, but I babbled for hours, as they got me on the couch and made me drink some kind of spiked tea. Words were coming out of my mouth as if I was a medium in a seance. When I was completely exhausted from crying, I left for home over their protests. "I'm okay," I promised them. "I just needed to talk to someone."

"Stay the night," Holly said.

I shook my head. "I can't."

I went home and got into bed, so completely exorcised that I fell asleep. Loud voices woke me up. Todd and Gustavo. I couldn't make out what they were saying. The voices stopped, and I heard a door slam. I pulled the covers over my head and never left the bedroom the entire evening.

I didn't see Todd until the following night, when he arrived home from the studio, courtesy of Gustavo, as I saw clearly from the window, although Gustavo didn't come in.

"Oh, Margo," Todd slurred after spending several minutes manipulating the key in the door. "I'm glad you're here. I need to ask you something." He fell into the sofa and extended his hand to me. "Come 'ere."

I stayed where I was. "What is it?"

"Need to borrow...money."

"Why?"

"Just need it."

"How much?"

"Five thousand." He passed out.

I was standing in the middle of the floor, shaking and hugging myself, watching him, when the phone rang. It was Holly. "Can I come over?" I asked her in a barely audible voice. Throwing some things into a bag, I ran out of the apartment.

Todd phoned the next night, sounding sober. "I called your pianist. I thought maybe you left to do a gig. What are you doing over there?" He didn't remember a thing.

"I'll be right there," I said.

"Do you want me to come with you?" Bobby offered.

"No. I'll be fine."

Todd was in his terry-cloth bathrobe, hair wet from a shower, when I arrived. "What the hell's going on?" he said, coming toward me.

"Why do you need $5000?" I shot back, keeping my distance.

"Oh." His face went blank. Then he said, "Sammy needs it."

"Is that what you're calling Gustavo now? Don't you get him confused with your son that way?" Before Todd could say anything, I continued. "I don't know the hold he has over you, Todd. I don't know why he's blackmailing you. But I can't be a part of it or you anymore. I'm going to stay with Bobby and Holly until I finish my club dates, and then I'm going back to New York." I swallowed, desperate to keep my composure. "I love you so much, Todd. I wanted to share your life with you, but you won't let me in. You want to drink yourself to death. I don't know why, and I can't stop you."

"You can't leave, Margo," he said, trying to come near me again. "I need you."

"Todd, I wanted to be your lover and your partner, not your crutch. And that's all I am to you now. There's no use talking about it, my mind's made up. I just needed a scorecard, that's all. You know, your three ex-wives, your pregnant secretary, Spain, Sammy, me. It was difficult to get it all straight. But I think I've got it now. Any port in a storm, except that, since all your money goes to alimony, payoffs to detectives, abortions, blackmail and child support, you'd rather the port was free. Not only financially, but emotionally."

Dumbfounded, he said nothing while I packed what I could and put the cats into their carrier. One by one, I carried my things into the hallway. When I was finished, I stood in the doorway.

"I love you, Margo," he said, his eyes meeting mine.

He was dead six months later.

Act III, Scene 2

1977 – 1978

By June, I was back in New York, homeless and unemployed. Finishing my engagements in my emotional and physical condition was excruciatingly difficult, and I arrived at Sulynn and Clark's for an extended stay, completely exhausted.

I was certain I had an ulcer, not that I knew anything about ulcers. It just seemed logical that an ulcer was the cause of my intermittent stomach pains. By the time I got to Connecticut, I was on the blandest diet imaginable and had dropped fifteen pounds I didn't need to lose in the first place.

I also hadn't had a decent night's sleep since leaving Todd. In order to cover the bags and circles under my bloodshot, swollen eyes that accompanied my pale complexion, I took to wearing hooker-type makeup on stage. It was better, I decided, to scare the audience than to worry them.

Sulynn's house was like an oasis in the desert to me, in spite of baby Nicole, a bad seed if I ever saw one. I had my own room, which housed most of Sulynn's considerable Beatles memorabilia, so I could think back to high school and wish I were still there, while staring at a *Hard Day's Night* poster. But the room had a door that shut firmly, enabling me to cut off the entire world, if necessary. And it was necessary. It was necessary to cry myself into a stupor, to sleep all day if I wanted to, to stay in bed if I decided getting up wasn't worth it. It almost never was.

My body ached for Todd, and it took every ounce of strength I possessed not to run back to him, not to call him or write him.

Sulynn declared that I was in a "clinical depression" and suggested it might be a good idea to "get back to work," even if it meant just singing at Clark's. At any other time, of course, she would have been right. But now, I didn't have the strength or the stamina to work.

"I'll be honest with you, Sulynn. I don't feel all that well."

"That's because of your depression. You're somatizing."

"I think *you* should go back to work," I said, "so you won't have time to watch talk shows and read all these cocktail hour psychology books."

Clark and Sulynn's efforts to get me to go to Clark's for dinner or atmosphere were in vain also. Lars was low on my list of People to See. I didn't even have the gumption to divorce him.

I called no one except Bobby and Holly. I didn't let Harry know I was back on the East Coast. I didn't call my sublet to check on the apartment. Instead, for almost a month, I read a bunch of cheap paperbacks, drank milk and chewed antacids for my stomach, watched television, played with the cats and baby-sat Nicole.

The stomach pain got so bad that one night, it woke me out of a sleep I had helped along with an over-the-counter sleeping pill. Flinching and sweating, I threw the sheet off of me, but when I tried to straighten up to get out of bed, I fell over and landed with a thump on the floor. The pain seared through me, and I couldn't get up. I yelled for Sulynn.

Nicole wailed, lights went on in the hall, the door flew open, and Sulynn and Clark stood over me. "Pain," I gasped. "Stomach. I...can't...stand."

Clark got me to my feet, although I remained hunched over, and assisted me back onto the bed. He and Sulynn were talking excitedly, but I couldn't concentrate on what they were saying. Sulynn touched my forehead and rubbed my hands. "You're going to be okay, baby," she kept saying over and over, softly. "We'll take care of you." Clark picked up me and carried me out to the car.

I must have passed out, because the next thing I knew I was on a gurney, screaming from pain as I was rolled down a hospital hallway. Everything went black again, and when I came to, I was in a hospital bed. Clark sat beside me, holding my hand. "Hey, kiddo," he said. "You scared the pants off us."

I drifted in and out of consciousness repeatedly. When I woke up for more than a few minutes, I saw Sulynn sitting across from the bed. Seeing I was awake, she ran out of the room and came back with a doctor.

"Miss Gaines, how are you feeling?" he said, retrieving a clipboard from the end of the bed.

I tried to sit up, but fell back on the bed. "Relax," he said. "You've had a rough time." Sulynn was on the other side of the bed, hand on my shoulder. "Miss Gaines," he continued, "you had an ectopic pregnancy, and we performed emergency surgery on you."

Sulynn shot the doctor a dirty look. "Do you know what that is, Margo? The baby was forming in one of your tubes. That's why you had so much abdominal pain."

"You can still have a baby, Miss Gaines," the doctor reassured me. "We have excellent techniques now, and I don't think in your case there will be a lot of scarring."

"But..." I felt like I was watching a foreign film and someone had forgotten the subtitles. "What happened to the baby?"

Sulynn turned her head away. The doctor said, "The baby couldn't possibly develop where it was, Miss Gaines. If you'd gone much longer, you would have died."

"But why did it happen?"

He shook his head. "We don't know. But occasionally, it does happen, and often the woman doesn't even know she's pregnant. The egg implants in the tube. The abdominal distress is the first symptom that something's wrong."

"When can she come home, Doctor?" Sulynn asked.

"Oh, three or four days." After he left, Sulynn looked at what must have been my very dazed face. "Margo, would you rather be alone?"

"No, but let's not talk, okay?" She nodded, and held my hand.

The next day, a social worker came in to see me, and I asked her to leave. I wasn't ready to talk. A priest came by. Apparently, I'd landed on a needy list. "There must be some mistake," I said, straight-faced. "I'm a Polish Jew."

Clark picked me up on my release day. "Here, sit in the back seat, or lie down if you feel like it," he said, getting me into the car. It was a brand new Lincoln Continental, so there was plenty of room to stretch out.

About two miles later, I felt nauseous. "Clark, I'm going to throw up." I had that horrible salivating sensation in my mouth.

Clark floored the gas pedal. "Hold on, Margo, we're almost home."

It was no use. "Clark, you have to stop the car. I'm going to throw up."

He pulled into a shopping mall, but not before I'd barfed all over myself. I hit the door release and made it out to throw up some more, kneeling on the ground.

Clark retrieved some rags from the trunk, so I could wipe myself off. He broke every speed limit in existence getting to the house.

"You're green," Sulynn observed as I dragged in, the entire front of me soaked.

"I think it's the medicine they gave me. I threw up on the way home."

"You didn't throw up in the new car!" she screamed, nearly dropping Nicole.

"ANGEL OF MERCY," I said. "No, your precious car is fine."

Clark came in behind me with my suitcase, looking worse than I did, I suspected. "She needs to go right to bed," he pronounced.

"After a bath," I said.

Sulynn helped me upstairs. "I'm sorry for what I said, Margo. It's just, Clark is such a maniac about that car."

"He was wonderful. You both are. Don't worry about it."

After my bath, she tucked me into bed. The Beatles were looking better than ever.

"Remember what we talked about, Sulynn," I said, before I drifted off to sleep. "If anyone asks you, this was an appendectomy."

"Already taken care of." She closed the door.

During July and August, I began to keep a journal of my thoughts and feelings, hoping it would act as a catharsis and help me come to grips with becoming pregnant by Todd, and then losing his baby. I couldn't let go of my love for Todd any more than I'd been able to let go of my love for Art.

"That's because you're a sadist," Sulynn told me. "You choose men who abuse you."

"Masochist, Sulynn."

"Whatever. And Todd has a narcissist complex."

It was better to agree with everything she said than to argue, and besides, I didn't have the energy for these discussions.

But the more I slept, the more tired I was; the more lazy I felt, the lazier I got. It was a vicious circle, and some of Sulynn's preaching finally got through to me. I had to break the cycle.

I started by going to Clark's on Sunday afternoons, and to my surprise, Lars was gracious, concerned and attentive, and turned out to be just what the doctor ordered. My third Sunday there, I got up and sang, appropriately, "Am I Blue?", one of the songs from my act. Slowly, I got my voice back into condition. It would be time to go back to work soon, I decided. If I could find work.

I was up in my room writing in my journal one Thursday, when Sulynn pounded on the door. "Guess who that was on the phone," she said. I hadn't even heard the phone ring. I didn't look up from my writing. "Who?"

"Arthur Gaines."

My pen stopped mid-sentence. "Where was he calling from?"

"New York. He asked about you, and he was angling for an invitation. So I told him to come out to the restaurant on Sunday, and I'd have someone pick him up at the train. You don't have to come, but I wanted you to know."

"I'll come. What else did he say?"

"Oh, not much. He's forming some sort of production company, and he's here to talk to some potential partners. And we talked about Bobby a little."

I smiled. "You miss the old gang, don't you?"

She shrugged. "I'm still mad at him for the way he acted, but..."

"But there's a history there, and you can't dismiss it any more than I can."

"I guess."

"We're getting older, Sulynn. We're thinking profound thoughts now."

"It's all that writing you're doing. It's aging you." She went back downstairs.

"MATURING," I yelled after her.

Lars was sitting with me when Art arrived at the restaurant, and immediately vacated his seat. "You don't have to go," I said, but he wouldn't hear of it, and escorted Art over to me. It was so ridiculous. My present husband bringing my ex-husband to my table. My life was like a French farce.

Art kissed my forehead. "How ya doin'? I heard you've been sick. A ruptured appendix or something?"

We exchanged pleasantries, but he wasted no time letting me know he was divorced. Holly had told me he was separated, but this was the first I'd heard of the divorce. I said I was sorry to hear it, and I meant it.

"It was for the best," he said. "We didn't want the same things."

"That's a recurring pattern with you, isn't it? Women who don't want what you want?"

"That wasn't it at all. Our goals for marriage were the same. But..." He lit a cigarette, then put it out. "I'm trying to quit."

"You were saying?"

"Oh. I wasn't in love with her."

"That's quite an admission." I glanced around for Sulynn or someone to rescue me.

"Well, I've made an admission to you. Now you can make one to me. What's the real story with you and Lars? I've never been able to get a thing out of my brother."

I laughed. "Okay, fair enough." I told him as much as I could, ending with, "I wasn't looking to get married again — really married — so it seemed like a good solution all around."

"I pretty much had it figured out." He seemed pleased with himself.

Sulynn approached the table. "I'm going to sing 'And This Is My Beloved.' Why don't you two do 'Anything You Can Do?'"

Art guffawed. "The Cape Codders was a long time ago, Sulynn. I'm not sure I remember it."

"That'll make it funnier. Come on!"

It was quite an afternoon, singing with Art like the old days and having a meaningful conversation with him. It was almost too much to take.

"Let's keep in better touch from now on," he said as he left. "Will you have dinner with me in the city next week?"

"Well, that's a little rough. I have no place to stay, and I don't want to come back on the train too late." Art was staying with Foss and her new husband. I knew plenty of people, but I didn't want any of them to know I was back in New York, and wanted less to have a conversation with them.

"Can't you stay at Harry's, or Howard and Fred's?"

"Howard and Fred live too far uptown, and I'm hiding from Harry."

"It's time you stopped, don't you think? Are you going to stay out here forever?"

"You're right." We made a date for Wednesday, which meant I had to call Harry on Monday. It was time to complete the healing process.

Harry greeted me with his usual warmth. "Margo, where the hell have you been?"

I went into my ruptured appendix bull. "I'm feeling much better now," I finished, "and I'm ready to do some auditions. Dinner theater, whatever."

"No dinner theater. It's better if you stay in town, and I'll line you up with something on or off-Broadway. Do your club act in the meantime."

"I really want to work, Harry, not sit around. And I can't do my club act. It's too exhausting for me right now. Send me out for whatever's available. I'm coming in on Wednesday. Can I stay overnight at the apartment?" He agreed, and said he'd call me at

Sulynn's if he got me an audition for anything.

"I wonder if I'm ready to make the rounds yet," I said to Art at Tavern on the Green Wednesday evening.

"I couldn't do an audition now if you held a gun on me," Art said.

He was full of plans for his film production company, and talked at length about his partners and projects. Suddenly deflated with tiredness, I gladly let him take over the entire conversation.

After dinner, we walked the short distance to Harry's. It was a beautiful night. For the moment, the suffocating heat seemed to have given way to a balmy breeze. It made me think of walking with Todd in Westwood, after going to dinner or the movies. I saw myself holding onto his arm and feeling so proud to be next to him. I stopped in the middle of the sidewalk.

"What's wrong?" Art asked me.

"I — I couldn't get my breath for a minute. I'm okay now." I'd only told Art I wasn't seeing Todd any more, no details.

When we got into the lobby of Harry's building, Art said, "Are you going right back to Sulynn's?"

"I don't know. I'll call Harry, and if there's nothing doing as far as auditions, I guess I'll go back. The heat's a little better in Connecticut. It's awful here." We stood at the door, awkwardly. I wasn't about to invite him up. All I wanted to do was crawl into bed, alone.

"I want to say something before you go upstairs," Art said. "About my divorce from Brownie."

I didn't want to hear it, but forced myself to be polite. "Yes?"

"My marriage to Brownie didn't work because I'm still in love with you."

I closed my eyes. "Art, you don't even know me anymore."

"Margo, I'm not asking you for anything now. But couldn't we just see each other from time to time? Get to know each other all over again? Talk about what happened?"

"As friends, yes. But as far as anything else, I'm still in love with Todd Lang." I watched the light go out in Art's eyes. Then I delivered the final blow. "You might as well know, I didn't have any ruptured appendix. I had an ectopic pregnancy." A sob shook my entire body. "I was pregnant with his baby, and it died." I leaned against the glass door, trembling and crying. Turning my back to him, I inserted the key in the lock.

"Margo, let me come with you. You shouldn't be alone."

"Thanks, but that's not necessary."

"Can I call you?"

"Sure." He looked as if he were about to cry himself. I forced a smile. "I'll talk to you soon, I promise."

The next day, just for something to do, I dropped in on Harry on Madison Avenue to see if anything was happening.

He perused some casting breakdowns. "The only thing going on now is a Long Island dinner theater production for *Sound of Music*, and it's mostly cast, except for Elsa. You know, the baron's fiancée."

"Perfect. Can you get it for me?"

"Hah! Are you nuts? It's a supporting role. It wouldn't look good for you to take a part like that."

"Harry, I gotta get back in the swim. Set up an audition for me, please."

He was firm. "You don't want to be in this production. The part of Maria —"

"I don't care about the part of Maria. Who wants to sing about a goatherd? Elsa has a big high C. Oh, Harry, *please.*"

He drummed his fingers on the desk. "I'll see if they'll give it to you without an audition. If you want to be a glutton for punishment, that's your problem."

The owners of the dinner theater, a thug-like man and his blonde bombshell wife, as well as the director, were thrilled to have a woman with a Broadway credit working for dinner theater money, and Harry got me special billing — my name in a box on the program: "And MARGO GAINES as Elsa."

I didn't quite understand the "glutton for punishment" bit until I walked into rehearsal on September 8th and discovered that Amalia Hayes-Winslow was playing Maria! I almost crawled out of the rehearsal hall in disgrace. I called Sulynn at the first break. "I've got to get out of this show," I announced. "I'm getting a doctor's note to say I'm dead."

Cooler heads prevailed. "Do what you've done since college," she advised me. "Wipe the stage with her. With her in the lead, the show's up for grabs."

I lived at Harry's apartment during the engagement. He wasn't very happy about Sammy and Deli living there, too, but I promised to keep their nails cut so they wouldn't ruin the furniture.

Once performances started, we were picked up each evening at 5:30 and driven out to the theater. For me, the brutality of this was second only to the meal they gave us when we got to the theater. During the eight-week run of the show, I went through five bottles of Pepto Bismol. Sulynn, Clark, Harry, Art, Howard, Fred, Foss — a whole host of people came out to see me, and they all went home with something close to food-poisoning.

Watching Amalia wreck the part of Maria was one thing, but listening to her infernal yakking was another. Amalia's only interest, as usual, was Amalia. She and my old college nemesis, Winslow, were trying desperately to get into Manhattan Plaza, the government-subsidized apartment complex for artists. In the midst of her attempts, a friend of hers who lived there came backstage after the show.

"I was hoping the show would cheer me up," he said to us. "I got some bad news today. A friend of mine down the hall, an older man, just dropped dead."

"That means his apartment's available, right?" Amalia asked.

Amalia was deeply jealous of me, as usual. This time, it was because I'd been singled out in all the reviews as being excellent, while her reviews had been mixed. Not only that, but *Blind Murder* was due out next month. I'd been invited to a rough cut, but couldn't face seeing Todd on screen, especially in our love scenes. But Harry attended the screening and assured me he could get me more work in film if I wanted it. I wasn't sure I did. Film work very often meant California, and California meant Todd Lang.

The show ended in late November, and it turned out to be the last show for that dinner theater. The IRS raided the place several weeks later, and the owners snatched a bunch of nickels from the cash register and escaped out the back door.

By now, my sublet had vacated my apartment, and I was back in, with memories of my marriages and Todd. Maybe it was a mistake to come back here, I said to myself. Hard as it was to find an apartment in New York, for my peace of mind, I considered looking.

Harry called me the morning of November 28th, 1977. He chit-chatted with me aimlessly for a while — totally unlike him — then said, "I need to see you at my apartment. Can you come over now? Sulynn is here, and I want to talk to both of you."

"Sulynn is there? What's she doing there?"

I heard her voice on the phone. "I stopped in. I'm shopping."

"Why didn't you tell me you were coming into town?"

"I decided at the last minute. I'll meet you here."

A half hour later, I arrived at Harry's. I knew the second I saw Harry and Sulynn that something was terribly wrong.

Sulynn indicated I should sit next to her on the sofa, and when I did, she put her arm around me.

Harry cleared his throat. "Todd died last night, Margo."

"I read it in the paper this morning," Sulynn said. "I figured you didn't know." I never looked at a morning paper.

The first thing that went through my mind was, Harry didn't say what I thought he said. The second thing I told myself was, at last I can have that nervous breakdown I've been promising myself.

"Are you okay, Margo?" Sulynn asked me.

"I — I don't know. How could Todd be dead? How?" I spotted *The New York Times* on the coffee table and took it, staring uncomprehendingly at the front page headlines. "Where — where's the obituary?"

"For corn's sake, Margo." Harry yanked the paper from my hand. "He wasn't Bing Crosby, you know. He's not on the FRONT PAGE OF *THE NEW YORK TIMES*." He rifled through it, stopping at last and handing me the one column item on page thirty, under an absolutely horrendous photo of Todd. When I saw the photograph, I sobbed, "Todd never looked like that. How could they print this?" Sulynn patted me on the back.

I tried to make out what the obit said, but none of it made sense. For one thing, it mentioned a widow. For another, an autopsy. Confused, I threw the paper down. "What widow? Why are they having an autopsy?"

Harry folded his arms across his chest. "He was found in a coma by the pool, with a gash on his head. He fell, I guess, but the coroner isn't sure of the exact cause of death. He was alone in the house."

"I don't understand any of this. What *house*?"

"Todd got married again a couple of months ago. I guess you didn't know. He married Janele Prendergast."

The name wasn't familiar to me.

"She's an ugly old souse," Sulynn said. "From the soap opera 'Monterey.' I met her a couple of times when I was on 'A Bright Tomorrow.' She's a member of the original cast, so they keep her on even though she's a horror."

"Why would Todd marry someone like that?"

"That's easy," Harry said. "She had a house he could die in."

"He didn't want to be alone," I cried. "I shouldn't have left him."

"Yes, you should have, Margo," Sulynn said. "You did what you had to do."

"But everyone was against him. He was being — blackmailed or something..."

Harry interrupted, "The only one against Todd was Todd, and that's the way it was from the day I met him, Margo. He was his own worst enemy, and you know it."

I couldn't bear it. As I convulsed with sobs, the incision in my stomach began to ache, and Sulynn put me in the bedroom to lie down, closing the door. I didn't stay there very long.

"The funeral," I said, coming back into the living room. "When is it?"

Harry and Sulynn exchanged glances. Harry said, "I don't know yet because of the autopsy, but whenever it is, Margo, it's not a good idea for you to go."

"He's right, Margo," Sulynn said.

"I have to go," I said, blowing my nose. "I have to say good-bye to him."

"Margo, Margo, Margo." Harry stood up and put his hands on my shoulders. "I'll get all the information on where he's buried, and the next time you're in Los Angeles, you can say good-bye to him. But I don't want you to even consider going to the funeral. You have to promise me that."

I was too upset to argue. I brought a bunch of newspapers with me to Sulynn's house, where I stayed a few days, bringing the cats with me. I couldn't face the apartment.

When I was calmer, I read each news account very carefully. Todd's obituary made the television page of *The Daily News* and was on page five of *The Post*. "Fall Kills Todd Lang," the *News* said. "*Nero* Star Todd Lang Found Dead at Pool," said *The Post*.

I was back to no sleeping and crying all the time. My tear ducts screamed for mercy, as I hadn't given them much of a break. Harry called a few days later. "Todd's being buried day after tomorrow, Margo. I'm going out to L.A. According to the autopsy, he had a stroke caused by a blow to the head incurred some days before he died..." he was reading from something — "...which later caused a cerebral hemorrhage and resulted in his death."

I felt as if I existed in a thick fog. "So, he didn't really die from the fall?"

"No. He passed out as a result of having a stroke, apparently. And he had the stroke because of this gash on his head."

"But how did he get the gash?"

"According to Janele, he fell in the house earlier in the week."

"Drunk, probably," I said.

"There was alcohol in his blood when he died. Also, his liver was a mess. Margo, are you still there?"

"Yes, I'm here."

"I'll call you when I get back."

"Okay. Harry? Would you — would you leave some flowers for me? You don't have to put my name on them."

"Sure, I will, Margo. Don't worry about it."

I went back to Manhattan on Sunday, and on Monday, I heard from Zelda Lasker. "The producers are interested in your taking over the lead in *Rosalind*," she said, referring to Foss's latest show. "Jocelyn Carlyle is leaving."

I couldn't have cared less. "Have you heard from Harry?"

Zelda's voice held a distinct "don't mess with me today" tone. "No. They want to see you tomorrow afternoon at two o'clock. Shall I set it up?"

"Yes, set it up." I hadn't even seen *Rosalind*, nor did I know one song from it. "I need a script and a score — fast," I said.

Maybe, I mused, as I worked with my accompanist that evening, this is just what the doctor ordered. I'd give it my best shot, at any rate.

The next day, I dressed the part. Rosalind spends most of her time disguised as a man, so I wore jeans, high boots and a tunic top, even going so far as to Ace-bandage my chest to make it flatter.

Quite a contingent turned out to see Margo Gaines audition for *Rosalind* — more than some of our showcase audiences for *Bloomin'*. Foss was there, of course, and the director, conductor, stage manager (Bertha again) plus Zelda, the two producers — Zack and another man, and an assistant. Howard, who had one of the leads, stood in the hall with Fred.

Being a quick study (not sleeping helps), I sang two songs from memory: "Like a Man," in which Rosalind describes how she's going to macho it up in her manly disguise, and "Venus," not the Frankie Avalon tune, but Ann Fossey's. "Like a Man" got a lot of laughs, and I could tell Zelda was concerned. A strong, positive reaction from auditioners usually meant they weren't going to hire you. The last thing one wanted to hear from potential employers was applause and compliments — the ultimate kiss-offs.

"Venus" touched my heart as few songs ever had, because of Todd. Singing it, I achieved what every performer dreams of, total commitment to the music and burning concentration. I let the song become my emotional receptacle.

"If you but knew how deeply I am in love,
But my love never ends.
I know no light without him, no stars above
I'll find a shadow, and sigh till he come
If you but knew how deeply I am in love."

For a few moments after I finished singing, no one spoke. I signed my contract two days later and went into rehearsal for my second Broadway show on Monday of the following week.

Harry escorted me to the theater after we had breakfast. He didn't have much to say about the funeral. "His parents were there. It was very sad. Very sad. Closed casket, naturally. I didn't go to the cemetery. Please don't cry, Margo. Put this behind you now."

Bertha was at the theater when we arrived, script in hand. "Where's Stan?" Harry asked, referring to the director.

Bertha was dumbfounded. "I don't think he plans to be here."

Harry became the Total Agent. "You mean you're supposed to put Margo into the show?"

I smiled weakly at Bertha, waiting for the fireworks.

"That's what I was told to do."

"Well, you can consider yourself untold," Harry barked. "No one puts my client into this show except the director. Margo Gaines is not a chorus kid." Almost crushing my elbow between his fingers, he dragged me out of the theater.

I, therefore, didn't rehearse all week, because the director was, by this time, out of town. He expected me to be blocked into the production by his return. He didn't know Harry Lasker, Agent to the Stars.

It was for this reason that I was at home, studying my script and singing through the music with the aid of a pitchpipe, when my buzzer rang on Friday of that week. My speaker didn't work, so I did what every New Yorker is absolutely never supposed to do: I buzzed the person in without knowing who it was and prayed the woman upstairs hadn't been in the foyer at the same time. She was constantly leaving notes on the mirror downstairs that no one was to be admitted without being announced, and she cornered me with another mugging story every time I left or came into the building. I swore she lay in wait for me.

When my doorbell rang, I looked through the peephole and saw a vaguely familiar face, one I couldn't quite place. I opened the door.

"Margo Gaines." The shortish, dark young man extended his hand to me. "I'm Sammy Spivak, Jr." He headed directly into the apartment, acting as if he owned the place and was just checking to see that his valuables were still there. Speechless, I stood at the door like a visitor.

"I'm here for a photo shoot and wanted to meet you." Sammy sat down in the chair by the window. I had a sudden vision of sitting on Todd's lap as he sat in that chair, and I physically shook myself out of it.

"My dad was in love with you." Sammy stated it as a fact.

"Did he tell you that?"

"Sort of. Were you in love with him?"

"Yes."

He indicated the couch. "Sit down."

I obeyed. There was something very Napoleonic about him.

"It's funny about Hollywood," Sammy the human said, petting Sammy the cat. "They don't know who the hell you are until you drop dead at a young age. Suddenly my dad is a myth or something."

Trembling, I reached for the white afghan next to me and wrapped it around myself, in an attempt to get warm. "He always had a kind of cult following," I said. "I think it was because of *Nero*."

"*Nero*." He nearly spit when he said it. "Anyway, there's all kinds of bullshit happening now, with this *Blind Murder* coming out next week. Is he good in it?"

"I thought he was wonderful."

"Hmm." Easily preoccupied, he continued to look around and fidget in his chair. "Well, some publisher called me. Do you know Raymond Delisle?"

"No."

"He's the guy. He wants me to write a book about my dad. I haven't got time to read a page of a book, much less write one. But I'm afraid if I don't write it, some stranger will. This Delisle told me there's going to be a lot of interest in my dad, that whole young tragic death thing, and with the movie coming out. Plus he read in the trades that my dad's producer in Spain signed a distribution deal to release some of my dad's films that haven't been seen over here. They're cheapies, you know, and they'll probably go straight to television, but still..." He paused. I waited.

"I wondered if you'd be willing to write about my dad. I don't want someone who didn't know him or care about him to say stuff..."

He was a strange combination of bravura and vulnerability, and there was something quite touching about him and maddening at the same time. Certain angles of his face were so much like Todd's, and yet, he had a nervous energy that bespoke a persona all his own. He was only a few years younger than I, but I felt like his mother. "I'm thinking about my grandparents, too," he finished.

I tightened the afghan around me. "I don't think I could write about Todd," I said. "I'm going into a Broadway show, so I have a time problem. Also — he had a lot of problems, Sammy. I wouldn't know what to write." I wasn't sure how much Sammy knew, so I left it at that.

"You mean the alcoholism."

"I don't see how it could be left out."

"I wouldn't ask you to do that. Everyone knew about it. I don't want a whitewash. I just want something..."

"Sympathetic?"

"Yes. Sympathetic." His face crumpled. "I loved him. He was my dad. I loved him so much." He buried his face in the arm of the chair. I touched his head, then gently massaged his neck as he cried.

He was terribly embarrassed. "Sorry," he muttered, reaching for a handkerchief. "The whole thing was real sudden, you know. Margo, will you just go talk to this Delisle guy? If I tell him I want you to do it, well, then no one else will."

I agreed to a meeting, and he said he would have the publisher call me. As he was leaving, I noticed the façade was back. He patted me on the shoulder. "Thanks. I'll be in touch," he said.

"Just a minute," I said. I went into the bedroom and came out with the charcoal drawing of Todd, his Christmas gift to me. "Your dad gave this to me. I'd like you to have it."

Tears rolled down his face. "I couldn't. I wouldn't feel right about it."

"Go ahead," I said. "I always thought you should have it. I want you to."

"I — I'm very grateful," he stammered. "I won't forget this."

Concentrating on *Rosalind* was impossible, and I was due to be put into the show by the director starting on Monday. I was in tatters. When I met Harry before the rehearsal, he was appalled at my appearance.

"I want you to see a doctor," he said, scribbling something on a piece of scrap paper he pulled from his pocket in the cab. "You call this doctor and you make an appointment."

I looked at the name: Dr. Martin Turner. "What kind of a doctor is he?" I knew damn well he was a psychiatrist. "I don't need a shrink."

"Yes, you do, dammit. You're not going to blow this show sky-high. Now you go see him, Margo."

I only went because I thought he might give me something to help me sleep. I went after rehearsal on Wednesday night, bringing a falafel sandwich with me to Dr. Turner's East 79th Street office. In retrospect, I was probably trying to antagonize the hell out of him. I sat in the waiting room and ate a falafel sandwich over his oriental rug, and dropped some of it.

When he came out of his office, his eyes moved from me to the sandwich I hadn't yet picked up off the rug. His expression never changed. "Throw that fucking thing away," he said. I did so. Immediately.

Once in his office, he got the couch, and I got stuck in a chair.

"I don't want to be here," I began. "Harry thinks I should talk to someone."

"What do you think?"

"I don't see why I need it. A lot's happened to me recently, but a lot happens to everyone."

"What's happened to you?"

At first, I didn't answer. Then: "I guess I should go back to the beginning," I said. "I married one of my best friends. He cheated on me, so I divorced him, but we still had to work together. We're back to being friends now. Then I married this gay guy so he could stay in the country and invest in a restaurant with some other friends of mine. I'm still married to him. I fell in love with an actor who was an alcoholic, and we moved to California together. He was being blackmailed or something. He's dead, and his son wants me to write a book about him. I'm in a Broadway show now, and Harry thinks I can't cut it."

I decided Dr. Turner wasn't disposed toward me. Either that, or he'd finally met his match. He asked me a lot of questions, undoubtedly trying to figure out if I'd fabricated any of what I told him.

"You think this is a fantasy," I accused him. "Unfortunately, this is my life." We verbally danced for a time, and I found myself making an appointment for the following week without being sure it was what I wanted.

The next evening, I had dinner with Raymond DeLisle, the publisher who had approached Sammy. Raymond DeLisle was full of "vision."

"I have a vision," he said, "of a book with a broader perspective than just Todd Lang. I envision a story placed in the '50s, using the story of Lang intertwined with the breakdown of the studios..." I mentally checked out at that point.

"I haven't had a lot of writing experience," I broke in eventually. "I also have some real conflicts. I'm not anxious to go public about my relationship with Todd, and I certainly wouldn't want it advertised that I'm doing a book about him. I told Sammy I'd talk to you, but..."

He waved his hands in the air. Two waiters rushed to the table, but he was only gesturing to me, so they retreated. "All this can be dealt with," he assured me. "I'll assign a top editor to you who will assist you in every aspect of the writing. If you want to write under an assumed name, that's all right, too. As far as the relationship with Todd, I have a vision that it can be handled as Margo Gaines' close friendship with Todd Lang, and as the author, interview yourself in the book."

I emoted about all this in my therapy session. "It sounds like, despite what you say," Dr. Turner observed, "you want to write this book. Why?"

"I'd like to help Sammy out. I wouldn't want to see someone who didn't know Todd write about him either."

"But you don't even know Sammy. And you didn't know Todd, did you?"

"No. And that's what hurts. I feel like I have to understand him, what happened to him, or I'll never be able to let go. I guess that's why I want to attempt to at least write about him. But — I don't even know where to begin."

"At the beginning." And for this, I was paying him $75 an hour.

My histrionics really began when I got a check from Delisle Publishing, Inc. for $10,000, as an advance. Supposing I couldn't write this book? I put the money in the bank, in case I had to return it.

Art was still putting a deal together in New York with his new partners and called me frequently. He planned to stay to see me open in *Rosalind* in January.

"You need a secretary and researcher," he advised me. "You can't do this and the show without help. Advertise at New York University and get a film student."

I called the University, and they placed the following on the student bulletin board: "Need research assistant for biography of actor Todd Lang. Call Margo." My service number was underneath my name. I received several calls and set up evening appointments to meet with prospects.

I'd pretty much decided to hire the first student that I interviewed. My second appointment arrived on her heels. As I opened the door to let her out, a chubby young man of medium height ambled into the apartment, rolling a luggage carrier with a large box on it behind him. He wore a suit and bow tie, and his Dr. Zorba hair stood straight up on his head.

"How do you do?" he said. "I'm Wyatt Bertolino."

"Wyatt Bertolino. You sound like you should be shooting up a saloon in west Italy."

"I'm an expert on Todd Lang. You both were great in *Blind Murder*." With a flourish, he indicated the box. "This is all Todd

Lang memorabilia."

I laughed. "You're an expert on Todd Lang? How did that happen?"

"Well, actually," he detached the box from the rope holding it, "I'm an expert on all movie stars of the '50s. The '50s are my era of specialization."

"That's quite an admission from a film student."

"How can you have that attitude and be writing about Todd Lang? The '50s are a great transition period in this country. Besides, I'm no longer a student. A friend of mine read me your ad from the bulletin board. Have memorabilia, will travel."

I couldn't believe the material he brought. Fan magazine article after article and photos of Todd with his first wife, Linda Wolfe, and baby Sammy; Todd and Linda moving into their first apartment; Todd and Linda at Lake Arrowhead. Todd in *The Misbegotten*, Todd in every other Hollywood film he made. Massive amounts of papers, photos and reviews.

"Would you be willing to sell some of this?" I asked him. "I think his son would like to see it."

"Sure. Do I get the job?"

"You bet."

"Does his son look like Todd?"

I picked up an early publicity photo of Todd. "Under certain lighting."

Like me, Wyatt was only half Italian, but his other side was Jewish, while mine was Irish. "I have the guilt of centuries," he told me. He had a work ethic second to none, and not only did research for me, but became my personal secretary.

Wyatt's many peculiarities surfaced a bit later. Shortly after I opened in *Rosalind*, he arrived for our afternoon work session wearing a light blue rayon sweater with brown, knobby plastic buttons. It was hideous. It was also a girl's sweater.

"It belonged to a girl I used to work with," he told me. "She left it at the office where we worked, and after she died, I took it."

"How did she die?"

"Avalanche in northern California."

"Why would you wear that sweater?"

"What else would I do with it?"

Everything Wyatt wore or furnished his apartment with, he either stole or bought from a garage sale or from the Salvation Army. He was the type who brought bugs into restaurants and put them on his food so he could get a free meal. He stole roses out of people's gardens. "Unless it's a small garden," he said. If it wasn't nailed down, Wyatt made off with it. But he was loyal beyond belief, and discreet. He told no one I was writing about Todd.

In February, *Rosalind* companies and tours were set up, and I immediately requested the Los Angeles company. I wasn't prepared for Harry's reaction. He hit the ceiling.

"You can't leave Broadway for Los Angeles," he insisted. "It's not a good move. I don't advise it."

I debated telling Harry about the book, only because he might be of some help to me, but decided against it. If I told Harry "Mighty Mouth" Lasker, I might as well take out billboard space in Times Square. The only people who knew were my psychiatrist, Sulynn, the Gaines family, Sammy, the publisher and, of course, Wyatt. As far as I was concerned, that already made too many people.

"I need to be in Los Angeles, Harry," was all I said. "So I'm going."

"You're making a huge mistake, Margo. I'm telling you." But I was firm.

Wyatt wrote to Sammy, explaining when I would be coming and what would be needed from him as far as setting up interviews. Wyatt also sent him a scrapbook of Todd Lang memorabilia. Sammy was deeply moved and called me more and more frequently as the weeks progressed, promising me his full support. Up to that point, Wyatt and I had only been getting a chronology of Todd's early life and career together, and Wyatt had conducted phone interviews with people from Todd's home town and college. Now it was time to get down to the nitty-gritty.

Fred and Howard sublet their apartment in Washington Heights and moved into mine. They liked the neighborhood better, and Howard could be closer to the theater.

In March, Wyatt and I left for Hollywood.

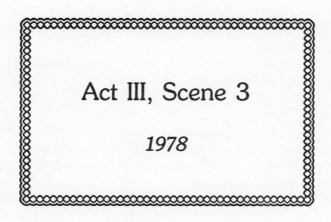

Act III, Scene 3

1978

At some point in L.A., my life went from being a French farce to a
Fellini movie.

When Wyatt and I arrived at the airport, Bobby was waiting.
"Hurry, hurry!" he pleaded with us, picking up some of our luggage.
"The last time I picked my mother up here, we got outside, and my
car was on blocks." He shot out ahead of us.

Wyatt's suit was padded with packages of smoked almonds from
the plane, as well as several magazines and the cat carrier, and as a
result, he had trouble moving fast enough for Bobby. I ran out to the
car, where Bobby was throwing our massive luggage into the trunk.
"Who's that character?" he asked me. "Is that the *secretary*? He looks
like he belongs in Bellevue."

"He does."

The production company of *Rosalind* supplied me with all sorts of
housing lists, but I paid no attention. Wyatt and I stayed with Bobby
and Holly for a week, until Wyatt found us an apartment. Yes, us. I
most certainly wasn't paying rent on a separate apartment for him.
We ended up in a fantastic place on Hollywood Boulevard. It had a
good-sized living room, eat-in kitchen, a dining room, with one large
and one small bedroom.

I was more impressed with the speed with which Wyatt furnished
the place. He had various sources, one of which was the theater where
Rosalind was playing. The theater had a room for sets and furniture,
and Wyatt picked out several items he liked, unbeknownst to me. To
Wyatt's credit, he didn't believe in being remotely surreptitious. He
liked doing things in the open. He backed my leased car up to the

front of the theater and had the maintenance man help him load a bureau into the car.

Then he decided he liked a drop leaf table. He disassembled it and carried it out in a hanging bag under his arm. It took two trips. He reassembled it in the apartment.

I didn't know where it came from until I invited a few people from the theater — including the theater manager — over for drinks. When they left, Wyatt told me he had really been sweating out the evening, thinking the manager might recognized the now-stripped table on which he was placing his drink.

Some years before I met Wyatt, he stole eight silver place settings from a hotel, not to mention chairs and a brass bed, all of which he now shipped to L.A.

I rented a bunch of furniture before he could steal anything else.

Wyatt's routine was pretty much the same daily. He fed the cats (I, of course, was still sound asleep), then set off for a bookstore near Grauman's Chinese theater, about a fifteen minute walk from the apartment, where he read a chapter of *Mommie Dearest*. Then he took a bus to the Margaret Herrick Library and did research on Todd for several hours. For lunch, he would go to a health food store that had barrels full of yogurt-covered raisins, carob items and sesame seeds, and eat his way from the entrance to the rear of the store. No one ever stopped him. The help was all too spaced out.

Despite his idiosyncrasies, to me, Wyatt was a godsend. He kept the apartment spotless, shopped and did the laundry, brought things to the cleaners, and as my "front man," conducted what interviews he could about Todd. I spent my afternoons before going to the theater organizing the material on Todd and writing. I found the entire process quite therapeutic. The young Todd had been a golden boy, his mother's pride and joy, the handsomest, smartest and most talented kid in his home town and college. When he got to Hollywood, he sat back and waited for everything to be handed to him, as it had always been. But it didn't work that way, and he found himself quickly slipping from the top of the heap to the bottom. His answer? Alcohol. Thus weakened, he let himself be dominated by his second and third money-hungry wives, who insisted he go for the quick buck. A disappointed Todd saw his dreams of super-stardom evaporate.

I'd lived with the man, lived with his nightmarish torment, and I wasn't convinced this was the whole story. The research was incomplete. For the big interviews, we needed Sammy Spivak, Jr.

Sammy in New York had been one thing. Los Angeles was something else again. It didn't take me long to figure out I wasn't going to get much cooperation from him. He was full of talk and gratitude for scrapbooks and information, but no hard help was forthcoming. The more I learned about him, the more turned off I became.

First of all, he was always, "REAL BUSY, SWEETIE." Sammy Spivak, as far as I was concerned, had it made in the shade. He was a pathetic photographer, but bombarded with assignments, because his stepfather was the head of an advertising agency, his mother was a working actress, and his occasional girlfriend was on the staff of a fashion magazine.

Some people, as Tennessee Williams wrote, are dependent upon the kindness of strangers. Sammy Spivak depended upon the pity of family to get him through. To this day, one of my favorite activities is looking through magazines and spotting his out-of-focus, off-center photos. In these days of point and shoot, Sammy Spivak has made lousy photography a new art form.

Over one of my major interviews with him — a ten-minute lunch — he informed me he was fresh from a drug and alcohol sanitarium, and in therapy with a woman who had her own show on cable access. That was the sum total of our "interview." Whenever there was a pretty girl around, his conversation was peppered with phrases like, "My friend, the editor of the Herald," so he was "REAL BUSY, SWEETIE" impressing the waitress.

Another time, he invited Wyatt and me up to his office at the ad agency. When we got there, he informed me he was behind schedule, that he didn't have an assistant for his next shoot, and would I mind holding some big huge aluminum-type thing next to the babe he was photographing. Wyatt lost his temper.

"This is Margo Gaines, jerk. She's here AT YOUR REQUEST to write about your dad, and on top of that, she's a Broadway star. Don't you talk to her like that."

I put a restraining hand on Wyatt's arm. Sammy appeared not to notice Wyatt's anger. "Honey, sweetie, I'm sorry. I didn't mean anything by it. I'm just..."

"REAL BUSY, SWEETIE," Wyatt and I said together.

Sammy didn't notice that either. "Yeah," he agreed. "I just can't talk today. But we'll have dinner soon."

I fumed the entire way back to the apartment. "He said he wanted this book written. It's obvious he's changed his mind. He hasn't introduced me to his mother or either one of his stepmothers. I haven't met Roger Carew. He doesn't have any old photographs, except for a mildewed bunch in his mother's garage, which he never has time to get. He doesn't seem to *know* anything about his dad unless it's something I tell him. And I don't know enough to write the important part of the book."

"You know," Wyatt said, putting a roll of film he stole from Sammy into another pocket, "he's very fascinated with you."

I stopped for a red light. "Why would I fascinate him?"

"He wonders about you and his dad, about your sex life and stuff. He's got a lot of sexual problems. I wouldn't be surprised if he's a closet case. If I might say so, I think the reverse is also true, and that's why you're not working together very well."

"You mean you think I'm interested in him?" The car behind me honked its horn. I jerked my car into motion.

"I don't think I said interested. I said fascinated."

Wyatt had rare insight. I smiled. Then frowned. "It reminds me a little of when I met Art nine years ago. He'd been to Europe, his mother was an ex-show girl, he was a whole year older than I was. To me, there was a mystique about him, and I was infatuated. I guess the same is true with Sammy. He's Todd's son, for one thing. For another, he leads this fast-paced lifestyle I don't understand, and he's a real California type, totally opposite from anyone I've ever met." I sighed. "I have a bad history with men, Wyatt. I can't afford any more trouble."

"When you're tempted, just think of his license plate." Sammy Spivak's license plate was N2DBZ (Into the Biz) and around the plate were the words, "Yes I do but not with you."

"If he weren't so pathetic, he'd be funny," I agreed.

When I wasn't occupied with *Rosalind* and the Todd Lang story, I was involved with the Gaines family. Art and his partners were trying to get funding for a film, and Art told me there was a role in it for me. I didn't need anyone to tell me that he was trying to get back together with me, but everybody told me anyway: Bobby, Holly, Lettie and Wyatt. I didn't think this was a good idea, but the others disagreed.

Out of friendship only, I occasionally accepted a dinner invitation from Art on Mondays, my free night. Art did everything he could to impress me. One evening, he took me to a gorgeous, expensive restaurant at the beach — Buckstone's. We'd been seated for about five minutes when the maitre d' approached us. Leaning very close to me, he said in a near whisper:

"I'm so glad you're out, Miss Hearst." Art's eyes were the size of saucers. He coughed to cover up his laughter.

I said, equally softly, "I'd rather not advertise it."

"Oh, my God," the maitre d' exclaimed, clasping my hand, "I

haven't seen you since you were a child. Your father used to love this place, and he brought you in here for lunch all the time. Do you remember?"

"Of course," I smiled.

"Welcome back," he said, leaving the table. He sent over a bottle of Dom Perignon champagne, and then all the waiters lined up with postcards from the restaurant for me to sign to their wives and kids.

Then the owner of the restaurant came by with this beautiful guest-book and opened it up. The last person to sign was Gerald Ford.

"I'm sorry," I said, "but after what I've been through, I refuse to sign after Gerald Ford. I want a virgin page." He turned the page, and I signed on the top of the new page, "MMM-good — better than bread and water. Patty Hearst."

The entire meal was free, and they gave us an exquisite dessert we hadn't ordered. At the end of the meal, we each were given a big bottle of Amaretto and some Amaretto cookies.

When we emerged from the restaurant, we ran to Art's car, where we could howl and scream with pent-up laughter, and no one could hear us. In the midst of this, Art kissed me full on the lips. I stopped him from doing it again.

"I can't," I said. "I've told you how I feel."

He tried to hold onto me. "But he's dead now."

"The way I feel isn't. It's with me every day, doing this book. And Art, I haven't forgotten what happened between us."

"I was stupid. I blamed you for my own lack of self-confidence. Things are so different now, Margo. Give me a chance."

Breaking away, I leaned against the door on my side of the car. "I'm begging you, Art. Don't push this. *Please.*"

To lighten things up, I asked him, as he drove me home, what he had planned after his latest project.

"I don't know," he mumbled. "My partners are pushing for some sort of disco film, like Bobby's involved in."

Since the success of *Saturday Night Fever*, producers were falling over each other to cash in on the disco craze. Bobby's hair was dyed two shades lighter than his natural sandy brown, and he was rushed into two quickie Travolta rip-offs: *Disco Dreams* and *Disco Heat*. The plots were interchangeable. Bobby played a Venice beach lifeguard in *Disco Dreams* and a Venice beach roller skater in *Disco Heat*. His character in both discoed his nights away and longed for the bright lights of Hollywood. In both films, he played opposite an eighteen-year-old blonde bimbo. Bobby was photographed through gauze.

His dancing was phenomenal, for which the critics applauded him, while crucifying the films. "*Disco Dreams* is a Disco Nightmare" one headline read, and "Disco Bobby Does it Again," another review proclaimed, critiquing *Disco Heat*. The best was an article in *People* magazine, entitled "Beach Blanket Bobby." But when I saw Bobby's air-brushed face staring up at me from *Teen Beat* magazine, I knew we were in trouble.

Bobby didn't see it that way. He was making piles of money and, within the disco disgust realm, enjoyed a certain cachet. "It's a waste of your talent," I whined. But it was no use. Bobby was forever from the "take the money and run" school. For that matter, so was Harry and, evidently, Bobby's new L.A. "manager." Some manager.

"I can get you a part any time you want," he bragged to me.

"Doing what?" I asked. "Playing your mother?"

I thought he had sunk about as low as he could, until he signed on as host of the "Disco Magic" TV show, a syndicated program featuring disco contestants, both soloists and couples, from all over the country, who would be judged by a celebrity panel.

I went to the first taping with Holly and Lettie and nearly tossed my cookies. "AND NOW" bellowed the announcer. "HERE HE IS — DISCO BOBBY GAINES!"

Bobby, dressed all in black, entered and was joined on stage by his dance partner, Lucinda, who was in real life a dominatrix. I would have guessed if he hadn't told me. Together, they did a sleazy number across the floor. Then Bobby introduced the "celebrity" panel: a bunch of has-beens who no doubt were promised five dollars and lunch. Then we sat through two chubby John Travolta look-alike contestants, stuffed into white suits; one couple from Queens, New York, whose hobby was bowling; and another couple from Ohio who also made a claim to being disco roller skaters.

Lettie was totally involved and took notes on the back of an envelope. "Who do you like?" she asked me in all seriousness.

"It's a toss-up," I said. "I might have voted for the first guy if he hadn't fallen."

After Bobby and Lucinda did another dance, the Ohio couple was awarded a trophy, $5000 and a chance to compete in the big Disco Finals.

"Come on as a guest," Bobby invited me.

"You're not serious," I said.

"Oh, do it," Lettie prodded me. "It'll be fun. I'd do it if I were asked."

"What makes you think you won't be?" I said.

It was too hilarious to pass up. Bobby made all the arrangements, and the production office sent some papers over for me to sign, then called and told me when to report.

"What shall I wear?" I asked the woman on the other end of the phone.

"Really, anything you want," she said. "No plaids or stripes, and keep the color neutral — brown, beige, ivory, that kind of thing."

On the day of the taping, I arrived in a beige blouse, narrow mid-calf-length brown skirt and brown boots. The skirt had a small slit on one side.

"Okay, let's rehearse," the director said, after I'd been to makeup and was coached on the scoring. "Miss Gaines, you'll hear your name, you'll come out. Bobby will dance with you here..." he marked a spot on the floor. "...Then you'll take your seat over there — the one with your name on it." Abruptly, his expression changed from all business to disbelief. "What are you wearing?"

I looked down. "A skirt?"

"But we can't see your legs."

"Nobody said anything about my legs."

He tapped his foot on the floor. "Get me a scissors, quick!" he hollered.

"Why?" I asked. He didn't answer.

Disco Bobby arrived when the scissors did. "Bobby," the director barked. "Dance with her. Make your entrance, Miss Gaines." I made my entrance. Disco Bobby twirled me around, then we went into a dip.

"Okay, hold it." He grabbed a piece of my skirt and cut up the leg. "That should do it. Nobody will see the threads." Bobby and I returned to standing position. "Do it again," the director ordered, opening and closing the scissors in his hand.

This time, when we went into a dip, he screamed. "Lift your knee, Miss Gaines." I did. "ALL THE WAY UP!" All the way up, uncovering my leg up to the thigh. "That's more like it."

"You owe me a new skirt, Disco Bobby," I said just before we came out of the dip.

Finally, "Disco Magic" began. "And now," Bobby said, after his dance, "I'd like to introduce our celebrity panel. The first panelist is, as a matter of fact, my ex-sister-in-law..." (titters from the audience) "...but still a very close friend. She was nominated for a Tony for her role in the Broadway musical, *Bloomin'*, and she's headlined in nightclubs all over the country. She's now appearing in Los Angeles as the star of *Rosalind*. Please give a big disco welcome to MARGO

GAINES."

Everything went fine, except that when Bobby and I dipped, the skirt ripped another inch or so, revealing a little more leg and probably part of my buttocks. Bobby and I heard the rip. "Less is more," he whispered, before raising me up.

Wyatt hadn't come to the taping, and when I got home, he wasn't there. Then, when I went into my bedroom, I saw Sammy and Deli sitting in front of the walk-in closet. I heard a lot of banging and noise from in there, but before I had time to even get frightened, Wyatt walked out, brushing dust from his jeans. He was carrying a small statue.

"Wyatt, what were you doing in there?"

"I can get into the landlady's apartment from the closet ceiling."

"You didn't steal that from her apartment!"

"No, I DIDN'T," he said savagely, throwing it on the bed. His face was twisted with rage. "I took what she promised me. She told me if I got a suitable tenant for the apartment across the hall, she'd give me $50. Well, I got her a great tenant, and when I asked her for the money, she acted like she hadn't said anything. She's a liar, a thief and a cheat."

"That's kind of the pot calling the kettle black, isn't it, Wyatt? Who did you get as a tenant?"

"Art."

I was very still. "Art. Art Gaines?"

"Yes. He's been looking for a better place."

I pushed Wyatt with such energy, he fell onto the landlady's object d'art which lay on the bed. "You got my EX-HUSBAND an apartment ACROSS THE HALL?"

"Well, what do you care? You're not seeing anybody."

In frustration, I jumped up and down, making Three Stooges noises which weren't doing my throat a bit of good. "Wyatt, you're a great secretary and researcher, but you go too far. I put up with your stealing since you've promised me you're going to return this furniture to the theater. And I INSIST that you bring that statue back NOW." I was hopping from one foot to another. "You're butting into things you have no right to butt into. What the hell is wrong with Art, that he'd agree to something like this?"

"He's in love with you."

"GET OUT OF MY SIGHT. OUT!"

"Do you mean I'm fired?"

"I mean get away from me for a while. Isn't your family here or something?"

"Yeah. They're going to be on a game show."

"Then go be on it with them. Stay with them wherever they are. Just get out of here for now, Wyatt. And return that statue."

I paced the living room, talking to myself, for at least an hour, my skirt continuing to rip. Should I make a big scene with Art and tell him I don't want him living there? Or should I just hang loose and pretend there was no problem?

I decided to be cool and friendly. But not too friendly. I also decided to kill Wyatt, but that would have to wait until the book about Todd was finished.

I grabbed at my hair. I had to do something about Sammy. I needed to interview at least a couple of his stepmothers and Roger Carew, Todd's nemesis from the '50s at Imperial Studios.

Why wasn't I more demanding of Sammy? I'm not cut out for this, I told myself. I didn't want to intrude — that was it. I felt like a voyeur. I hadn't been married to Todd, and I hadn't been his child. I wasn't really part of these people. I was waiting for Sammy to offer, which, of course, wasn't going to happen.

I called the Screen Actors Guild and found out who represented Roger Carew. After all, I was an actress with a good film credit, and I was starring in a major musical right here in Los Angeles. Within two hours, I had a lunch date with Roger Carew to discuss Todd Lang for "an article I was asked to write."

I met Roger at NBC, and he took me to lunch at Ma Maison. He was a most charming man and seemed very happy to talk about Todd. But he brought his publicist with him.

When Hollywood closes ranks, it shuts itself in with impenetrable iron gates. What I got from smiling, handsome Roger Carew, I could have gotten from any 1950s movie magazine. He told Todd not to play Nero. He tried to help Todd get work in Hollywood when his career was slipping. He used to date Todd's second wife. He even warned Todd not to marry her, because she was, in Roger's words, "a barracuda." No, they were never really competitors. Todd was too nice a guy to be cutthroat. There was none of that at Imperial Studios. He and Todd were good buddies. He always liked Todd. The turning point for Todd at Imperial Studios occurred when Todd lost an important role to Roger, yes, but Todd went on to do some fine films.

It was a waste of an afternoon, except that I got an autograph for my mother.

I went over to the ad agency and sat in the waiting room until Sammy walked through. "Hi, honey," he greeted me. He looked over at the receptionist. "Have I known you a year?" he asked her.

God forbid he should walk into a room without making a fool of himself. I interrupted his repartee. "I need to talk to you, Sammy. Can we get together tonight? Or can you talk now?"

"Come in my office, Sweetie." I followed him down the hall. His office was like his mind — tiny and chaotic. "I can't see you tonight. Actually, this girl's out here again. She's doing a book about my dad, she says."

"Excuse me. There's someone *else* doing a book about your father? I thought that was the point of me doing the book, so no one else would."

"Oh," he laughed, "she's not really going to write anything. She's a stripper from New Jersey. She comes out here and, well, she's got me confused with my dad." He raised his eyebrows and smiled.

"You mean she comes out here to sleep with you."

"Yeah. She's real cute."

Somehow, I controlled my anger enough to find my voice. "Sammy, I need an interview with Janele Prendergast. Will she talk to me? Will you call her for me?"

"My dad's death hit her pretty hard. She's the one who found him, you know. I could see..."

"Give me her address. I'll write to her." If I waited for him to call her, I'd be in a rocking chair by the time he got around to it.

He gave me what I wanted, and I left, muttering "good-bye" under my breath. He intimidated me. He had intimidated me from the day I met him. I was angry with myself, but determined just the same to finish what I'd set out to do.

I wrote a heartfelt letter to Janele, signing my own name, not knowing if Todd had told her about us or not, and at this point, no longer caring. I explained that I was doing the book at the request of Sammy, Jr. and would appreciate her input.

Wyatt reappeared three days later, the same day Art moved in across the hall, April 1st. He apologized all over the place. I didn't exactly accept it, and instead, told him about Sammy.

"Margo, I think that guy's back on drugs," he said.

Although I was a child of the '60s, I knew nothing about drugs, other than the effects of marijuana.

Wyatt went on. "His behavior is erratic, and have you noticed how he sniffs all the time? That's cocaine. And he's always either really busy or tired."

"You're probably right. I just need to get this done. I have a $10,000 advance, and I've gone too far to stop now."

"You're not doing it for the money, or even for him. You need to find some stuff out."

"And I'm not having any luck."

"This might help a little. I got it this morning."

It was a xeroxed report of Todd's autopsy. I read it over and over. The blow to his head, which later resulted in his stroke, was "not inconsistent" with the fall Janele Prendergast said he took in her home, banging his head up against the sharp edge of a wrought iron planter. He'd apparently started bleeding internally, and by the time he had his stroke, he couldn't be saved.

Janele Prendergast called the next day. She was very sweet and sounded a bit dotty. "I got your letter. I'm so thrilled that there's some interest in Todd. Would you like to come out here and talk?"

I made a date with her for the following afternoon. Wyatt, of course, expected to go with me. I shook my head. "I'd like to make it as casual and nonthreatening as possible," I said, "and go myself."

Sammy called that night. "You're probably really mad at me," he said. "I spoke to Janele. I'll go out with you tomorrow."

"That would be very good. Thank you, Sammy."

"I know I haven't spent a lot of time with you. I'll be honest, once you were here — there's a lot about me and my dad that I find difficult to talk about. And also about my mom and stuff..."

"Maybe you're just not ready."

"I really like you," he went on. "I consider you one of my best friends, and I want to get closer to you, but every time you ask me questions, I just freeze up."

"Sammy, I don't want to push you, but I won't lie. I need your help, and I haven't felt like I've been getting it."

"That's all going to change," he swore. "Starting tomorrow, I'll help you with Janele."

Wyatt, of course, was on the bedroom extension. "Now I'm sure he's on drugs," he said.

"Is that it? Or is it just that underneath all that Hollywood bullshit, there's a real person he's afraid to let come out? I can't figure him at all."

"I can," Wyatt answered. "He's on a banana boat going south."

There was a knock at the door, and Wyatt opened it to Art. "I'd like to talk to Margo alone," he said, and Wyatt disappeared into his room. The confrontations today were coming fast and furious.

"I just wanted you to know, Margo, I'm not going to be over here all the time or anything. But the apartment is exactly what I wanted, and I'll admit one of the tenants has a lot of appeal for me. But I'm willing to settle for friendship. I can see I've got no chance for anything else."

"Fine," I said, a bit frostily. "It would have been nice if you'd told me about this move beforehand, but now that you're here — welcome."

He grinned. "It's kind of like old times, isn't it, in New York? Except for Sulynn, we're all in the same neighborhood again."

I didn't answer. Nothing would ever be like New York, and he knew it as well as I did.

Sammy called at ten o'clock the next morning. I was still in bed. "Sweetie, I can't go with you to Janele's. I was up all night photographing a Diana Ross concert. I was nearly trampled to death, too, by TOQs..."

I was still groggy. "TOQs?"

"Tired Old Queens. And I haven't been to bed yet." After listening to my breathing at the other end of the line for a while, he said, "I'm really sorry, Margo, I'll just never make it. If you want to cancel..."

"I'm not canceling." He would always have some excuse, I realized. "I'm hanging up now, Sammy. I have nothing more to say." I slammed down the phone, and switched on my new answering machine.

Janele had been all sweetness and light over the phone, but after what I'd heard and read about her, I wasn't anxious to meet her alone. From what I gathered, after twenty years on the soap opera, the producers got sick of her K-Mart wig and morose expression and offered her a lowly, "don't call us — we'll call you" day player contract.

Given all this, it was hard to catch her on "Monterey" in order to check out her acting ability, but I had a few times. A day player contract was more than she deserved.

She looked even worse in person, without her wig, than she did on television. Her house was a mess. It looked like she hadn't cleaned it since before Todd's death. I wondered if the chaos and all his garbage all over the place wasn't some sort of memorial to him.

"My housekeeper quit," she explained, as if reading my mind. "The new one isn't starting until Wednesday."

I doubted very much if she'd ever had a housekeeper, but I played along.

"Sammy isn't coming?" she asked.

I kept the sarcasm out of my voice. "No, he was up all night photographing a concert." Subtext: snorting coke. "He seems to be busy all the time."

She'd lost interest in casual conversation. "Let's sit in here,

Margo." She threw some newspapers off the couch and indicated a place for me. "I understand you're interested in writing about Todd."

"Absolutely," I said. "I've already done a good deal of the research."

"Well, if you do write about him, I'll sue the pants off you."

Boy, the sweet, dull-old-broad bit died a fast death, I noticed. I licked my lips and tried to quell the panic in my stomach. I wished fervently that Wyatt were with me.

"Why do you feel that way?"

"I want him to rest in peace, and I don't want any slander written that will hurt his son."

Had "his son," who had allowed me to see this shrew alone, been in front of me at that moment, he would have known hurt that reached a new level. Dizzy, I expelled a long breath.

"What makes you think I'm going to write slander? Todd was a friend of mine."

"Oh, that's what they all say," she laughed. "Then the book comes out and it's nothing but garbage and lies. I won't have it."

"Mrs. Lang..." I almost choked on the words. "Why would I want to do a number on Todd, of all people?"

"Because that's what sells books. I'm warning you, I'll sew this town up so tight you won't be able to get in to see even a secretary."

Fighting words from a woman practically barred from the set of her own soap opera. It was beginning to appear that I wasn't going to get my interview. She was a terrified wreck. Why?

Unsteadily, she made her way to the bar and poured herself a straight scotch. "Would you like a drink?"

"No, thank you." As I watched her, I noticed a desk up against the far wall. There, in its full glory, was my gift to Sammy, the charcoal that Todd gave me. Lying against a stack of books, not even facing out into the room. Sammy, evidently, didn't have time to finish his Christmas shopping.

"Where did you get that charcoal of Todd?" I asked her, trying to hide the fact that my blood was boiling.

"From Sammy." She took a deep, long drink (mother's milk). "I know you gave it to him."

So she knew everything. There was no point in sticking around.

She shakily walked toward me. Was it fear or true unsteadiness? "I'm asking you to give up this idea of a biography of Todd. No one's interested."

"Well, I'm sorry you feel that way, Janele." I wasn't about to call her "Mrs. Lang" again. "The book will suffer a little from not having your input, but if that's the way you want it..."

"You're not serious," she said. "You're not going to still do it, after I've asked you, begged you, not to?"

"I've put a lot of work into it, and frankly, Janele, I don't see how you can stop me."

"You don't? You're in for a shock, lady. A bad one. I wonder if Sammy knows what a snake you are, how you've taken advantage of him."

I smiled. "Quite the opposite, I think. If it weren't for me, Sammy wouldn't know anything about his father. You act like you care so much. He didn't have one photograph of his dad before he met me. No one, including you and his own mother, ever talked to him about the kind of man his father was. All you've all done is keep your secrets. You talk about not hurting him. He's already so destroyed from neglect, there's probably no hope for him."

I was almost out of the house when she grabbed my arm and, small and frail as she was, yanked me around to face her. Her face was purple with rage, and she held a fireplace poker. "You can't write that book," she said.

"Put it down, Janele," I said quietly. "You don't want what happened to Todd to happen to me, do you?"

Mesmerized, she let the poker drop to the floor. "That's what happened, isn't it?" I went on. "You hit him and you really injured him, probably while you were both drunk. Hit him so hard that he had a stroke a few days later. Isn't that what you were afraid someone would find out?"

"It's not true," she said in a hushed voice.

"I don't know if it's true or not, Janele. If it's any comfort to you, Todd was a goner whether you conked him on the head, or not. How much longer did he have, the way he drank and the way he wanted to die?" I left.

Art — who wasn't going to be hanging out at my place — was there with Wyatt when I got home. I was glad to have them to talk to.

"It's obvious to me," I said, "that I can't do this book. Janele Prendergast is capable of anything. I was lucky to get out of there alive. But there's more to it than that. She thought I knew something else, I'm sure of it. She got so scared that she threatened me, and then I guessed what happened to Todd. But I had no way of knowing about that beforehand. No, she was scared about something else when I walked in. I was wrong when I accused her of being afraid someone would find out she hit him."

"You think she knows about that Gustavo character?" Wyatt asked me.

"She knew Todd and was married to him for a much shorter a time than I knew him. But still, they *were* married. In many ways, Todd thought of me as a kid. He might have told her something..."

"I think there's a good chance he did," Art said. "Especially if they were drinking buddies."

"You can't give up on the book," Wyatt said. "That's just what everybody wants. All the more reason for you to keep digging."

"Or write a whitewash. Maybe not dwell on the end of his life so much. Except, of course, Raymond Delisle wants a book people would be interested in reading. I'll think about it."

Wyatt clenched his fists. "I'd like to bash that Sammy, Jr."

I arrived home after that evening's performance of *Rosalind* to find Art — who wasn't going to be hanging out at my place — and Wyatt in the living room with three huge garbage bags filled to the brim.

"What's all this?" I said.

"Sammy, Jr.'s garbage," Wyatt announced proudly. "We thought we'd go through it and see if there's anything of interest. We've been casing his neighborhood for days, trying to figure out when they put the garbage out."

"You've got maggoty garbage in my living room?" Art, the cleanest human being in captivity, felt differently, it appeared, when it wasn't his apartment. "Get that stuff down to the garage. I'm not interested in one piece of paper that's in it."

Laughing and joking, they carried it out. Sending them down there turned out to be a mistake. Wyatt appeared a half hour later with Rosenthal China. "The landlady had this stuff in one of those closets down there. She probably doesn't even remember it's there."

"Aren't those units padlocked?"

"I picked it. Art held the flashlight."

"Why are you showing it to me? You know you have to put it back. Now." And what the hell had gotten into Art? Now that he was thirty, he was getting downright playful.

A few nights later, I was in my dressing room after a performance of *Rosalind*, when the stage manager told me "a man" was waiting to see me. "Please send him in," I said, wondering who it was and hoping he didn't have a sawed-off shotgun.

It was Harry Lasker.

He wasn't smiling, and dispensed with a greeting. "What the hell is all this business about a biography of Todd Lang?"

In spite of myself, I chuckled. "Gee, this thing has a lot of support. I can tell you also are thrilled. How'd you find out about it?"

Harry looked as if his blood pressure was shooting to the skies as he spoke through gritted teeth. "From Roger Carew and Janele Prendergast."

"I never told Roger Carew I was writing a book."

"You didn't have to. Margo, you're insane. You get off this, right now."

I dug in my heels. "What is it with you people? I have an advance from a publisher, and I was asked to do this by his son."

"His son doesn't know his ass from his elbow, and neither do you. You don't have any idea what you're stirring up here."

"Well, just supposing you tell me." I glared at him.

"I've been trying to tell you since you met Todd. I warned you not to get involved with him. He was into some pretty raw stuff in Spain. If you keep upsetting people and making noises like this, I'm warning you, Margo, you're in *way* over your head. You won't want to write about what you learn. But knowing about it, and having people think you *might* write it, is enough to get you in a lot of trouble."

"IT. IT. What is IT?"

Harry put his hands to his bald head. "Look, Todd was — he was a weak man. I told you when you were cast in *Blind Murder* that he didn't know how to play the Hollywood game. That doesn't mean he didn't try. He — well, you know what a gorgeous man he was. A couple of producers were interested in him..."

"Male producers, I assume."

"Male producers. And Todd slept with them. And one of them gave him a lead in a good film in the old days and later wanted to help him get back into Hollywood. He was one of the producers of *Blind Murder*."

I laughed, more from relief than anything else. "That's it? He had a couple of bisexual experiences, and for this I have to look over my shoulder?"

"No. The thing is, Roger Carew has had more than a few bisexual experiences — lots more — and he certainly doesn't want you nosing around into the good old days at Imperial Studios."

I crossed my legs, folding my robe across my knees. "Harry, you've made an impressive attempt here, but I can't buy any of it. Janele Prendergast almost clobbered me with a poker, and she didn't do it because Roger Carew is a homosexual. You can try to tell me Todd was gay, but I lived with the man and I slept with him — he wasn't. I certainly don't care that he was with a couple of guys to further his career, and even if I wrote that, or anybody else did, I can't believe it would stop traffic. So quit dancing around."

Harry hesitated, then said: "You asked me right before you left for L.A. who Gustavo Ochoa was. I'm going to tell you now. He was Todd's pimp in Spain. Todd needed money desperately — back taxes, alimony, his accountant was suing him — and Gustavo set him up with some rich old men who paid him for sex. *Nero* was a big hit in Europe, and everybody lined up for Todd. His last ex-wife hired detectives to investigate him in Spain and used all this to get a big settlement. Then Gustavo followed him over here and blackmailed him with photographs. Janele knows about it."

My throat closed off. "How he must have hated himself," I gasped. "How could he? How could he do that to himself?"

"So you understand now, Margo, *there can't be any book.* Give Raymond Delisle his advance money back."

"How did you know about Raymond Delisle?" No reply.

Lightning struck. Everything made sense. I walked up to Harry and stared at him. Then I slapped him — so hard, my hand left a red imprint on his cheek.

"You've been behind this from the beginning," I said. "There was never supposed to be a book, was there? You sent Sammy to me and told him to keep quiet about it. Because if I knew the suggestion to write a biography came from you, I would have been suspicious.

"You figured I'd never get around to writing a book. But no one else — no *real* writer — would try, so long as the family was cooperating with another author. Todd Lang wasn't Clark Gable. The public wouldn't support two or more books about him, only one. So get Margo, Sammy. And you told yourself, airhead, distracted Margo is no writer. She won't get anywhere, and when she hits a brick wall, she'll come home with her tail between her legs. By then, there won't be any more interest in Todd Lang.

"You really covered all the bases. You got me into a Broadway show. I can just hear you now: 'You know what Margo's like when she's working. Why, her own husband cheated on her in front of God and the entire world, and she didn't even notice.' You must have died when the producers set up an L.A. company and I insisted on going. And then I hired a secretary. 'Oh, my God, she can't be serious, can she? She's not really going to do this thing.' For years you've been screaming at me to grow up, Harry. Didn't you think I'd ever do it?"

He pursed his lips. "I was thinking about Sammy, Jr. He can never find out."

"Oh, I see," I said. "I'm now to be held responsible for Todd Lang's mistakes. Kill the messenger. It's my fault that Todd lived as he did. You had no part in it. You took someone with a schoolteacher's temperament out of his small town, and because he was a knockout, that alone made him movie star material. But it suddenly becomes *my* problem that he couldn't handle it. I'm the big threat to the keepers of the flame.

"Well, Harry, you're right about one thing. I'm not doing any book. But not because I'm intimidated by a bunch of Hollywood bullies. I'm not going to write something half-baked. And because I loved Todd, no matter what he did, I won't be the one to write about his self-destructive mistakes." A look of satisfaction crossed Harry's face.

"However —" I continued, "Todd lived as he did, and you're out of your mind if you think it's going to stay hidden forever. And when it comes out, Harry, it won't be written by someone who loved him and wants to understand his pain. It'll be written by some trash writer going for a quick buck. All you assholes are doing is buying some time, and you know it. And don't throw Sammy, Jr. in my face. Janele tried that. None of you give a damn about Sammy, or about Todd, either. You only care about your own guilt and your own secrets. Now, please leave. And by the way, you're fired."

The next day I got up early, bought a bunch of flowers and drove to the cemetery where Todd was buried. I sat in front of his grave for a long time, holding the flowers in my hand. Then I laid them across his headstone.

"Rest in peace, Todd," I said. "If you can."

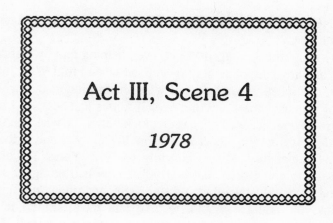

Act III, Scene 4

1978

Wyatt was furious that I returned the advance for Todd's biography to Raymond Delisle. However, I kept Wyatt as my personal secretary, and I actually did write about Todd, a good article called, "Todd Lang: The American Dream Gone Wrong," which appeared in *Film Monthly* to a great response. In the article, I wrote about Todd's promising career and how, through bad judgment, mismanagement and alcoholism, it had all gone sour for him. I was pleased with it, and I then didn't feel as if all my research had gone to waste. *Film Monthly* said they were interested in more articles.

Wyatt was hell-bent on destroying Sammy Spivak, Jr., and I felt powerless to stop his little games. Wyatt's point was that Sammy, while he may have suspected the dark side of his dad's life, actually didn't know anything, and therefore, it was cruel of him not to have helped me more than he had. No amount of my psychoanalysis of Sammy's passive-aggressiveness helped his case at all.

"I might back off him," Wyatt said, "if he hadn't given Todd's Christmas gift to you to that head-basher."

He started by deluging Sammy with junk mail. Anything that said "bill me" or "send me free information" on the card was submitted with Sammy's name on it.

The junk mail was only Phase I of Let's Ruin Sammy Spivak's Life. Next, Wyatt put up signs announcing a garage sale at Sammy's house the following Sunday, scheduled to begin at 7 a.m. That Sunday, Wyatt gleefully took my car and drove by Sammy's. "Lots of cars," he reported when he returned.

Then he and Art advertised in a free rag, *Cheap Buys*:

"PIANO — Baby grand. Owner must sell, $250." With Sammy's phone number.

Bobby and Art encouraged Wyatt, even helping him by tearing out coupons and devising plots. It only stopped when I told Wyatt he was fired if it continued. I asked myself why I hadn't interceded with this Threat of Threats earlier and told myself it was just because I hadn't thought of it, not because I got a secret kick out of the whole thing.

Rosalind was ending its L.A. run in September, and I thought, somewhat reluctantly, about returning to New York. Sulynn was begging me to come back, but after all, I now had no agent and no work, and Fred and Howard would stay in my apartment indefinitely.

"I think you should stay out here," Art said one afternoon, relaxing in my apartment. "Do my film, and get an agent out here." He still didn't have funding for his first movie venture and was working as an assistant producer.

"The problem with that is, I don't care for film or television work. I like the live stage."

"Things are really opening up out here," he said. "There's no reason why you can't do stage work. Besides, you have a lot of friends out here now."

"A lot of them are the same friends I had in New York. Do you sometimes feel we're all following each other around?"

"Well, I know my mother is," he said, and we laughed. He pulled me down on the couch and kissed me again and again. I let him. It had been a long time since I'd been kissed like that.

Art put his lips against my cheek. "Margo, I can't compete with a ghost, but I'd sure like to try."

"There's no more ghost," I said. "And you know something funny? He was a ghost while he was alive, too. I — I can't tell you, Art, that I'll ever really get over Todd. But I'm not in love with him anymore."

"But you can't say you're in love with me either."

"Hmm..." We kissed. "I can't — right now."

"Margo Gaines, you've already got the last name. Can't we make it legal again?"

I broke away from him. "Oh MY GOD!" I screamed, jumping up. I scared Sammy and Deli, who ran from the room.

Art was hurt. "You think it's funny?"

"No," I said, gasping for air. "It's just that — you just proposed to a married woman! I never divorced Lars!"

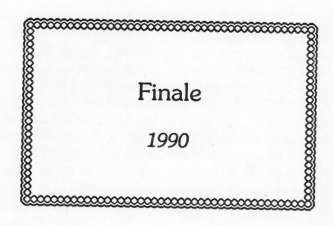

Finale

1990

It was impossible to concentrate backstage. I was quickly going crazy.

"I thought Lettie was going to watch the kids," I said to Sulynn. "Where did she go?"

"I don't know. What happened to Nicole? She promised to baby-sit."

I found Sulynn's daughter, Nicole Davidson, now a sullen fifteen going on twenty-five, casually painting her nails in the empty dressing room next door. It was supposed to be Sulynn's dressing room, but for moral support, we were sharing a room. There were no small children anywhere in the vicinity; instead, they were screaming through the halls. Sighing, I ran into the wings, where I saw Lettie and Holly talking as if they didn't have a care in the world.

"Excuse me," I said. "But Sulynn and I are trying to get ready for a performance, and the kids are out of control. Could one or both of you *please* help us out?"

As I walked into the dressing room, Art, Jr. was trying to reach his toy tiger on the makeup shelf. "Lila," he kept saying.

I handed it to him. "Here's Lila, honey. Where's Sammy?"

"I have Sammy." My eight-year-old, Megan, came in holding Art, Jr.'s toy dog.

"S'mmy, S'mmy," he gurgled, taking it in his other hand. He named his favorite toys after our cats, Sammy and Deli — actually, Sammy II and Deli II, the original Sammy and Deli having died within a few months of each other, shortly before his birth three years ago. We'd given our new cats other names, but ended up calling them

"Sammy" and "Deli" anyway.

"Megan, take Art and the other children, and go find Nana Lettie and Aunt Holly, okay? Mommy and Aunt Sulynn have to get ready."

I shut the door and looked in the mirror. "I can't do it."

"Well," Sulynn said, "you're stuck now, honey. We both are."

We had our telegrams from Bobby taped on the mirror: "Doing AIDS benefit of *Bloomin'*. Need cheap and horrible women from original cast. Afterward, planning knock-down Margarita Bash at El Terjita for sloppy drunks. Come if you're not on the wagon. P.S. Don't tell Veda."

Bloomin' had cashed in on the baby-boomer audience with a revival in 1989, which was choreographed by Bobby Gaines, and in 1990, the original cast was asked back to do a special benefit performance to help actors with AIDS.

Bloomin' had been especially touched by AIDS: our lyricist, Tom Scardino; our original director, Len Magnuson; and most tragic for us, Howard. After Howard's death two years earlier, Fred moved to San Francisco, where he worked in an AIDS clinic and practiced "healings." But he'd come in especially for this performance, which was dedicated to Howard, Len and Tom. The current cast member in the part of the rocksinger, Larry, Howard's original role, would be doing it with us today. That was fine, except that he was twenty-two and we were forty. Beverly, now forty-two, was playing his love interest and referred to it as "the ultimate May-December relationship."

"What kills me," Sulynn said, "is how fifteen years ago, we applied age makeup at the end of the show. Now we have to apply *youth* makeup at the beginning of the show."

Fred stuck his head in. "Need any help, MIZ Margo Girard Gaines Andersen Gaines?"

"So that's it," I said. "You came three thousand miles to abuse me. You can help me with this awful wig."

"And what am I, chopped liver?" Sulynn complained. "I could use some help, you know."

"Margo's the frail one." Fred helped me ram the long-haired wig on my head. "Jesus," he said. "You look like you looked twenty years ago. This is your exact hair color, too."

"Do I look like I looked twenty years ago?" Sulynn threw on her Shirley Temple wig.

"You should thank God you never looked like that off the stage," Fred said. "Margo, you're using a henna now?"

"Yes, to cover the gray. I don't have much, but what I have, I hate."

"*Gray?*" Sulynn said. "You want to talk *gray*? I'm not gray. I'm *white*. I pulled out sixty *white hairs* in the car on the way to the first rehearsal. My mother's hair was white by the time she was thirty-six."

"Mommy, mommy," Sulynn's ten-year-old, Ariadne, ran in. "Have you seen Barbie?"

"Which one? And where's your father?"

"I see it," I said. "It's on the top of the coat rack. Can you get it for her, Fred?" Ariadne dashed out of the room, yelling, "I FOUND IT!"

"We've gotten her every Barbie doll in existence," Sulynn said. "Or so we thought. She came home down in the mouth the other day and said, 'Jennifer has the Golden Dream Barbie.' I turned to Clark and said, 'Is it possible we've missed one?' But I'm the one who suffers. Have you ever dressed one of those things? I'm the one who's got to zip those tight pants up over Barbie's fat hips."

"Speaking of fat hips," Fred said, combing the back of my wig. "I can't wait to hear the audience when Amalia walks, or should I say *waddles*, onto the stage."

"She does look gross," Sulynn agreed, with relish. "I mean, okay, I'm no sylph myself, but *brother*."

"Okay, everybody, quiet for a minute," I said, waving my hands. I got the guitar from the corner. "Let's see if I can remember these fingerings. I've loused them up at every rehearsal. I just can't seem to get it. I don't think we've had enough rehearsal."

"Honey, we did the show for two-and-a-half years. And that was just on Broadway," Sulynn said.

"Oh, this is ridiculous." I threw the guitar down and flung the door open. Spotting the stage manager, I said, "I need to see the conductor right away, please. Right away."

Bobby came down the hall. "I can't remember my guitar fingerings," I told him.

He followed me into the dressing room. "I don't know what you're crabbing about," he said. "I can't do my own choreography." He did some steps, followed by a jump. It looked fine to me.

"See?" he said. "My balance is off or something. The name of this performance shouldn't be *Bloomin'*. It should be *Wiltin'*."

"How about *Agin'*?" I suggested.

Bobby had quit dancing about five years ago and, out in L.A., choreographed throughout the *Dirty Dancing* phenomenon, as well as stage shows in L.A. and Vegas. Then he, Holly and their three children, who thankfully were sitting with Holly's parents in the audience, came to New York, where Bobby started to do Broadway choreography as well, becoming a true bicoastal. *Bloomin'* was his third show.

I hadn't set foot on a Broadway stage since *Rosalind* and, as a matter of fact, never came back to New York after the *Rosalind* company closed in L.A. Art and I were re-married in 1979. I'd appeared in many plays and musicals out in Hollywood, as well as, thanks to nepotism, TV movies and feature films produced by The Delilah Company, which was run by Art and several partners. They didn't make huge-budget films, but instead, strived for quality, and had done very well.

We lived in Pacific Palisades, where, when I wasn't acting or singing, I worked on my writing. I'd collaborated on a few screenplays, nothing major, and had written a few articles. At this point, I preferred writing to performing, so I could be home for the children.

Now, I was about to "do Broadway" again, and I was irrationally nervous.

The conductor politely knocked on the door. "You wanted to see me, Margo?"

"Yes, you'll have to double the guitar in the pit. I can't remember the fingerings."

"No problem."

"Maybe not for you," I muttered. "But I think my brain is going."

"Places," the stage manager called. "Break a leg, everybody."

"OH, DON'T WORRY," I heard Bobby yell.

Foss, looking exactly as she had twenty years ago, stood at the wings. "I'm so excited," she said, hugging me. "Just think — it's almost like the old days."

I stood in the wings. Two arms grabbed me from behind. "I hope that's Art," I said.

"Got that right." He turned me around and kissed me. "We've been in this show under so many circumstances — friends, married, divorced, not speaking, married to other people..."

"It's pretty crazy when you think about it. We were so young, too. And we thought we were *so* mature."

He grinned. "With that wig on, you look like you did when I first met you."

"Disgusting," Sulynn said, interrupting our smooching. "Just like newlyweds. It's not hard when you keep getting remarried."

The overture started.

"Those fingerings just went out of my head again," I moaned. Art ran across the back of the stage to get to the other side for his entrance, and Bobby replaced him behind me.

"Do you think I'm getting arthritis?" he said. "I swear I used to be able to kick higher. And nothing used to hurt."

"Just don't give yourself a shot of insulin in front of me, that's all I ask," Sulynn said. "Remember that time?"

"Please don't make me laugh," I pleaded with them.

The spotlight hit my stage left spot. I walked out, guitar in hand, and sat down.

The fingerings came back.

"We're all bloomin'," I sang. "Flowers starting to rise..."

CURTAIN